Thrones We Steal

Jessica Jude

Contents

Author's Note

W ESBOURNE IS A FICTIONAL island country set in the middle of the Atlantic Ocean between North America and Europe. While the country is a fantasy concocted in the playground of my mind, all of my books are contemporary and take place in the modern world.

The following book contains mature content and potential triggers, including: sexual abuse of child (off-page), death of parent (off-page), death of animal, terminal illness (off-page), substance abuse and overdose (off-page), verbal / emotional abuse, language, and explicit sexual content (chapters 37-38). It is not intended for readers under 18.

Each chapter is named after a song that fits its vibe. Access the entire playlist on Spotify by going to https://jessicajude.com/thrones-playlist

And finally, I am not responsible for any damages inflicted upon books or reading devices by the consumption of this book.

xoxo Jess

1

"I Dare You" - The Regrettes

I T'S JUST AN OLD diary, exactly like a thousand others that have passed through the Historical Society: decrepit, brittle, and smelling like a musty attic. Much like the people who donate them.

One thing is certain—it doesn't have the power to change my well-organized life. The thought is laughable. But Maisie isn't laughing.

"I'm telling you, Celia. Once you read it, you'll never be the same."

Sighing, I glance at my watch. "I need to leave for my meeting, but I'll get to it Monday." I close the task manager on my screen and shut down the computer.

"That's too long. It's gotta be now." When I don't respond, she adds, "Like, right away. I made a copy." She places a stack of papers next to the antique journal on my desk.

"Maisie, I swear I'll do it first thing next week." I swing my bag onto my shoulder. "Before you go, can you search the archives for anything we have pertaining to a J. Thompson? Mrs. Kelley thinks there may be a link to her grandfather who was killed in the First World War."

Maisie moves to block my way before I can reach the door. "I don't think you understand. This is, like, really important." She grabs the pages and shakes them. "There's information in here that will change everything."

I take another step forward. "I can't afford to be late just to read about life in the nineteenth century. Also, make sure Ethan gets access to the online database. He was having some trouble earlier." She refuses to budge, and I find myself close enough to smell her lavender and vanilla body spray.

She shakes her head, sending her blonde ponytail wagging. "It's not just an old diary. You have a personal interest in this one. It'll change your life, I promise. Like, big-time change. As in, a read-it-and-never-look-back kind of thing. And not just you. All of Wesbourne. This country as we know it will change if this diary becomes public knowledge."

She's either being melodramatic or buzzed from caffeine. One option is as likely as the other.

"Just give me a quick summary. And maybe lay off the coffee." I look at my watch again. I need to leave now if I want to make it on time.

"Okay, okay. How about this?" She brackets my face with her hands like she's framing a portrait. "Right now you're Celia Chapman-Payne, Duchess of Whitmere and director of the Wesbourne Historical Society. After you read these"—she shakes the papers once more—"you will no longer be any of that."

"I don't style myself like that anyway."

"That's not the point! Everything will be different. I can't tell you how, though. You'd never believe me."

I doubt her already, but I purse my lips and extend my hand. "Fine. I'll read it tonight."

"Trust me, okay?" She shoves the photocopies at me. "You won't regret it."

My mother's throwing a dinner party tonight, and I was planning to duck out early to draft a proposal for the next board meeting of the Wesbourne Nature Conservancy. Now it looks like I'll be reading through someone's daybook instead.

As I leave my office, the reception area of the Historical Society murmurs with quiet activity, typical for a late Friday afternoon. The receptionist hands a brochure to a middle-aged couple at the front desk with information about the kinds of items the Society will accept. One of our interns is carrying a cardboard box to the archive room.

Sunlight streams in through the building's glass front and reflects off the marble floor. It gives everything a chic, modern look that belies the centuries of history preserved within these walls. The Society had been housed here for over a decade before I became its director two years ago. If I had my choice, we'd be headquartered in a building like the Allerton Hotel, rich in history and architecture, but some battles aren't worth fighting.

A group of high school students descends the staircase after their tour of the second-floor museum. Their guide, Dame Adelaide Mansfield, follows. Her white hair is cut into a wavy bob, and she looks as regal as a queen, although her closest connection to royalty is having been knighted in 1994 for her work in foreign relations. She shoots me a look of exasperation.

I step back to let the students to file out of the building and wait for her to join me at the door.

"A bunch of bloody twits. All of them more engrossed in their phones than in the genuine history right in front of their faces." She rolls her eyes at the kids' retreating backs. "How are the wedding plans coming along, poppet? It's been ages since we talked."

"Let's grab tea together soon, and I'll catch you up on everything," I say. "I've got to hurry if I'm going to make my meeting with the petition committee."

"I won't keep you, dear. You're going to need all the favor you can get."

I'm terrified she may be right.

As always, Adelaide is right.

I scan the half dozen men surrounding the table in front of me, stuffed into their suits like sausages threatening to burst their casings. The Crown must have scraped the bottom of the barrel for this committee.

"Sirs, please."

Their low chatter quiets as they turn in my direction. "If I could have a few more minutes of your time, I think you'll be very interested in this footage." It's a stretch, but one can hope. I aim the remote at the ancient television in the corner of the room and press play. The news anchor leaps into action.

"—body of fourteen-year-old Kira Radbury, found in her home on the east side of Wesbourne City on Wednesday." A girl's picture fills the screen next to the anchor. Her lips are curved into a smile around her braces. My vision blurs at the sight, and I blink to clear it. "Preliminary reports say that Radbury had large amounts of insidion, Wesbourne's most popular drug, in her system, which caused the death of the young teen in the early hours of Wednesday morning. This is just one of the many cases of insidion overdoses in Wesbournian youths—"

I click the power button, and the screen goes black. Waiting a few beats, I hope to allow Kira's photo to stick in their minds. That pink-cheeked, strawberry blonde girl could have been any one of their daughters.

No, that isn't true. All of their daughters are safely ensconced in private schools Kira's single mother had no hope of ever affording, leaving her at the mercy of the public school system. There, the currency of choice among students is insidion, a lethal and temperamental drug that is almost always addictive, if it doesn't kill you first.

I turn around to face the committee—all men, not a single woman—and say, "Surely you can all see the need to do something about the rise in illegal substances entering our ports."

Lord James clears his throat before replying. "It's not that we don't think something should be done about it, Your Grace. It's simply your proposition to increase security at the ports that raises concerns."

"And what do you propose we do instead?" I ask.

Evidently having completed his duty, Lord James looks around at his colleagues on the special committee assigned to my petition.

Lord Sutton sighs. "Why not simply incorporate more teaching in schools?"

"As I mentioned earlier, the schools are already pushing a large amount of anti-drug education. While proving somewhat effective, there is still the matter of large supplies of insidion making it onto school grounds and being sold to children. If we could cut these off before they ever enter the country—"

"Sorry to interrupt, Your Grace, but adding more security personnel to the ports would not only slow down processing, but also increase costs exponentially. It would require a raise in taxes." This from Lord Barton, possibly the most understanding member of the entire group, if not for his single-minded focus on inane matters like cost.

"I think most citizens would be in favor of a slight tax increase if it meant protecting their loved ones from the devastating effects of drug use," I counter.

"With all due respect, Your Grace, I hardly think a woman in your position could know what the people of Wesbourne would or would not be in favor of," Lord James says.

The stuffy room becomes as still as death. My throat grows tight, and I choke for air.

He seems to regret his words immediately and stammers, "My apologies, I simply meant—"

"No apology needed. I'm sorry to have wasted so much of your time." I gather the stack of files I brought with me: accounts of insidion-related teen deaths in the past five years, detailed spreadsheets that received only cursory glances from the committee members, and the reports of the estimated future results should they approve my petition. I shove everything into my bag and march out the door without a backward glance, heading to my car.

Good riddance to the lot of them. I'll find another way to save this country from going to hell in a bloody handbasket.

This is the problem with a class system so deeply entrenched that even a century of modernism hasn't completely rooted it out. There are those who think social status is the only thing that matters, the ultimate protection, even from the law. Rumors trickle—a military deserter who got off with only a hefty fine because he was a member of the House of Lords; a baroness whose temerarious driving endangered innumerable lives, but her record remained spotless.

And there are those of us who believe in earning what we have, in equal opportunities for everyone, regardless of how many times their family is mentioned in *A History of Wesbourne*.

Despite our differences, Wesbournians fight with a relentless determination for what we believe in, and we're proud of having one of the strongest monarchies to survive the twentieth century. This nation isn't perfect, but it also isn't afraid to confront its problems.

Which is exactly what I'm trying to do.

My car takes a wheezing breath as I turn the corner onto Browning Street. I make a mental note to call the garage. It's been making funny noises the past few days, and I promise it a full detail if it'll hold out a little longer. I just need it to get me home in time for my mother's party tonight. I'm twenty-five years old and hold a dukedom, for crying out loud, but that woman can still put the fear of God into me.

St. John's Cathedral comes into view on my right. My heart gives a little burp of anticipation. Just four more months, and I'll be walking through her doors in an exquisite white gown.

My phone trills from my bag, and I hit the button to accept the call.

Maisie doesn't waste time. "How was the meeting?"

"Stellar."

"Sooo, not good?"

"If you consider wasting my time and effort in front of a bunch of spineless prats who don't give a damn about anything but their pocketbooks, who then insult me simply because I'm a woman, 'going well,' then it was a smashing success," I tell her, accelerating through the intersection as the light changes from yellow to red. Orange, my mum always calls it.

"Yikes. Do they have any idea what they've done?"

"Likely not, but they'll soon find out it will take more than their measly excuses to stop me. What's up?"

"Lady Rosalind called. She said you weren't answering your mobile."

"My mother believes the earth stops on its axis when she calls. What did she need?"

"She wanted to ask if you could pick up a few more bottles of wine for tonight. Something about there being a mix-up with her order?"

I stifle a groan. That means going back downtown and delaying my return home. "Lovely. With any luck, I'll get there just in time for her to roast me and serve my carcass for dinner."

"Just remember, if another queue seems to be moving faster, as soon as you switch to it, it will slow down."

"Helpful as always, Maisie."

"I do what I can," she sings.

I turn the car around and head to the nearest wine shop. A large poster attached to a light pole catches my eye. I recognize the picture of Kira Radbury beneath the words *Protect Our Children*.

"I should send flowers to Kira's mum," I say. "Maybe even meet with her, give my condolences. Let her know there's someone on her side."

"I'm writing it on a Post-it note as we speak," Maisie says. "It'll be on your desk Monday. Don't forget about reading the diary."

My gaze shifts to the pages tucked in my handbag. "Don't worry. My unofficial assistant won't allow me to forget."

Her laugh echoes through the car. Maisie and I have worked together for two years, and if my arm ever needs amputating, I'll see about getting her attached instead.

I buy the wine for my mother and nestle the bottles in the back of the car with the blanket I keep there for emergencies. The large diamond on my left hand snags on the delicate fibers, and I smile as I untangle it. Everything is going according to plan—as long as I'm not late to dinner. My career is off to a great start, I'm in love with a man who couldn't be more perfect for me if he tried, and I'm overflowing with ideas to improve this beautiful country I'm lucky enough to call home.

I hate to tempt the universe, but it's hard to imagine anything strong enough to ruin this life I've built for myself.

2

"I Knew You Were Trouble" - Taylor Swift

THE BUZZING STREETS OF Wesbourne City fall behind me as I wind my way home. I crest a hill, and the landscape unfurls before me like a giant 3D map. A travel blogger once described Wesbourne as "the land of fairy tales." They were right. We have it all: crumbling castles, cobblestone streets, cottages with thatched roofs, brooding forests. We even have a royal family, although it's hard to say if they're the heroes or villains in this story.

My father is to blame for my love affair with this country. She does that to a person, sneaks up behind you and steals kisses like a forbidden lover. Beyond her gorgeous surface—sloping emerald hills, craggy cliff faces, icy crystal waters—her heart runs as deep as the precious gems mined from her core. She's a witch's brew of the red-hot passion of an Irishman, the elegant sophistication of a Frenchman, the traditional reserve of a Brit, and the powerful ambition of an American.

Who could help but love her?

I turn off the principal street leading out of the city and onto one that leads to my family's estate. The roads around here seem to be shrinking over time while the cars only get bigger. I've often wondered what will happen when the two finally become the same size.

My car sputters a sigh, and a thin wisp of white steam rises from under the bonnet. I smack my palm against the steering wheel. "Not tonight." I try coaxing it to go just a bit farther, and it obliges by taking me another mile before finally groaning to a stop, depositing me too far from the main road to attract help and much too far from home to walk. I manage to steer to the side, but between the narrow strip of asphalt and the steep bank, I'm still taking up half of the lane.

I slump into my seat and press my eyes shut. Stupid, stupid car. Maybe it's an easy fix, a loose cap or something that I can tighten and then be on my way again. It's a ridiculous thought, considering my complete lack of knowledge about engines, but I climb out anyway. Steam is still hissing from underneath the bonnet as I fumble for the release and lift it.

The hot vapor smacks me in the face, and I jump back, losing my grip on the metal, which slams shut with a loud crash. That's what I get for thinking I could fix anything.

The only thing to do is hire a car to take me home. I root through my handbag for my phone, then pull up the ride-sharing app. Because I'm in the countryside and the closest thing to a town is a coastal village to the west with a population of roughly sixty, a driver will have to come from the city to pick me up.

Terrific. That means waiting at least thirty minutes for their arrival, on top of the thirty it will take to get home from here.

My phone pings with an incoming message. It's from my mother, right on schedule.

> **Mum:** You didn't forget about the party tonight, did you?

> **Me:** No, Mum, I didn't forget.

As if that was ever an option.

Mum: And you got the wine?

Me: Wouldn't dare come home without it.

As I lean against the side of my car, the sunshine-flushed metal warms me through the thin fabric of my trousers. I accept the ride that will get here the fastest and ignore the cost. Avoiding one of my mother's guilt trips is priceless.

Mum: How soon will you be here?

Me: TBD. My car broke down. Waiting for a ride.
X

I imagine how irritated she will be as I stick the phone into my pocket. Lifting my face to the sultry afternoon sun, I let its rays seep into me. The scent of saltwater floats on the breeze, and I inflate my lungs with it. If I squint hard enough, I can almost make out the jagged coastline in the distance. A bank of dark clouds hovers over the horizon. When you live in the middle of the ocean, storms that pop up out of nowhere are as much par for the course as pimples before a big date.

Wesbourne sits between the United States and the United Kingdom like a mid-Atlantic taunt. Both neighbors have tried to add our small nation to the *United* in their names at one point or another, but they underestimated the extent to which a Wesbournian will fight for what he wants.

The purr of an engine running much smoother than mine shakes me from my thoughts. A sleek black sports car careens down the hill toward me. A quick glance at the app confirms my driver hasn't even left the city yet, and my fear wrestles with my desire for help. I'm all alone beside the road, with no one even remotely close enough to hear my screams. And it's too late to hide now.

The car slows to a stop behind mine, its windows too dark for me to see inside. Then the door swings open, and a familiar figure steps out. My heart plummets. *No.* No, no, no. I try bargaining with the universe for an ax murderer instead.

The waning sunlight highlights the jawline Buzzfeed recently dubbed the most attractive in the world. I've always wondered about the kind of person who has the inclination to evaluate things like that. Do they take anything else into consideration when coming up with those rankings, or are we liable to find Ted Bundy under "Men with the Sexiest Eyes" next?

Henry is literally Prince Charming, and I don't mean that in the postmodern way ignorant people use the word "literally" to mean "figuratively." He is next in line for the throne of Wesbourne, he's obnoxiously good-looking, and his charm triggers the gag reflex if you get too close.

"Celia." He shuts the door and makes his way toward me. "Car trouble?"

"No, just enjoying a picnic."

"Interesting shoes for picnicking." Grinning at my heels, he swings my car bonnet up. No face full of steam for him, the bastard. He fiddles around with a few things, then steps back. "It's overheating, which caused a host of other issues. It'll have to be towed."

"And I should believe you because . . . ?"

He shrugs. "Suit yourself. Have fun on your picnic." He slams the hood and heads back to his car.

I watch him walk away. He might be my only chance of making it home on time. I glance down at my phone again. The blinking dot that represents my ride is still in the city, and it's not moving. Is there a red light? I wait a few more seconds, but there's no further progress. What if there's been an accident or something else holding up traffic? *Damn it.*

"Henry, wait!"

I run after him, my heels wobbling on the loose gravel. He continues walking but spins around at the last second. I have to catch myself to keep from crashing into him.

"Are you accosting me, C?" He pushes his sunglasses into his hair and stares down at me.

"Of course not." I grit my teeth. "I need a ride home."

He squints at the horizon and winces. "I don't know. I've got a date tonight, and I don't want to be late."

"Henry, so help me god—"

He grins, which reveals the small gap between his front teeth, the result of not wearing his retainer after his braces were removed. I've worn mine religiously every night, but I'll still never achieve that megawatt smile.

"Hop in," he says.

After I collect my things from my own car, I slide into Henry's luxurious coupe. A cocktail of leather, vanilla, and amber hits me. He flicks down the volume on Elvis's voice pouring from the speakers, and the car becomes quiet except for the whir of the engine.

"I don't know why you insist on driving one of those," he says as we pass my vehicle.

"They're not that bad."

He snorts. "They were ranked the second-most unreliable cars in the world, right after Chrysler. Let's face it: Wesbourne's future does not lie in car manufacturing."

"At least I'm willing to support my country through thick and thin."

"How many times have you had it in the shop in the past three months?"

"Zero." The real answer is two, but he doesn't need to know that.

"God, Celia. You are too dedicated for your own good."

"Rich, coming from someone who professes an allergy to the word *dedication*."

"Hey, I can be dedicated. Have you seen my whiskey—"

I hold up my hand. "Please stop talking." I cancel the ride on my app, leave the driver a generous tip for their trouble, and slide my phone into my bag. My eyes fall to the console between Henry and me, where a slim leather wallet is wedged. I don't need to touch it to know just how soft it is. My stomach clenches as I turn away.

Of all the people to be driving by—on a mostly deserted road, at that—it had to be him. The anticipation I felt earlier is sucked away. The car throbs with a sickly silence.

He slices through it. "How's your fiancé?"

"Fine."

"And wedding plans? Coming together well?"

I shoot him a look from the corner of my eye. "Yes. My mum helps a lot."

"She approves of him, then?"

"What are you driving at?"

"Just that if he has Lady Rosalind's stamp of approval, he must be pretty great." Henry raps his fingers on the steering wheel. "But I wonder—is he really everything you want?"

"Implying what?"

He gives me an exaggerated wince. "Just questioning whether you're ready to spend the rest of your life with the same person."

"You just insulted my level of dedication. I should think the answer would be obvious."

"We also addressed your inability to choose a reliable car."

"For your information, Beck is everything I've ever wanted. He's incredibly smart, he has strong values, he's loyal and kind. Responsible."

"Sounds like a job resume."

"At least he has a job."

Henry's laugh is abrupt. "Yeah, he works for me."

"He doesn't work for you. He works for the Crown. There's a big difference."

"There's a *slight* difference. And I have a job too, by the way."

"Last I checked, seducing women and partying all night weren't considered jobs."

He pulls a package of gum from the console and offers it to me. When I shake my head, he pops a piece in his mouth. "Sometimes there's more than meets the eye."

"And here's me thinking your looks paved your way through life."

"Nope. That would be my sick dance moves."

"So you're admitting that partying is your job?"

"No, that's what I do for fun. You should try it." He blows a tiny bubble with his gum and snaps it. "Fun, that is."

"One doesn't need to drink half a dozen shots and hang out in a strip club to have fun," I counter.

"Fine. Fun that doesn't involve a spreadsheet or a book."

I open my mouth to reply, but he holds up a finger. "Or anything to do with history."

"Just because my version of fun doesn't make the front cover of *People* magazine doesn't mean I don't have it."

"Ah. So you think I do it for attention."

"No, I just think you're selfish."

The car begins the trek up the long, paved driveway of my family's estate, over one hundred acres of gorgeous Wesbourne countryside. Maison de Lierre has been in the Chapman-Payne family for more than a century, and when my father died nine years ago, it became mine. Primogeniture laws were updated retrospectively a few years before his death, allowing the oldest child, regardless of gender, to inherit their father's estate and title. If he had died three years sooner, everything would have passed to his first cousin.

In the distance, the three-story manor's white stucco gleams in crisp contrast to the slate-gray shutters flanking the windows, which are lined up like soldiers. A row of columnar trees border the path to the double doors. The house looks like the love child between an antebellum mansion in the American South and a French chateau in Provence.

The estate is beautiful but expensive. It should have enough capital to sustain itself, but the money vanished years ago, into thin air for all I can make out. My mother, sister, and I all have our own trusts, but they're small. My father's life insurance policy and my income from the Historical Society allow us to live comfortably but not lavishly—proof that titles don't equal money, and old estates often take more than they give.

Regardless, I love this place and wouldn't trade it for all the wealth in the world.

Henry's voice is hushed. "Everyone's selfish, C. Some are just afraid to admit it."

"Don't insult others just to make yourself feel better."

"I'm not trying to insult anybody. It's the truth. We're all selfish. We only do something if there's a clear benefit for us."

A brittle laugh bubbles up in my throat. "Speak for yourself. I doubt Nelson Mandela held his 'selfishness' responsible when he was sentenced to life in prison."

"He felt better fighting for his country, even at the risk of punishment, than sitting back and doing nothing."

"So by your reasoning, Mother Teresa was selfish too?"

"To a certain extent, yeah."

"You get more despicable with age." Just a few more seconds and I can get out of this car.

"There's an endorphin rush, isn't there? When you do something good for someone else?" Henry shakes his head as if trying to find the right words. "All I'm saying is that ultimately, we do the things that make us feel good. It's how we're wired."

When we pull up by the front entrance, I don't wait for him to open my door. As soon as the car stops, I jump out and march to the house. My mother would berate me for my lack of manners, but some things demand a break in protocol.

Henry happens to be one of them.

3

"Electric Love" - Børns

L ADY ROSALIND IS A sight to behold under the best of circumstances. Increase the stress load, ensure people are watching, throw in a late daughter or two, and she becomes something else altogether. She's waiting for me when I walk through the door.

"Where is it?" She casts a panicked look at my hands.

I glance at them myself, but they are empty save for my handbag. "Where is what?" The words leave my mouth at the same instant I remember. *The wine.*

My breath makes a hissing sound as I inhale through my teeth. "I left it in my car." I was so distracted by Henry's appearance that the bottles in the back seat didn't cross my mind.

My mother closes her eyes and presses her narrow fingers against her temples. At forty-eight, she is still a classic beauty. She passed her slender, white neck on to both of her daughters, but neither Beatrice nor I were fortunate enough to inherit her burnished copper hair, which she now pats to mask her irritation.

"I'm so sorry, Mum. I'll go without wine tonight, if that helps?"

"No, it doesn't help. I'm short six bottles."

"It'll be okay." I grasp her shoulders and turn her around, steering her toward the drawing room, where the hum of voices is audible. "No one will even notice."

The cocktail hour is underway, and it's unusual for my mother to leave her guests. She must have been watching for my arrival.

I move to open the door, but she claps a hand on my arm. "What are you doing?"

I gesture toward the door. "Attending your party?"

"Not dressed like that, you're not."

I blink at her, then down at my outfit. I'm wearing wide-leg cream trousers and a silk blouse. Not exactly evening wear, but surely good enough.

"Dinner won't be for another hour. You have time to freshen up."

She opens the door herself, and I can see several people in the room, drinks in hand. I recognize one of them as an outspoken advocate for those living at or below the poverty line.

"You invited Lord Rosenbaum?" I've attempted to secure a meeting with him on multiple occasions but have yet to be successful. "I need to speak to him."

"Celia, you're not attending dinner like that," Mum repeats in a hushed tone.

"But if I can get his support for my petition—"

"Go change. You smell like old books." Without another word, she slips back into the drawing room and pulls the door shut behind her.

I sigh and spin on my heel. With any luck, I can clean up well enough to meet Rosalind's approval and still have time before dinner to talk to Lord Rosenbaum.

I end up taking a shower. Turns out, not only do I smell like old books, but waiting in the sun added a tang of sweat as well. I'm zipping up the back of a long navy-blue evening gown when the door of my bedroom bursts open and my younger sister tumbles inside.

"A knock is universally accepted as a prerequisite for entering an occupied room," I say.

She laughs, a tinkling, bubbly sound, like champagne in a flute, and I realize how much I've missed it. Taking the zipper from my fingers, she tugs it to the top. "You would've just told me to come in. I saved us both time."

We squeeze onto the padded bench in front of my vanity, and she dumps an appalling amount of makeup onto the dressing table. It nearly obscures the surface and sends more than one bottle rolling to the floor. She either doesn't notice or doesn't care—both are 100 percent Beatrice.

She launches into a dramatized account of her semester, the heart-breaks and friendships and finding yourself that make that first year of uni so bittersweet. Bea is a whiz at math, so getting into the University of Cambridge wasn't difficult for her. How she's managed to keep up her grades since then is beyond me. Every story she tells me sounds straight out of an episode of *Gossip Girl*.

"How do you have time to study?" I say, dragging a mascara wand through my lashes.

"People don't go to uni to study, silly." When she sees the look on my face, she adds, "I'm kidding!" But she doesn't answer my question.

I study our faces in the mirror. At first glance, we'd hardly pass for sisters, but on closer inspection the similarities become more distinct. We both have our father's smallish, upturned nose and our mother's high cheekbones. Our mouths curve into the same slightly lopsided smile. But where Bea has gorgeous flaxen waves that cascade down her back, I've got a chocolate-brown mane that hangs just past my shoulders.

It's considered a terrific investment for a Wesbournian to study abroad, either at a Russell Group university in the UK or one of the

Ivy Leagues in the US. For the rest of your life, you can dangle it like a diamond bracelet from your wrist. *Yes, darling, I studied at Harvard. It was such a bore.*

But I can't argue with the fact that Bea's time in England seems to have been good for her. There's a rosy bloom on her cheeks, and her eyes—one brown, one blue—dance with the excitement that comes from being nineteen and believing you own the world. She's the type that will stay friends with her flatmates for the rest of her life, swapping Christmas cards and baby announcements and holidaying together in Greece.

I think of my own uni friends. I can't remember the last time I've spoken to any of them. Our WhatsApp thread has been quiet for an eternity.

"What are your summer plans?" I say, even though it's pointless to ask. Bea has never made a plan more than twenty-four hours in advance.

"Fran said her uncle might be able to find something for me at WBC, but I don't know if I want to waste my holiday in a stuffy news station."

"What's Andrew doing? Are you two taking any trips?"

Bea has been dating Andrew Piedmont for the past two years, and our mother has high hopes for the match. Landing the future Earl of Hansford would be no small feat, and getting your daughters married to men with titles and money is, unfortunately, still a thing Wesbournian mums worry about. I have disappointed her on this count, and she's redirected her energy toward Bea.

"I broke it off."

"You what?"

My sister begins applying her favorite shade of lipstick, Chanel 426 Roussy.

I watch her, transfixed. "Why? You guys were great together."

"There's someone else." Her hand shakes, and she has to wipe a smudge above her lip.

I'll castrate the bastard myself. "He cheated on you?"

Her eyes fly to mine in surprise. "No, *I* met someone."

"What do you mean? I thought you liked Andrew."

"Andrew's great, but he's not what I really want." She tosses the tube of lipstick onto the cluttered dressing table. "I want someone to worship me, to give up everything to be with me. Someone who will write me songs and fight battles for me and tell me he'll die if he can't have me. I want a Heathcliff."

The clawing scent of makeup coats my nostrils. "Heathcliff and Catherine were toxic and unstable."

"They were madly in love. They couldn't function without each other."

"Bea, it's not normal to feel that way about a person."

"That's what makes it so beautiful."

"You can't truly want that. All of those emotional highs and lows—they'd eventually wear you out."

"The highs would be worth every single low. To have someone who loves you like that . . . It'd be the most glorious drug in the world." There's something ethereal in her tone, which scares me.

"You'd have to come down some time," I say.

"Not if I could help it."

"You can't be serious. There's no stability in a relationship like that." I turn to dust my face with powder as if her words aren't slowly carving a hole in my chest.

"Stability isn't the most important thing."

"Happily-ever-afters are make-believe, Bea. Every relationship is work, but it's a lot easier with someone you trust."

"Like what you have with Beck?"

"Yes! Exactly."

"You're with him because he always lets you have your own way."

"That's not true," I say, and catch her cocked brow in the mirror. "Okay, so he often does, but that's not why I'm with him."

"Don't get me wrong. You and Beck belong together." She stands and gathers her scattered makeup. The bottles make hollow clunks as they knock together in the bag. "But Andrew never made me feel this way. Like I'm on top of the world."

"So you're already with someone else?"

She toys with a makeup brush, skimming its bristles across her palm. "We're not together officially, but it feels like the real thing. I think I'm in love with him."

There's a prickle behind my ears. She's too young, too inexperienced. She still has three years of university ahead of her. She's not ready for love.

"Who is he?" I ask. "Someone at school?"

She shakes her head, and her blonde tresses bounce. "He's older, more mature than a student."

Now doesn't seem like the right time to point out that she is, in fact, a student herself. I don't want to think about the words *older, more mature.*

"We were at a party in London, and things just clicked," she says.

I teeter on the edge of composure. "He's British?" Rosalind will have a coronary if Bea leaves the country for good.

"Nope, he's from Wesbourne." Her face splits into a stunning grin. "See? He's perfect."

I very much doubt that. "Are you going to tell me his name, or do I have to wait for an introduction?"

"Actually, you'll meet him tonight. He's coming to dinner. In fact," she says, glancing at her phone, "he should be here soon. I'm going to finish getting ready in my room. I'll see you downstairs." She presses her lips into my hair before walking out. The scent of her honeysuckle shampoo trails behind her.

It takes me five minutes to find my phone under my discarded clothes. When I finally check the time, it's seven forty-five. Rosalind plans to serve dinner at eight, and thanks to Bea's unceremonious waltz into my preparation and her forthcoming introduction, I completely forgot about talking to Lord Rosenbaum. But right now, that petition is the furthest thing from my mind.

My little sister thinks she's in love for the first time in her life, and with someone who is the Heathcliff to her Catherine, no less. She expects me to approve of this man who has stolen her heart so thoroughly, but we will see about that.

4

"Why Do You Love Me"
Charlotte Lawrence

MY MOTHER HAS OUTDONE herself tonight. By that I mean I'm slightly afraid to walk through my own house for fear of knocking over a centerpiece or upsetting the balance of her carefully constructed universe. She habitually goes above and beyond what is considered normal for these kinds of highbrow events. The fish will be halibut, not peasant food like *salmon*, and no, we won't skip the sorbet course, because "image is everything, Celia, everything." I don't have hard evidence, but experience suggests she has also measured the distance between each table setting like she's Mr. Carson from *Downton Abbey*.

But tonight feels different. I peek into the dining room to gauge what we're dealing with and—is that an *ice sculpture*? The official occasion for this party is Bea's homecoming—not that Rosalind ever needs anything as vulgar as a *reason* to entertain—but even that doesn't seem significant enough to warrant the giant swan perched in the center of the long table, water dripping from its frozen beak.

I move to the drawing room, where several dozen guests are mingling. I spot Lord Rosenbaum near the fireplace, but he's deep in conversation, so I scan the room for the only other person I'm interested in seeing tonight.

Beck isn't hard to find, standing a head taller than everyone else. His face is drawn in fascination, brows pulled together, head tilted forward as he concentrates, and I know whomever he's talking to is receiving his full attention.

Ten years from now, he will be one of the top legal advisors to the Crown, with his straightlaced, buttoned-up advice and knowledge about all things law. Even gravity can't keep someone like him from rising in rank; loyalty and dependability are trophy-winning racehorses. He will drive a newer model of his current Volvo—still a frosty silver—and every other week, the interior will be meticulously cleaned by an acne-ridden teen at the detailing shop, whom he'll tip more generously than necessary. While he waits for them to finish, he'll call me to ask if he should bring home chicken biryani from our favorite Indian take-out, and after we tuck our two kids into bed and let the dog out and empty the rubbish bins, we'll end the day on the couch binging a historical TV show that's just come out.

It's the best kind of beautiful.

I'm startled from my reverie by the sound of something shattering. Lady Colette has dropped her goblet, and pieces of broken glass glint like diamonds on the floor. Before anyone else can react, Beck steps over the mess to pull her away. She can't stop babbling apologies.

One of the waitstaff appears beside me with a broom. Beck walks over and takes it from her. "I'll clean up." Then he turns to me and brushes a kiss across my lips. "Hello, lovely."

He's gone before I can respond, sweeping the shards into the dustpan and bringing it back to the girl still waiting in the doorway. After she takes it from him, he grabs both my hands in his. In their largeness, they completely engulf mine, and warmth spreads through me. I become the recipient of that trademark smile I love, the one that makes his eyes shine

and crinkle at the corners, making you feel like you're sharing an inside j
oke.

"Four more months," he says, "and you'll be Mrs. Harrison." He snags
a drink from a nearby tray and hands it to me.

"Chapman-Payne-Harrison," I correct.

He gives a mock frown and adjusts the delicate chain around my neck
until it lies straight. "You don't think three last names is extravagant? We
wouldn't want anyone to think you were pretentious."

I smile and take a sip of wine. "My aim is always to be as pretentious
as possible."

We've agreed that since my father had no sons, one of the best ways to
honor him is for me to keep his names in addition to Beck's. Our children
will share them as well.

"You still haven't told me where we're honeymooning," I say.

"I have no intention of doing so."

"How can I prepare if I don't know where we're going?"

"You mean, how can you make sure everything is perfect?" Beck's eyes
sparkle like the glass he just swept up.

"I promise to behave," I tell him. "No spreadsheets, no research."

"None?"

"None."

"How will you survive?"

I pinch him lightly through his jacket. "I'll be fine. Just tell me. Please."

"You really want to know?" When I nod, he says softly, "Croatia."

Images of Roman ruins, walled cities, and sienna-tiled roofs dance
across my mind in a mini theater production. I squeeze his hand and grin.
"Croatia sounds amazing." I can already see us exploring Diocletian's
Palace, spelunking the various caves, hiking through national parks. "Do
you already have the activities planned?"

His face falls. "Celia, you promised. No research."

"I won't! But I need to know what to pack."

He sighs and shakes his head, but he's still smiling. "I thought we could stay on the beach. Eat seafood, read, drink martinis in the ocean. Relax after the stress of the wedding."

A tiny pebble of disappointment—it's minuscule, really—drops into my stomach. Normally I would show Beck how much more the place had to offer, but I promised. This is his project. I am planning every last detail of the wedding, and he's taking care of the honeymoon. If he wants to spend it getting fried to a crisp on the beach while ignoring the ancient ruins and natural wonders behind us, I will eat all the bloody oysters he wants me to.

"I can't wait." I rise up on tiptoes to press a kiss to his lips. I will trust him with this.

Bea's words from earlier come back to haunt me. She thinks I'm with Beck because he always lets me get my way. If that were true, I'd be trying to convince him to change his plans, to do things the way I want. Of course, there's always the possibility of subtly dropping hints between now and then. But my sister is wrong. I am perfectly capable of accommodating others, especially the man I love.

My mother's ambitions for me have always been much higher than my own, and I know she was disappointed in my choice, even if she's too well-bred to say as much. Beck isn't titled, and his job as a solicitor will never provide more than a comfortable lifestyle for us. But even she now agrees that he and I are meant to be together.

We met through an online dating app that gathers in-depth details from its users, including results from various personality tests. When I came across Beck's profile, I was stunned by how high our compatibility was. He's been married once before, to a superficial woman who didn't appreciate what she had. But I can't hate her too much. After all, her loss is my gain.

"Have you met Bea's date?" I ask Beck, scanning the crowded room for anyone who seems like he's trying to get into my sister's pants.

"I don't think he's here yet." He tugs at the cuff of his jacket. "And where is our lovely Brit?"

"You know Bea. Arriving late makes a bigger splash."

"I assumed being abroad for six months would be splash enough."

"Thou can never attract too much attention when thy name is Beatrice."

Above the murmur of the room, a faint knock can be heard from the front hall. "That must be the date. I'll be right back," I say, and slip into the foyer to answer it. I can't believe my good fortune. Bea's not down yet, so I can interrogate this "older, more mature" man alone. With luck, I can drive him off before dinner even begins.

The wind has picked up outside, and the front door pulls heavily. But instead of the investment banker with slicked-back hair I'm expecting, I find Henry standing on the portico, looking dangerous in a navy dinner jacket.

"What are you still doing here?" I frown. "I thought you left an hour ago." I scan the path behind him, which is turning inky now that the sun has set. Bea's date is even later than she is. Major red flag.

He holds up several bottles of wine in each hand. "I told your mum I'd get the wine from your car."

I ignore the guilt that niggles at me. "I thought you had a date tonight."

"I do. That's why I'm here."

"What are you talking about? My mother is hosting a dinner—"

I take in his fancy jacket again, the velvet lapels looking soft in the light from the house. Rosalind's strange obsession with this party becomes crystal clear. "No. Absolutely not."

"Will you just let me in?" he says.

"You are *not* dating my sister," I hiss.

"Celia! Don't keep him waiting outside." As if summoned by our words, Beatrice herself floats down the stairs and over to the door like the ballerina she used to be. She has the keen ability to always sense whenever she's the topic of conversation.

She squeezes past me and drags Henry into the house. Her bubblegum nails wrap around his arm like he's a prized trophy. Adoration flows from her face as she beams at him, then swivels to me. "Were you surprised?" To Henry, she says, "I'll bet her jaw hit the floor when she opened the door."

He does his best to affect a laugh, but the air is cardboard. His eyes meet mine as she presses a kiss to his cheek. Bile pools in my stomach, and there's no longer any space in my lungs. I'm going to be sick, and Rosalind is going to murder me for ruining her party.

Out of deference for my mother, I will not wreck anything right now. But give me two more hours, and then I kill him.

In true Rosalind fashion, the seating arrangement prevents couples from sitting next to each other, even though this practice is as outdated as landlines, which she also still swears by, claiming cell phones are too personal. "Imagine if the *prime minister* called me while I was in the *bathroom*!" I didn't bother pointing out that the prime minister hasn't yet had a reason to call her, in the bathroom or otherwise.

In her efforts to put her best foot forward, which I now know is all part of a plot to help Beatrice land the crown prince, she has staggered the men and women, putting me between Lords Havensport-Barton and Poast. I'm acquainted with both, but the conversation is so dull even the middle of the desert sounds like paradise right now. The most intriguing thing happening is the storm rolling in, which causes the lights to dim several times and coaxes manic giggles from several of the women.

Rosalind's eight courses drag on, until finally the pudding is served and the end is in sight. I glance across the table to find Henry's eyes on me. He's spinning a fork between his fingers, and the *flick-flick-flick* is arresting. I narrow my eyes, and the faintest hint of a smile lifts his lips before he looks away.

When dinner is over, we move to the drawing room again for yet more obligatory small talk, but this time with the companions of our choice. I'm torn between discussing my petition with Lord Rosenbaum and saving my sister—who is currently super-glued to Henry's side—from destruction.

"What is she doing with him?" Beck says next to me, following my line of sight. His dislike of our future monarch matches my own.

"What do you think?"

Beatrice radiates under Henry's attention, and I know she's misinterpreting it as something it will never be. He leans close and whispers something in her ear, which teases giggles from her lips. Why can't she see that he flirts like this with every woman he's with? Then he chooses a new victim the very next day.

It's an age-old story. Bea thinks she can change Henry, tame him. She hopes she's different enough to be the one to turn the bad boy into a good boy. But it's futile. Henry cares about no one but himself, and Beatrice will simply be collateral damage.

My petition can wait. My sister's heart may not be able to.

"I have to do something," I say to Beck.

It doesn't take long to catch Henry's gaze. I flick my eyes toward the doorway, and after a few seconds, he detaches himself from Bea's grasp.

When he walks into the hall, closing the door behind us, I pounce. "What the hell do you think you're doing?"

"Calm down. We're just friends."

"Don't tell me to calm down. That's my sister!"

"Fully aware."

"How dare you drive me home and not say a word?"

"I thought you knew. You asked me for a ride." He holds out his hands like an innocent little boy, but the last thing he is is innocent—or little.

"There's no way in hell you thought I knew."

"Okay, fine," he says. "I had my suspicions when you didn't jab your stiletto into my eye. But what was I supposed to do? Bea practically begged me to come tonight."

"Because she thinks she's in love with you!"

"She's not in love with me."

Part of me is relieved to hear his nonchalance. But when I talked to Bea a few hours ago, she was far from nonchalant. How can he brush aside her feelings so casually?

Because this is Henry we're talking about, that's how.

"That doesn't mean your intentions are anything but despicable," I say.

"I didn't realize you were so well-acquainted with my intentions."

"The entire world is aware of your reputation. I won't stand by while you tear my sister's heart to shreds."

He gives me an unnerving smile. "I told you, we're just friends. She asked me to come tonight, and I felt bad saying no."

"We all know how hard it is for you to say no."

"Believe it or not, I'm not quite as desperate as you think."

"What makes you think I'll believe anything you say?"

He runs his fingers through his hair, tousling it into a roguish heap. "We used to be friends."

"Yeah, well, we're not anymore, are we?"

"Celia."

I ignore the pain in his voice. "Stay away from her, or I will kill you. With my stiletto."

"You can't protect her forever, C."

I know that. But it doesn't mean I won't try.

5

"Lone Warrior" - Mindshift

I WAIT UNTIL MOST of the guests, including Beck, have gone home before slipping away to the library. A person can only handle so much small talk before their brain cells start to deteriorate. Mine are on the verge of total extinction.

I didn't get a chance to talk to Lord Rosenbaum, and he and his wife left early. But the party has given me an idea for a blog post, one on dinner customs evolving over time. I've been running *Wesbourne in Time* for four years as a pet project. The income that trickles in through the handful of sidebar ads helps cover the cost of keeping the site up.

The library is my favorite room in the house, for more reasons than the floor-to-ceiling walls of books. It's where my father spent the most time when he was alive. If I stand close enough to the half-empty box of cigars on the mantelpiece, I can still get a whiff of his scent, that combination of moss and tobacco I would recognize anywhere.

A fire burns low behind the grate, hardly necessary with spring in full swing, but it lends a cozy atmosphere to the room. The storm outside is raging, and claps of thunder shake the windowpanes. I'm sitting at the giant rolltop desk that used to be my father's, which has now become my own workspace. More blog posts, fundraiser expense sheets, and board meeting agendas have been drafted here than I can count.

The clock says it's just after eleven. That gives me a solid three hours to do research for this post. I'm excited to jump in, but before I can do more than wake my sleeping computer, a familiar ping comes from the other side of the room. It's my phone, but I can't remember where I set it down. It's not on my desk anywhere.

I debate ignoring it, but I'm afraid it's Beck texting good night. I find the practice a little cheesy, but he thinks it's important, so I go along with it.

I finally locate it on the fireplace mantle. It's not from Beck. It's from Maisie, along with a bunch of others sent during the party.

Maisie: Have you read it yet?

Maisie: I'm not going to let you forget, remember?

Maisie: Are you ignoring me?

Maisie: CELIA!!

Maisie: You need to read it! You promised!

Maisie: I'm not sure if I should be mad or worried that you're not answering my messages but given your propensity to lose your phone I'm giving you the benefit of the doubt. But I'm not going to stop until you assure me you are READING THAT DIARY!

I completely forgot. Between my car breaking down, the disastrous ride home with Henry, Bea's startling announcement, the dinner, and attempting to keep my sister from becoming another one of Henry's victims, it drifted into the dusty and cobwebbed recesses of my mind.

It's not that I'm opposed to reading it. I wouldn't be the director of the Historical Society if history didn't fascinate me. It's that Maisie lives in a world where drama lurks around every corner, waiting to be discovered (or manufactured). The diary is probably a semifictional account of the founding of Wesbourne, in which it's revealed that—surprise!—"Wesborne" should actually be spelled without the *u*.

But I know this isn't fair. As melodramatic as Maisie can be, she wouldn't make this big of a fuss over nothing. I now have a burning curiosity to know exactly what she discovered in that little book.

I retrieve the pages from my bedroom, where they lay forgotten in my bag. Back in the library, I settle into an armchair near the fire and text her back.

> **Me**: I'm starting it right now.

Less than a minute later, there's a reply.

> **Maisie**: It belonged to Queen Helena's lady-in-waiting. Yes, your 4th-great-grandmother, Helena. Start at the entry dated 16 May 1837. Prepare to have your world turned upside down.

Why didn't she tell me this sooner? I would've blown off my meeting and the dinner party. Maisie knows Helena is my family's last link to royalty.

A movement in the doorway catches my eye. I look over to see Henry leaning against the heavy, wooden frame, hands in his pockets and watching me. I glower at him.

"Escaping?" he asks.

"I don't know what you're talking about."

"Come on. We both know you couldn't leave that party fast enough."

"Correction: you don't know anything about me."

"So you suddenly enjoy small talk?"

I ignore him and start riffling through the pages, looking for the date Maisie mentioned.

"That's what I thought," he says. "You'd rather peel off your own toenails."

"You're disgusting. And egotistical," I tell him, still focused on the diary.

"Admit it. I'm right."

"I won't because you're not."

The thick Persian rug muffles his footsteps, but I sense him entering the room. "So this is where you spend your time," he says, and I finally glance up.

He's at my desk, running his hand over the smooth surface of my private sanctuary, seducing it right in front of my eyes. I can almost feel him dragging that same hand up my arm. Goosebumps break out across my skin.

Henry bends over as if he's looking for something. "Where's all of your stuff?"

"What stuff?"

"You know, pens and sticky notes and stacks of paper. Normal-people stuff."

"In the drawers, where it should be." I clear my throat. "Do you need help finding the door?"

He doesn't move. "Nope."

Since he apparently has no intention of leaving, the only thing to do is pretend he doesn't exist. I turn back to the photocopies on my lap.

"Do you still think about him?"

He's holding a framed photo of me and my dad, taken at our favorite spot in Herrington Forest, the emerald-green pine trees providing the perfect backdrop. For my fifteenth birthday, he planned a special picnic for the two of us, complete with champagne and my favorite cheddar from Le Comptoir du Fromage in Paris. We asked a stranger to photograph us. I can still picture her bright green souvenir T-shirt flapping in the breeze, *Wesbourne* across the front in big blocky letters.

Little did either of us know the brain tumor that would snatch him from me less than a year later was already forming inside him.

"All the time," I whisper.

They say time heals all wounds. It's a lie. He's been gone nine years, and sometimes I still come downstairs, expecting to find him in his dressing gown and slippers, reading the newspaper right here in this chair. The shock of finding the room empty, even his scent gone, is enough to drag me under waves of grief all over again.

Henry's eyes catch mine, and if he were anyone else, I would say concern flashes in them before he turns away. He pulls a volume of fairy tales from the bookcase and flips through it. "Do you still read these?"

"Not really."

I look down before he can see the tears in my eyes. It was our favorite Sunday tradition: popcorn and fairy tales in front of the fire, my dad's baritone changing for each character in the story.

My fingers twirl the hammered silver bracelet around my left wrist. In the center, two hands clasp a heart between them, a royal crown resting on top. My dad brought it back from Ireland when I was ten. I can still hear his velvety voice explaining that the heart represented love, the hands friendship, the crown royalty. An inexpensive claddagh, easily sourced from any of a hundred different shops dotting the streets of Dublin, but still one of my most treasured possessions.

Henry continues his perusal of the room, lifting objects and fiddling with them like a seven-year-old hyped on sugar. I let go of the bracelet and try to focus on the dates in front of me, looking for the entry from 16 May 1837, but my eyes keep straying to Henry's fidgeting. Watching him is like a scab you can't quit picking at. When will he leave?

The room dims momentarily before the lamp beside me returns to its normal wattage. Henry replaces the antique hourglass he's been studying. "I need to go. I don't know what I'm still doing here, to be honest. Everyone else has probably left by now. This room is just so interesting, I got sucked in. Sorry for keeping you from . . ." He waves a hand at my lap. "What are you doing, anyway? Are you *working*?"

If I could just get him to leave, I'd be able to focus on this diary and whatever secret it may or may not hold. "Yes, I'm working. Sort of."

"It's Friday night." He lifts his wrist to check his watch. "Actually, it's almost Saturday."

"Great. I'll be sure to ask next time I need the date."

"What's so important it can't wait until tomorrow?"

There's no way I'd be able to accomplish everything I do if I didn't stay up late, but this would be beyond his comprehension. It's not like he goes to bed early, but it has nothing to do with work.

"I promised my colleague I'd read this tonight." I finally locate the entry from 16 May and squint to make out the words. The handwriting is tall and slanted—very common in the nineteenth century. Fortunately, I've seen my fair share of old documents, or I would be having even more trouble deciphering it.

"What is it?" he asks.

"A diary someone donated to the Historical Society. Maisie thinks it will be life-changing, although I fail to see how." My manners are too ingrained for me to demand he leave, but I'm strongly considering abandoning them.

The lamp beside me flickers once, then goes dark. Through the doorway, I can see that the rest of the house has lost power as well. Henry's silhouette is still visible, the light from the fire dancing across his face.

He moves closer to the hearth. "Guess we should have anticipated that."

I stifle a massive groan. I can't ask him to leave now, so I may as well accept his presence.

Grabbing a throw blanket from the sofa and wrapping it around my shoulders, I move to sit in front of the fire and allow it to illuminate the pages in my hands.

"Aren't you going to read aloud?" Henry has found another object to study—this time a shadowbox holding my father's butterfly collection—and looks over at me when I don't answer right away.

It hadn't even occurred to me. "You want me to?"

"For old times' sake. I'll be the Watson to your Holmes."

I arch a brow but comply. He settles into the armchair I've just vacated as I begin to read.

16 May 1837

There was a garden party today. Helena was very fidgety, nearly anxious. I kept smelling salts nearby all day. She seemed especially excited about the ship newly arrived from Ireland. Asked me all manner of questions about it, as though I would know something. I presumed she might have some family visiting, since she is Irish herself, but I struggled in vain to get an answer from her about it.

18 May 1837

There have been a few new hires. The ship from Ireland brought several maids and a footman. A ball was held at the palace tonight. Helena wore her scarlet gown and black diamond necklace. She looked radiant.

5 June 1837

A storm this afternoon made the walkways wetter than usual. Helena and I had to cut our walkabout short. I came into her bedchamber later to find the hem of her gown soiled much more than would have been possible during our short jaunt. She must have gone back out later.

"Wait a second," Henry says. "Helena, as in *Queen* Helena?"

"Way to keep up."

"You could have told me. She's my ancestor."

"Breaking news from Captain Obvious."

Helena had married William I in 1834, who ascended the throne after his father's death later that year. They had two children, Catherine and

William II, and that's where Henry's and my shared family tree splits into separate branches.

"Forgot I'm talking to the expert. Go on." He leans his head against the back of the chair. "I can't wait to find out more about Helena's soiled dresses."

"You're such a child," I mutter under my breath before starting again.

The diary continues in much the same manner, accounts of Helena not acting like herself, flighty and nervous. One particular entry catches my eye.

16 October 1837

Helena is a different person these days. She cannot sit still for more than a few minutes at a time, and when she does sit, she gazes out of the window, and I see that her mind is a million miles away. Today I caught her tracing the path of a raindrop on the windowpane. When I spoke, she simply looked at me and smiled, her cheeks flushed and her eyes sparkling. She is hiding something, I am sure of it.

More cryptic entries follow. What in the world does Maisie want me to find? Finally, the entry for 4 December hints at something more.

4 December 1837

Today was beautiful. The sun shone all of its glory down on the freshly fallen snow that came during the night. When I asked Helena if she would like to venture outside after the full fortnight of overcast weather we have recently had, she said she was not feeling well. I had a cup of soup brought up, but she emptied her stomach shortly afterwards. I do hope she is well soon.

25 December 1837

Helena is still not well. King William insisted she attend the Christmas party in the Grand Ballroom. She asked me to loosen her stays, and it is a good thing I did as she requested. She was weak and shaky the whole time, the poor dear, and could not manage more than a bite or two before needing to be escorted out. One of the footmen helped me get her upstairs. The whole thing was a wondrous embarrassment for her.

31 December 1837

Helena is on the mend, although she tells me she still feels weak, and just in time for the new year. She is more reserved than she has been for so very long. I fear the sickness has drained the life from her. King William does not seem to have noticed and requested she join him in his bedchamber this evening. It has been nearly a year, and it is no secret he has no regard for her, preferring the company of his mistress.

The pieces are starting to fall into place, and I do not like the final picture.

28 February 1838

A small birthday celebration was held for little Catherine today, marking two years since her birth. Helena asked me to have her seamstress let out the waists on her dresses. She has never had her gowns altered except during her confinement, and I know there is something she's not telling me.

"Hold on." Henry's elbows are on his knees, his brows drawn together in a quizzical frown. "Are you thinking what I'm thinking?"

My ears are ringing with the blood pounding past them. "No. Definitely not."

He runs a hand through his hair, causing it to stick up at all angles before falling back into place, like a perfectly choreographed dance. "What else, C? First she's sick, and now she needs bigger clothes?"

I refuse to believe it. Helena can't have been pregnant. "It was probably a virus of some sort. Before people knew about the importance of hygiene—"

"The dates line up with William the Second's birth."

I take a deep breath. "But it says she hadn't been with the king for a year. Think about what you're implying."

"It's the only thing that makes sense."

"Not if they hadn't . . . you know." I can feel my face flame.

"You do realize it's possible to have sex with someone besides the person you're married to, right?" He smirks at me, the bastard.

I glare at him. "Thank you for that intel. If you don't mind, I'm going to continue." It's the only way to prove this ridiculous theory wrong.

29 March 1838

Helena has shared her news with me, although I have so many questions I dare not ask. I have pondered the calendar at length but cannot make sense of it. She said the end of July, but how can that be? Unless . . . But I cannot consider it.

15 May 1838

A downpour has taken over the country for the past three days. The fields are flooded and the roads are impassable. Helena remains in good spirits, but I know she is anxious for her time to come. Things are not as they used to be between us. I know she is not telling me all that is on her heart.

8 August 1838

Helena has been delivered of a son. He was christened William, and one day he will be king, William II. He is a bonny lad with dark red hair. She has not said a word to me about her secret, but I pray she knows it is safe with me all the same. I would never tell another soul. It shall go to my grave with me.

I lay the stack of pages beside me on the floor. I can't read any more. A cold heaviness expands in my stomach as I process what this means. It isn't possible. It *can't* be possible.

If William II was illegitimate, that meant King William I only fathered one child—Catherine.

I mentally trace a path down the family tree I know like the back of my hand, following the oldest male, or female when there were no males, in each family: Catherine to Elizabeth Anne, to Joseph, to Frank, to Theodore.

Maisie is right. This changes everything.

Henry sits motionless in the chair. His eyes are glued to the floor, unseeing. What is going through his head? If this is real—which it can't be—it's as life-changing for him as anyone.

"There's no way it's true," I whisper.

He raises his eyes with effort, as though they weigh a hundred pounds. "You think someone made this up?"

"I don't know what to think."

He shakes his head and rubs his fingers over the creases on his forehead. "It's pretty obvious the writer of that diary thought Helena had an affair and gave birth to another man's baby. We're in agreement on that, right?"

"It seems that way," I say. "And if the baby wasn't William's . . ."

"Then my father is not the rightful king," Henry finishes.

I study his face for a sign of what he's feeling, but it gives nothing away. Then his brow furrows again, and his head swivels up. "If my father doesn't belong on the throne, who does?"

Guilt plays at the edges of my conscience—guilt over something I didn't do, something I couldn't have prevented if I'd wanted to.

I watch Henry scan the room, finally finding the framed family tree that hangs in a place of honor over the fireplace. My father was proud of his lineage, even if he wasn't close enough to the throne for bragging rights. Henry uses the torch on his phone to illuminate the diagram and works his way over to the correct branch, then follows Catherine's lineage down, down, down.

Because if William II was illegitimate, that means his older sister, Catherine, should have reigned instead of him.

I know the instant Henry figures it out, the same thing I realized just moments ago. The room becomes as still as a coffin, waiting breathlessly for what comes next.

"It's you, isn't it? You're the rightful monarch of Wesbourne."

6

"Part of Me" - Katy Perry

MOST PEOPLE DON'T KNOW my family is descended from royalty. It isn't the kind of thing you bring up in conversation—"Yes, my great-great-great-great grandfather was the king, small world, huh? Would you like another glass of wine?"

It's not like I'm considered in line to inherit, although technically I hold the impossible twenty-second spot, after Henry's Aunt Margaret and a bunch of dodgy cousins. It's been nearly two hundred years since a direct ancestor of mine sat on the throne. But if this diary is right—and I'm highly skeptical that it is—I should be ruling Wesbourne. It's staggering at best, debilitating at worst.

If the truth had come out back then, my life would look completely different right now. Bea and I would have been raised in the palace as princesses. When my father died, the whole country would have mourned the loss of their king. I would have been crowned queen on my twenty-first birthday. Would I be planning my wedding to Beck right now? Would we even know each other? Or would I be engaged or married to a man chosen for his suitability as my prince consort?

"Only if it's true," I say in answer to Henry's question. "Although it can't possibly be. Do you know the kinds of lengths Helena would have had to go to in order to have an affair? It's preposterous. It's more likely the diary was forged."

"C, if there's even the remotest possibility—"

"Think about what you're saying."

"I can't think. I need food." He pushes himself from the cushy recesses of the chair.

"You just ate an eight-course dinner a few hours ago."

"Exactly. It was hours ago. Please let me raid your fridge." Henry doesn't wait for an answer, just leaves the room, presumably headed for the kitchen.

I roll my eyes and follow him into the dark hall. Someone has to do damage control. All of the guests have left, meaning we must have been in the library much longer than I realized. The kitchen looks eerie without so much as the light from the microwave clock broadcasting the time in glowing numbers.

I find Henry standing in front of the refrigerator, both doors gaping open as he shines the light from his phone over the shelves. In a few swift movements, he gathers a small pile of food beside the stove.

He spins around to face me. "Frying pan?"

"You couldn't just grab a bag of crisps like a normal person?"

"I have a craving." His voice is muffled by the cupboard he's currently sticking his head into. He reemerges, skillet in hand. "For a toastie. Want one?"

I shake my head, both in answer to his question and in incredulity at the situation. Who in their right mind could eat after everything we just discovered? I say as much.

"Food helps me focus. Here, come hold the torch for me." He hands me his phone.

I hop onto the countertop and watch as he uses a match to light the gas range and sets the pan on top. "Is this an avoidance technique?" I ask.

He glances up from the bread he's spreading with butter. "I'm a stress-eater. And that stuff in there"—he uses the knife to motion in the general direction of the library—"is enough to tank even me."

"Henry, it doesn't change anything."

"It changes everything. We can't just bury something like this."

"It's been buried this long. We can just rebury it, pretend we never found it." I watch in fascination as his sandwich grows: brie cheese, slabs of cheddar, pancetta, a spoonful of blackberry jam—necessary on all toasties in Wesbourne, although the variety depends on the region—and anchovies.

"Please tell me I did not just see you put anchovies on that thing." I move the light closer. Yep, they're definitely there.

"Don't criticize my masterpiece." He carefully lowers the whole thing into the hot pan. The scent of butter and cheese caramelizing almost makes my mouth water. "We have to think about this from all angles. If my father isn't the legitimate ruler, I sure as hell don't want him on the throne."

Opinions on our current monarch are divided. Some despise him, others hold him up as a hero for the things he's done in his two-decade reign. I don't have to wonder which camp Henry falls into.

"As far as everyone knows, he is the legitimate ruler," I say.

Lifting my leg, Henry grabs a spatula from the drawer beneath me. I feel goosebumps instantly rise at the contact. "At least four people know about the diary now."

"I'm willing to forget about it if you are. And Maisie won't say a word if I tell her not to." That leaves the old lady who donated it, but who will believe the ragings of someone with one foot in the grave? Maybe she hasn't even read it.

"But think about what you'd be giving up."

I count the advantages on my fingers one by one. "A lifetime in the public eye, enough stress to turn me prematurely gray, and no chance at a normal life. Practically paradise."

He slips the spatula under his loaded toastie and flips it gingerly onto the other side. "Okay, so it wouldn't be a walk in the park. But you'd do a better job than my father."

My laugh is abrupt. King William isn't my favorite person on the planet, but that doesn't mean I'm better qualified to lead a country, for god's sake.

What's disconcerting is that Henry has guessed that I want this—which I do, so much it shocks me, but I can't let him see that. No matter how badly the thought of leading the nation pulls at me, I can't do this. It would be too destructive.

"Coming forward with this would tear the country apart. You can't just go around flinging two-hundred-year-old bombshells without a nasty fallout," I say.

Henry slides his concoction onto a plate and cuts it diagonally. "It'll come out eventually. Secrets always do." He holds the plate toward me. "As much as it pains me to do this, are you sure you don't want half?"

"Positive. But I would appreciate being relieved of my duties as your torchbearer." I shine the light into his eyes.

He takes the phone from me and sticks it in his pocket. "Oh god," he moans, after biting into the sandwich. "This is divine."

"Spare me your food orgasm."

"You have to try it."

"Sorry, you lost me when you put anchovies on a perfectly good toastie."

"C, I promise this will change your life." He waves it close to my nose.

"I've had enough life-changing revelations for the night, thanks."

He moves to stand in front of me, close enough that a hint of pine rises above the scent of burnt cheese. "Open up." He moves even closer and shrugs, his hips brushing against my knees. "Unless you're scared."

This situation is careening toward a cliff edge. I lean forward blindly and manage to bite into the toastie he's holding in front of me. An explosion of flavor ricochets in my mouth—sweet, salty, tangy.

"Well?" Henry says, as though he's an artist who's just spent twelve months on a painting.

I offer a noncommittal grunt. "It's okay."

"Celia Eleanor, you lying twit. You loved it."

Covering my mouth while I finish chewing, I grant him a small nod. "It's pretty good."

He spins away from the counter and pumps a fist in the air. I use the opportunity to slip down from my perch and start putting things away. The sooner I send him on his way, the better.

"I still think we should come forward with all of this," he says a few minutes later as he loads the dishwasher.

"And I think we shouldn't." I swipe a wet cloth over the countertop.

"Is it really because of Wesbourne? Or is it something else?"

My hand freezes mid-wipe. "Like what?"

"Like maybe you're scared?"

"This isn't a stupid sandwich, Henry. We're talking about an entire country."

"I know that. I also know that you would sacrifice everything if you thought it was the right thing to do."

"I don't consider severing that tenuous and potential thread *sacrifice*. The right thing to do here is to say nothing."

"And give up the opportunity to make a real difference in this country?"

My skin heats with the rage starting to boil inside. "Implying what I've done so far can't be considered a 'real difference'?"

"You know that's not what I meant. I just think you could do so much more."

"That's rich coming from a guy whose only contribution to Wesbourne to date has been an enormous number of broken hearts and probably more than a few STIs."

His tone turns steely. "What I do is none of your business."

"But what I do is yours?"

"Would you calm down? I just want you to think about this before throwing it all away."

"Stop telling me to calm down! The press would drag me through the mud. And then they'd hang me. Throwing out a curveball like this will affect everything." I take a stabilizing breath. "Why do you want it so badly?"

Henry doesn't respond, and those few seconds are all I need for the truth to smack me between the eyes.

"Oh." My breath comes out in a rush, and a sick knot forms in my chest. "Doing this would relieve you of your own responsibilities. You're unbelievable." I throw the dishcloth at him and walk out, not bothering to find out if it hit him or not.

In the library, I gather up the diary pages from where they're scattered on the floor. Henry's footsteps sound behind me.

"C, that's not why I want this."

"Save me the bullshit. I should have been suspicious from the very beginning."

"If we let this go, it will all be a lie."

I slam the papers onto my desk. "Since when are you such a proponent for the truth?"

His face puckers with hurt. "That's low, even for you."

"Even for me?"

He tousles his hair, and the firelight glints off the strands like they're interwoven with gold. "I didn't mean it like that. Just that your barbs usually hit the mark."

"Words are the most effective way to let people know exactly how you feel." I refuse to let him guilt-trip me. "You should know."

"Fine, I deserved that. But maybe you should sleep on this before deciding."

"There's nothing to decide. This conversation is over, and this"—I slap my palm onto the stack of pages—"doesn't leave this room." I push past him, then turn back before walking out the door. "And stay the hell away from Beatrice."

Henry can go fuck himself.

7

"Royals" - Lorde

M Y PHONE RINGS BEFORE the morning light has even had a chance to slither its way past the curtains in my bedroom. As I should have expected, it's Maisie.

"I waited as long as I could," she says in greeting. "But I can't take it anymore. You read the diary, right? All of it?"

I push myself into a sitting position and rub the sleep from my eyes. "What time is it?"

"Five thirty. So, did you? Because I've been thinking, and we need to come up with a game plan. The best thing to do is to go into this fully prepared. But first, tell me your initial reaction. Were you shocked? When did you figure it out? I had my suspicions pretty early on, but it's so unexpected, I still find it a little hard to believe. What—"

"How much coffee have you had?"

"I don't know. Five or six cups, why? Oh, and how did you—"

"God, Maisie. Slow down. Not everyone has a caffeine drip in their arm."

I swing my legs over the side of the bed and stumble downstairs. Neither my mother nor Beatrice are up yet, because in the Chapman-Payne household we follow normal-people hours, like rising at seven a.m.

I start the coffee maker before lifting the phone to my ear again. Maisie is still talking as fast as ever, and I'm not sure she even knows I haven't been listening. I let her continue to ramble as I grab a mug from the cupboard.

Last night hurtles into my mind like a wrecking ball. The diary. Helena. William II and Catherine. Family trees. Henry. Me. The monarchy. God, what a mess. Did the whole thing actually happen? I'd write it off as the craziest dream I've ever had if it wasn't for Maisie's incessant chattering about it through the phone.

"—which seems like something to consider too. Are you even listening to me?" She finally stops for a breath.

I fill my mug and take a sip. "I am now."

"So what do you want to do?"

"Right now, I intend to enjoy every drop in this cup of coffee. Then I'm going to take a shower."

"I mean about the diary!" she says impatiently.

"I think we should keep it in the Society's safe. I don't like the idea of displaying it in the museum."

"You want to put it in the safe."

I take another sip. "Correct."

"Just until the news is out though, right? After that, I thought we could have an entire feature wall dedicated to it, with the pages detailing the pregnancy blown up so people can read it, along with pictures of Helena and maybe some of her gowns—"

"No, I mean for long-term safekeeping."

"You don't think people would be interested in seeing it?" There's confusion in her tone. "It's going to become a historical sensation overnight. I just thought—"

"It's not going to be anything besides another daybook someone found in their attic."

There is a beat of silence. I imagine her blinking repeatedly behind her glasses.

Finally, she says, "You want it to stay quiet."

"Now you're catching on."

"I see." Maisie's voice is almost too hushed to hear.

"Did you really think I would want to tell the world?"

"To be honest, yes, I did. I thought this would be a dream come true."

"Disrupting the country, informing people they've had the wrong monarchs for almost two centuries? Becoming Wesbourne's pariah? It sounds like a nightmare." An involuntary shiver passes through me, and I take another drink.

"It wouldn't need to be like that. We could approach it properly, have a detailed plan before we make a move."

"A detailed plan to blow up the country? We don't even know if the diary is legitimate. People would only need a shred of doubt to tear me to pieces over this. I like myself too much to let that happen."

"We'll find substantial proof. There must be things we can check—records, evidence, *something*."

"Why don't we ring up Helena and ask her."

"This isn't funny, Celia."

Of course it isn't. It's as unfunny as something can get, but try explaining that to the part of my brain that's short-circuiting. "Just trying to help," I say.

"I don't understand why you're responding this way. I thought you'd be thrilled. Imagine what you could do as queen!"

I did. For almost an hour last night, lying in my bed unable to sleep, my brain playing the scenes on repeat as though they were actual memories. Meeting foreign dignitaries; sponsoring charities I'm passionate about; traveling across the country to meet my citizens, listen to their requests, and find a way to make their lives better. But none of that changes the fact that sharing this diary with Wesbourne will bring more harm than good. And that's something I can't stomach.

"It's too big of a risk," I say.

"Think of Kira. You could make a difference for people like her."

The thought stabs at me, but it's one I've already considered. As queen, I'd have the power to push laws through Parliament without getting signatures on petitions. Still, there's no guarantee I would ever become queen, even if the diary were made public. Most likely, it would only cause me to lose all credibility I've earned to date.

"You won't change my mind. The diary stays secret."

"But—"

"I'm serious."

Maisie sighs. "You're giving up an incredible opportunity. Do you know how many people would kill for this?"

"Too many, I'm afraid. Why do you care so much?" I'm beginning to suspect everyone has ulterior motives concerning my future.

"I—" She's momentarily speechless, but she recovers in perfect form. "I'm your friend. I want to see you reach your highest potential."

"Then, as my friend, please respect my decision concerning this."

"Don't you at least want to talk to your mum about it before you decide?"

I shudder. "My mother is never to catch wind of this." That would provoke a level of maternal interference even Elizabeth Bennett would be in awe of.

"Okay." Maisie's tone is subdued. It's so unlike her that for a brief moment I wonder if I'm doing the right thing. But all I have to do is picture the aftermath of revealing the diary dynamite to reassure me I've made the right decision.

It doesn't matter how good anyone thinks I would be at the job. It doesn't matter that I might change things for the better. It doesn't matter what I want at all.

What matters is Wesbourne. It's the only thing that's ever mattered.

8

"The Sound of Silence" - Disturbed

T HE SOUND OF ANGRY shouting filters through the windows of my mother's car. She graciously allowed me to take it to work this morning since my own is at the repair shop for the foreseeable future, but there will likely be recompense to come.

On the block ahead of me, where the Historical Society is located, a crowd of people is boiling like a pot of stew. Some are holding handmade signs. Some are cupping their hands around their mouths as they yell. All of them appear angry. Probably another labor union strike, although I don't know why they'd be in front of the Society.

I circle the block to the back of the building, but it's almost as surrounded as the front, the sidewalks and streets throbbing with an almost palpable rage. I briefly consider turning around and going home, but I need to get to work today. After reading the diary, my arguments with both Henry and Maisie, my car breaking down, and the twenty minutes I spent searching for my phone this morning, I am counting on a long list of to-dos to get my mind off things.

I find a parking spot, grab my purse, and head for the door. Maybe I can help these people in some way. If this is another labor strike, I might be able to initiate negotiations, but first I need to get inside and clear my head.

I pick my way through the crowd and am almost halfway to the back entrance when someone shouts, "Hey! Aren't you Duchess Celia?"

Some people will never learn the proper styling of titles, nor respect those who choose not to use them. I swallow the urge to correct him. "Yes, I am."

"That's her," another person yells. "She's the one trying to steal the crown!"

The tone among the protesters changes. The shift is small at first, like a pebble thrown in a pool, then grows bigger and bigger. Slowly, as people realize what's happening, they turn and begin hurling insults in my direction.

"Throne robber!"

"Liar!"

"Power hungry!"

For the first time, I read the signs they're holding up along the street.

Our King, our monarch.

No stupid notebook is going to change anything.

Love Wesbourne, love the king.

A sharp pain shoots through my chest. Someone has gone public with the diary.

A reporter blocks my path and tries to shove a mic into my face. "Miss Chapman-Payne! What are your plans? Do you think you'll be successful in taking the throne?"

I push past her and stumble on, keeping my head down.

My legs are as limp as Jell-O, but I force them to carry me past the protesters to the back door of the Historical Society. I pray my key magically won't stick for once, and fate smiles on me for the first time all morning.

I burst through the door and relock it behind me, then collapse against the cool steel. It's a relief against the hot flashes taking over my body. My heart pounds like waves against a rocky cliff. Yoga breaths, I remind myself. Slow and steady. Calm and collected.

Maisie walks in from the archive room and startles when she sees me. "What are you doing here?"

"I work here. What in god's name is going on?"

She follows me down the hall to my office. "Didn't you see the news this morning?"

"No. I didn't have time." I think of the twenty minutes I spent combing every inch of my bedroom for my missing phone before finding it on my desk in the library. Today is already shaping up to be fantastic. "Have you called the police?"

"There are a few officers out there, but there's nothing they can do at this point. The crowd is peacefully protesting."

I can still feel hands clamoring at me, and I shudder. "That is anything but peaceful."

"Didn't you get my texts? I even tried calling you."

I unlock my traitorous device to see a missed call from Maisie and four from Henry. Maybe I should start tying the thing to my body. "I couldn't find my phone, and by the time I did, I was already running late."

All weekend, Henry bombarded me with messages. He seemed to have made it his personal mission to change my mind about the whole diary business. When he wasn't successful, he must have decided to take more extreme measures and gone to the press. I will have his head before the day is over. What a bloody disaster.

Maisie walks over to the window and peeks through the miniblinds. "There are so many people out there."

"And they're very angry." I blow out a breath. "What am I going to do?"

"I think you just have to ignore them. They'll eventually lose interest and go away."

"I mean in the long run. So much for burning the diary and pretending it never existed."

She turns around, fear in her eyes. "You don't—you don't think I had anything to do with this, do you? Because I *swear* I didn't say a word to anyone. You know I would never do that, right? I promised you I'd take this secret to my grave. While I think you'd make an incredible queen, and obviously I would kill to be your private secretary . . . I mean *imagine*. It would be a total dream come true." She shakes her head. "But that's not the point. Because I would *never* do that to you. I can't even—"

"Maisie." I put up my hand, motioning for her to stop. "I never thought you were responsible." It took me all of two seconds to put the pieces together. "I know exactly who is to blame for this mess."

Just like that, my plan to hide the past has disintegrated with a poof. Wesbourne is going to take matters into her own hands, without stopping to consider the cost to herself. How many people will be hurt by the time this blows over?

Maisie walks back to the door. "I'll get you a coffee. We'll both think better with some caffeine in our systems."

"You're a saint."

After she leaves, I take her spot at the window and peer out at the crowd, which has grown in size and is still quite animated. Someone is giving an impromptu speech. What is the Crown making of all this?

Like some kind of creepy telepathy, Henry's name lights up my phone, his fifth call this morning.

"You have some nerve," I say.

"Why didn't you answer earlier? Don't go to work today."

"Too late."

"You're already there? Bloody hell, C."

"I had no idea there was anything going on."

"If you would have answered your goddamn phone—" He breaks off, and I picture him pacing, his hair disheveled from his roving fingers.

"I cannot believe that after everything I said, you still went behind my back," I tell him. "What kind of bastard are you? This will completely ruin me, to say nothing of the repercussions for the whole country. You're even worse than I thought."

"God, Celia. Why don't you tell me how you really feel?" A muffled curse floats through the phone. "Do you actually think I had something to do with this?"

"What do you expect me to think? You pester me all weekend about it, then expect me to believe someone *else* leaked the story?"

"Yes, that's exactly what I expect, because it sure as hell wasn't me. Who else did you tell?" Anger bleeds through his voice.

"I didn't tell anyone. Maisie already knew, but she swears she didn't say a thing."

"It had to be her."

I let out a humorless laugh. "She's the last person on earth to say anything, right after your dog."

"I don't have a dog."

"So what happens now?" I turn as Maisie reenters my office with a steaming mug of coffee. *Bless you*, I mouth.

"We have a meeting with the press secretary and prime minister in an hour," Henry says. "Hopefully we'll get a plan in place to stop this madness."

"Good luck. Keep—"

The sound of breaking glass reverberates through the room as an object tears through the window and slams against my computer screen, shattering both. I instinctively scream and duck. I do my best to avoid the shards on the floor around me. If I hadn't moved a few seconds earlier, pieces of my brain might be splattered across the marble.

"Celia? Celia!" Henry yells from my phone, now lying across the room where it landed. I turn to see Maisie curled into a ball near the door behind me.

"Are you okay?" I ask her.

She nods.

"Go ring the police station. Quickly!"

She scrambles to her feet and leaves the office. Hunching over so I'm below the window, I gingerly pick my way over the glass to my discarded phone. When I lift it to my ear, I can hear Henry on the other end barking orders to someone.

"Henry?"

"Celia, thank God. Are you okay? What happened?"

"I'm fine." I stay in a crouch but peek over my desk to see what was thrown. "Someone launched a rock through the window. Maisie and I are fine, but my office is a wreck."

"If you can get to a room without windows, do so now. I'm on my way." He hangs up before I can object.

"The police are on their way. The officers outside are too busy making arrests to come in and take statements," Maisie relays when I meet her in the foyer.

Someone has thrown a rock through the glass wall at the front of the building as well, and the shards are scattered all the way to the edge of the reception desk. Fortunately, Maisie contacted all of our staff and volunteers earlier to let them know to take the day off.

When the officers arrive, they take both our statements in small offices away from the main entrance. After we've finished, I follow them back to the reception area, where Henry is waiting as promised. He is joined by several armed men that can only be bodyguards.

"You didn't need to come," I say, but the relief at seeing him nearly cripples me. I force myself to remain upright and in control. "The police have it handled."

"Are they going to handle that, too?" He points to my forehead.

I raise my hand to find a small gash, only an inch wide. The blood has already dried. "I'm fine. It's nothing serious."

"Regardless, you look like Frankenstein. Let's get it cleaned up." He leads me to a nearby chair and pushes me into it.

"Frankenstein was the creator of the monster, not the monster himself."

"You're delirious. I'll be right back with a first-aid kit."

I close my eyes and lean back. It's all creeping up on me, and my nerves are so heightened the sensation is almost painful, a tingling that both tickles and hurts. What I wouldn't give to undo everything that's happened since Friday.

I startle awake when Henry comes back with the medical bag from the front desk. "When's the last time you slept?" he asks, pulling out an antiseptic wipe.

"Last night." I remember seeing 2:27 on my alarm clock before closing my eyes. I haven't slept more than five consecutive hours in years.

"Hold still." He leans over and gently wipes away the blood on my face. The scent of his cologne tickles my nose, and I drop my eyes so they can't meet his.

"Ouch!" I squirm under his feather-soft touch. "That stings."

"Don't be a baby. I'm almost done." He tosses the wipe aside, sticks a bandage over the cut, and carefully rubs his thumb over it, causing a million goosebumps to rise on my neck. "There, as good as new. Come on, I want to introduce you to your new personal protection officers." He helps me out of the chair.

Two men, whose suits can't hide their muscles and who must have aced the class "Twenty-Five Ways to Hide Your Emotions," are waiting for Henry to snap his fingers and command them into action. "This is

Davies, and this is Lane. They've been assigned to your security detail," Henry says.

I shoot them a forced smile before turning back to him. "Can I talk to you for a second?"

"That's what we're doing."

"I mean in private. Without the security."

He narrows his eyes, then leads me several paces away. "What?"

"I don't need bodyguards."

"Today proves otherwise."

"Fine. I don't *want* bodyguards."

"Too bad. You've got some now."

"You don't get to make decisions like that for me. I'll just dismiss them."

I march past him to do just that, but he grabs my arm, restraining me with ease. "You can't. They've been hired by the Crown. They answer to me, not you."

Wrenching my arm free of his gasp, I snap, "You have no right to interfere with my life."

"Hate to break it to you, but you became a matter of great importance to this country when that diary was leaked this morning. So whether you like it or not, you will be accompanied by personal protection officers whenever you leave your home. Got it?" He moves toward the two PPOs, grabbing my arm again and dragging me with him. "Escort her to the car, please."

I freeze as he releases me. An image of the protesters parades across my vision. It sucks at me, yanking me down into a swarming black vortex of grappling hands and horror and hate.

I've never felt hatred like that before. It was a writhing beast, eyes glowing like Lifesavers against the wheezing dark. Those people—the ones I had been cranking out plans to help—they want me silenced. They want me gone.

A strong hand envelops my elbow, a lifesaver of a different sort. I meet Henry's gaze. "They hate me."

"They don't know you. They wouldn't be able to if they did."

He shelters me against his chest, and we step outside to face the ugliness of this country I once thought beautiful.

9

"We Fall Apart" - We As Human

MY MOTHER AND BEATRICE are waiting for me when I get home. One look at their faces tells me everything I need to know.

"Oh my god, Celia! I can't believe what they're saying. Is it true?" Bea cries, launching herself at me as I walk through the back door. Lane and Davies remain outside to "secure the perimeter."

"Let her breathe, Beatrice," my mother says, freeing my neck from my sister's overeager grip. "How are you holding up?" She gives the bandage on my forehead a pointed look.

"I'm fine. Just a scratch. Everything else will need more than a sticking plaster."

She nods, and I can tell she's already concocting a scheme. It's obvious from the way her eyes flick back and forth across the tiled floor, not really seeing anything. My worst fears have just collided with her highest hopes, and there is nowhere to hide. The one upside is that if anyone can find a way to spin this so that we come out looking like heroes, it's my mother.

"We'll get through this. I'll make sure of it," she says.

I move down the hall, hoping for some time to myself to figure out what to do next, but Bea has other plans. She follows me into the library.

"Not now, Bea. Please. I just want to be alone."

She bites her lower lip, normally covered in gloss but now uncharacteristically bare. I realize she isn't wearing any makeup at all, something I've rarely seen since our mother began allowing it when Bea turned fourteen—a whole year earlier than she did with me. "I need to talk to you," she says.

"What about?" I pick up the stack of mail on my desk and flip through it.

"It was me."

"What was you?" Pulling out several items that are destined for the rubbish bin, I set them aside.

"I gave those papers to Fran. She took them to WBC."

I turn to study my sister. She's picking at her nails, pink flecks of polish peppering the rug. "What papers?"

"The ones on your desk. The ones you fought with Henry over." She raises trembling fingers to her eyes and presses them into her sockets. "That's why this all happened. It's my fault."

Comprehension sifts into my foggy head. I scan my desk for the photocopies that I somehow failed to miss all weekend. "You turned the diary over to the press?"

Hands still covering her eyes, she nods.

"What the *hell*, Beatrice?" My voice crescendos with each syllable.

A trembling sob slips past her lips. "I didn't know! I had no idea what it was. I came downstairs to get a cup of tea, and I heard you and Henry in the kitchen. I was jealous, so I stayed to listen. I heard you fighting about something, and—"

"You thought you'd take your jealousy out on me?"

"I wasn't really thinking."

"You don't say."

"I knew that Henry wanted to come forward with whatever was in those papers and you didn't. I wanted to help him out."

"You betrayed your sister for a *fling*?"

"No!" She clasps her hands together as though in prayer. She'll need a prayer before I'm through with her. "I just . . . lost myself for a moment. I thought I could help Henry out, and . . ." Her shoulders droop as her words trail away.

"And you thought he'd be *so* grateful to you for it. Well, the joke's on you, because you made as big of a mess for him as you did for me. Even if I had let him come forward with this, he wouldn't have gone to the bloody WBC."

"I know that now. I—I'm sorry for everything. Please say you forgive me. I'll do anything."

Before I can answer, my phone rings. It's Beck. "I need to take this, but we are not done here." I push past Bea, accepting the call on my way out of the room.

"I heard about everything that happened. Are you okay?" he says.

"I'm fine. Just a little shook up."

"I'm outside your house, but two angry-looking men won't let me inside."

"You're here?" I walk to the front door and pull it open. Beck is standing several yards away, apparently as close as Davies and Lane will allow him. "He's my fiancé," I tell them.

They step aside, and Beck brushes past them and into the house. Once the door is closed, he lowers his lips to mine. His kiss is warm and reassuring. He's exactly who I needed to see.

"I can't believe this madness. Are you sure you're okay?" he says.

I entwine our fingers and lead him to the back of the house. "Let's go for a walk. I feel like I might explode in here." Maybe I'll get lucky and the shrapnel will puncture one of Bea's lungs.

We stroll through the garden, which is donning its summer finery in a seductive dance. The sweet, heavy fragrance of warm flowers hangs in the air.

"Do you have an enemy out to tarnish your name?" Beck says. "Who would concoct a story like this? And worse yet, who would believe it?"

I hear my blood roaring the way it does when you hold a shell to your ear. Of course it's all rot. I never believed it myself. I force a chuckle. "A bunch of idiots, I suppose."

There is silence for a few minutes as we wind our way through the hedgerows. When he finally speaks, his voice is hushed. "It *is* just a story, isn't it?"

"God, I hope so." It comes out in a whoosh. My heart is balancing on the edge of a precipice, and the slightest nudge will send it toppling over.

"Have you spoken with anyone from the Crown yet?"

I nod. "Henry told me there was an emergency meeting scheduled with the prime minister, but that's all I've heard."

"They won't hesitate to throw you under the bus to save their own skin," Beck says.

He's probably right. Isn't that what I've suspected all along? "I'm already under the bus. A few more hits won't matter much."

"We'll take legal action if we need to. Those kinds of fabrications could be considered libel."

"Even if there's truth to them?"

He stops, which pulls me to a halt as well. "What are you talking about?" The warmth has leached out of his voice.

"There is a diary," I say. "Maisie was the one who read it first."

"You knew about this?"

"Only recently."

"How long, Celia?"

"It's not important. It—"

"How long?"

Damn it. I should have told him. "Since Friday night."

Beck looks at me incredulously. "You knew the entire weekend and didn't say a word? What was your plan?" Frustration rolls off him. The heat of it mixes with the sunshine to create a stifling cocktail. "Were you ever going to tell me?"

What can I say that won't sound foolish and offensive? *Sorry, I didn't think it mattered? I assumed you wouldn't care if I made this decision without telling you? It never crossed my mind to ask your opinion?* In the end, I settle for: "I was hoping no one would ever find out."

"For god's sake, Celia. There's a chance you should be our queen, and you thought you'd keep it to yourself?"

"When you put it like that, it sounds pretty stupid," I mutter.

He barrels on. "What I can't reconcile is the fact that you weren't going to tell me about this. We're getting married. I imagine this is the kind of thing couples share with each other."

"Can't imagine very many people having this conversation."

His nostrils flare. "You know what I mean."

"You're right. I'm sorry. I should have told you." I grab both his hands in mine. "I was hoping if I stuffed it away, I could pretend didn't know anything."

Beck pulls me into his arms, his embrace a solid wall of security. "I only wish you'd allowed me to help you through it."

"You're here now," I say against his suit jacket.

"And I'm not going anywhere, okay? We're in this together."

I squeeze him hard and pray he's right, even as part of me wonders how quickly he'll regret those words.

By evening, my WhatsApp is blowing up. My uni flatmates have watched the news and are struggling to reconcile the girl they used to dig out of the history stacks with the one whose face is currently splashed across all major news outlets—a diva who's trying to steal the crown.

Despite my mother's best attempts, I attended the University of Wesbourne rather than going abroad to Yale or Oxford. My argument was that she'd raised me according to her standards for the first eighteen years. The rest were mine to do with as I pleased.

My memories of uni are mostly of the sprawling modern campus, the giant vat of peanut M&Ms that was always on the buffet, and a group of girlfriends who were the perfect antidote to my slight obsession with my studies. They dragged me to soccer matches, where we'd sit on the bleachers in our hoodies and sip spiked hot cocoa and flirt with cute boys. Those nights were the most carefree of my adulthood, but they weren't really me.

Friendships have never come easily for me. When you show people your vulnerable side, you give them the opportunity to hurt you. It's much easier to keep your distance, even if it means not having close friends you can turn to when your world blows up because you might be the rightful monarch of your country and that country now hates you.

I know they get together without me. I can't blame them. I'm a bore because I never have more than one drink, and I criticize everything around me. They always invited me out during the year following graduation, but the club scene has never appealed to me. And between the various charities I joined, my relationship with Beck, and eventually my position as the director of the Historical Society, I more often than not had an excuse for not going. Eventually the invitations stopped coming, and the chat thread that includes me only lights up when someone has a birthday or starts dating someone new.

Or when someone makes breaking news nationwide.

Ally: Oh my GAWD, Celia. Is it true?

That depends on what you've heard.

> **Jasmine**: Of course it's not true. You can't believe anything on the news these days.

Jasmine, ever the conspiracy theorist.

> **Rachel**: What are you planning to do, Cece?

I hate that bloody nickname.

> **Leslie**: How could you not tell us? We're your best friends!

That's debatable. Do best friends go for months without speaking?

> **Ally**: Let's do a girls' night! It's been AGES since we've hung. I heard Fire on 79 is FANTASTIC.

The new club downtown, sure to be crawling with reporters more than happy to capture all of us on camera?

> **Leslie**: Imagine if it is true! Can we be your ladies-in-waiting when you become queen?

Oh, god.

The news story has turned into a political nightmare in the space of one day. Citizens across Wesbourne are taking sides. Some, mostly those who have always supported the monarchy, are completely dismissing the diary and will do anything to keep King William on the throne. Others are outraged at the thought of an illegitimate king reigning.

With rioters still camped outside the Historical Society, we have opted to remain closed until things die down, hopefully within a few days. I can't risk jeopardizing our employees or volunteers. The truth I don't confess to anyone is that I'm not sure I have enough courage to face that angry mob again. Henry glimpsed the chink in my armor, but we haven't spoken since that day. He's likely been advised to keep away from me, and you won't catch me complaining about that arrangement. Distance from me means distance from Bea.

But it turns out even my own home isn't the safe haven I thought it was. On Wednesday, I receive a letter, tucked in a stack of bills and junk mail like some innocuous invitation. I open it, and the message makes my blood run cold.

STOP THIS MADNESS OR WE'LL STOP YOU. WE KNOW WHERE YOU LIVE.

It's not like the location of the estate of Whitmere is a secret, but that doesn't negate the obvious malice behind the missive.

"What is it?" my mother asks as she enters the library. She must've read something on my face.

I hand her the sheet of paper, and her face blanches as she reads it. "This is nonsense," she says, but I can see she's as shaken by it as I am. "No one would actually try to hurt us."

"They threw a rock through my office window. I don't think anyone knows what they will or will not do."

Since the first article, photos of the royal family and me have cropped up everywhere. Nauseating headlines accompany them: *Two Royal Families Wage War Over Crown. Duchess Celia Barred From Palace. The Ultimate Game of Thrones.* According to many sources, I'm nothing more than a grubby crown-snatcher, intent on ruining the nation if it means finding my way to the glory and power of the throne.

I was expecting this. If it was someone else in my shoes, I would be leading the chorus of naysayers. How dare anyone mess with our beloved

Wesbourne and her monarchy, regardless of how much we like or dislike her current king?

What I didn't see coming was those who proclaim me a national hero. They've become information whores for anything they can find on "Princess" Celia—the name doesn't even make sense, but they love it. Videos dissecting my fashion choices are going viral, and my blog crashed under the heavy traffic it is now receiving. I'm getting so much fan mail I've had to open a new email account. I've even heard that a local designer sold out of a particular dress I wore several weeks ago.

The whole thing is utterly ridiculous. I just want life to go back to normal. I have over a million wedding details to take care of, but with tensions running high, I've been advised to lie low for the time being. Read: stay locked inside my house, which would have felt like punishment regardless of what was happening outside.

The Crown is reluctant to acknowledge the issue. It's as if they think that by addressing it, they're somehow giving credit to the diary or to my supposed claims, neither of which I expect them to do, but their lack of response has only left the people more confused and distressed.

I can't count the number of requests I've received for interviews, some polite, others downright demanding. I ignore them all, because what am I supposed to say? By giving an interview, I'd be giving weight to the diary regardless of what I said, and the last thing I want to do is further drive a wedge between my family and the Crown. Despite the headlines, I have no intention of making any demands on them. So until the palace acknowledges the scandal and gives me a clue as to how to handle everything, I intend to remain silent and away from prying eyes.

It's been two weeks since the news about the diary broke, and I'm in the library working on wedding invitations. I've already met with the calligrapher twice. Deciding between the final three sketched designs is proving to be the most difficult part of this whole process. The problem isn't that none of them are perfect. It's simply that there are more pressing issues at the moment than choosing between copper holographic or silver foil.

"Celia, you're going to want to see this."

I look up from my desk as Beatrice walks into the room. Her steps falter when she glimpses my face. I'm still smarting from her betrayal and the havoc it wreaked, and as a result, am keeping her at arm's length. "I very much doubt that."

She holds out her phone. A news video dominates the screen. "Someone set fire to the palace."

"What?" I take it from her hand.

A reporter is stationed outside the palace gates as a cloud of smoke billows from the side of the building in the distance. "—confirmed there was a fire in the east wing earlier this evening. Police are unsure if it was deliberately set, but early reports are pointing to an act of terrorism. Fortunately, the east wing is used very infrequently, and no casualties have been reported. We're seeing an increase in violent acts, and we advise all citizens to stay inside unless absolutely necessary. Caution is recommended in all—"

I stop the clip, and the reporter's face vanishes. I wish I could make the churning pit of bile in my stomach disappear as easily.

Bea looks like a broken toy as she takes her phone back. "What's happening? It feels like the whole world is falling apart."

"I wish I knew."

I call Henry, and he answers on the first ring.

"I heard about the fire," I tell him.

"A bunch of lunatics. Things are getting bad," he says. "There was a shooting downtown too, a confrontation between two different groups that ended badly."

"Because of the diary?"

"Seems so. There's even been talk of taking up arms and storming the palace."

Acid rises from my stomach and burns the back of my throat. How did things escalate so quickly? And what is it going to take to regain the peace we had less than a month ago?

"I got a threatening letter." I don't know what has prompted me to bring it up; it seems silly to mention in light of everything else that has happened.

There's a pause, then Henry asks, "When?"

"A few days ago."

"And you didn't tell me?" His voice takes on a lethal edge.

Bea's mouth has popped open. She's probably wondering the same thing. I didn't say anything because I knew she would freak out, and because I'd rather face whoever sent the letter than my sister at the moment.

"It's not a big deal," I say to both of them. Clenching a pencil between my fingers, I begin doodling on the paper in front of me, hard, heavy lines swirling together. "Nothing happened."

"For fuck's sake, Celia," Henry growls. "You are not to go anywhere without an armed escort, understand?"

I want to tell him where he can stick his armed escorts, but even I recognize the common sense behind his directive. "I know how to take care of myself."

"For once in your life, just do as you're told. I've got enough on my plate without worrying about you, too."

"I never asked you to worry. I'll be fine."

"But if something happens to you, the Crown will take the fall for it."

The tip of my pencil snaps. Henry's never exhibited such regard for the Crown's reputation before. "Your concern is touching."

"Just stay safe, okay? I'll let you know if there's anything to report." He ends the call abruptly.

I remain in exile, and by the time another week passes, a bomb threat has been made against the palace, several businesses broken have been into and looted, and a police officer has been shot during a particularly nasty riot. The Wesbourne I know and love has turned into an ugly monster.

I wonder if I've been mistaken all along. Is there any good in this country worth saving, or have I been living in delusion? Half the nation wants me out of the picture entirely, and the other half thinks I should be crowned her queen without further ado.

None of them care what I want.

Someone has taken a giant black crayon to my beautiful drawing and scribbled on it, until the beauty has been obliterated and only the ugly remains.

10

"Fire Save Us" - Iliya Zaki

IT SEEMS THE CROWN is facing her demons after all. My mother, Beatrice, and I have been invited to attend a meeting at the palace. They give no details, simply ask that we arrive at the Green Drawing Room at 2 p.m. It's worded as a request, but when a summons comes from Wesbourne Palace, a temporary restraining order is put on your free will.

A hushed quiet fills the drawing room when we walk in, like at a wake, everyone afraid of speaking above a whisper for fear of resurrecting the dead. A footman ushers us to chairs at a large table in the center of the space, and a server brings us tea and coffee. The wheels of the drink cart fracture the silence like a high-pitched giggle as she pushes it around the room.

The prime minister is already seated across from us, in murmured conversation with someone I assume to be one of the Crown's advisors. The palace's press secretary is seated near them, as well as a few other people. No one from the royal family is here, but I can't imagine we'll be meeting without them.

I accept a cup of tea and use it to warm my icy fingers. I chose it in hopes it would calm my nerves, but I probably should have asked for coffee instead. Because let's be honest: nothing is going to calm my nerves at this stage. The next hour could very easily determine my future. I might be sick before it's over.

Henry enters the room, which prompts Beatrice to sit up straighter. He winks at her before unbuttoning his suit coat and sitting down on the opposite side of the table. "Good afternoon, ladies."

I sip my tea and visualize ramming a hundred darts into that pretty face of his. Beside me, Beatrice runs her fingers through her hair before toying with the ends. Does she have any idea how obvious she's being?

"Why are we here?" she whispers to Henry.

Before he can answer, King William and Queen Olivia walk in. Henry's parents are as dissimilar as any two people I've ever met, like opposing chess pieces.

William is dark and brooding, his face lined with a hard anger he'd look naked without. But if he's a storm cloud, his wife is the sun. Olivia is petite and polished and looks more blue-blooded than her husband does. Her blonde hair is flawlessly swept away from her face, leaving it free to smile and radiate warmth in the wake of William's storminess. Wesbourne loves her. They tolerate him.

But no matter what you think of his tax hikes or the permanent scowl on his face, you have to admire the guy. Anyone who can mastermind the institution of ten thousand new jobs during a global recession, all while backing the implementation of more trade programs in public schools, can't be all bad. Of course, the more people hold jobs, the more the Crown collects in income tax, which subsequently lines William's own pockets. But you won't catch me complaining about something that has so significantly improved this country.

Everyone now stands in deference while the king and queen take their seats. The prime minister opens the meeting and recounts the recent events that we are all too familiar with already, which have culminated in the need for some kind of action on the part of the Crown. Are they just coming to this realization, or is the intention to give the rest of us the impression that they've simply been too busy in the past month to care?

"The most concerning of all of these events is the call to arms that has recently been broadcast throughout this city, as well as the other major cities in Wesbourne. It appears the citizens have decided to take matters into their own hands. We have no idea how many people would actually rise up, but any number is too many.

"Our country cannot withstand a war of any kind. If we are divided, we become ripe for invasion. Although the United States is our ally, our treaty specifically stipulates that they will not offer aid in the event of a civil war. It is imperative we avoid that at all costs." The PM clears his throat and continues.

"As some of you know, Parliament held an emergency session yesterday. During that session, several suggestions were made as to how we might maintain the peace in Wesbourne. Of these suggestions, only one was voted by the majority to be in the best interest of our country and her people. Only one seemed to carry the potential to ultimately diffuse the ticking time bomb we are facing right now and hopefully eliminate all talk of civil war. Parliament voted to go ahead and present this option to the parties who will be affected and who will ultimately need to decide on the course of action they are willing to take.

"Prince Henry and Celia, Duchess of Whitmere." He pauses and looks down the table at the two of us. "Parliament is asking both of you to consider your loyalty to your country of utmost importance right now. You both have a claim to the throne, depending on the perspective. With that in mind, a suggestion has been made that would require sacrifice, but that may, in fact, save this country."

Oh god. My stomach is wound into a ball so tight, I'm afraid to move for fear of rupturing it. I clasp my shaky hands together in my lap and try to imagine what the PM is going to say next. Will Henry and I have to enter some kind of competition for the throne? A sword fight, or an obstacle course? I know the idea is absurd, but whatever he's about to suggest, it's obvious I'm not going to like it.

The prime minister continues. "The only solution that appears to stand a chance of preventing a civil war is for the two of you to get married."

The room is silent.

And spinning.

And suddenly very warm.

Too warm.

But somehow I am cold, my fingers icicles. I'm frozen—a literal statue.

Everyone can hear my racing heart. It's impossible not to. It's so loud.

I can't turn my head to look at my mother, but I can see her hands from the corner of my eye. They are clenched and white. I glance down at my own lap, where my hands mirror hers.

I refuse to look at Henry. His eyes pull at me like magnets. He wants me to meet his gaze. I can feel it. We're a set of Tricky Dogs. He's the black Scottie. I guess that makes me the white one.

I look everywhere but at him.

The wood grain of the table scurries away from me in both directions. My salmon-colored teacup is missing a tiny fleck of gold from its rim. A piece of dust floats down and lands silently in my tea. Beatrice is shredding a napkin on her lap beside me.

"Forgive me, sir, but I'm not sure I understand how that would solve anything."

Henry's voice shatters the silence like a wrecking ball. The effect is immediate: people begin to breathe again, to fidget.

"No apology needed, Your Royal Highness. The marriage is only the first part of our proposal. The second is a joint coronation in three months. This would be announced to the public in hopes of appeasing both parties, those who wish to continue the current lineage and those who wish to"—he glances at me, and a red flush creeps up his neck—"see Catherine's descendant on the throne."

"But I'm only the heir. What does this mean for my father?"

"King William has agreed to abdicate for the good of Wesbourne."

I dart a quick glance at the king's face. He hasn't done so willingly, that much is clear. But then I've never actually seen him smile, so maybe his face simply doesn't know how.

"Of course, since Celia would be rising to the rank of crown princess and then queen, the duchy would be passed down to the next heir in line," the PM says.

More silence follows. The processing part of my brain is currently experiencing a malfunction. "You must be joking, sir." The sound of my own voice shocks me. I didn't realize I was capable of speech. That opinion must have been shared, because I can almost hear the eyes collectively turning in my direction.

"I understand the predicament this puts you in, Your Grace. I know you are engaged to be married to someone else. Parliament was in session for eight hours over this. If there was another way, we would've found it."

"But there must be another option. Can we not persuade the people to keep peace? Surely there are enough level-headed people in this country who are willing to see reason." The more I fight the hysteria threading my voice, the thicker it grows.

"Even if it were that simple—which it's not—but if it were, there's still the matter of the diary's allegations. People aren't simply going to forget about it."

This is absolutely preposterous. They are actually proposing that I marry Henry.

Henry.

No horror movie in the world could inspire a nightmare this horrendous.

One of us would end up dead. Within a week. Probably him. Which means I'd go to prison for life. Maybe I could plead self-defense? If

I could hold off until I became queen, could I exonerate myself? Do queens even have that kind of power?

"Couldn't Beatrice do it instead of me?" If the depths of my desperation weren't already apparent, the fact that I've just offered up my own sister to a wolf flips on the flood lights.

Bea jerks her head up at my words, and a sharp pang flares in my chest. She's actually hoping it's a possibility. But let's be honest—so am I.

The PM shakes his head. "I'm afraid Lady Beatrice is too young. The law dictates a ruler must be twenty-one before being crowned. So even if you were to abdicate your potential right to the throne, Lady Beatrice couldn't take your place for several more years."

Of course. I knew that. My fight-or-flight response is firing on all cylinders and skewing my ability to remember the name of my country, let alone the intricate nuances of her ascension laws.

Another thought grips me. "You said I would have to give up my dukedom. That includes our home, doesn't it?"

The PM has turned a bright, mottled red. Apparently, upending people's lives isn't something he does with any regularity. "Since Maison de Lierre is the seat of the Duke or Duchess of Whitmere, I'm afraid that, yes, the entirety of it would go to"—he consults a paper in front of him—"your cousin, Benjamin Chapman-Payne, the new Duke of Whitmere. Should you choose to accept this responsibility," he tacks on to the end.

How comforting. I have a choice. Which door do you choose, Celia? Hell or Hades? "But that's our home!" I blurt out.

I worry at my bracelet, a fragile link to sanity between my fingers. My mother tenses beside me. Raising your voice at the prime minister, in front of the king, is *not* an acceptable thing for a lady to do. But I'll wager no lady has ever been put in my position before.

"I know how shocking all of this must be." The PM fixes his attention on my mother, who is sitting as though a broomstick has been superglued to her spine. "A set of rooms in the palace would be readied for each member of your family, ma'am. The three of you would assimilate into the royal family."

She nods but doesn't say a word. Her fairy godmother has just granted her deepest wish. What is there to say except "thank you"?

The prime minister's face couldn't possibly get any redder. It is now the color of a ripe beet. He resumes his attack on my world. "Which brings us to another matter. Your Grace, you would, of course, be asked to resign from your position at the Historical Society, effective immediately."

The last support beneath me gives way, and I fall. "Excuse me? You do realize I'm the *director* of the Society?"

"I do, Your Grace. But if you choose to go through with this, your duties as a working royal will keep you much too busy to hold a job outside the palace. Not to mention, under the circumstances, it seems best to cut your ties with the diary and the Historical Society indefinitely."

It's too much. My fiancé, my home, my career. My entire life and identity. They want everything. Every single bloody thing.

"Parliament is aware of the enormity of this request. It will require sacrifice and a dedication to your country. We don't expect you to jump into this quickly. We ask that you give it serious thought before making a decision."

"How long do we have?" Henry is cool and collected. I am a deranged mental patient.

"Parliament is willing to give you three days to come to a decision, Your Royal Highness."

"And if we say yes?" Henry again.

"The wedding will be in one month from now."

I sputter a cough into my hand. "Just to clarify, we have three days to decide our future, then we'd be married in a month and crowned in three?"

"That is correct, Your Grace."

"What a generous offer."

The prime minister tightens his lips. "I'm not asking you to choose who you want to marry or what you want to do for the rest of your life. I'm not asking what you *want* at all." His eyes soften infinitesimally. "I'm asking you to decide how much you're willing to sacrifice for your country."

"What if we decide we're not willing to do this?" Henry's voice startles me out of my downward spiral. Is saying no actually an option?

"Parliament is putting measures in place to attempt to maintain peace, but the likelihood of them being successful is thin. As a backup, we are preparing for an outbreak of war."

My heart lurches downward. It hits my toes with a *thunk*. I have two choices: either follow through with this ridiculous plan, or drive Wesbourne to a civil war and, ultimately, ruin.

I've been grappling for a solution, anything, to prove there are other options. But it's clear now.

Preventing a civil war is up to me and that intolerable human being across the table.

11

"Courage to Change" - Sia

I T'S A GOOD THING Davies is acting as driver as well as security, because there's no way I'd have the presence of mind to get us home without veering off the road and into the steep embankment beside it. By all appearances, neither do my mother and sister.

We don't speak. What is there to say? If I refuse this proposition, I will single-handedly be responsible for the destruction of Wesbourne. If I consent, it will mean the destruction of my entire life.

But just because our mouths aren't talking doesn't mean our bodies aren't. I'm sandwiched in the back seat of the SUV that came as part of the package deal with the PPOs, and while alike in our silence, the feelings radiating off the women on either side of me couldn't be more different.

Beatrice sulks on my right, looking out the window with her chin in her palm. She hasn't so much as glanced at me since the prime minister presented Parliament's solution for Wesbourne's redemption. Her body screams its irritation like a siren, either because she wasn't consulted before her boyfriend was offered up for an arranged marriage or because she isn't eligible to marry him herself. Probably both.

On the other side of me, my mother, the duchess dowager, sits as erect and poised as ever. Her neat auburn French twist is the final period in her paragraph of elegance. I don't need to guess at her thoughts either. This marriage would be the culmination of her dreams, her magnum opus. It no longer matters that her obsession with my skin, hair, weight, and education didn't pay off in a proposal from Henry when I turned eighteen. In the end, this is almost as good, and she isn't complaining. From the slight lift of her chin, I can tell she's already plotting—likely something to do with the wedding or how I can shed ten pounds in the next four weeks.

From my position in the middle, I am considering prescription drugs as an alluring alternative to facing this situation like a mature adult.

When we arrive home, it's to a house that won't be ours for much longer if Parliament has their way. A family of strangers will put their own fingerprints all over it, obscuring the years we've spent here, smudging them out as if they were nothing. I learned to walk on these parquet floors, using the mahogany wainscot for balance. The door that leads into the back garden still has a nick from the kitchen knife I hurled at it during the ninja phase I had when I was seven.

As we step inside, Bea and my mother dissolve into the recesses of the house, which leaves the library to me. Neither of them uses it the way I do, and I've never been more grateful for that than I am right now. There is only one person's presence I crave, and even though I'll never be in it again, this is as close as I can get to having him here with me.

I lift the lid of the cigar box and breathe in the musty tobacco scent, then move to the photos lining the bookcase. The room is a hodgepodge: part cozy home library, part office and lounge, part shrine to the late Duke of Whitmere.

My father would have gone his whole life unobserved if it hadn't been for his older brother's death at nineteen, when the duchy of Whitmere passed to the spare. He was happy living in the shadows, content to contribute to the glow of his wife and daughters without needing any of it himself.

"What do I do, Dad?"

I pick up one of the pictures of us together. In it, I'm six years old, the top of my head barely reaching his elbow and my gap-toothed smile broadcasting my excitement. It was taken right after the King Frederick's Day parade in the city. My mother had stayed home with a newborn Beatrice, and having my daddy to myself all day was the best thing I could have imagined.

I can still hear the green-and-white flags snapping in the wind all around us, feel the pebbles encrusted on my cotton-candy-sticky palm from scooping up a handful of strewn flower petals. There was a whiff of peppermint in the air, intermingled with the scent of fried fish and crushed roses. Since then, I've only smelled that particular combination twice, and each time it smelled like pride.

I thought my heart would burst with it as I stood there next to my father. He was so tall I had to crane my neck to look up at him. When the troops started passing on the street, I straightened as much as I could, saluting them the way he'd shown me.

He taught me what it is to love your country. Nationalism flowed through his veins, and he joined the military as soon as he was old enough. He resigned when I was a few years old, when my mother's nagging him to be closer to home finally wore him down. He would have given his life for Wesbourne without batting an eye. He would expect no less from his daughter.

I put the photo back with a sigh and pick up another one, this one of my father before I was born, before he even married my mother. He looks sharp and handsome in his dark green uniform, grinning broadly at the camera alongside the rest of his squad. I trace a thumb over the lines of his face, which has grown hazy in my memories. What I wouldn't give for one more day.

"I thought I might find you here." My mother's voice is quiet, but it startles me anyway. She hands me a tissue, and I realize my cheeks are wet with tears.

I wipe them away and turn the photo toward her. "He looks so young."

"Only eighteen," she says. "We met several years after this was taken."

"I still can't believe he resigned. He always seemed so proud of his service."

As much as I loved all the time I had with him as a result of his early retirement, I've always imagined that he harbored a small resentment toward his wife for making him quit. And if he didn't, I do.

"He changed in those last few years," she says. "He never told me about the things that haunted him, just kept them bottled up inside. It was best that he came home when he did."

"Did he ever mention going back?"

"Not that I recall." She claps her manicured hands together. "Now, let's talk about what we're going to do with the bomb Parliament dropped."

It's such a classic Rosalind move, I almost break into a sob, but I catch myself at the last second. She won't sympathize or appreciate the lack of composure. Ultimately, it doesn't matter which of her daughters walks down that aisle and marries the heir to the throne. She pinned her hopes on me, and when that didn't work out, Beatrice made for a nice replacement. But Parliament has presented a plot twist, and she's more than happy to revert to the original plan. It's like she's waved a wand and cast some magical spell over the kingdom.

"Not now, Mum. I just need time to think."

"Time is the one thing you don't have," she says.

"I have seventy-two hours," I remind her. "And I intend to use every one of them."

I waste the next eight hours eating my way through an entire Hawaiian pizza—picking off the pineapple and eating it separately—binge-watching *Poldark*, and crying every time something terrible happens to Ross or Demelza, which basically means once the opening credits roll, the tears don't stop. Mum is likely downstairs looking for therapists with last-minute openings.

I wake the next morning groggy with sleep, the way you do when you take a two-hour nap in the afternoon and rouse to find the day wasted and your mouth tasting like roadkill. My bedroom looks like the aftermath of a high school slumber party, with one stark difference: this mess belongs to a party of one.

It's time to pull myself together. I decide to try a Katniss Everdeen. "My name is Celia Chapman-Payne," I tell the mirror. "I am twenty-five years old. I am the Duchess of Whitmere and the director of the Wesbourne Historical Society. I live in a beautiful home, and I'm engaged to the man I love. I've just been informed that I'll need to sacrifice all of these things if I have a single decent bone in my body. Otherwise, my country will be destroyed and I'll become known as the most selfish human being alive."

How is this supposed to help? Maybe I should put myself in Parliament's shoes. If the goal is to do what's best for Wesbourne, what's one measly young woman in the grand scheme of things? She comes from good bloodlines, is less likely to be an embarrassment than about 80 percent of the population, and has good teeth. Cut her off from everything she knows and loves, marry her off to the nation's biggest disgrace—two birds, one stone—and throw a crown on her head. Problem solved.

I scowl at my reflection. None of this is making things any easier. How in the bloody hell am I supposed to make this kind of decision? My formal education, while exceptional, did not prepare me for finding out I might be the rightful queen of Wesbourne. I have a newfound sympathy for Mia in *The Princess Diaries*. If only I had a queen grandmother to shout "shut up" at.

This sparks an idea. She may not be a queen, or my grandmother, but Dame Adelaide could easily pass for both, and she sure as hell will let me yell at her if I want to.

"Sure, come over, love," she says when I call her. "I'm at Englewood Manor for the weekend." I can hear the tide crashing in the background muffling her voice. "Bring your wellies."

"What?" I say, louder so she can hear me over the waves. "Why do I need my wellies?"

A garbled reply is all I get before she hangs up. Walking to the mud room, where my Le Chameau rubber boots are standing along the wall, I stuff my feet into them, then pluck my waxed jacket from its hook. I guess I'll find out what she's up to when I get there.

The estate Adelaide shared with her late husband is located in the country, about an hour southwest of Maison de Lierre. It is situated on a bluff overlooking the sea, the large manor nestled at the end of a long gravel road that winds through the craggy countryside like a child's scribble.

The housekeeper answers the door when I knock and directs me to a rocky path leading to the beach, where the mistress of the house is supposedly "busy foraging." I follow it down the steep cliff, clutching the rock face to as I try to keep my footing on the loose stones. The wind billowing in from the ocean tries to filch my breath when I reach the bottom, so crisp you could snap it in half, and the tang of saltwater permeates my nose and mouth.

I climb over the massive boulders studding the coast and spot Adelaide further down the shore with a tall, blue bucket at her side. Like me, she's dressed in knee-high wellies—although hers are Hunters—and a wax jacket, navy to my dark olive. She glances up as I approach, the wind whipping her short white hair into her face. Pushing it back with one hand, she uses the other to wave a greeting.

The first time I saw Adelaide, I did a double take because I thought she was Helen Mirren. We were at a charity gala during my final year of university, both madly intent on winning the same eighteenth-century Pierre Redford landscape that was up for auction. All of his paintings are evocative, but this particular piece is said to be his best. You can almost hear the waves slamming against the rocky coastline as you gaze at it. I would have sold my car to obtain it, and nearly had to by the time Adelaide bowed out—and none too graciously, either. She later called a truce, saying she couldn't hate anyone whose taste was as good as her own. We've been friends ever since. It was thanks to her recommendation that I got the director position at the Historical Society, where she not only serves on the board but also volunteers three days a week.

"You're just in time," she calls now, then motions for me to join her on the flattish rock she's perched on before squatting down beside a large crevice.

"What are we doing?" I can't see what she's looking at, aside from a shallow pool of water gathered in the fissure. Some sort of algae is growing along the bottom of it.

She gestures toward a small overhang, which creates a sort of cave-like opening inside the rock. "Stick your hand in there for me, love. I'll have the bucket ready."

I bark out a laugh. "Stick my hand in there? I don't think so."

"Oh, come on. Don't be a coward."

"What exactly is in there?"

She waves her hand as though I've just asked the most ridiculous question in the world. "Nothing but a pair of harmless edible crabs."

"Oh, is that all?" I grab the handle of the pail. "I'll opt to hold the bucket, thank you very much."

Adelaide chuckles, then, bending over so she can reach it, slowly sticks her hand into the narrow nook. Several seconds later, she pulls out a large brown crab, grinning victoriously. "There's the female." She drops it into the bucket and reaches back in. "Now, for your husband."

Several crabs later, we venture further down the shoreline toward what she calls a mussel patch. "All right, poppet. Tell me what's on your mind."

How do I even begin? "You've seen the news?"

"I can't imagine there's a person in Wesbourne who hasn't."

"Parliament has a plan they think will bring about a ceasefire."

Her brows meet together above her sharp eyes, and she studies my face. "What kind of plan are we talking about?"

I couldn't ask for a more trustworthy confidante. Adelaide's work in politics depended on her ability to safeguard confidential information. Even now, years later, she's still sitting on a myriad of governmental secrets. Might as well cut right to it.

"They want Henry and me to get married and ascend the throne together. In three months."

If she's shocked, she doesn't show it. Her face remains as expressionless as the rocks surrounding us. Turning toward a large outcropping on our left that's covered in mussels, she says, "Ah, look at all of these scrummy fellows."

She has either chosen to ignore what I said or is taking her time processing it.

"Several things about collecting mussels," she tells me. "Only take the biggest one from the patch."

I nod in agreement. It's the first rule of responsible foraging: never take everything.

"Secondly, try to keep the beard on the mussel as you're removing it from the rock. If you pull it off, you kill the mussel." She demonstrates by carefully prying a large black shell from the rock face, a brown, hair-like clump clinging to it. She tosses it into the bucket of seawater at our feet. "Your turn."

I follow her directions and climb over to a patch of mussels on the other side of the outcropping. I gently tug on one, and a ridiculous euphoria shoots through me when it comes loose, stringy beard still in place. Adelaide's grin makes me swell with pride.

We continue scouring the shore for more mussels, stopping once we've collected several dozen. She sets the bucket down and sits on a large rock.

"I'd have to be stupid not to deduce why you're here."

I perch beside her and wipe my wet hands on my jeans. "Does it make me a terrible person if I don't know what to do?"

"Don't be absurd. It makes you human."

"How do I choose between two right options?"

Adelaide gives me a wry smile. "Once you figure it out, let me know."

"My mother thinks I should do it."

"Of course she does. Rosalind would wither away if she didn't have ambition to keep her alive." She pins me with her sharp eyes. "But that doesn't mean you should."

"In some ways, having a choice makes it even worse. If they had just told me I had to do this, at least I could avoid all of this agonizing."

"It wouldn't be like our government to make things easy, would it? What's your heart telling you?"

I pick a piece of seaweed off the rock and drag my fingers through it. "Depends on which side you ask. Part of me can't imagine leaving Wesbourne to ruin if it's in my power to potentially save her. And of course there's the lure of being queen, of finally making a difference. The other part of me—" My voice breaks, and I take a stabilizing breath. "The other part is horrified that I'd even consider doing that to Beck. What kind of person am I?"

"You've been asked to make a terrible choice. I don't think there's a right or wrong answer."

"You're not the one who has to tell my fiancé I'm considering breaking it off with him so I can marry someone else. Doesn't the fact that I'm even having this conversation break all of the trust in our relationship? Even if I decide not to do this, how will our marriage hold up if he knows I struggled to make up my mind?"

"If he can't understand that, poppet, he doesn't deserve you." Adelaide reties the silk scarf around her neck, and I catch a glimpse of the large birthmark she always keeps covered. She pats my hand where it rests on the rock. "Beck is a good man."

I squeeze my eyes shut against the tears. "The best. To give that up, to never have a satisfying marriage . . . What am I thinking?"

"You're thinking of the greater good."

"Sometimes I'd like to tell the greater good to bugger off."

She laughs, and the wind snatches away the musical sound. The ocean spreads out before us, shocking in its limitless expanse. The waves crash further out at sea.

The tide will be coming in soon. It makes me think of one of our weekend trips to the coast as a family when Bea and I were little. We found a live starfish on the beach, and my father scooped it up and threw it back into the water. Then he told us the story of an old man who used to walk along the seashore after the tide went out, picking up starfish after starfish and throwing them back into the ocean.

One day, a younger man asked him why he bothered. He wasn't making a difference, he said, because the beach was full of washed-up starfish. He'd never be able to save them all.

The old man bent over, picked up another starfish, and threw it into the sea. Then he straightened and said, "It made a difference for that one."

The only question I have is: which starfish do I save?

12

"All Too Well" - Taylor Swift

I'M NOW OFFICIALLY PROCRASTINATING. My first of the three days is gone, and I'm no closer to making a decision than I was when I walked out of the palace, dragging the ruins of my demolished world behind me. Henry keeps calling, but I always let it ring through. I can't talk to him until I know what to say.

I haven't talked to Beck yet either for the same reason. What do I tell him? *Hey honey, how would you feel if I broke off our engagement because a better opportunity came along?* If our situations were reversed and he said that to me, he'd be lucky to leave the room with all his appendages still attached.

I consider flipping a coin. I even spin it on my desk, but the circles make me dizzy. I imagine explaining to the prime minister that I made my decision because the coin landed face up, but I have a bit too much pride for that.

Speaking of pride, if I'm being truly honest, that's one of the biggest issues at stake here. It's what kept me quiet about the diary in the first place, has prevented me from doing a single interview since, and is now complicating this whole thing by rearing its atrocious head again.

If I do what Parliament is requesting, some people will see me as heartless and cruel for leaving my fiancé behind—all in a bid for power and fame, they'll say. This bothers me more than it should. I'm also worried that I'll lose the faith of the people whose interests I've been championing these past few years. My opinion on the outdated class system is no secret, and I've been a vocal advocate for equality. I will lose their trust entirely if I accept the position as their queen, lording over them like I'm somehow their superior.

On the other hand, if I say no to this whole thing and try to get my life back to what it was, I'll still be ostracized by those who think I've made the wrong decision. And, of course, I'll have to live with the knowledge that I could have saved Wesbourne from a civil war.

No matter which way you spin it, my life will never be the same again, and now there will always be people who hate me. I'm trying not to let this bother me, but it does.

By the time noon rolls around, I haven't done anything to get me closer to a decision besides accept Beck's dinner invitation. There's a sickening dread simmering in my stomach at the thought of what I'm going to say to him, but I push it aside. Until I know how to proceed, there's no use stressing over it.

Maisie calls to ask if I'm willing to meet with Kira Radbury's mother. She has unofficially stepped into the role of my private secretary/gatekeeper-to-the-world since the Society closed, and I couldn't be more grateful. She had the foresight to send flowers to Ms. Radbury because she knew I was too preoccupied to remember.

"She says it won't take long. I think she wants to thank you in person for the flowers and for what you're doing to protect children like Kira."

Which to date is nothing, thanks to that failed meeting with the petition committee.

"I'm heading into the city this evening," I say. "I could meet her then."

Beck and I agreed to have dinner at his flat. I didn't relish the idea of Davies and Lane, or any other restaurant patrons, being privy to our conversation.

Maisie offers to arrange everything and get me the details. Four hours later, I'm once again riding in the back seat of the obnoxious Crown-issued SUV, which might as well be a military tank, on the narrow country road.

I don't know what I'll say to Kira's mother, and I don't have a bloody clue what to say to Beck. I'm hoping my fairy godmother will transform me into a pumpkin by the time I get there so I can avoid both situations.

Maisie has arranged for me to meet Ms. Radbury at Flynn Park. It's one of the less frequented ones in the city and has the benefit of being close to Ms. Radbury's home in the eastern district.

I'm shadowed by my favorite PPOs, and when we arrive, they insist on securing the area before allowing me to exit the car. It's complete overkill because this section of the park is clearly deserted, but I do as I'm told and stay in the vehicle while Lane scouts the perimeter like he's 007.

When I'm finally permitted to get out, I see Ms. Radbury waiting for me on a wrought iron bench. She stands as I walk over, my guard dogs sticking to my side like Velcro. I plan on stepping in if they try to pat her down, but they stop about ten yards away from us, offering the illusion of privacy.

"Thank you for meeting me," Kira's mother says, and gives a short bob that I belatedly realize is supposed to be a curtsy. She is young, only a few years older than me. She must have been just a teenager when her daughter was born.

"You don't need to do that," I tell her. "Why don't we sit down?"

"I don't mean to take much of your time. I just wanted to thank you for what you're doing for Kira. Not enough people care about what happens to kids like her."

On impulse, I reach out and wrap my fingers around Ms. Radbury's. They're icy. "What happened to your daughter was terrible, and I will do everything in my power to prevent it from happening to other children."

She offers me a sad smile, and my heart breaks again at the tragedy this woman has endured at such a young age. "If only things had worked out differently, and you were actually our queen."

Her words jolt through me, but there's no way she could know about Parliament's proposition. She's only referring to Helena's secret. "I'm not sure how much good I'd do from the palace either."

"Why not? You'd have more power."

I look at the trees around us, glowing like embers in the light of the setting sun. "I'd feel like such a hypocrite. I'm not sure people would trust me anymore."

"Sure they would. It's different when those in power are on your side."

Is it? Maybe. I'll have to mull this over later, since I'm going to be late getting to Beck if I don't leave soon. I thank Ms. Radbury and ask her to let me know if there's anything else I can do. She agrees, and I'm ushered back into the car by my attentive hounds.

As the city sweeps past us, I use the precious minutes to think about what I'm going to say when I see Beck. He deserves the truth. The problem is, I'm not sure what the truth is anymore.

Do I want to be queen? Am I willing to give up everything for Wesbourne? Will I be able to live with myself if I don't save her? I don't have the answers to any of it.

As we pull up in front of Beck's apartment building, in a small hippie village near downtown, my eyes snag on a piece of Mylar caught in a bush beside the front door. A shudder crawls down my spine. It's just a deflated birthday balloon, I tell myself. But that does nothing to dissolve the taste of death in my mouth.

Beck has made individual beef Wellingtons, a green peppercorn sauce, fingerling potatoes, and fresh green beans—which he picked up at the farmer's market this morning, along with strawberry almond baklava from the confectioner's stand. He's capped the whole thing off with a very nice bottle of Cabernet Sauvignon.

I feel sick.

I was surprised the first time I saw his flat. I'd been expecting a stark and cold bachelor pad, but his warm gray walls are tastefully hung with art in a variety of styles and mediums. A supple leather sofa faces a television he only turns on when I'm here, and three stools sit at a bar that separates the kitchen and living room. All of the surfaces are free of junk mail, magazines, and odds and ends, and are instead decorated with pictures of the two of us and his sisters. An impressive collection of books takes up a good portion of one wall, and they aren't there for vanity either. He's read nearly all of them.

During my time at uni, I came across a study that showed that couples who live together before marriage have a higher divorce rate than those who wait until after their vows. When we got engaged, Beck and I decided we had everything going in our favor already. It seemed crazy to tempt the universe. After the wedding, we were planning to live in at his place for a year or two before moving to Maison de Lierre for good.

Life with him would be easy, comfortable. I wouldn't have to nag him about leaving his wet bath towel on the floor or putting the milk carton away empty. He'd indulge me with *Gilmore Girls* and foot rubs, and I'd buy him a hardcover political thriller for every birthday and holiday. And to think I'm considering dousing the whole thing in gasoline and lighting a match.

"Aren't you hungry?" He points at my plate with his fork. I've managed to take two bites of the incredible pastry he's prepared.

"It's delicious. I'm just not feeling the best."

"Do you want to tell me what's on your mind?"

I nod. That's why I'm here, but the words refuse to form.

He watches me, and when he realizes I'm not going to say anything, he adds, "I'm assuming you're still thinking about the diary?"

I bite my lip and nod again. I'm a coward, pure and simple. The least my fairy godmother could have done is load me up with courage when she rejected my request to be transformed into a gourd.

"Are you also thinking about the emergency Parliament session?"

My head snaps up. Of course he knows about the meeting. He works at the palace. Maybe he knows about everything. Maybe I've been stressing, running myself ragged over how to tell him, and he's known all along. Maybe it's not as big of a deal as I'm making it into; maybe there's a legal loophole or the situation has died down since the meeting or—

A glance at Beck's confused face ends my fantasy. He doesn't know anything.

"Yes, that too." I clear the cobwebs from my rusty voice. "They've proposed something they hope will end the riots and acts of terrorism. Something they feel is the only viable option. They were in session all day trying to find another solution, but this was the only thing they came up with."

I'm stalling.

I can't do this.

The words won't leave my mouth.

Beck stabs a forkful of green beans while he waits for me to continue.

Then the words tumble out on top of each other like gumballs from a busted machine. "They want me to marry Henry."

He freezes midchew and looks at me like he doesn't remember who I am. Now it's his turn to be mute, and he stares at me for what feels like an eternity.

Finally, I can't take it anymore. I whisper, "Please say something."

He drains the contents of his wine glass. "I don't understand. How would you marrying Henry solve anything?"

I explain as best I can, but I must be failing miserably, because instead of comprehension, a steely coldness settles over him. "It sounds as though you've already made up your mind."

"No! That's the problem. I don't know what to do."

"You don't know what to do," he parrots.

"I've been going back and forth in my mind the last two days, and I'm no closer to knowing what I should do than I was. Please help me, Beck."

He's quiet for so long I can feel each one of my nerves splitting into a frayed end. I know he's still processing all of this, but I wish he would do it out loud so I could know what he's thinking. It's always been one of the more frustrating differences between us. My words hit a greased slide to my mouth, bypassing my brain altogether. His marinate in his cerebral juices for a while until their flavor is just right.

"Let me get this straight," he says, adjusting his knife and fork so both are at exactly six o'clock on his plate. "You were asked several *days* ago to break our engagement and marry Henry. Since then, you haven't breathed a word of this to me and have instead been debating *what you should do*?"

"What would you have had me do instead?"

"Call me immediately? Tell them right then you wouldn't do it? Anything but fret about it like there's a decision to be made."

"But there *is* a decision to make," I say, palms up. How is he not getting this?

Beck sags into his chair. "You're actually considering this."

"You think I should abandon Wesbourne when I have it in my power to save her?"

"It's not your problem, Celia."

"It became my problem the day I was born into a royal bloodline. Possibly the only royal bloodline."

He scoffs. "Does that somehow make you nobler than the rest of us?"

"No, it makes me required by *blood* to give everything I am to this country."

"No one would blame you for saying no to this."

"No one except me." I don't realize how true the words are until they're out of my mouth. Would I really be able to hold my head up if I walked away from my country when she needed me most? It would negate everything I tried to do in the future. If I only contribute to society when I stand to benefit from it, it means Henry's right. I am selfish.

"Isn't this the kind of thing we decide together? We're on the verge of getting married, for fuck's sake," Beck says, and I flinch. He never curses.

"You're right. I'm sorry." I take a deep breath and brush my hands across my trousers. "What's your proposition?"

"Tell them you're not willing to do this, then marry me like you promised. It's as simple as that."

My eyes flit to the enlarged portrait hanging above the table. It's from our engagement shoot. We're standing in front of St. John's, the oldest cathedral in Wesbourne, the exquisite architecture creating a gorgeous backdrop. We look happy and in love, because we are. Will this break us forever?

"And if I choose that option, what happens to Wesbourne?" I say it softly, not sure I'm ready for the answer.

"I don't know, but we can leave, go live somewhere else. America, England, France. We'll buy a villa in Fiji. It doesn't matter. What matters is that we'll be together."

My tongue is numb, a heavy, dead weight in my mouth. "That's not all that matters, Beck."

If you had asked me five minutes ago if he felt the same way I do about this nation, I would have said yes without hesitation, but it's becoming apparent his devotion to her is vastly different from mine.

"I can't believe you would do this to me," he says. "To us."

"You make it sound as though I'm in this situation by choice."

He shakes his head. "It wouldn't be hard to get out."

I gape at him. "How can you say that? Everything about this situation is hard."

"If I were in your shoes, we wouldn't even be having this conversation."

He's right. I'm a fool to not have seen it before.

Beck wasn't raised the way I was. He's had to fight for everything he has. A mother who deserted their family, an alcoholic father who all but left his twelve-year-old son to raise his younger sisters, an ex-wife who divorced him after what he thought were three happy years of marriage—life hasn't been kind to him. He had to work three jobs just to put himself through university. While he's succeeded against the odds, he's not willing to sacrifice everything he has for a country that did little to help him when he needed it. And now I'm considering leaving him as well, cementing his belief that he is unworthy of love.

I can't do it. If I love him, I can't destroy him like this. There has to be another way.

"What if we found a compromise?"

"A compromise."

"We wouldn't be legally married, but . . ."

He looks at me without blinking, and I know the wheels in that brilliant head of his are spinning fast. Without a word, he tosses his napkin onto his plate and pushes away from the table. The action knocks over my glass, which is still half-full, and the wine oozes into the stark white tablecloth and dribbles onto the hardwood floor. He doesn't even notice.

"Beck. Can you please say something?"

He's now leaning against the countertop. Tension ripples through the muscles in his back, but he doesn't answer.

I stand and move to the cupboard under the sink, where I know I'll find a bottle of white vinegar and a roll of kitchen paper. He doesn't even glance in my direction. "Beck?"

Grabbing the supplies, I mop up the spill on the floor, then turn my attention to the purple-red splotch on the tablecloth. "How am I supposed to know what you're thinking if you won't talk to me?" I pour vinegar onto the stain to neutralize the pigments.

"I assumed my thoughts on your"—he pauses, as if searching for the right word—"*suggestion* would be a foregone conclusion." Tight ropes in his arms strain beneath his rolled-up shirtsleeves.

"It's not all cloak-and-dagger these days," I say. "We could make it work."

He spins around to face me. "Do you think so little of me that you assume I would be happy to play second fiddle to another man?"

"Of course not."

"And yet you propose this preposterous arrangement, assuming I'd be thrilled."

"I am trying," I say, "to find a way to keep my world from completely imploding. This is the only thing I can think of!"

"Your mistake was thinking I'd consider being your *mistress*. I'm supposed to be your husband, but for some reason, you've taken that option off the table!"

The slap of his words reverberates through me. I keep dabbing at the wine-and-vinegar-soaked tablecloth and duck my head to hide my brimming eyes. "My mistake was thinking you loved me enough to do whatever it took for us to stay together."

"You're the one tearing us apart."

I am losing my grip on my tears. Where do we go from here?

"I still have another day before I need to give them my answer," I say. "What if we talk again tomorrow?"

Beck moves his hands to his narrow hips, hands that I love, that have cradled my face so many times. "You seem perfectly capable of deciding on your own," he says. "Once you walk out that door, don't bother coming back."

13

"Anxieties" - The Regrettes

IF I WERE A better person, I wouldn't have suggested that Beck and I start an affair. If I were a better fiancée, I wouldn't have considered breaking off our engagement. If I were a better citizen, I wouldn't be wavering back and forth about this decision.

I should know what to do. And I should have anticipated Beck's anger.

He's the Chandler to my Monica, and life without him doesn't feel like a life at all. Was it really so farcical to suggest that we might be able to find a small amount of happiness in spite of the circumstances?

When I get home from dinner, there's a faint glow emanating from the library. I enter, eager for anything that will remind me of my dad, remind me that there are more important things at stake here than what I want. Someone has lit a fire in the hearth, and it crackles and hisses, the mellow aroma of burning pine filling the air. God, I will miss this room when we leave.

Is that it, then? Have I made my decision subconsciously? Was there ever a decision to make?

I stand in front of the blaze and allow its gentle warmth to saturate my bones, trying to drive out a cold I'm not sure will ever leave. I hold out my hands in an attempt to thaw them, and Beck's ring sparkles in the light, flames reflecting in the two-carat diamond.

Since he slid it on last fall, it's become a fixture on my finger, one I never thought I'd take off again. He saved up for nearly a year to buy it; enlisted the help of both of our families, a photographer, and a cellist; designed the perfect opportunity to say those four words I'd dreamed of hearing since I was young. *Will you marry me?*

The whole holiday was exquisite. Strolling through Galleria Borghese. Exploring the Colosseum and the Pantheon. Indulging in plate after plate of pasta and an endless supply of wine. Finally, it culminated in front of the Trevi Fountain on our last night. As strains of music surrounded us in a haze of happiness, Beck dropped to one knee, and I promised him a future. A future I yanked away almost as quickly. Am I really as heartless and cruel as he thinks I am?

I slip the ring from my finger and allow myself one more admiring glance before dropping it into my pocket.

"You're going to do it, then?"

I spin around to find Bea sitting in the corner, deep in the recesses of an armchair. "I don't expect you to understand."

"That's good, because I don't." She snaps the book on her lap shut, and the harsh sound echoes through the room. "How can you live with yourself?"

"Let's not forget who got us into this mess in the first place."

Her soft features harden into stone. "Don't worry. You can't possibly regret it more than I do right now."

"There wouldn't have been a future for you and Henry anyway." The fact that she's only succeeded in pushing him out of her grasp forever is a small consolation now.

"Is that supposed to make me feel better? I love him!"

"Bea," I say. "We both know he would only have used you, then tossed you aside when he got bored. Look at his track record."

"I suppose you think it'll be different with you."

"I beg your pardon?"

"You've always wanted him, even back when we were kids. This is your dream come true." It comes out it with so much venom, I blink and take a step back.

"Are you out of your mind?"

"You think the world revolves around you," she spits. "Isn't it ironic that as soon as I want Henry, you become engaged to him? Why do you always need to win at everything?"

A strangled cough bolts from my throat. "You think this is some kind of *competition*? If I could get out of this mess, trust me, we wouldn't even be having this conversation."

"They're not forcing you to do anything. You're the one throwing away your fiancé to steal the man I love."

"You want me to allow Wesbourne to fall to pieces because my sister has a crush on the prince? Bea, most of the women in this country think they're in love with him."

"But they're not your sister." She sinks even further into her chair. It's like it's swallowing her whole. "I love him, Celia. I think I always have. He's always been so sweet to me, so funny and playful. He never treated me like I was just a little kid. He's protective too, and I feel safe when I'm with him. Who wouldn't fall in love with him?"

She's right—who wouldn't?

"He's not that boy anymore," I say. "He's manipulative and selfish. You see the way he lives, the things he does."

Bea snorts. "Maybe we should be more cautious of people whose flaws aren't blatantly obvious. We all have them. Some just feel the need to hide them. I'd rather have someone who is brutally honest about who they are."

I fill my lungs with air and fight for strength. She's devastated and delusional, but I've already hurt Beck tonight. Is there a chance of ending this evening without hurting my sister too? "I'm sure you're right. What are you looking at anyway?"

She sniffs and swipes her hand under her eyes. "Just some old photo albums." She hands me one. "Looking for pictures of Dad."

I flip through it. It's full of snapshots taken when we were young: Bea in the bathtub, me blowing out the candles on my tenth birthday, both of us dressed in poofy white dresses for Aunt Eleanor's wedding.

"Sometimes I forget what he looks like," she whispers. "I've already forgotten the sound of his voice. The way it felt when he held me." A long sniff punctuates her words. "I come in here because it's the only place that still feels like him. I've tried sniffing his cigars like you do, but they're too strong; the other notes of his scent are gone. But sometimes when I close my eyes, I can almost picture him sitting in his chair."

I wipe at the tears on my cheeks. Will I ever stop crying tonight? "I wish I could freeze his presence, but every year it seems to vanish more."

We sit together for a few minutes, flipping through the albums and revisiting a childhood that feels like a lifetime ago. How has so much transpired in such a short period of time?

"Why does losing someone have to hurt so bad?" she says. I know she's referring to more than our father.

I swallow, unsure whether I can trust my voice. It comes out warbled. "The greater the love, the greater the loss."

Bea waits a long time before saying softly, "I guess that makes it worth it, then."

"Does it?" I think about Beck standing in the kitchen earlier, not bothering to turn around as I left his flat.

"Of course."

"The happiness is only temporary," I say. "The pain lasts a lifetime."

A frown creases her smooth brow. "But doesn't the happiness outweigh the pain?"

I think of the grief I feel for my dad. It's agonizing, crippling, debilitating. Nothing can overshadow it, not even the mess I'm currently in. "I'm not sure it does. Not always."

"What about memories?" Bea rubs her hand across the album cover. "You'll always have those. Thinking back to the good times can at least diminish the pain."

"Yeah, sometimes those help." And sometimes they only intensify it. A haunting reminder of what could have been, should have been.

"I'll always be a believer that it's better to have loved and lost than to never have loved at all." She stands and reshelves the albums.

I smile. "You've always been more of a romantic than me."

"Do you have a single romantic bone in your body?" she asks wryly.

"Not anymore."

"Why can't you see that you're hurting people by doing this?" She says it quietly. I should've known the moment we just shared was only a temporary reprieve.

"I see it better than anyone, Bea. I've got a knife buried up to the hilt in my own heart."

"We're going to lose this house." Her voice breaks. "So not only are you taking Henry from me, you're also taking Dad. What kind of sister does that?"

Her words hit their mark, bullseye, dead center. Henry is no loss—he was never hers. But our father . . .

"We've established that you're willing to hurt everyone you love." She brushes the tears from her cheeks, but she's not done doling out wounds like they're party invitations. "But what makes you think Henry will agree to marry you at all?"

14

"Mr. Brightside" - The Killers

U NTIL BEATRICE SAID THE words, the thought never crossed my mind. *What makes you think Henry will agree to marry you at all?* Why didn't I take his calls? If he isn't willing to go ahead with this whole arrangement, I've destroyed my own future without cause. Beck will never take me back if he thinks Henry rejecting me is the only reason for my return, and I can't blame him.

After my conversation with my sister, I manage to get a few hours of sleep, and the next morning I call Henry. Parliament is expecting our decision first thing tomorrow. We make plans to meet at the palace tonight, because there's no way I'm having this conversation over the phone.

The day leaks by, and I mark the passing of each hour with a spoonful of cookie dough from the tub Rosalind thought she'd hid in the back of the refrigerator. I've managed to avoid any real conversation with her about my decision, but that's probably because she assumes my despondency can only mean one thing.

Eventually, the time comes. I should have demanded that Henry clear his schedule and meet me earlier, but I'm putting off seeing him for as long as possible. The last place I want to be is at his mercy—which is exactly where I'm going to find myself in a matter of minutes.

Is it possible to taste dread? Because the sour flavor in my mouth won't go away, no matter how many times I brush my teeth.

A footman ushers me through a series of furniture-stuffed chambers, each winding further into the heart of the palace. I'm going to need a map of this place, or I'll meet my demise by getting lost and starving to death in a room that hasn't been touched in the last decade. It's been ages since I've played hide-and-seek here, and the further we walk, the more confused I become.

I glance up at the sound of voices and giggling above me. Henry is escorting two women down the staircase to my left, both wearing dresses that should be considered underwear. My high-waisted trousers and navy sweater are a nun's habit in comparison.

When they reach the bottom, Henry spots me and has the decency to flush. "Celia." He attempts to disentangle himself from his companions. "I'll be just a minute."

The women give me mocking smiles and toss their hair over their shoulders as he leads them away.

I silently call him every foul name I can conjure, including a few I've never used before and am surprised come to me with such rapidity. I follow the footman into a small drawing room and accept the drink he offers me. It's dim in here, the handful of lamps giving off only a tepid light, leaving the corners shrouded in shadow. I ignore the stiff-as-a-board leather sofa in the center of the space and cross to the single window, then shove aside the heavy velvet drapes that smother the view of the night sky.

My fingers find the bracelet at my wrist and twist the charm round. The whiskey scorches a blissful path down my throat, and my shivering abates. The awful taste in my mouth remains, though.

A few minutes later, Henry walks in and closes the door softly. I can smell him without turning around. Amber, pine, vanilla—and the gagging hint of floral perfume. I take another gulp from my glass.

"I didn't know you drank," he says. The slosh of liquid being poured is the only other sound in the room.

"I don't." I take another sip. I'm still facing the window, and his gaze on my back is like the tip of a knife blade. I rub at the goose bumps that have risen on my arm in spite of the sweater I'm wearing.

"Are you okay?" he asks.

"Not in the slightest." The remainder of my whiskey slides down my throat like hot lava.

"Trouble in paradise?"

"Whatever gives you that idea?"

The sound of a match being struck pulls my attention across the room. Henry is kneeling before the fireplace, where logs are stacked and ready for burning. "Just a hunch," he says.

I walk over to the bar and top up my glass. "I don't know why the bloody hell I'm here."

"Surely it has nothing to do with the fact that Parliament is expecting our answer tomorrow."

I glare at him. "It's certainly not for the company."

"I'm assuming you talked with your fiancé?"

"Yep."

"What happened?"

"What do you think?" I hold up my naked left hand.

A frown creases his brow. "He let you go? Just like that?"

"What was he supposed to do after I told him I was considering marrying someone else?"

"I sure as hell would have fought harder than that for the woman I love."

"I wasn't aware you've ever loved anyone besides yourself," I say.

"Would you know if I had?"

"It doesn't take a genius to figure out that a guy who sleeps with a different woman every night doesn't know what it's like to truly love someone."

"Unless, of course, he does."

The look on his face begs me to feel guilty, so I move to refill my tumbler instead. Again. Why has it taken me so long to enjoy hard liquor? This buzzy warmth is really quite nice.

"Maybe you should slow down," Henry says.

"Maybe you should mind your own business."

"C, we have a lot to discuss. I just think you should have a clear head for it."

I slam the glass down on the bar. "Don't you dare tell me how to conduct myself. Not when you're a disgusting, drunk manwhore yourself."

He chuckles mildly, like he can't believe I just said that. I can't either, come to think of it. "At least come sit down." He gestures to the sofa.

"I'll stand, thanks."

Sighing, he shoves a hand into his hair. "The sooner we talk about this, the sooner you can leave."

"Then just stop!"

"Stop what?"

"Stop being a pain in the ass. Stop making it impossible for me to feel normal around you."

He moves toward the bar, and I take several steps backward until the wall prevents me from going any further. Soon, he's within inches of me.

"What are you doing?" I ask. It sounds more breathless than it should.

Damn that whiskey. He's taking up every inch of space, and I can't draw a breath that doesn't contain him.

"Making it impossible for you to feel normal." His voice brushes my skin like a silky-soft feather. He props his hands against the wall on either side of my face. "I want you to feel alive, on fire. Passionate. Excited. Animated." He shakes his head. "Anything but normal."

I'm not sure the last time I saw Henry this closely. His eyes are burning through me like a forest fire looking for something—anything—to consume. His irises look nearly black, the color of a lush velvet night, with tiny specks of gold flecked throughout.

"Why do you care how I feel?"

"Because when you're on fire, you bring people to life. You bring me to life." He smirks, and that familiar glint comes back into his eyes, obliterating the glow that was there just moments ago. "And because I'm a pain in the ass."

I shove him away and escape his suffocating presence, which, combined with the whiskey, is doing weird things to my head. "I can't do this." What the hell was I thinking in even considering it?

The door seems a long way off, but I do my best to walk toward it without stumbling or veering too far off track. My fingers close around the knob at the same time Henry's clasp my wrist.

"C, wait, please. I'm sorry."

"I can't, Henry. Let go of me."

He does, his fingers slipping from my skin. "Don't go."

I hesitate, still turned away from him. If I leave, I will lose everything. Beck is already gone. My pride, my dignity, and Wesbourne will soon follow. If I stay and we go through with this, I'll lose my home, and most likely my sanity, but I'll have a chance at saving my country.

"Don't throw this away just because you're mad at me," he adds.

"Sounds like a terrific reason to me."

"You'll never forgive yourself." He's right, so I don't say anything. "We could do this, you know. Make this work."

"Sawing off my arm sounds more appealing."

"God, liquor sharpens your tongue." He lets out an amused exhale. "Let's sit down. Your swaying is making me nervous. Plus, you'll be warmer by the fire."

I'm still shivering, so I let him lead me over to the sofa. "You actually think we should do this?" I say once he's seated at the other end.

"It doesn't really matter what I think."

"Why not?"

"You have a lot more to lose than I do. I'm unattached, and I've known my whole life that I'll be king someday. I'll have to get married at some point. This moves up the timeline, but I always saw it playing out something like this." He leans his forearms on his knees and clasps his hands. "Minus the bride who hates my guts."

"I don't hate your guts," I tell him. "Although sometimes I fantasize about carving them out and feeding them to the fish."

This makes him laugh, and his laugh makes me smile. Just a tiny little flick of the mouth, gone before he has a chance to notice. "I'll be sure to lock my door," he says.

I hold up my finger. "I have some conditions."

"I'd be shocked if you didn't."

"Before I agree to anything, I want to make sure we're on the same page."

His left brow inches upward. "Do elaborate."

"This marriage will be on paper only. Obviously."

He stares at me, faint creases appearing near his eyes. I'm amusing him. For the first time in my life, I actually wish he would say something. But like always, he does the opposite of what I want.

"I just meant—I mean, I— Nothing is going to happen. Between us. Nothing changes." I wait for his agreement. There's nothing but the slightest twitch of one nostril. "You do understand what I'm saying, right? We're not— It's not going to— This is not—" I can't get the right words to line up and march out of my mouth.

"As much as I'm enjoying watching you bodge this up," he finally says, "I feel the need to put you out of your misery." He doesn't even attempt to hide his smile. Asshole. "If you're afraid I'll try to force myself on you, rest assured. I only sleep with women who want me."

"Don't forget the ones who are drugged."

The creases around his eyes deepen for just a second. "Would it be the worst thing in the world to be loved by me?" he says quietly.

"We're not talking about love. We're talking about sex—something that for you is just an entertaining diversion, but that's important for me." The list of people I want to be having this conversation with is short, but my mother, the prime minister, and an orangutan all rank above Henry.

"Lots of people have sex without being in love."

"I am not 'lots of people.'"

"Thank god for small mercies," he says. "Any other demands? Designated corridor space? Hazmat suits? Shared custody of the dog?"

"When did you get a dog?"

He pinches the bridge of his nose. "Is that your only condition? You're ready to go ahead with this?"

"I am the opposite of ready. But since my self-induced food coma did nothing to get me out of this mess, I don't see what other choice I have." I pause. "Unless you have some ice cream?"

Henry stands and pulls me to my feet, and my skin sizzles where it touches his. I sway as the room spins, and he pushes me back into the chair. "On second thought, maybe you should stay sitting." Before my sodden brain can comprehend what's happening, he drops to one knee and pulls something from his pocket.

"What are you doing?" It comes out in a whisper, because I know exactly what he's doing.

"You ask too many questions. It's my turn."

My heart jackhammers in its cavity. "No, really. What are you doing, Henry?"

"Relax," he says, and runs his thumb over the back of my hand. It has the opposite effect. "I want to do this right."

I pull away from him and wipe my clammy palms on my trousers. "You don't need to do this. It's a business transaction, nothing more."

"I know that. But since this is the only proposal I'll get, I'd like to do it right."

I can't very well say no to that.

I peer down at the red velvet box he's holding. A lump the size of a hedgehog dislodges itself from my stomach and crawls up my throat. He pries the lid open to reveal an antique band of yellow gold filigree, set with a diamond the size of a small coin and surrounded by clusters of emeralds. In spite of myself, I gasp. It's exquisite.

"I brought it with me just in case. It was Helena's. Seemed appropriate." Henry removes the ring from its box. "I know you hate me and think I'm an arrogant jerk. We drive each other crazy, and you'll probably kill me before the year is over."

He reaches for my hand again, and goosebumps scurry up my arm all the way to my hairline. "We don't need to like each other to do this. We can do it because it's right for our country," he says.

My lip trembles, and I bite it to keep it still.

"Celia Eleanor Chapman-Payne." He pauses, his eyes locking on mine. "Will you marry me?"

Will you marry me?

Eight months ago, those same words. Another beautiful ring. Another pounding heart. Another handsome man.

How can I put another man's ring on my finger before it's even adjusted to being bare? It's a betrayal, but I don't know how to survive otherwise. I must do this, and so I nod.

Henry slides the massive diamond onto my hand, and its weight settles into my heart. This is it then. We're actually doing this.

He presses a chaste kiss to my knuckle, his lips warm next to the cold metal. It's the final seal. I have promised to marry this man to save my country. Does that make me noble or cowardly?

Because no matter what it looks like from the outside, I know that I never really had a choice. My fate was determined the moment that diary was discovered.

15

"Something Just Like This" - The Chainsmokers + Coldplay

MOST CITIZENS ACCEPT GOVERNMENTAL decisions with acquiescence. My mother is not most citizens. She vehemently objected to Parliament's announcement that the wedding will take place in four weeks, on the grounds that a month isn't enough time to *look* at gowns, let alone have one designed. Parliament does not have the same fear of my mother as I do, and so the date remains.

After the engagement announcement was made to the public, the outbursts, fires, and riots stopped. I think everyone was too stunned to remember what they'd been so mad about. Frankly, I'm surprised there hasn't been an uproar protesting the marriage of the country's most eligible bachelor.

The riots may have stopped, but the tension is still as thick as pudding. Everyone is holding their breath, waiting to see what's going to happen. Waiting to see if Henry and I will actually tie the knot and be crowned. They say you can feel it when you walk in and out of the small shops downtown, when you stop to fill your car with petrol, when eating lunch in a cafe.

Not that I do any of those things. Going out in public these days requires an entire security team, and I find myself missing the marvelous times Davies, Lane, and I spent together, just the three of us. The whole entourage attracts more attention from the media and pedestrians than I want to receive in my entire lifetime, let alone an hour of shopping. I'll have to get used to it eventually, but for now I'm putting it in the box marked "problems for future Celia."

The press is eating the whole thing up, and you'd think they could cut me some slack, considering I've just given them job security for the rest of their careers. They're desperate for any morsel of information Henry and I deign to throw them, and when we refuse, they make it up. My favorite headline so far? *Princess Celia Spotted Buying Pregnancy Test.*

I'm praying Beck still avoids tabloids.

Finding a wedding dress is the least of my concerns. If it were up to me, I'd wear something off-the-rack from David's Bridal, although that would likely send my mother to an early grave, which seems unfair. She's been spending every minute of her days—and doubtlessly her nights, too—poring over the details of the event, unable to trust the crew of wedding planners hired by the Crown to do their job.

"I have been preparing for this since the moment you were born," she told me at one point.

Unfortunately, it's the truth. She and Henry's mother, Olivia, were flatmates when they were at university. While they weren't all that close during the first semester, when the crown prince began paying more and more attention to Olivia, you can be sure the wheels started turning in my mother's head. Never one to let an opportunity slip through her fingers, she did everything in her power to ensure a lifelong friendship with the woman she hoped would one day become queen.

It worked. Her plans always do. She remained friends with Olivia even after William was crowned upon the death of his father, only two years into their marriage. Henry once told me it's difficult, if not impossible, to form new friendships as a royal. It's such an isolated and unrelatable role.

I am fond of Olivia. Disliking her would be like disliking a songbird. She exudes a "Grace Kelly mixed with Michelle Obama" vibe, and she's known around the world for her impeccable style. She once confessed to me that the accolades really belong to her stylist, because she wears everything he chooses without question.

A month before the wedding, Olivia solves the dilemma of my wedding gown. "It was Helena's," she says as several maids remove the dress from its vacuum-sealed bag. "It will need altering, of course, but I know how much you love history and thought it might work."

I want to squeeze her. It's such a small, inconsequential thing. I couldn't care less what I wear down the aisle, but this gesture almost undoes me.

The dress itself is incredibly gorgeous, in spite of its age. While nothing like the Caroline Spencer gown I'd planned to marry Beck in, it shines in its own royal way. It has long sleeves of lace, which continues over the bodice, a high collar, and a full skirt with a train that will require several page boys to carry it.

If I had doubts about being accepted into the royal family, Olivia eases them with her gentle welcome, ensuring I have at least one ally in the palace. It's been over a decade since I spent any considerable time in her home, but she acts as though I was there just last week.

In truth, I've always envied Henry his mother, with her cheerful smile and offer of cookies whenever I visited. I love my own mum dearly, but Rosalind's demand for perfection extended even to my sleeping position—*on your back to prevent wrinkles!*—and sometimes I just wanted to be a kid. Through her friendship with Olivia, she secured a spot for her child as royal playmate long before I was even conceived. When that child turned out to be a girl, she could practically hear the wedding bells ringing in St. John's Cathedral.

I should feel grateful to my mother. I wouldn't be equipped for the role I'm about to play had it not been for her careful preparation. I spent the better part of my childhood learning French, Italian, German, Russian, and Mandarin and am still moderately fluent in all of them. While other girls vegged out watching the latest *Pretty Little Liars* episode, I was learning how to exit a vehicle without showing too much skin. Back then, hanging out with Henry was the Miralax to my bloated weeks, even if our time together was highlighted in red as part of the "ultimate mission" in the two-inch-thick spiral planner my mother kept for me.

Of course, her plans eventually fell through. Not only did I *not* become engaged to Henry, but I stopped spending time with him altogether. At fifteen, I had little control over my calendar and commitments, but even my mother couldn't argue when they told her Prince Henry had more pressing obligations than our weekly afternoons together. She floundered momentarily, but now she's is back at the wheel, finally able to prepare for the wedding she's envisioned in perfect detail since the day I was born.

One day, she walks in while I'm packing, frowning at the clipboard in her hand. "Which do you prefer for your bouquet, roses or lilies? Roses are classic, of course, but lilies signify elegance in a way a rose never could."

For my ceremony with Beck, I was planning to carry white hydrangeas.

"Mum, I don't care, honestly. Why not let the wedding planners handle it? We've still got so much sorting to do." I gesture around the library. There are a million items to go through before the movers come to pack things up.

As if planning the wedding of the century isn't enough, we're also in the process of packing up three decades' worth of belongings and memories before relocating to our personal apartments at the palace. Much of the furniture and artwork belong to the estate, having been in the family for more than a century, and will pass to the next Duke of Whitmere. Still, we have enough personal possessions to fill several moving vans.

"I think we'll do both," she says, stepping over an open box on the floor. Before I can say anything else, she pulls out her phone to place a call, probably to one of the wedding planners with the update on the flowers.

I sigh and reach for my father's box of cigars on the mantel. What would he make of all this? Of course, if he were still alive, things would be more complicated. It's not like *he* could have married Henry. Maybe Parliament would have ordered a duel between my father and the king, swords drawn as though they were Manet and Duranty.

Bea walks into the room, eyes glued to her phone. She has made herself scarce since our argument, presumably still enraged that I put my country before her budding relationship, which was destined for failure before it ever started. I clear my throat to let her know the enemy is present.

She looks up in surprise, and disdain colors her features. "I hope you're enjoying destroying our lives." She brushes past me to grab the photo albums from the shelf. "Thanks to you, these photos are the only thing I'll have to remind me of Dad."

I let her go in silence. It won't help to remind her that this estate is not only my childhood home too, but the one I planned to share with Beck and our future children. She may be in love with Henry, but I'm giving up the man I was going to build a life with.

What exactly does she think I'm gaining from this arrangement?

My new suite in the palace is like something out of a fairy tale. The whole apartment consists of a private sitting room; a lavish bedroom with a gilded bed; an enormous bathroom featuring both a soaker tub and glass-walled shower; and a closet and dressing room that are nearly the size of my entire bedroom at Maison de Lierre. Everything is tastefully decorated in cream and gold, but I feel like Catherine being removed to Thrushcross Grange and longing only for the simplicity and memories of Wuthering Heights.

When we were packing, I smuggled my dad's cigars into the cartons of things destined for my suite. The familiar box brings that nauseating twinge of sadness and impending doom you get when you're five days into your holiday and you want nothing more than to bury your face in your own pillow in your own bed and suck in the familiar scent, but you've still got another week at the seashore. So you do your best to enjoy it, even though you know the ache will come back with more and more frequency until you're finally back home.

Except I'll never be home again.

Wesbourne Palace could have come straight from the pages of a picture book: spiky turrets puncturing the cloud cover, windows upon windows grinning like teeth in the stone walls, and an overall stateliness that shouts "Important people reside here!" It's Hogwarts on steroids, with less magic and higher expectations.

A dozen of those expectations are marching through my door right now. Leading them is Maisie, who accepted my offer (aka plea) to officially become my private secretary before the words even left my mouth. I thought it would be comforting to have someone familiar beside me, but looking at her now, I wonder what she's done with the girl I worked with at the Society. She's in black pumps, her hair styled into a low chignon, and she's ditched the grandma cardigan she always used to wear for a chic, tailored day dress.

Behind her follows an entourage of expressionless staff members, all carrying what upon closer inspection appear to be magical props to turn the ugly duckling into a beautiful swan.

Maisie begins the introductions. "This is Cynthia. She's going to work her magic on your brows. Stefano will add extensions to your hair. Liz will do your nails, and Kerry is in charge of waxing."

My nutritionist will measure me, chart my weight daily, and craft a diet plan to "shave off the rounded edges." Royals can't show softness, after all, in spirit *or* body.

I also have a personal trainer, a posture consultant, an etiquette specialist, a wardrobe stylist, a publicity manager, and a language tutor to help keep me fluent. And finally, there's my personal maid, Daphne, who will do things for me that I'm suddenly incapable of doing myself, like removing my clothes from their hangers and flipping down the coverlet before I crawl into bed.

Over the next two hours, I'm analyzed, dissected, and clucked at. Everyone wants a turn at me, and given our tight time frame, they have to share. Someone pinches the underside of my arm—gauging fat content, no doubt—my hair is tugged from its loose ponytail, and icy fingers lift my chin higher.

I snatch at their fleeting directives and stuff them away in my memory, hoping at least a few will do as they're told and stay put.

Never hold champagne in my right hand so it's always dry for greetings.

Always smile, even when I think no one is looking. Someone is always watching.

Never remove my coat in public. It's unladylike.

Always hold my bag in my left hand to leave the right free for waving.

Never speak to the press, and if I absolutely have to, say as little as possible. Words are so easily manipulated.

Always use a clutch bag to cover my decolletage when exiting a vehicle. The king doesn't want to see my cleavage in his breakfast newspaper. (Nor do I want him to, but that's irrelevant.)

Never look down when walking, but keep my chin in line with the floor. Always, always, always remember that appearances matter. Make it impossible for the press to find fault with me. They'll do it anyway—they always do—but I should give them a run for their money.

Over the next few days, I'm buffed, straightened, fluffed, painted, plucked, and squeezed to within an inch of my existence. I've practiced French, German, and Mandarin until my brain is swollen. My daily workouts leave me weak, trembling, and craving cookie dough—which is strictly off limits. The binders of information I'm supposed to memorize threaten to break the desk they're perched on.

I'm not sure I'll recognize myself a year from now.

16

"It Ain't Me" - Kygo + Selemz Gomez

B ECAUSE WE'RE GETTING MARRIED in less than a month, Henry and I don't have time for the traditional royal wedding tour across Wesbourne. Instead, the Crown is throwing a large garden party in honor of our engagement and has allowed members of the public to apply for an invitation. There were over one hundred thousand applications. Of those, seven thousand were approved.

The sprawling green behind the palace has hosted hundreds of parties over the years and will serve as the place for our official presentation as an engaged couple this afternoon. Through the window of my sitting room, I can already see a large crowd has gathered. In their pastel dresses and hats, the women look like a box of French macarons spilled across the lawn, and the men like Cinderella's coachmen with their morning coats and top hats. Large floral arrangements dot the grass. The crowning glory is a long white tent, open on one side, where guests will be able to help themselves to a buffet of tea and finger sandwiches.

Despite the nausea that's been plaguing me ever since this whole thing started, excitement bubbles up inside me as I watch the people congregating. They are here to see *me,* and soon I will be responsible for their welfare as citizens. I will protect their rights and do my best to make Wesbourne a nation they can continue to be proud of.

I give my reflection in the mirror one final glance, adjust the pleated skirt of my pale pink day dress, and, satisfied that I look the part of a queen-in-waiting, leave to join the rest of the royal family.

They're waiting near the formal back entrance. Henry and his father both look dashing in their long tails, hats tucked under their arms, and Olivia and Rosalind glow like spring blooms in their sage and lavender dresses and fascinators. Even the coat of the royal chocolate Labrador gleams as he sits at William's side like a page boy. Beatrice is not down yet. At least there's something I can depend on.

A few minutes later she appears, not remorseful in the least about her tardiness, but wearing a smile so blinding I nearly squint. She's wearing a snug-fitting baby-blue gown with puffed sleeves, the hemline falling far below the acceptable knee-length and hitting her midcalf. The reason for this seemingly demure choice soon becomes apparent. A long slit inches its way up the side of her dress and stops daringly short of revealing more than her beautifully tanned thigh as she moves. A miniskirt would be more modest. My sister has no intention of giving up without a fight.

The crowd awaiting us outside is a welcome distraction. After our small processional, people clapping on either side of the informal aisle, I wind my way through them, greeting both dignitaries and average citizens, chatting with members of Parliament and stay-at-home mums. A group of university students excitedly exclaims that my "modern fairy-tale romance" is extremely swoon worthy. I offer them a tight-lipped smile. More like modern Gothic horror.

When my hand threatens mutiny if it has to shake one more person's, I retreat to a grouping of trees, desperate for a few minutes to myself. Although we were encouraged to greet guests individually to cover more ground, I can't help but notice the natural pairings that have emerged from our cobbled-together family. Olivia and Rosalind's long-time friendship has drawn them together, the queen subtly showing my mother the ropes. King William isn't a people person, but he's accompanied everywhere by his dog, Argos.

And then there's Henry and Beatrice. They have spent nearly the entire party together so far, linking arms, giggling together, and looking to all the world like *they* are the ones getting married. The now familiar pang of homesickness punctures my stomach.

I watch them talk with a small group of people near the tea tent. Bea places her hand on Henry's arm and tosses her head back to laugh at something he says. They look divine together, a couple you'd see splashed on magazine covers and billboards.

My nails dig into my palm. I release the tight grip and toss the contents of my teacup into the nearby hedge.

"He's a damn fool." The voice startles me, and I find King William standing just behind my shoulder, Argos faithfully pressed to his side.

I process his words and turn back to see who he's talking about. He's staring in the same direction I was, where Henry and Beatrice have moved into the tent and are collecting a small array of sandwiches on a plate.

I decide against voicing my agreement and instead lick my lips several times. I will probably never get used to having lipstick caked onto them. "It's been a good turnout, don't you think?"

The king grunts, and I wonder if it's his usual contribution to conversation. He hands a sandwich to Argos, who swallows it in one entire gulp. "I've told him to keep his nose clean until I'm blue in the face, but it doesn't do any good," he says.

I look into my empty teacup, unsure what response he hopes to get from me. "He's never cared much about his image, sir."

"Like I said, a damn fool."

"Do you think the press will run a smear campaign?"

Just last week, rumors that the crown princess of Norway is having a dalliance made it to the front pages of all the major tabloids. A select few reporters and camera crews have been allowed access to this event, and they're sliding through the crowd like slippery eels. For the first time, I'm relieved that Beck turned down my offer of trying to maintain a relationship.

William scoffs. "They have to run their stories past us before publishing. It's outside these gates you should be worried about. Out there we have little to no control. Free press and all that hogwash." He takes a long drink from the cup in his hand. The scent that wafts toward me testifies to it being something other than tea.

"You think I should be worried, then?" I turn to fully look at him.

He returns my gaze with a hard one of his own. "Henry will never stay satisfied with one woman. May as well look the other way."

My mouth drops open at his insinuation. Does he think I'm interested in Henry romantically? "I beg your pardon, sir, I—"

"The staff knows better than to talk. It's not too difficult to get what you want."

Confusion settles over me like a fog. "I'm not sure I understand you, sir."

His attention has returned to the crowd. Henry and Bea are once again floating through it as though they're in an ad for a bloody timeshare in Bora Bora. Unexpectedly, William swings his eyes back to me, his gaze hard as flint. "Better find your happiness somewhere else."

I take a step backward. "And where do you suggest I look for it?"

"I understand you left a fiancé behind."

"That is correct." I reach down and stroke Argos's velvety head. He presses his muzzle into my palm, begging for more.

"Is he discreet?"

"I'm sorry, *how* is that relevant?"

From the corner of my eye, I see William lift his shoulders in a shrug. "Like I said, with enough discretion, you can have what you want." He drains the dregs of his cup.

He is seriously suggesting I start an affair with Beck. Obviously, that thought has occurred to me already, but I never expected to hear it suggested so blatantly, and certainly not by a member of the Crown.

Before I can think of anything to say, Henry approaches us from behind. A strange feeling washes over me, like a child in a grocery store spotting his mum after thinking her gone. Which is unexpected, considering I want to strangle him at the moment.

"What's going on?" Henry asks, giving his father a wary look. Argos whines and comes over to lick Henry's hand. Bea has unglued herself from his side and is nowhere to be seen.

William bristles at his son's interference. "Just giving Celia a bit of advice."

Henry looks to me for confirmation.

"We were just talking," I say, and avert my eyes. I have no intention of getting in the middle of whatever beef they have with each other.

"Leave her alone, Father." Henry's voice carries a sharp edge, and I imagine it pricking my skin, a bead of blood oozing out.

"Need I remind you who you're speaking to?" William hisses, giving a swift tug on his morning coat. "Not that you've ever had a sense of propriety between your ears."

I clear my throat rather loudly at the sight of a photographer making his way toward us. No matter what William says, I don't trust the press further than I can throw them, which, looking at the beefy man wielding the camera, wouldn't be far. "It might be time to wrap up this discussion," I say.

With a glance at the photographer and a surly one in Henry's direction, the king turns and walks away. Argos follows closely at his heels. Relief steals over me as I watch him retreat. My energy has drained away like suds at the bottom of the shower.

The photographer gestures for Henry and me to move closer together. I try to step away as soon as he's captured his shots, but Henry's arm remains snug around my waist.

"Get your hand off me."

He lowers it slowly. "Relax. What did my father actually want?"

"He was giving me a few tips on happiness."

Henry snorts and kicks at the grass with the toe of his dress shoe. "What the hell does he know about being happy?"

"Nothing, if his face is any indication."

"And how did he advise you to be happy?" He takes a sip from his teacup, and I wonder if he's smuggled in something stronger as well.

"He suggested I take Beck as a lover."

Henry chokes on his tea—it is, in fact, tea. "Good god," he says once he's caught his breath. "And he says I have no scruples."

I rub a thumb along the gilded handle of my teacup. "Guess I don't either."

"What do you mean?"

"I thought about it long before he suggested it."

Henry stares at me. He seems to think I live in a box—a very tiny, secure box that doesn't allow room for hormones or emotions of any kind. "And?"

"And what?"

"Are you going to do it?"

"No."

"Conscience get the best of you?"

"Apparently, Beck's conscience is loftier than mine."

"You actually asked him?" The look on Henry's face tells me he'd be less surprised if I'd thrown my tea at him.

"Yes, Henry, I did." Irritation seeps into me like water in a leaky boat. "Not that it's any of your business. But rest assured, he wasn't interested."

"He's a fool."

I consider telling Henry his father made the same comment about him just a few minutes ago. Instead I say, "What's the deal with your dad? Is he always like that?"

I didn't see William much when I was younger. He was always attending events or meetings when I visited the palace. In recent years, we've had minimal interactions, and they are always in public. I'm not sure I've ever had a conversation alone with him before today.

"You mean charming, gracious, and full of sunshine?"

I smile in spite of myself. "I assume you're his usual victim?"

You could cut yourself on the sharp edge of Henry's jawline. "That became my role the minute I was born. But don't worry," he adds, his face brightening. "I make sure he never runs out of ammo."

Our conversation is cut short as someone pulls him aside, and I can't help but feel like he isn't telling me everything. I nearly walked in on an argument between him and his father last week. I was on my way to the massive library, but the sound of raised voices stopped me right before I entered the room. I had no intention of eavesdropping, but when I heard the two of them arguing inside, curiosity got the best of me.

William sounded angry. "Do I need to remind you of what will happen if you let this get out of control?"

"I'm well aware, Father," Henry said. "Nothing has changed."

"We both know the temptation anything in a skirt poses for you. Your reputation speaks louder than your words."

"Well, I learned from the best, didn't I?" Henry again.

"Don't patronize me," the king yelled. There was a sound of a thump, like palms slapping a table. "I'll be watching you." I imagined him jabbing his finger at his son. "And you know exactly what I'll do if you break our agreement."

Afraid they were about to leave the room, I scurried down the hallway. My guess is Henry and his father both have some deep-seated issues to deal with, and neither will appreciate me sticking my nose in. But just how deep do those issues run, and what kind of fallout will result if they're ever addressed?

17

"Set Fire to the Rain" - Adele

DESPITE THE CROWN'S CONFIDENCE in their working relationship with the press, they failed to take into consideration the amount of cell phones that would be at the garden party. The general public don't follow the same rules of decorum as the peerage, and it turns out they won't hesitate to sell incriminating photos of the royal family to the tabloids in order to buy another month's worth of groceries.

That's how pictures of Henry and Beatrice ended up gracing the covers of no less than six different tabloids, accompanied by headlines speculating about everything from Henry having chosen the wrong girl to him having a threesome with the two Chapman-Payne sisters.

Maisie has waited three days to show them to me. Upon seeing them, I wait three seconds before marching into Henry's office.

It's the kind of room you'd expect a posh banker to have. The scent of leather, woodsy spice, and coffee greets me as his private secretary, Sidney, leads me inside. Three of the walls boast floor-to-ceiling bookcases, all made from a rich, dark mahogany. A fireplace is nestled between the shelves opposite three large windows that overlook the palace grounds.

Henry is sitting behind the massive desk at the center of the room. He glances up as I enter. His suit jacket is draped over his chair, and he's sporting a pair of tortoiseshell glasses, looking more businessman than rogue prince.

He stands and pours himself a cup of coffee from the minibar in the corner. "Want some?"

I shake my head.

He takes a sip and winces as if he's burned his mouth. "What can I do for you?"

"You can stop making advances on my sister, that's what." I slap one of the magazines onto the desk. It makes a very satisfying thwack, causing Henry's shoulders to twitch.

He flicks his eyes to it, then returns them to me. "They write whatever they want."

"Everyone at that party saw the way the two of you acted. Not only are you playing with Bea's heart, but you're ruining her reputation."

"Maybe you should give your sister more credit. She can take care of herself."

I clench my jaw. The last time I thought Bea could take care of herself, she was five. She ended up lost in the woods for hours, looking for her big sister, who'd been so eager to get rid of her she hadn't given any thought to the consequences. That isn't going to happen again.

There is only one way to handle Henry.

"I'm here to strike a deal. Name your price," I say.

His eyebrows float upward in amusement. "My price?"

"We've established you're too much of a scoundrel to do it out of the goodness of your heart, so I'm here to appeal to your selfishness."

"You're overreacting, Celia. There's nothing going on with Bea, I swear."

"She thinks she's in love with you."

"I'd be more flattered if you didn't make it sound like she's caught the bubonic plague," he says.

"Your ego would collapse under more flattery."

He tosses his glasses onto the desk and studies me until tiny little bumps run up and down every inch of my skin. His eyes linger on my lips, and my whole body hums like a plucked guitar string. I'm acutely aware of how alone we are and of every flicker of movement he makes.

"Fine. I'll make you a deal." His voice is quiet, too quiet.

Regret is a tidal wave. What was I thinking, bargaining with the devil? "On second thought—"

"Scared?" Henry chuckles into his mug before setting it down. "You know me well."

"What do you want?"

"One kiss."

I sputter out a cough. "Excuse me?"

"I promise to stay far away from Bea in exchange for a kiss."

"You must be out of your bloody mind."

"Consider it practice."

"For what? We agreed this marriage would be in name only."

"At some point we'll have to show the public we're not secretly plotting each other's murders."

"I don't condone lying."

"Kiss me, C." His eyes dance with challenge.

"Not if you were the last man on earth."

"Okay, then. I'm sure Beatrice will happily oblige me." He winks and moves in the direction of the door.

"You're depraved."

"Maybe so. Or maybe I just know how to get what I want."

"Henry, please." *Not this.* Anything but this.

"It's just a kiss. It won't kill you."

It might. "How do you sleep at night?"

His grin threatens to split his face. "Just fine, thank you. It'll be over in no time, and we both get what we want." There's no question why he wants to kiss me. He thinks it'll be the most effective way to screw with my head. He's right.

"You're despicable. Who asks for that kind of exchange?"

"That's the deal. You can take it or leave it." He's dead serious, all traces of the grin now gone.

I hesitate, consider whether protecting Bea's heart is worth it. With the way she's been acting lately? Probably not. But I'd be lying if I denied the animalistic curiosity surging through me. Does kissing the prince deserve the hype it gets? I hate that I'm dying to know what that mouth feels like, taste like.

His lips part ever so slightly under my stare, causing my core to clench tightly. I can't trust my sister to stay immune, but at least *I* won't fall for Henry's charms.

I close my eyes, unsure if I hate him or myself more right now. "Fine. Deal." I say it quickly, before I can change my mind.

A mischievous glint lights his eyes. "Should we do it now or would you prefer a more romantic setting?"

"Just get it over with," I hiss.

"Your wish is my command."

"In that case, why don't you go squat in a cactus patch?"

He throws back his head and laughs. The effect is magical. Henry comes alive when he laughs, truly laughs. My insides clench with a familiar ache.

The corners of his eyes are still crinkled in amusement as he approaches. He keeps his gaze locked with mine and slowly slips a hand around my waist. The other slides up to cradle my jaw.

I forget my own name.

He leans forward and rests his forehead against mine. His scent swirls around us like a cloud of intoxicating vapor.

"Preferably some time in this decade," I whisper, no longer able to take a full breath.

He smiles and whispers back, "'Patience is bitter, but its fruit is swee t.'"

Then he lowers his lips and presses a kiss to the corner of my mouth, producing instant goosebumps. I suck air into my lungs as he moves his head to reach the nape of my neck. His stubbly cheek brushes against mine, and nerve endings I didn't even know I possessed come alive. His mouth continues its journey at a leisurely pace, kissing my earlobe, my eyes, my jawline, my chin.

I can't stop trembling. He lingers over my lips, hovering, his warm breath tantalizing, his nose nuzzling mine, until I crave him like a starving man craves food. The only thing I want, the only thing I can think of, is tasting him.

Suddenly, finally, powerfully, his mouth crashes into mine, and fireworks explode inside a keg of gunpowder. I give a muffled whimper as heat tears through my body, radiating with every pulse of my blood.

I'm being scorched, but I don't care. I only want more.

Fingers tangled in my hair, Henry draws me in and angles his head. He tightens his grip on me, pulling me impossibly closer, until I'm not sure where the seam of fusion is. He tastes like warm coffee, strong and powerful. I'm no longer earthbound as he tugs on my mouth with his own, his lips teaching me what it's like to be kissed until you feel it in your toes.

My hands find their way to his shoulders, his neck. I simply cannot get enough of him. He groans against my mouth as my fingers glide into his hair, and he drags his own hands over my body, creating an insatiable blazing path of fire everywhere they touch.

After a lifetime contained within a too-short moment, he pulls back and presses his face against mine once more. Our breaths mingle; we're both gasping for air. He drills into my soul with a look so intense I know he can see everything. It makes me quake.

Finally, he lets go of me and backs away. It's like stepping outside naked in a blizzard—biting and disorienting.

"That was more than a kiss," I manage to get out between pants. My body still surges with electricity, but without grounding, it courses through my veins, back and forth, until I'm on the brink of explosion. I can feel the high flush on my cheeks as my heart pumps triple the amount of blood as usual.

"I wanted you to experience a real kiss." Henry's voice is gruff, as if he hasn't used it in a decade. "I bet your ex-fiancé never kissed you like that."

Anger quickly replaces what I mistook for desire. He's right, of course. Beck has never kissed me like that, because *Beck* is a gentleman. And no gentleman would ever take advantage of a lady the way Henry just did.

I slap him across the face.

"Ouch!" He rubs a hand across his cheek, which is already turning red. "Was that for starting . . . or for stopping?"

"You know exactly what that was for."

"You seemed to be enjoying yourself."

My face grows hotter at the insinuation. "You flatter yourself. If I was enjoying myself, you would know it." My denial is futile, a dying man's attempt at survival, but necessary all the same.

"In that case, we could have another go at it and you could tell me what you like this time."

"Or we could both go jump into a volcano."

Not even if I were dying would I admit how badly I want to do that again. My lips are still throbbing with the memory of his, my skin chafed from his stubble, and a homesick ache twists through me. I miss him, and he's standing right in front of me.

A knock sounds on the door, reminding me where I am. It's followed by Henry's secretary sticking his head into the room. "Mr. Beckham Harrison is here for your appointment, sir."

Panic shoots through me. Henry meets my eyes, then turns back to his secretary. "Give me a second."

Sidney nods and closes the door again.

"You did this on purpose." I point my finger at him. "You knew he was coming, and you wanted to play some sick game with my head."

"And what game was that?" Henry folds his arms over his chest.

"Whatever manipulative tricks you play on women."

"I dare you to find one woman who says I tricked her into spending time with me."

"You're looking at one."

He sighs. "If I told you I forgot he was coming, would you believe me?"

"Not a chance in hell." I comb my fingers through my hair, trying to undo the havoc Henry has wreaked. I still tremble thinking about his hands.

"Relax, C. You don't even look like you've just had an earth-shattering experience. Here, let me at least help repair the damage I did." He reaches out a hand, but I bat it away.

"Stay away from me."

"Calm down. I just want to help."

"Give me a break. I know what your help looks like."

He leans close and whispers, "Your lips are swollen."

I grit my teeth and take a deep breath through my nose. "There are no words in the English language strong enough to convey how much I loathe you."

"Then please don't overexert yourself trying." He pulls a small mirror from one of his desk drawers and holds it in front of me.

I use my reflection to tame my mussed strands. "Do I even want to know why you have this in your desk?"

"Do you always think the worst of me?"

I look up at him. His tone is light, unaffected, but his eyes tell a different story.

Before I can respond, he calls to Sidney. I use the remaining few seconds to smooth down my dress and put as much distance between myself and Henry as possible. I pray I'll be able to slip out without any awkwardness.

Beck enters the room, and his eyes alight on me. He covers his surprise quickly, but not before I catch a glimpse of it. Is my shame sizzling like a neon sign above my head? I was still engaged to him just a few days ago.

"Your Royal Highnesses." Beck's normally warm, friendly voice now sounds like a blast of frigid air. His eyes meet mine once more, and this time I notice a small glimmer of something hard in them. I want to sink into the floor.

"Mr. Harrison," Henry says. "Please, come in. Celia was just leaving."

"Hello, Beck," I say before excusing myself from the room.

Fresh air. I need fresh air like a politician needs votes. I walk through the palace halls as fast as is acceptable for a royal family member wearing heels—which isn't fast enough.

The sun hits me like a spotlight once I step outside, and I turn my face to catch its rays. I wander through the gardens, led by my feet alone, my thoughts much too conflicted to pay any mind to where I'm going.

Ten minutes later, I stop short, regretting giving free reign to my body, which is clearly still living on the mountaintop of Henry's kiss, or else it would never have brought me here, of all places.

The stone steps descending into the Sunken Garden are clothed in moss and lichens, like a subtle warning to stay away. I ignore it and carefully pick my way down. I'm here now, so I may as well rip off all my plasters while I'm at it.

A koi pond sits at the center of the green lawn, complete with lily pads. The goldfish seem to have disappeared, though. Plants spill over the flagstone path, disregarding the border, which was once neatly edged. Weeds poke their heads rebelliously through the cracks, and years of dirt cake the surface. The palace employs a crew of gardeners large enough to staff a bustling restaurant. There's no reason this particular garden should have been neglected for so long.

The memory of my last time here swells around me and threatens to suck me down into even further humiliation. I won't let it. I have to stay strong. The future depends on this.

Birds chirp in the nearby branches, oblivious to the chaos raging inside me. I drop to my knees on the path, the stones warm from gulping up the rays of the sun. It was sunny that day, too.

I tug at a cluster of weeds. This place makes it easy to shut out the outside world. The whole garden is four feet lower than the rest of the grounds, and it's surrounded on all sides by a wall and a thick hedge. I've spent more hours here than I can count, creating make-believe fantasies, playing schoolyard games, lounging in the sun, and conjuring enough freckles to give my mum an ulcer.

And Henry at the center. Always Henry.

Even now, ten years later, I can't escape his magnetism. What possessed me to kiss him the way I did? Because, while I'd die before admitting it to him, I participated in that kiss as much as he did.

I yank on a particularly stubborn weed and nearly tumble backward when it finally comes free.

Beck and I were on the verge of getting married, and we've never kissed with half as much passion. That is the trouble with Henry—he doesn't think. He just does whatever he wants in the moment. And when he pulls you into his circle, you can't help but do the same.

Guilt eats at me, much like the caterpillar making quick work of a leaf on one of the nearby plants. This isn't who I am. I'm Celia Chapman-Payne, doer of what's right and good and just. Follower of plans and maker of lists. Kissing Henry like we were the only two people left on the planet does *not* fit into the picture.

I look at my nails. They're now thoroughly chipped and dirtied, as if I'm a little ragamuffin let loose outside rather than the queen-in-waiting who just spent an hour getting a manicure. Liz—and probably Maisie—is going to kill me when I return to the palace.

I toss the small pile of weeds I've removed aside. The rest will have to wait for another time.

No matter how badly my body might try to convince me otherwise, kissing Henry has to be strictly off-limits. It doesn't matter that those few short minutes may have been the best of my life. It doesn't matter that he tasted much better than I ever imagined anyone could. And it certainly doesn't matter that when he looked at me, I saw shadows of the old Henry.

It will not happen again.

18

"Illumination" - Jennifer Thomas

ON THE MORNING OF the wedding, the sky is ominous with clouds as a storm rolls in. Isn't there a saying about not getting married during a thunderstorm? If not, there should be. The weather never lies.

I'm in my sitting room watching the downpour through the window, a princess locked in her tower. The wind blows the trees outside nearly sideways, until I'm convinced they'll snap in half, but they never do. The howling gusts are chilling, and I rub my arms through my lace sleeves.

My hair is arranged in a cascade down my back, a veil and tiara over it. Helena's dress has been altered to fit me like a glove. My bouquet of roses and lilies teases my nose with its cloying perfume.

Everything is ready. Everything except my heart.

I've been avoiding Henry since that stupid, incredible kiss. And while it hasn't been too hard to forget about when on the brink of the wedding of the century and preparing to rule a country, the memory still torments me when I'm trying to fall asleep.

As if conjured by my thoughts, a text lights up my screen.

Henry: I'm sorry about everything. I'll make it up
to you, I promise. x

I toss the phone back onto the table. Typical. He thinks everything can be forgiven with a box of chocolates or tickets to a movie premiere. He doesn't know that I'm just as upset with myself as I am with him.

There's another ping.

Henry: I know you've been avoiding me. Please
don't let your feelings about me change what
you do for Wesbourne.

Damn the man for thinking he can read my mind.

An efficient knock sounds at the door, and my mother steps inside before I can answer it. "All set?" she asks. One would be forgiven for thinking today is *her* wedding day, given the colossal smile on her face and her bridezilla insistence on perfection.

"I don't know if I can do this, Mum."

She clasps my shoulders and spins me around so we're both facing the window. "Do you see those trees out there? The wind is doing everything in its power to destroy them. But look at them." She squeezes, her warm hands imparting strength. "It's going to take more than wind to break you, too."

I stroke the lace at my wrist. "Is it silly that I've always wanted a fairy tale for myself? Not the falling for a prince part, but feeling like fate smiled down especially on me, giving me a life I don't deserve?"

"Who says it hasn't?"

I swivel around. "I don't want this. I want to marry the man I love, to have a family with him, and to spend the rest of our lives making a difference. That's the fairy tale."

"Sometimes we write our own fairy tales," she says.

"Don't pretend to sympathize. This is *your* fairy tale."

"I'll admit, I think fate has not only smiled on you, but rained its bounty upon your head." She spreads her arms. "You'll make more of a difference as queen than in a thousand lifetimes as anyone else. You can have anything you want."

"Except the man I love."

"Love the man you've got."

"Like it's as simple as that," I say.

"It's not as difficult as you might think."

"How would you know?"

"Because that's what I did."

The room swirls around me, and I take a step back. "You loved Dad."

"Of course I did." She shrugs, as if we're discussing which variety of potatoes to have for dinner. "But not at first. Not for a long time."

"Okay, but at least you didn't have to marry him before you loved him."

"My mother would have said I *got* to marry him. In spite of love, or the lack thereof."

A desert storm twists through my mouth. "What are you talking about?" I say quietly.

She sighs and sets her mouth into that all-too-familiar line. She's shoring up for battle. "Your father was a catch. I was not. One does what one must."

"You seduced him?"

"Let's just say I hid my lesser qualities and overlooked his."

"You just said he was a catch."

"Of course. He was the Duke of Whitmere."

"But—" Hot, angry tears warp the room. It's all a lie. She's just trying to keep me from backing out. "Dad was a good man. There's no way he would have married you unless he loved you." It's too frighteningly plausible that my mother married him for his title.

"Theodore was a good man, yes. But he wasn't perfect."

"I never said he was."

"Come on, Celia. It's no secret you idolize him. But the danger in putting someone on a pedestal is that sooner or later, they're going to topple off."

She hands me a tissue, and I dab at the corners of my eyes carefully. Best not to mess up the work of the team that just spent three hours on my makeup.

"I brought you something," she says, holding out a small velvet box. Inside is a tiny charm, my father's face in a gilded frame. "For your bouquet." She helps me attach it to the ribbon wrapped around the stems.

"Thank you," I murmur.

"He would want you to do this." She gives my hand a final squeeze. "Dry your tears and lift your head. You have a wedding to attend and a country to rule."

A limousine is waiting to take me to the cathedral, where the whole country will be waiting, breathless, to see if "Princess Celia" will actually work up the courage to marry her nemesis.

My mother helps me lift the train of my dress into the car, then climbs in after me. We ride in silence, her seeming to sense I want to be left alone, and me too absorbed in the severity of what I'm about to do to pay attention to anything she might say.

The rain is still coming down in torrents, and the sky occasionally cracks open in a bright flash. Water splashes up from the wheels as we drive, and we're slowed by the blinding downpour. The storm is a symphony in its final movement: loud, dramatic, and emotionally wrecking.

As we pull up to the curb in front of St. John's, a fiery ball forms in my chest, and my tears threaten to fall again. Thousands of people are gathered in the streets, dressed in slickers and hats and carrying umbrellas of every color. They seem incognizant of the storm beating down on them. Many are also holding signs, and my heart drops. I remember the angry messages from before and at first thinking they're here to protest the wedding. But when I squint to read through the rain, I realize they're all variations on the same theme: they're congratulating me on my wedding day.

A few weeks ago, I was the Duchess of Whitmere and the director of the Historical Society. My biggest achievement was having saved the old North Chapel from being leveled to make way for an apartment complex. Today, everyone in Wesbourne knows who I am and will be watching my wedding broadcast on live television.

I have to do this for them.

I glance toward the church. A sidewalk canopy has been erected as protection against the rain, although it looks as effective as tissue paper in a hurricane. A soggy green carpet lies beneath it. Personal protection officers are hovering near my car door, waiting for my signal.

Taking a deep breath, I tap on the window. The door opens, and someone holds an umbrella above me as I climb out.

"We'd better hurry, Your Royal Highness, if you wish to remain dry," the man says.

I'd like to see him hurry in a two-hundred-year-old, ten-pound wedding dress and heels.

"One moment." I motion for my mother to keep my train inside the car. Then I turn to the crowd behind me, raise my hand, and wave. They'll never know the turmoil that has brought me here. To them, I am privileged beyond comprehension—about to be married to the most sought-after bachelor in the country, if not the world, and crowned Queen of Wesbourne. It's enviable, really, when you look at it like that.

They cheer above the din of the rain and wave back at me. Several women throw bouquets in my direction, which are immediately pelted by the downpour. What would they think of me if they knew how close I came to deserting them less than an hour ago?

"Okay." I turn back toward the church. "I'm ready."

My mother follows behind me and keeps my train from dragging on the wet carpet. PPOs flank us on every side as an innovative shield against the rain whipping under the canopy.

As I climb the steps where Beck and I had our engagement photos taken a few months ago, my throat tightens. I try not to think about what he might be doing today, whether he'll watch the wedding, if he feels as sick as I do.

Inside the dry interior of the cathedral, hairdressers and makeup artists swarm me to ensure their work survived the trip. My train and veil are given a quick blow-dry. My mum slips away to her seat at the front of the church.

It's almost time.

Behind the closed doors leading into the nave, the organ plays, but the music does little to calm my anxious heart or dry my sweaty palms. Beatrice steps out from the shadows and gives me a perfunctory peck on the cheek. She looks gorgeous in her emerald dress. Every maid of honor in every royal wedding since Wesbourne's founding has worn the national color. We couldn't exactly break tradition now.

My father is supposed to be here, offering his steady strength as he leads me down the aisle. God, what I wouldn't give for five minutes with him. Instead, I have to make that terrifyingly long journey by myself.

The attendants swing the doors open, and the music shifts to "Prelude to the Te Deum." Taking one shaky step after another, I begin my walk to the front. Has the aisle always been this long? The page boys follow with my train, and the guests rise and gaze at me, smiling. If I block out everything else, I can almost imagine this is the wedding of my dreams.

Except the wrong man is waiting for me at the chancel.

When I reach the front, Henry turns to take my hand, and I see his face for the first time. He is breathtakingly handsome in his military uniform, and he's looking at me strangely, like he doesn't know what to say.

The knife that's taken up residence in my gut twists sharply. What am I doing here?

Henry squeezes my trembling hand. "You got this," he whispers. It has an unexpected stabilizing effect on me, and the realization hits me like a ton of bricks: I'm relieved I'm not doing this alone.

We face the front and read the Preface with the congregation. During the hymns, the Scripture reading, and the wedding address, my mind drifts. When it's my turn to recite my vows, I'm surprised to hear myself speaking the words after the minister, promising to love Henry for as long as we both live. Will God forgive my lie?

The rest of the ceremony commences, but I don't hear what is read. I kneel to pray at the appropriate time, exchange rings with my new husband, sign my name on the marriage certificate, and walk back down the aisle, but it holds as much meaning as brushing my teeth. The only way to survive this is to block it out.

The rain has stopped by the time we get outside, and the crowd goes wild as we step through the doors. We stand at the top of the steps for a few minutes for photos. My hand is wrapped in Henry's, and I force my lips to curl into a smile. After all, I'm doing this for the citizens of Wesbourne, and they want a picture of a beaming princess on her wedding day.

No one cares if the princess doesn't want to be there.

Something like a chant rises up from the throng of people. "What are they saying?" I ask.

"They want us to kiss." The weight of Henry's eyes is heavy as he watches me. "What do you think? Should we give them what they want?"

My smile falters, but I save it just in time. I don't look at him. "Not on your life," I say through my grin.

"Why not? Afraid you'd like it?"

"On the contrary, I'm confident I wouldn't."

"That's not what your body said the other day," he murmurs quietly.

That same body betrays me by flooding with heat. "That's where you're wrong."

"You forget, I am very familiar with the female body," he says. "Besides, you owe it to the people. They're here to see you. The least you can do is give them what they came for."

That's what I'm doing by posing for these insipid pictures and pretending to be a blushing bride whispering sweet nothings to her husband. At least this conversation is making the blush authentic.

The crowd refuses to let up. If anything, their enthusiasm is growing. *Kiss her, kiss her, kiss her!*

Bloody hell. The last thing I want is a big scene. I dart a quick glance at Henry, which is the wrong thing to do, because my body begins its own chant. Damn that jawline of his.

Guilt kicks me in the stomach. Even if Beck isn't watching the live broadcast, he will certainly see the coverage later. I can't do that to him.

I straighten my spine. "Not happening."

My smile melts under the inferno of the chants, like an ice cream cone on a hot July day. If we wait long enough, they will eventually give up.

The crowd, however, does not take the hint. Instead, they increase in momentum and volume, now adding clapping to their raucous chants.

"They're undeterred," Henry says, as if I'm a toddler, illiterate to social cues.

If I give in, at least they'll stop yelling, and we can be released from this mortifying situation. I can deal with the fallout. We're married now. A tiny peck won't destroy anything.

"Fine," I say through my teeth. "But make it quick. None of that stuff you pulled last time."

He grins and angles his body toward me. The people start to go wild. Wolf whistles and cheers ricochet through the air as Henry cups my face in his large hands. My heart begins a high-speed chase with itself the instant his skin touches mine.

Slowly, he bends over until his lips catch mine, then lead them in a soft, sensual dance. He slips one hand behind me and swings me backwards, much to the pleasure of the crowd.

It's a gentle kiss, the kind you'd expect on a first date. He raises me back up and smiles, a taffy-sweet smile that's only for me. I know this because it's not on his mouth but folded into the creases around his eyes, where only I can see it. And just for a second, I see the Henry I used to know.

Despite the fact that this was a public kiss between mature adults rather than two lust-driven teenagers making out under the bleachers at a soccer game, it still leaves me breathless. For a span of five seconds, I existed in the center of the rainbow.

"You just became even more envied and adored than you already were," he says. "You're welcome."

He releases me back into a world now drained of color.

Our limo pulls away from the curb, the cheers still audible through the bulletproof glass. Henry twists the shiny gold band on his ring finger. "Well, we did it. You okay?"

I stare out the window. The trees are drooping, heavy from the rain, and their leaves glisten with droplets of water that dribble to the ground in synchronized movements. The earth is soggy with their offerings.

"I will be," I say quietly.

Silence hangs in the air like a forgotten melody, thick and oppressive, keeping peace just out of reach. I sense Henry's fidgeting in the seat beside me.

"C." That single letter holds concern.

"I'm fine."

"We did the right thing."

"Did we?"

"Of course we did."

"Beck wanted me to run away with him."

Henry's quiet for a few moments, then: "Did you consider it?"

"Yes." I trace the trail of a raindrop on the window.

"What stopped you?"

"My father."

"Hey." Henry reaches for my hand, which has unwittingly clasped my bracelet. "Your father would have been proud of whichever decision you made."

"You don't know that."

"He loved you more than anything." Henry stops, and I hear him swallow. "I often wished—"

I move my head just enough to see him in my peripheral vision. "You wished what?" I ask when he doesn't continue.

"It's stupid. But sometimes when I was younger, I wished he were my dad."

I tug my hand back into my lap. "At least your father is still alive."

"As if that's any better," he mutters.

I swivel to face him. "Maybe if you'd try to make him proud instead of only thinking about yourself, you'd have a better relationship."

Henry's fist tightens into a hard ball, turning his knuckles pale. "You don't know the first thing about my relationship with my father."

"That doesn't give you the right to compare your pain to mine."

He punches the leather upholstery, which lets out a small puff of air. "That's not what I was trying to do."

"Forgive me. Your intentions have always been impossible to read." I feel the weight of his gaze but keep mine focused on the rain-sprinkled window.

"Is this about the kiss?"

"Wow, mind reading. What other skills do you have?"

"C, what choice did we have? It would have been worse to ignore the crowd."

"Not *that* kiss, you idiot."

The car is silent as he processes this.

"I apologized for the other one," he finally says.

"Why do men think an apology magically fixes everything?"

"I already told you, it was just a kiss."

I gape at him. "That may have been 'just a kiss' to you, but it was highly inappropriate, considering I'm in love with someone else."

"I'm confused. Are you mad at me or yourself?"

I slug his arm hard enough to send pain radiating through my hand. With lightning-fast reflexes, he catches my wrist. One quick tug and I'm practically in his lap. I pull back, but his fingers are like a manacle.

"Fine." His eyes narrow with intensity. "That wasn't just a kiss for me either. As a matter of fact, it was the best kiss I've ever had. And I've kissed a lot of women." He releases his grip on me, and I tumble backward into my seat.

I haven't had a lot of experience in that department. Beck and I were together for years, but kissing was never our thing. I didn't even think I liked it much, not until the one in Henry's office.

Of course it was the best kiss *I've* ever had. Henry is a pro—a thought that makes me crave a toothbrush. But the best he's had? Bullshit.

"I imagine women usually fall for that line," I say, rubbing my newly freed wrist.

"It's not a line."

"I think we can both agree it shouldn't have happened," I say. "And promise it never will again."

"I have no regrets." His turns his attention to the window. "And I'll make no promises."

19

"Without Me" - Halsey

OUR WEDDING NIGHT IS as anticlimactic as one might expect from an arranged marriage in which both parties can barely hold a civil conversation that isn't full of snide comments and deranged looks. I retreat to my suite soon after dinner. Henry does whatever he normally does, which is to say, I don't have a bloody clue.

I'm brushing my teeth when my maid, Daphne, knocks on the bathroom door. "There is someone who wishes to see you, ma'am," she says.

"Who is it?" I mumble through a mouthful of toothpaste.

"It's your husband."

I nearly choke. Henry may legally be my husband, but that doesn't mean he should be referred to as such. I spit into the sink. "Tell him I've gone to bed, please."

She returns a few minutes later. "He says it's important that he speak with you."

I smirk at my reflection in the mirror. If Henry thinks I'm going to be duped into believing a word out of his mouth after everything he's done, he's about to be sorely disappointed. "I'll talk to him soon. Thank you, Daphne."

Tonight is the perfect night to do an advanced skin care routine, I decide. Cleanser, face mask, rinse, toner, every jar of anti-aging cream in my bathroom, facial serums, moisturizers, massage, gua sha, and finally a jade roller. By the time I'm done, my skin has never felt better.

After spending some quality time with my cuticles and nails and moisturizing my whole body, I finally approach the connecting door between Henry's and my suites, which I'm tolerating only because it can be locked. Without opening it, I say, "Henry?"

"Congratulations, I'm an old man."

I bite my lip as it curls into a grin. Victory tastes sweet. "What do you want?"

"Open the door, and I'll tell you."

No way is he regaining the upper hand. I won it fair and square. "I'm tired. I was just going to bed."

"Fine, I'll go without you then."

"Go where?" I ask before I can stop myself. There's no answer. "Henry?"

He's hoping my curiosity will get the best of me, but there is nowhere to go this late, and certainly no place I'll go with him. It's nothing but a trap.

I know this, I swear I do, but I still knock. "Henry, answer me."

Only silence greets me. I take a few steps away back, but the niggling fear of missing out does an annoying *rat-a-tat-tat* on my shoulder. I let out a frustrated huff and turn toward the door again. Unlocking it, I swing it open to reveal Henry propped against the frame, a devilish grin stretching across his face.

"You infuriating prick." I grab the folds of my dressing robe and pull them a little tighter.

He slips his fingers into my tied sash and tugs me toward him. "Let's go." He walks toward the double doors leading to the hallway.

"Excuse me? I'm not going anywhere like this."

He throws a glance over his shoulder. "You look fine. Come on."

"Not until you tell me where we're going. And probably not even then."

"It's our wedding night—humor me. Unless you'd rather go in there?" He jerks a thumb over his shoulder in the direction of his suite.

"Sure, let me just stab a fork in my throat first. If you think I'm following you anywhere without more information, you are grossly mistaken."

"Always with your need to know everything." He sighs, as if that's somehow an obnoxious request. "Trust me, you will want to see this."

"Trust you? Because you're such a trustworthy person?"

"Despite what you may think, I actually do know you pretty well. You won't regret this, I promise."

"Do you give that caveat every time you make a move on a woman?"

The hint of a smile dances on his lips. "You don't regret that kiss as much as you wish you did."

I hate that he's right. That kiss has had me lying awake for hours and woken me in a tangle of sheets and sweat. I hate that in spite of everything, sparring with Henry is actually a great distraction from what has become of my life.

"Fine. I will go with you on whatever evil errand you're on, but I must remind you that I am perfectly capable of removing your favorite appendage if you try anything."

This elicits a chuckle, the kind that warms your insides just listening to it.

I stick close to him as we make our way to the opposite end of the palace. I've never been in many of these rooms before, and given the map in his hand, I don't think Henry has spent much time in them either.

We stop outside a set of doors, not unlike the hundreds of others we passed on the way here. He opens them, then steps inside to flick on the light. I walk in after him, still unsure what to expect.

Yellow silk damask covers the walls of the large bedchamber, which evidently hasn't been redecorated since the nineteenth century. A massive, curtained bed dominates the room. Several pieces of antique furniture, including a hand-painted French armoire and a Victorian dressing table with a curved mirror, seem to hint that the room once belonged to a woman. There's a stale, forgotten odor in the air, reminding me of the archive room of the Historical Society.

"Why are we here, Henry?" I move closer to the armoire with its exquisite floral designs.

"This," he says, sweeping an arm around the room like a showman, "was Queen Helena's bedchamber."

"You're joking."

"Nope. This is where my great-great-great-grandfather was conceived."

"Just the mental image I wanted."

"I thought you might want to look around. I know you've always been interested in Helena."

The room does hold a certain appeal, not the least of which is the fact that my personal hero and ancestor spent considerable time in it. When will I get another opportunity like this?

"That's a nice way of putting it," I say.

"You're right. Borderline obsessed would have been more accurate."

I narrow my eyes at him before continuing my exploration of the armoire, but there's nothing inside, other than some old linens that have yellowed with time.

"The craftsmanship on this is incredible." I rub my hand over the intricate carvings in the corners. "It looks mid-eighteenth century. It was probably made right before all the forest fires in 1761."

"Should I get your laptop so you can write a blog post?" My face heats, but Henry's smiling. "Come here," he says.

I brush the dust from my hands onto my silk robe. The whole time I've been inspecting the armoire, he's been fiddling with the dressing table between the two windows on the east-facing wall.

"See how this part seems too wide?" Sitting back on his heels, he looks up at me as I join him.

He reaches inside the open drawer, and there's a faint click. The back panel releases to reveal a hidden compartment.

A stack of papers bundled together with ribbon is nestled in the opening.

"Are those letters?" I say as he sticks his hand in and tugs them out.

"Looks like it." He offers them to me.

I run my hands over the thick stack. My fingers are trembling like I've just had an entire pot of coffee. "They've got to be hers, right?"

Henry grins, and my heart jolts. When did his smile start doing that to me? "Only one way to find out," he says.

We settle on the floor against the foot of the bed. The bed itself would have been more comfortable, but I trust a used car salesman more than I trust myself on a bed with Henry right now.

I pick up the bundle of letters, but his hand stops me. He touches the silver ring threaded onto the ribbon binding them together, then reaches for my wrist. "Isn't that the same thing as your bracelet?"

"Yeah, it's a claddagh," I say. "They're Irish."

His fingers sear my skin, and I hope he can't feel my pulse snag. I gently tug my hand free, then carefully open the first envelope and begin reading aloud.

18 July 1836

My dearest Helena,

You cannot know how I felt upon receiving your letter. After all, it has been three years since you left, since I saw your face for the very last time. I never thought I would see or hear from you again, and even though my heart has hardly beat since the day I heard the news, I did not dare believe it could really be from you.

But how could I live with myself if I did not respond, even if it turns out to be nothing but an evil trick designed by a cold heart? I will take this risk and face the consequences, come what may. My body may be in Ireland, but my heart will always be in Wesbourne with you.

You do not know me if you think I do not forgive you for the vows you have spoken to one who is not me. We swore our love to one another, and whilst a woman's heart is a fickle thing, you have never had the heart of a woman but of an angel.

Not a day has gone by that I have not thought of you, my love. How could I not, when you are my entire world, everything I long for? A singular hope has kept me alive these years, and it is this: that your heart remains as true to me as mine does to you.

A great, churning sea lies between us, my dear Helena, but it is nothing in the face of the love we share. I would cross it today to come to you, but I would rather walk through the depths of hell itself than to put you in danger. We may be parted in life, but we shall never be parted in spirit. It will take more than mere mortals to destroy what we have.

I can hardly bear the danger you are inviting upon yourself in writing to me, but I do not think I can suffer the silence a minute longer. My heart beats for you and you alone. I can only trust that you have taken care to conceal all traces that could lead back to you, and I truly hope your maid can be trusted. I will do as you ask and direct my letters to Margaret Smith, trusting they will find their way into your hands.

I am alive and well, with the exception of the gaping hole in my chest that once held my heart, which flew across the ocean with you when you left.

I am yours for all of this life and the next.

Your dear Philip

I refold the letter and place it with the others. "I wish I could have seen their reunion," I whisper.

Henry leans back in faux surprise. "I didn't know you were into porn."

I jab my elbow into his ribs. I've never before encountered such raw, powerful love. Nearly two hundred years later, it still has the power to change the atmosphere in the room.

"Maybe great love really does exist," he says.

I sigh. "That doesn't mean it's sustainable or realistic." But in the face of that impassioned letter, I might be forced to concede my stance. Those weren't the words of a man infatuated. His love had withstood the test of time and harsh reality.

"Helena's mysterious lover finally has a name," Henry says.

"There must have been thousands of Philips living in Ireland in 1836."

"Maybe the rest of the letters will tell us more." He plucks the next one from the stack and reads it out loud, then we work our way through the rest of them.

From what we can surmise, Helena had been secretly engaged to Philip Anderson in 1833. Her aristocratic family did not approve of the match and sent her to live with a family friend in Wesbourne, where she was introduced to Wesbournian society. When she caught the eye of the future king of Wesbourne, William I, her father wouldn't allow her to refuse him. She was forced to marry William less than a year after her removal from Ireland.

Helena finally worked up the courage to write to Philip three years later, in 1836, asking his forgiveness and his correspondence if his feelings for her remained true. Still madly in love, he started writing Helena letters but directed them to her lady's maid, the same Margaret who had written the infamous diary.

Margaret would slip the letters to her mistress, who began putting together a plan to see her lover again. The two of them corresponded for nearly a year, arranging all the details for Philip to sail from Ireland to Wesbourne. Helena even sent him the money to purchase passage to Wesbourne.

Finally, in the spring of 1837, Philip wrote one final letter telling her his ship was set to sail on the third of May.

"I guess we know what happened next," Henry says once we complete the stack.

"Just because they made plans to be together doesn't mean they actually pulled it off."

"Why are you so skeptical? We have the diary. Now we know that a lover did exist and that Helena made arrangements for him to meet her in Wesbourne."

"So far it's just a hypothesis. We can't prove Philip ever left Ireland, let alone that he made it to Wesbourne. And even if he did, what proof is there that they had an affair?"

We're still sitting on the floor, and my feet are falling asleep. Henry nudges me with his shoulder. "I can't tell if you want it to be true or not."

"I can't either," I say.

"Do you have doubts about being queen?"

I slide the tarnished claddagh ring over my finger. "You know I do." It's a whisper, echoing through the still room.

Slipping his arm behind me, he tugs me against him. He is familiar, warm, and solid—stability incarnate. It's nothing but a façade, since he's the most irresponsible human being I've ever met. Nonetheless, I allow myself to soak up his strength for just a moment.

"What's the worst that could happen?" he asks, keeping his voice hushed. I guess neither of us is willing to disturb whatever ghosts might linger in this room.

"Tarring and feathering comes to mind."

"Okay," he says. "What's the worst that could happen in this century?"

I attempt to shrug, but with my shoulders trapped under his arm, it comes out as more of a snuggle. "I go down in history as a terrible queen. I waste this opportunity."

Henry is quiet for a moment, and I'm grateful that he doesn't offer the glib response I expect. Finally, he rests his chin on my head and says softly, "C, you couldn't be terrible if you tried."

It's so unexpected, and so sweet, that for a second I'm left spinning. He smells like a pine forest and soap, and I can't help the way my head inclines toward him. I need to feel his warmth through the thin fabric of my robe. I need his reassurance that I can do this, that I have what it takes.

"How do I know this isn't just a ploy to sabotage me?"

"You don't," he says. "Therein lies the fun."

"The fun will have to wait." I shift out of his embrace. "Right now, I need to get to bed before I fall asleep in a sitting position." *With my head on your shoulder.*

He stands and grabs my hands to pull me up. Pins and needles torment my feet as blood returns to them. I stamp them on the floor and follow him out of the room.

When we reach the door of my suite, Henry waits while I unlock it. "Thank you," I say, turning to face him. "You were right. No regrets."

"You're not alone in this, C. I hope you know that." The look in his eyes converts my knees to Jell-O. He brushes a strand of hair from my face, and his fingers linger, tracing my neck and drawing goosebumps to the surface of my skin.

It's a betrayal, the way my body responds to his touch, craving it while my mind screams "run."

"Henry," I whisper. It's meant as a warning, to both of us, but comes out sounding like aching desire.

He understands it all the same and drops his hand. His eyes are laced with pain.

"I'm sorry," I say. "But I can't handle it if you hurt me again."

I manage to get inside and close the door before sinking to the floor and allowing my tears to fall. I am doing everything right, or bloody well trying to, but it still isn't enough.

No matter how long I stay away or how well I avoid him, he can crumble my defenses in the space of an hour. He's always had that ability, even when we were young. It's what made him the best friend I've ever had. It's also what destroyed my whole world.

Henry is my kryptonite. I know that. He knows that.

And for that reason, for my own safety and well-being, it's imperative I stay away. If I don't, the result will be a hurricane, destroying absolutely everything. Just like the first time.

20

"Wildest Dreams" -
Taylor Swift

"**T**HE SEAFOAM GREEN IS classic," I say, holding the tea-length dress against myself while looking in the mirror.

"Yes, but the yellow is a total showstopper." Maisie waves the bold pencil dress in front of her. "You'd look like a babe in it."

"I'm not sure *babe* is the look I'm going for at the hospital opening."

Now that I'm officially a working royal, I am bound by a calendar that puts the one my mother used to keep for me to shame. I'm expected to attend various events on behalf of the Crown, sometimes with the whole royal family, other times on my own. In the four weeks since the wedding, I've already become a patron of three different charities, lending my name, and thereby my support, to their causes. Maisie estimates my schedule can accommodate roughly five hundred more.

There are also public events that require glad-handing and a smile that hurts my cheeks within two minutes of being locked into place. You can go to the royal family's website to find a full list of these engagements, filtered by family member, if you're one of those people who likes to lurk at public events in the hope of meeting a royal. It's one of these I'm currently preparing for.

The entire royal family will be at this one. Apparently, the Wesbourne Cancer Institute is considered important enough to warrant an appearance from each member. God knows how many dollars it took to buy that level of importance.

Maisie shrugs, undeterred by my argument against the dress she's chosen. "Let's face it. The green is your safety net. It's longer, sleeves to the elbows, and has a nice boatneck collar. But the yellow pushes you out of your box. Which we both know you've grown too comfortable inside."

What part of this box does she think I'm comfortable in? I open my mouth to reply, but she cuts me off.

"Come on. The color is eye-catching, and you're one of, like, three women in the world who can pull off lemon yellow. It's knee length, which means it will show off your legs, which are looking great, by the way, thanks to that new trainer. And the dipping bodice is still modest without being prudish." She blatantly ignores the irritation on my face.

"I'm more comfortable in the green," I say.

She isn't wrong. It *is* my safety net, but right now, safety is one thing I could use more of. The night Henry and I found the letters in Helena's room was far too dangerous, and I'm doing my best to forget it ever happened.

"Because you're scared to take a risk!"

"I'm not scared. The green just makes me feel more confident." And I could use more confidence right now. Having one's entire life upended would make anyone waver. Before I lost Beck, I would never have let my guard down around Henry.

Maisie sighs. "You wore it to the boat-christening ceremony. The press will rip you into juicy shreds for re-wearing it, and they'll enjoy every minute of it."

"You're right. It's inhumane of me not to have considered them before. Let's replicate the entire outfit so they have enough gossip to fill *two* editions." I pluck the dress off the hanger.

"If I turn gray by the time I'm thirty, I'm blaming—and charging—you," she says, but obediently helps me into the seafoam-colored dress.

I haven't seen Beck since that godforsaken day in Henry's office, but he's sure to have had his fill of me since then. I can't go anywhere—in the city or online—without being greeted by my own face. Even the post-wedding kiss is still being splashed around like next season's fashion trends.

If Beck didn't hate me before, he definitely does now.

"Which shoes?" Maisie startles me out of my thoughts, dangling two pairs of heels in front of me. I point to the nude Gianvito Rossi pumps. She rolls her eyes and hands them over. "Again with the safe choice." She slides the white slingbacks back onto the shelf.

"Sorry I'm such a bore. Maybe you should apply at a fashion magazine."

She affects a horrified look. "You know I'd rather die than leave your side. Oh, by the way, I looked into that garden you asked about, the one that was looking a little shabby?"

Several weeks ago, I asked her to find out why the Sunken Garden wasn't being taken care of, but I'd completely forgotten about it. "What did you find out?"

"It seems our good prince doesn't want it touched." She picks up the electronic tablet that goes everywhere with her, and which she lovingly refers to as her "backup brain."

"Henry asked them to stop taking care of it?"

"That's what I was told."

This is an interesting development.

My phone pings from somewhere nearby. I glance around, hoping to get lucky and find it lying on my bed. It's not.

"Closet, second shelf from the right," Maisie says without looking up from the tablet.

She's right as usual, and I unlock my screen, expecting to find a text from my mother reminding me to wear pantyhose. The woman will never forgive my visiting the Equestrian Foundation with—*gasp!*—bare legs. I do not expect to see a text from Beck.

Beck: Can I see you? Winchester Park, 11am.

A thousand thoughts swirl through my head. I reach out and snag one, and it's this: How can seeing him do anything but further complicate this mess I'm in?

Because I am a glutton for punishment, because I still miss what we had so badly it's a physical ache, and because what else can I possibly do, I text him back.

Me: I'll be there. x

The Wesbourne Cancer Institute is world-renowned for its groundbreaking research and innovative treatments. A new wing was just added for their youngest patients: children.

We walk down the quiet halls on our private tour. The colorful artwork on the walls, the glassed-in indoor playgrounds, and the soft music being piped through the speakers are all designed to deceive you into thinking you are at a very large and squeaky-clean daycare.

But there is nothing to be done about the scent.

No amount of crayon drawings, nurses in Eeyore scrubs, or soft block towers can mask the fact that this is a hospital. And despite what everyone says about them being places of healing, hospitals are where people come to die.

Although I vaguely recall Maisie going over the itinerary for our visit in the car, I was so consumed by the idea of seeing Beck again that I wasn't paying attention. If I had been, there's no way I would have agreed to step through those doors without putting up more of a fight. As it is, I am now being herded down the corridors with our whole entourage, the chief medical officer pointing out the things we should be impressed by. This is met with murmured approvals and quiet questions.

I don't understand why we can't stop in the rooms and meet some of the patients. What better way to bring cheer than a visit from the king himself? But we pass each door without slowing. Apparently, we are too busy or too important to be bothered by dying children.

One of the doors we pass is open, and I peek inside. A tiny boy is lying in bed watching TV, a stuffed bear tucked under his arm. I smile and give him a little wave. His face lights up in return. I'm about to step into the room when my eyes are drawn to the large Cat in the Hat balloon bobbing above the bed. I freeze.

I hesitate just long enough for the nurse tending to the child to stick her head out and close the door with a gentle smile. I steel my jaw as the memory sweeps over me. I will not fall apart here. I can't.

It taunts me behind my closed eyelids: a sad red balloon with *Get well soon!* scrawled across the foil, as though the forced cheerfulness could somehow convince a body to eradicate the sickness sucking the life from it, one long slurp at a time.

It was the first thing I saw when I walked into his hospital room. His cold, ashen face was the next.

I was too late. And the sadistic balloon mocked me for my absence.

My stomach heaves as we round another corner, and a nurse sweeps past us, pushing a triage cart followed by a gust of antiseptic air. I need to find a bathroom and then an exit.

"You okay?" Henry says softly, wrapping his fingers around my elbow.

I cannot let him know how much the gesture makes me want to crumble into his arms. I glance up at and give him my best to smile, although I can't be sure it doesn't look more like a grimace. "Fine. Why?"

"You're in danger of snapping your bracelet."

He's right. I lower my eyes to my wrist and realize I've been twisting the thin metal band so hard it could have snapped. I let go. "It's this place," I say.

"I assumed." He scans the hallway, then whispers something to one of the PPOs behind us. "Come with me." He steers me to a bathroom.

After splashing cold water on my face, I attempt a deep breath, but quickly give up that idea. Even hospital bathrooms smell like death. My watch says it's already 10:40—I'm supposed to meet Beck soon. My heart picks up speed like a car merging onto the highway.

I have to get out of here. The only problem will be sneaking past both Henry and the PPOs. I may be able to convince Henry to take me to the park, but there's no way he'll leave me there alone, even with Beck. *Especially* with Beck. Regardless, it's my only option at the moment.

"I need some air," I say after exiting the restroom. "There's a park a few blocks away. Walk me over there?"

Fortunately, he agrees, and we excuse ourselves from the tour and step into the sunshine.

Winchester Park isn't your average city park. It's more like a small national park plunked into the center of the city, skyscrapers growing around its perimeter like a hedge. A rocky bluff overlooks the expanse of Wesbourne suburbia, and evergreen trees line the winding asphalt paths. We see few people as we walk, the towering pines and rock boulders offering plenty of privacy.

My phone vibrates in my bag, and I pull it out.

Beck: *I'm at the bluff.*

My palms suddenly sweaty, I tuck my device away again and wipe them on my dress. My heart is now jackhammering in my chest. "Do you mind if I walk alone?" I ask without looking at Henry. My lying skills aren't exactly first-rate. "I just need to . . . Thinking about my dad—"

He hesitates, scans the area around us. It's deserted. "Don't go far. You never know who might spot you." He gives my seafoam dress a pointed glance. "You don't exactly blend in with the trees."

At least I didn't wear the yellow.

Moving down the path as quickly as I dare without seeming like I'm hurrying off, I find my way to the edge of the park. I don't encounter a single person. When I reach the bluff, Beck is standing there with his back turned to me, and I take a minute to study him. He looks taller than I remember, but has that same lean build. His hands are in his pockets as he looks out over the rocky ledge, causing his elbows to jut out at sharp angles.

"Beck." It's tentative, almost a whisper, but he hears it.

He turns to face me but doesn't move any closer, so I stay where I am, arms dangling awkwardly at my sides. He must have come directly from the office. He's wearing his usual uniform of navy suit, white shirt, and gray tie.

"Celia." His voice sounds like it's been dragged over a cheese grater. He clears his throat and covers the distance between us in three long strides. "When I saw that you were going to be at the hospital this morning, I was hoping you'd be able to slip away."

I don't know what to say. What is the protocol for seeing your ex-fiancé? Our last conversation held so much anger and disappointment and hurt, and I am not the same person I was two months ago.

"How have you been?" he asks.

"I'm okay." I'm surprised to find it's actually true. My new life isn't easy, not by a long shot, but every day I'm settling into my role more.

"I miss you." He tugs his sleeves down. "I was a fool. A damn fool."

The blame for this mess falls squarely on my shoulders, but there's a part of me that's still smarting from his rejection. "It's all in the past."

"I've had time to think," he says. "And I want you back."

I blink at him. Is he serious? Of course he is. Beck would never joke about something like this.

"It's a little late for that," I whisper.

"I never should have asked you to choose between me and Wesbourne."

This is the speech I wanted from him two months ago, not now that so much has changed. "What's done is done. It never would have worked anyway." I envision the headlines broadcasting Princess Jacqueline's affair.

"You said yourself that these things aren't uncommon."

"I was grasping at straws."

He frowns and props his hands on his hips. "I'm not ready to let you go."

"Beck, I'm married now."

A murmur of voices signals the arrival of a group of walkers. I turn to face away from the path until they disappear around a cluster of trees.

"Are you sleeping with him? Is that why you won't consider it?"

"Excuse me?"

"It's a simple question, Celia. Are you or are you not having sex with Henry?"

"Why in the bloody hell would you ask me that?"

"Just answer the question."

"Of course not!"

Beck deflates slowly, and I think of the balloon in the hospital again. For the first time, I see how fatigued he looks. Older. "Please tell me you'll at least give it some thought," he says.

I open my mouth to respond, but the words won't come. My skin prickles with the memory of Henry's hands on me, my head on his shoulder. It feels like a betrayal, thinking of it now, when I should be rejoicing that Beck still has feelings for me.

"I'll think about it," I squeak out.

He moves then, and before I can tell what he's about to do, his lips are pressing against mine. His hands cradle my waist, and he explores my mouth like a man returning home after a long trip.

That annoying sound some phone cameras make ricochets through my subconscious. With it comes the realization that not only are Beck and I in a compromising situation, but we are no longer alone.

I break off the kiss as the horror sets in. There's a flash as someone darts around the curve in the path, but they're past the trees before I catch more than a glimpse.

"Bloody hell. They'll burn us alive," I say, and press my fingers to my temples.

"Should I run after him?" Beck asks.

"No need." A very angry Henry rounds the bend, the shirt of a young man clasped in his fist. "Give it to me." He holds out his free hand, palm up. "What the hell do you think you're doing?"

The kid grimaces and pulls his phone out. After placing it in Henry's hand, he says, "I didn't mean any harm, Your Royal Highness." It's surprising the guy hasn't toppled over from the weight of Henry's glare.

Henry shoves the phone into his jacket pocket. "Don't you ever," he says, his teeth clenched tightly, "take another photo of her, or I'll see to it you lose both thumbs." He shoves at the same time as he releases his hold, and the kid goes stumbling back the way he came.

Tension is rolling off Beck in waves. This is his worst nightmare. He won't even ask for an adjustment of his receipt at the grocery store if they charge him for two gallons of milk instead of one.

"Henry, don't you think you're being a little dramatic?" I say. "You didn't have to threaten him."

"You'd prefer I left him to sell the photos to the highest bidder?" He levels his gaze on Beck. "It's time for you to leave."

Beck leans toward me. "Do you want me to stay?"

I hesitate. I don't relish the thought of seeing the two of them duke it out in the middle of Winchester Park, and if the look on Henry's face is any indication, it's liable to happen if Beck sticks around.

"Do I need to get a box of crayons to spell it out for you? I said, it's time to go." Henry's voice is thin ice.

"You'd better leave," I say, squeezing Beck's arm. "I'll call you."

He looks down at me, and I can't tell what he's thinking. After a few seconds, he pulls away and disappears down the path, leaving me in the company of a volcano on the brink of eruption.

"Was that really necessary?" I move to edge past Henry, but he sticks out his arm.

"Not so fast. First, you can explain what the hell you're doing."

"I don't have to explain anything to you."

"On the contrary, I think you do. You *lied* to me," he says through his teeth.

"You never would have let me come if I'd told you the truth."

"You're bloody right I wouldn't."

I glare at him. "I did what I had to in order to make my meeting."

"A meeting with Harrison? Or with the tosser taking your photo?"

"You're a child."

"The least you could say is thank you."

"I didn't ask you to do that. I didn't ask you for anything," I spit out.

"You're my *wife*. You didn't need to ask."

My pulse thrums loudly in my ears. "I don't need you to save me, or whatever it is you think you're doing."

"Admit it. You're glad I showed up and made both of them leave."

"What's that supposed to mean?"

"Come on, Celia. We both know Harrison bores you."

"How dare you talk to me like that." It comes out shakier than I'd like, my fists trembling at my side.

"Because it's the truth, but you're too scared to admit it." He takes a step toward me, and his dark eyes probe mine.

"Don't make assumptions about how I feel."

"Assumptions?" Scoffing, he shakes his head. "God, C. I know you better than you know yourself." His voice is the richest velvet. "I know that the last time we were together you scared so badly you've done everything in your power to keep away from me ever since. Because you're terrified."

"I hate you."

"I know that too. Now, why don't we talk about what was happening before I walked past the trees?"

"There's nothing to talk about. Why did you follow me anyway?"

"I was worried about you. I knew being in the hospital was hard for you, and I wanted to make sure you were okay. Let's not forget, you implied you needed time to yourself because of your *dad*, not because you were meeting your lover."

My chest grows warm and tight under his glare.

"Speaking of—" Henry reaches into his jacket pocket and pulls out the incriminating phone. His face is a cool mask as he scrolls through the pictures. "Getting pretty cozy with the staff, C."

"Oh, please," I say. "Don't play that card. It's beneath even you."

"Okay," he says, putting the phone away. "Then tell me how many more of these destructive situations I'll have to save you from."

"I never asked you to follow me, and I bloody well didn't ask you to save me."

"Since you're so unappreciative, you won't mind if I hand this phone over to the press then, right?"

"Sure, go ahead."

The corner of his mouth twitches. "All right. *The Sun* should have lots of fun with it."

"Damn it, Henry!" I say as he starts walking away. "Can you for once not make me want to strangle you?"

He wheels around to face me. "As soon as you quit being a pain in the ass."

I desperately want to hit him with something heavy, like my car. "You smug son of a bitch."

He moves closer until he's only inches away. I refuse to take a step backward, refuse to show him how he affects me. Cupping my jaw in his palm, he yanks me to him with his other hand.

"I ought to kiss you until you can't see straight."

Electricity zips through my blood. At his touch, my body responds the way I knew it would, rising up and begging him to make good on his threat. My mind grabbles for control.

"But I won't," he breathes, and brushes his lips over mine. It nearly sends me into cardiac arrest, but he doesn't appear to notice. "I'll settle for drinks. In my suite. Tonight."

I jerk away from him. "Are you out of your mind? I know what you do there."

Raising both palms, he says, "I swear, drinks only. You owe me for bailing you out."

"No way. I'm not coming to your room." I'm still buzzing from the high voltage coursing through me.

"Come on, C. Just as friends. Aren't you tired of fighting?"

I study him. He isn't hiding laughter—always a sign that he's up to no good. Instead, his eyes hold a smudge of a plea, and Henry doesn't make a habit of asking for things. His lips are slightly parted, as if he's waiting with bated breath for my answer.

I do a quick gut check on myself. My traitorous body is already waiting in his suite, praying he didn't mean his "just as friends" comment. My inner skeptic is surprisingly silent. It seems the general consensus is that Henry can be trusted this time.

And the truth is, I *am* tired of fighting with him. I bite my lower lip, now cold with sweat. "Okay. Just drinks."

"Just drinks," he says with a grin.

21

"Stranded" - Plumb

I T TAKES ME LESS than thirty minutes to regret my decision to meet Henry in his room, but he will never let me back out now, not after I've agreed.

I need an escape plan. I'll go and have one drink with him, claim a headache, and return to my own suite. He can't force me to stay longer than I want, and if he actually thinks I have a headache, he'll let me go. The trick is to be convincing enough.

After dismissing Daphne for the night, I circle my closet, debating what to wear. It's best to be on full defense. Henry is not to be trusted, no matter how guileless he appeared earlier. I finally decide on a black cashmere sweater and jeans. Comfortable, unassuming, and best of all, modest.

I'm pulling my hair into a loose ponytail when soft music floats through the wall from his room. My blood hurtles through my veins at top speed, and I curse my past self who stood in the park and agreed to this. Stupid girl.

If I delay any longer, he'll come looking for me, so I summon up the courage to knock on the door connecting our suites. He doesn't answer, although I can still hear the music. Maybe he didn't hear me.

I knock again, louder this time, but there's still no answer. We didn't agree on a time, so maybe he expects me to let myself in when I'm ready?

I turn the knob and step inside, able at last to satisfy my curiosity about the prince's lair. Candles flicker on all available surfaces, making shadows dance on the dark walls. I briefly consider running, but—let's be honest—wild horses can't drag me away before I see more. I'll leave soon enough.

Henry's sitting room looks much like mine, except it's decorated in shades of navy and taupe. There's also a baby grand hogging an entire side of the room. A small grouping of candles sits on top, their flickering reflected in the glossy black lid.

The most incredible melody surges from the instrument's depths. It's dramatic, sad, hypnotic, and I quickly realize Henry is responsible for it. I stand mesmerized, watching him play, a hot ball of emotion welling up inside me as his fingers draw out the haunting music. Despite the years of lessons I've taken in both piano and violin, I've never produced anything this beautiful.

He is unaware of my presence, of that I'm certain. He's playing with complete abandon, eyes closed, his body leaning into the music like they are one. I know he feels it in the depths of his soul, the same way I do in mine.

Watching him is magical.

After several more minutes of playing, he pauses, and in doing so, notices me standing there. The serenity drops from his face as if I've embarrassed him.

"That was beautiful," I whisper, letting my fingers graze the lid of the piano. "I didn't realize you still played." I'm having trouble reconciling the image of Henry, playboy prince, with Henry, heartfelt musician.

He rises from the bench. "It's my escape."

"Don't stop on my account."

He walks around the piano, wearing a thin white T-shirt and soft light-wash jeans. He looks nothing like the Henry that decorates the front of the tabloids and every bit the boy he was at seventeen. Unease crawls down my spine. I can handle playboy Henry, but the one standing in front of me scares me senseless.

He studies me. As he slides them across my body, his eyes on me feel just like his fingertips did. He might as well be trailing his hands down the length of me.

His extensive perusal ends at my feet, which are bare—a choice I regret as his gaze lingers on them. I curl my toes, and a tiny smile tugs at the corner of his mouth.

"What? What's wrong?" I double-check the fly of my jeans with panicked fingers.

"Nothing." The small smile blossoms into a full one. "You look perfect." He moves to the bar near the window. "Can I get you wine?"

"Yes, thank you." Look at us, being civil like normal people.

Henry uncorks a bottle of red. "To be honest, I didn't think you'd come tonight. I was expecting a text saying you weren't feeling well."

Accepting the glass from him, I say, "I almost did." Now my cover is blown. I'll have to think of a different reason to leave early.

Chuckling, he motions for me to precede him to the sofa. "You're as predictable as the sunrise."

Despite my apprehension, I'm also strangely excited. I take a seat, clutching my goblet like it's a life preserver.

"When was the last time you had fun?" He settles at the opposite end of the couch, leaving an appropriate amount of space between us. A buffet of snacks is spread across the coffee table, and the tub of cookie dough does not escape my notice. Henry reaches for a bowl of peanuts.

I take a sip of wine before answering. "When I slapped you. That was exhilarating."

His laugh is glorious, rich and full of depth. "That's not quite what I meant." He tosses a handful of nuts into his mouth.

"Too bad. It's such a stress reliever." Am I *flirting* with him? The alcohol must be going to my head. Time to slow down. I set my glass down and grab a scoop of cookie dough.

"I have a better idea." He walks to a closet on the far side of the room. When he returns, he's carrying a dilapidated Monopoly box. "You up for a little trading?"

I choke out a laugh. "You mean am I up for kicking your ass?"

"Hey, I won a few times."

"Yeah, because I felt sorry for you."

Frowning, Henry places the game on the table. "Well, a lot of things have changed since then."

Isn't that the truth. "I guess we'll just have to see if your hustling skills are one of them."

He refills our drinks while I set up the board. "No cheating."

Pressing a hand to my chest, I give him a horrified look. "I wouldn't dream of it."

An abrupt laugh slips out of him. "You forget I know you."

Ignoring the pang that vibrates through my chest, I toss a little plastic hotel at his head as he sits down. "Things have changed, remember?"

He holds up the Scottie game piece questioningly, and I greedily swipe it from his hand. "Not that, apparently," he says with a grin.

As we begin playing, we slip into our natural groove, the years melting away until we're simply Henry and Celia again, best friends and fierce rivals. I'd forgotten how much fun it is to spend an evening around a board game. Not relaxing, at least not if I want to beat Henry, but definitely fun. For a few hours, I don't have to think about the responsibilities and future awaiting me.

"I can't believe how long it's been since I've played," I say, adding another house to Boardwalk.

"I should've picked Candy Land. At least then I'd have a shot at winning." Frowning at my growing empire, Henry stands up. "I think it's time for something stronger than wine."

Now is my chance to leave, to find some excuse for why I can't stay any longer. I *need* to go, before things become even more dangerous. The problem is, I have the strongest urge to stay.

"I really should be heading to bed," I say before I can talk myself out of it.

"We haven't even finished the game yet."

"It's Monopoly. Does anyone ever finish?"

"Come on, you're so close to obliterating me. The least you can do is finish the job." He hands me a glass of whiskey.

"Fine." I take a sip. The alcohol burns a hot trail down my throat and joins the butterflies in my stomach, now fluttering in a pool of warm gold. My backbone melted into that same pool a while ago.

We play until Henry declares bankruptcy. "Every time," he says, tossing the last of his mortgaged property cards into the box. "I don't know how you do it."

"I'll never tell." The alcohol is making me bold. I need to leave, but my body isn't listening.

He reclines on the couch, his face shadowed and hard to read in the dim lighting, but he looks relaxed.

"Tell me something I don't know about you." My words surprise me even more than they do him. I face him and tuck my feet under me.

He gives an uneasy chuckle. "What do you want to know?"

"Your deepest, darkest secret." I take a sip of liquid courage. "What's the biggest skeleton in your closet, Prince Henry?"

He stares at me for a moment, then into his glass. "Some skeletons aren't meant to see the light of day." The amusement has bled from his voice.

I stretch out my leg and nudge him with my bare toes. "Come on. We're friends tonight, aren't we?"

He wraps his fingers around my ankle. I forget to breathe as he strokes it with his thumb, sending tremors into my core. Finally, he releases me, leans forward, and clasps his hands in front of him.

"Henry? What's wrong?" I set my drink down and scoot across the sofa until I reach him. Touching him feels like the most natural thing in the world, and I rub my hand across his back, relishing the feel of the thick muscles under his T-shirt.

He looks at me then, and I hardly recognize the mournful look that has crept into his eyes. He shakes his head, then kneads the furrows in his forehead. "The past can be a dark, ugly thing, C."

My eyebrows pull together in sync with my stomach. "Now you're scaring me." I tuck my hand back into my lap. It still tingles from touching him.

His eyes are dark and stormy, a vortex pulling me in. I feel myself drowning. The hurricane begins to rage inside me, and my heart fractures more the longer I look at him.

Please don't hurt me. Please don't hurt me.

He rips his gaze from mine and rubs his palms together. "I think you should go, Celia."

"Not until you tell me what's wrong."

"I can't tell you, okay?" he snaps. It's as harsh as a slap, and I flinch.

"Can't, or don't want to?" I should take his advice and leave. I should stand up and walk out the door. But something about this unseen side of Henry draws me in like a slot machine after a small win.

"You don't know what you're asking. You'd never look at me the same way again."

"You can't know that."

"C, if I told you what he did—" He breaks off.

"Who? What who did?" I pause. Think. Guess. "Your father?"

He doesn't respond, but his steely eyes flash. I have my answer.

"What did he do, Henry?" My voice is quiet, almost a whisper. "You know you can trust me."

"I can't tell you, C. It's too nasty, too repulsive." He squeezes his eyes shut and pinches the bridge of his nose. "Let's just say he has a thing for little boys."

Without meaning to, I recoil. Something drops into my stomach, and I realize it's my heart. Henry doesn't need to elaborate any further.

Who could do something like that? To an innocent child? I swallow to keep the vomit at bay. Our conversation after the wedding flashes through my mind, when I accused him of disappointing his father. God, I am such an unfeeling jerk.

I reach for one of his hands, intertwining our fingers. "You can tell me whatever you want or need to. I'm not going anywhere."

His fingers tighten around mine, but he remains silent. After several long minutes, he says, "I've never told anyone."

"Not even your mum?"

He shakes his head.

"How old were you?"

His Adam's apple bobs as he swallows, probably trying to suppress the bile the memory stirred up. "The first time? I was five."

Dear god, it happened more than once? Tears burn at the corners of my eyes. What kind of monster is he? My voice doesn't sound like mine right now, but I manage to squeak out, "How long?"

Henry's voice is cold as ice. "Six years. Until I was strong enough to fight him off. Or maybe he just lost interest, I don't know." My hand is still clenched in his and slowly turning numb from his tight grasp.

Despite my best attempts to hold them back, tears run down my cheeks. I bury my face in that space between his shoulder and neck, sharing in his pain, his trauma. All those years we were friends, spent countless hours together, and I never knew. Never even suspected.

Henry brings his hand up to cradle my head, gently caressing my hair as though I'm the one who needs comfort. He presses a kiss against my temple. I know it's the thank-you he can't voice.

Silently, he strokes my leg, the touch of his hand words enough. We remain that way for what seems like hours. I lose track of time.

When my body begins to tingle from staying locked in the same position for too long, I whisper, "Thank you for trusting me with this. I'm sorry I wasn't there for you back then."

He stiffens beneath me. "You have nothing to apologize or be grateful for. I never should have told you."

"You shouldn't have to carry this alone, Henry." My left hand is still clutched in his death grip, but I run the other along the collar of his T-shirt. A thrill shoots through me at the way it makes him swallow, having my fingers so close to his skin.

"I should go," I say. It's true even if I make no move to act on it. I've never felt so close to another person before, not even in the throes of intimacy with Beck.

"Yeah, you should," Henry says. He slides his palm up my leg until he reaches my hip. Pauses. Waits. "But I don't want you to."

He begins rubbing circles on the back of the hand he's still holding, his thumb tracing rings of fire. The touch is so faint it's barely perceptible, except to my racing heart.

"Celia."

The way his voice caresses that one husky word makes me quake until I'm jealous of my own name. He tilts his head until his lips are only a hairbreadth from mine, and then hesitates as though he's waiting for permission.

My body doesn't need another invitation. I incline my head the millimeter needed, and our lips meet in a tumultuous reunion, hungry and passionate. His fingers dig into the back of my head, losing themselves in my hair, my ponytail a distant memory. I move my hands to that stupidly incredible jawline and pull him closer. He groans against my mouth.

Henry yanks me against him and begins to explore my body. Everywhere he touches explodes with crazy desire. I slide my hands over the chiseled planes of his chest, then slip them underneath his shirt. My sweater becomes putty in his hands: wadded, tugged, lifted, removed.

He breathes my name again as he gazes at me, and then *I'm* putty in his hands. The look on his face is a mixture of painful desire and awe, even though I know he's seen plenty of women wearing much less than I am. He glides his hands around my waist and captures my mouth with his once again.

I can feel how much he wants me as I swing my leg over and straddle him. His lips are hot and possessive on mine, and I cannot believe that I am here, doing this, with him. I take back the curse I issued on past Celia from earlier in the park. She deserves praise instead.

I knew there had to be a reason for everything that happened back then. I've been afraid to admit it, but there's always been a part of me that wants to excuse him, wants to write him a "get out of jail free" card. Because if he had a reason for what he did, it wouldn't hurt so bad. It would mean the Henry I've always known is still there. Everything else is just a facade.

I scoot as close to him as I can, suddenly unable to get close enough. He groans as I rub against him.

"Baby," he says. His teeth gently bite my lower lip. "Are you sure?"

I growl at the loss of his mouth, and he chuckles, then slides nimble fingers up to the back of my bra. But before he can unclasp it, there's a knock at the door. We both freeze.

I pull back just enough to meet his eyes. My thoughts are reflected in his face: *Maybe they'll go away.*

The knock sounds again, a steady *rap, rap, rap*. He sighs and shifts me off his lap. "I'll be right back," he says, before dropping me a quick kiss on the lips.

I hold my sweater against my chest while I wait for him to return. He opens the door just wide enough for his still-clothed frame to be visible. Muffled voices float over, but I can't make out what's being said.

After a few moments, Henry shuts the door and walks to the far side of the room, carrying a bottle of wine in an ice bucket. He places it on the bar. Keeping his back to me, head bent, he runs his fingers through his hair. His chest expands with what appears to be newfound resolve, then he walks over to me.

"What was that about?" I can't control the tremors shuddering through my body.

He remains standing, his hands on his hips. "Nothing. Just a bottle of champagne."

"Are we celebrating something?"

He doesn't even look up. "I didn't order it."

"Okay." I drag out the word. The humming just under my skin skids to a stop. "Who did?"

"My father."

A fuse sparks inside my belly at the mention of him. "We don't need to drink it. Just don't freeze me out like this."

"You should go." Henry lifts his eyes from where they've been burning a hole in the rug under our feet.

"What?" My voice wobbles. A cold disquiet steals over me as I rise, my sweater still gripped in my hands. "What's wrong?"

"Nothing's wrong. I thought I could do this. I realized I can't."

Everything snaps into sharp focus. Henry standing there, hard and unrecognizable, not at all the person I once knew. The candles flickering, their glow turned eerie. My bare skin, chilled in a room that has lost its warmth.

I shiver. "You're right. This was a terrible idea." I slip my arms into the sleeves of my sweater and pull it over my head. It's a poor cover for the humiliation crippling me. "I don't know what the hell I was thinking anyway. You and I could never work. This has always been your game."

He doesn't say anything.

"I knew you would hurt me, but I wanted to trust you so badly. You broke down all of my defenses, just so you could watch me bleed. Some things never change."

I stalk out of the room and slam the door behind me. Bloody hell. Henry be damned. I never should have trusted him—the man feasts on destroying hearts.

But despite the monologue running through my mind, my heart is on a different wavelength. It knows the truth. The truth that I can't ever seem to escape, no matter how hard I try.

I'm in love with Henry. I always have been. And like always, he doesn't feel the same way.

22

"White Horse" - Taylor Swift

S OMEONE IS KNOCKING AT the door. I ignore them. They keep at it for a few more minutes but eventually give up and go away. The sun saturates the drapes covering the west window like a bucket of gold poured in from outside. It will soon turn to shades of pink, orange, and red.

I'm still dressed in my jeans and bra from last night, my sweater discarded somewhere on the floor. I'm going to burn it, along with all traces of Henry's scent.

My mouth feels dry, and I know without looking in a mirror that my eyes are puffy. I feel like something rising from the dead, barely alive, barely breathing, heart still cold.

It's like existing in a dream world: you think you should be able to feel things, but you can't because you're trapped in another reality, one that doesn't feel real at all because it can't possibly be real. But the gaping hole in your chest, the one that's impossible to ignore, is still there, still aching, still reminding you that you're alive, even if just barely.

They've been coming all day—Maisie, Daphne, Rosalind, even Beatrice. The only person who doesn't is the only one I want to see. If he did show up, I don't know whether I'd carve his heart out with a rusty spoon or demand an explanation. But it doesn't matter, because the door between our rooms remains shut. There's only a gaping silence on the other side.

I knew, of course, that Henry can't be trusted. It's in his DNA. But he caught me unawares and captured me so completely, I assumed something had changed. I forgot the most important thing: a wolf is still a wolf, even in granny's clothing.

How is it possible to have misread so many signals?

I now recognize his concern, his thoughtfulness, his tenderness, his vulnerability—all of the things that chipped away at my resolve to keep him out—for what they actually were: traps laid for my poor heart to stumble into and be fatally ensnared by.

I am angry. Angry at him, sure, but mostly at myself. Because no matter how hard I try, I can't murder the flicker of hope that there's some explanation. Approximately how many times can a meat grinder be used on a heart before it finally relents and accepts reality?

I need to know why, need to understand. Does he have a fear of commitment, or does he just get off on stealing and breaking hearts? Maybe if he explains, I can move on. But more than anything, I need to see him again, to breathe him in once more, to feel his hands on me. Just once more and I'll be able to get him out of my system for good, out of my head.

I recognize the toxicity of my own thoughts, but there's no reasoning with an addict.

I pull myself out of bed and wash my face. Makeup can't redeem me, but it helps. Slipping into my crumpled sweater, I inhale a deep lungful of Henry's scent—I'll burn it later—and brush the tangles from my hair, squeezing back tears at the thought of his fingers putting them there less than twenty-four hours ago.

God, when he looks at you like that, you feel like a goddess.

After brushing the wrinkles from clothes as best as I can, I walk to his door. My heart thrums loudly enough to pass for a knock. Will he throw me out again or will he at least have the decency of offering me an explanation first? I quietly knock on the door and wait for the sound of his footsteps.

Everything is quiet.

"Henry?" I hate the trepidation in my voice. "Please, I just want to talk to you. I promise not to throw anything." *At least not right away.*

Still no answer. I try the knob, and it turns under my hand. The room is dark. Without giving a thought to what I'm doing, I walk inside and flick the light switch. There's no sign last night ever happened—the Monopoly game cleaned up, the wine glasses gone, the candles snuffed out and cleared away. It's like the whole evening was a dream. Or a nightmare.

I won't be getting any answers tonight. As I turn back toward my own suite, my eye catches on the bucket on the bar, the champagne still inside. The ice has melted and is now nothing but a lukewarm bath. I can't help feeling like this stupid wine ruined everything, even though I know that's ridiculous. It was simply the catalyst for the next act in Henry's game: tear Celia's heart into a myriad of minuscule pieces.

I lift the bottle, water dripping off it into the bucket. At least he didn't open it after I left. I swivel the tag strung around the neck around and read: *Best wishes to the happy couple.* It isn't signed. Somehow William must have known about Henry and me, and as much as I dislike him and want to see him rot in prison for what he did to his son, it was a thoughtful gesture.

It's a shame to let such nice champagne go to waste. I carry the bottle back to my room. I may not be getting any answers, but at least I'll have some company.

Once the wine and I have become thoroughly acquainted with one another, I pull out my phone. Henry might be able to avoid me by not coming home, but his cell goes everywhere with him. It takes reaching his voicemail twelve times before it occurs to me that he can just as easily ignore my calls as my knocks on his door.

Damn him.

Damn the way he can shatter me with a single word. Damn the way he makes me feel electrified. Damn the way the world turns technicolor just because he's in the room. Damn the way my heart keeps insisting *just one more time*. Just one more kiss, one more night, one more adventure. Once more in his arms, once more seeing that look in his eyes, once more hearing him say my name like he's caressing the word itself.

And damn the fear that's rising in my chest.

Fear that I'll never be whole again.

I wake with my very first hangover, although fortunately it's a mild one. The empty champagne bottle taunts me from my bedside table. I sit up and rub my temples gently so as not to disturb the beast.

My phone is lying next to the wine, and the embarrassing number of phone calls I made last night trots across my memory. Drunk Celia makes a lot of really dumb decisions, and I suspect she's not done making an idiot of herself. I delete Henry's number from my contacts and erase my call log and our text thread. Call it saving me from myself.

I'm in love with a fantasy. The Henry that fills my head is nothing but a projection of my desires onto a phantom that looks an awful lot like him. The real Henry is selfish and manipulative and breaks hearts like he breaks the tops of his soft-boiled eggs at breakfast.

I can't do this anymore. Wesbourne isn't worth it.

I drag a large suitcase from one of the numerous cabinets in my dressing room and hoist it onto the bed. It's time for a strategic retreat.

Fifteen minutes later, when I answer the door to find my sister on the other side, the suitcase is nearly full. Only a few more items, then I'll be ready to leave. I let the door gape open and return to my task.

Bea follows me into the bedroom. "Where are you going?"

Until she asked, I hadn't given it any thought. "I'm not sure. Maybe New York? It's large enough to get lost in, right?"

"And you want to get lost because . . . ?"

"Because I've had enough." I toss a pair of sneakers into the bag. Not much use for heels when you're hiding from society. "I need to get out."

"You're running? For how long?"

I slam the lid of the suitcase and zip it shut. "Indefinitely."

To her credit, Bea looks stunned rather than gleeful. "I don't understand," she says.

"That makes two of us."

"You'll be back in time for the coronation, won't you?"

"Not if I can help it."

"But—"

"I'm sure Parliament will figure something out. They always do, don't they? Maybe they can find another victim to throw at Henry."

Her eyebrows draw together, and for a second, I see our father reflected in her face. "Does this have something to do with him?"

I turn away to grab a few books from the nightstand, even though I gave up reading them weeks ago. I'm not sure how much I can trust my face and its propensity for honest expressions right now. "Why would it be about him?"

"Because you're acting strange?"

"I'm perfectly normal." To prove my point, I look at her chin and smile. It's the kind of smile you give your great aunt June when she kisses you for the third time and tells you that you remind her of a cat she once had. You wonder if her mind is getting foggy or if you should be concerned about the vibe you're giving off, so you plaster a grin on your face that you hope conveys not a single one of the thoughts running through your head at the moment.

Bea points to my bag and the shoddy job I've done packing it. A bra strap and several shoelaces peek out where the zippers meet. Several items managed to escape the tornado of my manic packing and are still on the bed.

I lift my shoulders, then let them drop. "I'm in a hurry."

"You're not following him, are you?"

I meet her eyes for the first time. "Following who?"

"Henry."

"Why would I follow him? Where's he gone?"

"The last I heard, Monte Carlo."

This is news to me, but I school my features into indifference. "Good riddance," I say, and adjust my suitcase to look more like a reasonable human packed it.

"I don't understand why you're so determined to hate him."

The irony of Beatrice's words is not lost on me, but I am in no state to set her to rights about my actual feelings for Henry. "Because he's a lying, scheming, manipulative bastard. He doesn't care about anyone but himself, and he thrives on inflicting as much hurt as possible." I close the bag a little more violently than necessary.

"There's more to him than that."

"You are so blinded when it comes to Henry that he could chew your heart up, spit it out, and you'd thank him for it."

I sense rather than see her bristle at this implication. "You make it sound like I can't think for myself."

"I only meant that Henry is good at this. He has years of experience toying with women."

"Most of those women are only looking for a fling. Hardly anyone would actually want to be *married* to a prince."

I shake my head. "Regardless, Henry isn't capable of being in a normal relationship."

"He's never tried."

"He would destroy you, Bea."

"I'm stronger than you think! You still look at me like I'm a little girl who can't take care of myself. It hurts that you think I'm so weak I could be broken by the only guy I've ever loved. Why can't you trust that I know what I'm doing? Why are you so convinced he'll break my heart?"

"Because he broke mine!"

The room grows thick with silence as we stare at each other. Bea's mismatched eyes widen slightly, and the blue one turns the color of the sea during a storm.

Slapping her would have led to less shock than this admission.

"Are you satisfied?" I ask. "I fell for it, every bloody bit of his beautiful charade. I love him. Like head-over-heels, sell-my-soul kind of love. And it's slowly sucking the life from me." I grasp the handle of my luggage and yank it off the bed. "I can't hate him, no matter how hard I try. I have to get out of here."

A knock at the door prevents Bea from answering. I step through the sitting room to open it to find Maisie on the other side, backup brain in hand.

"Good morning," she says, scooting into the room. "Glad to see you feeling better today."

Better might be a stretch, but I don't correct her.

She doesn't leave me time anyway. "I know it's a bit early for our morning meeting, but I just got the news, and I knew you'd want to hear right away." She takes a dramatic pause. "Your petition for increased security at the ports has just passed through Parliament. It must have been marked high importance, or else there's no way they could have rushed it through so quickly. It turns out—"

I don't listen to the rest of her thoughts on the matter, because the significance of this is staggering. I was expecting another year or two of working on this petition before making any headway on it. There's no doubt in my mind that my sudden rise in status is responsible for the priority of the request.

Maisie's play-by-play of the Parliament session comes to a halt when Bea steps out of the bedroom to join us. "I'm so sorry," my assistant says. "I didn't know you had company. We can have our meeting as soon as you're done." The door closes behind her before I have time to say anything else.

"I'm actually leaving," Bea says. "I just came to ask if you've seen Dad's watch. I couldn't find it in any of my boxes after the move, and Mum hasn't seen it either."

"Yeah, I think I know where it is."

The ornate wooden box in my sitting room contains mementos of our father that I haven't had a chance to go through yet. Sure enough, the heavy wristwatch is among them. I hand it to her, but my eyes stay on the picture of Dad at eighteen with his squad. In it, he's in danger of exploding with pride. Pride at serving Wesbourne, no matter the cost to himself.

What would he think of me now, on the verge of deserting my country, fleeing just because my heart had been broken? After his death, I used to comfort myself with the thought that our loved ones can see what we're doing from heaven, and I'd think about him watching over my shoulder, murmuring words of encouragement when I took a difficult test at school or bit my tongue to keep from saying something nasty.

Now the thought fills me with shame.

I let the lid of the box drop, shutting away the image of his pride. I look up to find Bea still in the room, looking at me like she knows me from somewhere but can't remember my name. I can't handle her censure, so I move toward a cord on the floor and start winding it up.

"What are you doing?" she says.

"Currently, I'm packing my charger. A fugitive still needs her phone."

She walks over and places both hands on my shoulders. The genetic gods probably snicker to themselves every time my younger sister dwarfs my five-foot-five frame. I'm not short, but Bea is willowy and graceful. And right now, she's determined. "You can't leave."

"You can't stop me." It comes out much weaker than I intend.

"You're the one who taught me to get back up when someone knocks you down." I know she's thinking of Stacey Evans in primary school. "Are you seriously going to quit that easily?"

"This isn't a mean-girl fight, Bea."

"I don't care what it is. No man has the ability to destroy you. You're about to become queen of the nation, for god's sake."

I've never seen her so dead set on anything. In fifth grade, she won a ticket to see Selena Gomez in concert for getting the highest score on a math test, then proceeded to give it to her classmate who'd thrown a nasty fit because she came in second.

No man has the ability to destroy you. "I think this one might."

She shakes her head, and her hair flows over her shoulders like a golden cape. "I won't allow it. You've always protected me. Now it's my turn to do the same for you."

A lump the size of Spain slips from my stomach and takes up residence in my throat. Little sisters aren't supposed to be the ones doing the protecting. "I don't know how to get through this. It hurts too bad."

"I know." She pulls me against her chest, and the scent of jasmine floats around me. "I'm here for you, I promise. Whatever you need. You'll come out stronger on the other side."

A sliver of suspicion threads through me. "You're not just saying that to get Henry for yourself, are you?"

"Why would I want anything to do with a guy who can break my sister's heart and then flee the country? You were right. He doesn't deserve either one of us."

I stay. And it's bloody awful.

Over the next few weeks, the gossip rags are full of Henry's exploits. They feature articles with his picture front and center, always with a woman draped over him, always smiling in that way that suggests their plans for the evening are far from over. The only thing that changes is the locale: he's in Austria, Greece, France, Portugal, Belgium, even the United States—thank god I didn't go—with a supermodel, actress, or celebrity in hand.

Playboy Henry is living large, and I'm a fucking idiot.

I pore over each article, desperate for news of him and dying to see who he rejected me for. It's a futile mission, but I have to know. That's the thing about addiction—it never makes any sense, but reason is the furthest thing from your mind. In the same morbid way traffic slows to a crawl around an accident as people rubberneck, I'm drawn to this. I analyze each woman's hair, body, fashion choices, lip shape, eye color, makeup, and curves. I question everything about them, then scrutinize myself.

It never helps. Seeing Henry's face grinning at another woman makes me want to hurl. Their long nails and tanned skin touching him breaks my heart all over again, splitting the fissure even wider, if that's even possible.

Why did I ever think for one second it would be different with me? I warned Bea against the danger but didn't see it coming myself. If I could, I'd take it all back. I'd return to the day we sat in that room with the prime minister and he told us about the decision we needed to make. This time, I'd tell Parliament I would have to be dead before I'd even consider marrying Henry.

But I didn't agree to marry Henry because I was in love with him. I did it for Wesbourne, and—loathe as I am to admit it—I'd do it again to save her. Some things are just bigger than us, bigger than our problems, our love lives. Some things require sacrifice.

Loving him will always be my biggest mistake. I want to tear his incredibly handsome head right off his shoulders, to scratch him until he bleeds, to hurt him as badly as he's hurt me. But at the same time I also desperately want to give him a chance to explain himself. Maybe the pictures are photoshopped. Maybe I misunderstood him that night. Maybe, maybe, maybe.

I'm delusional and refusing to see reason. An addict.

I miss him the way you miss your heart when it's no longer in your body.

And that's the most dangerous thing of all.

23

"The Heart Wants What It Wants" - Selena Gomez

How to get over someone. There are more than eight billion search results for this simple query. I estimate it would take me roughly six months to get through them all, and by then I should be sufficiently over this heartbreak.

But I can think of anything better to do with my time, and after reading about how self-love can help heal the heart for the fourth time, I'm ready for some different advice.

Adelaide is in the kitchen when I arrive at Englewood Manor. She's wearing a red-and-white-striped apron and swaying her hips to Nina Simone.

"What are we cooking?" I say, giving her a peck on the cheek.

She could afford to hire a personal chef, but she chooses to make her own food. She could afford a full live-in staff for that matter, but she resents the idea that wealth means you don't do anything for yourself anymore. And I suspect she also cherishes her privacy too much to have all those people in the house.

"Cullen skink." She tosses me an apron. "You can chop the leeks."

I take my place at the cutting board, and we work in companionable silence for several minutes. She directs me to sauté the leeks and onions in butter, and when they're soft, she adds a bowl of diced potatoes.

"Poach the haddock in the milk and cream," she instructs. "But be careful you don't burn it."

To date, my experience in the kitchen has been minimal. My mother didn't consider cooking a necessary pillar of education for the future bride of the crown prince, and she didn't have a backup plan in the event said match didn't work out. I can, however, make a mean piece of toast.

Adelaide keeps an eye on me and my pan of fish and eventually directs me to gently break the fillets apart.

"You want these in with the potatoes and leeks?" I ask.

She nods and holds the lid while I pour the two mixtures together. After giving everything a quick stir, she says, "We can talk while this simmers."

As Nina crows about feeling good, Adelaide and I perch on two wooden stools near the stove. The soup smells like the sea. My stomach burbles in anticipation.

I scratch at a small scuff on the counter. "How do you get over someone?" The words tumble out. Preambles are overrated anyway.

She waits a beat, until the silence becomes nice and uncomfortable, then says, "Darling, I could tell you a million things to try, but the only one that actually works is time."

"Time." That's as bad as self-love.

"Breakups require a grieving process, just like any other kind of loss. Nothing will speed it up."

"How much time are we talking?"

"Every relationship is different. The stronger it was, the longer it takes."

I feel myself deflating. "It's been weeks. I was hoping I'd feel better by now."

"You have a hard time letting people in. When you eventually do, your attachment is strong, which in turn makes letting go that much harder."

"There's got to be a way to speed things up."

"Well, you could always consider taking a new lover."

I laugh abruptly. "You make it sound like shopping for a new pair of shoes."

"But even more fun." Adelaide winks. "There is an exceptionally enticing option living right under your nose. He might be just the ticket."

It takes me a second before it finally clicks into place that she means Henry. My disdain for preambles has landed me in this situation. Right now, I hold the status of *giant ass*. "I, um, I wasn't— Well, I wasn't referring to Beck." I mumble this to the countertop, as though it can somehow help me.

She takes this in, and there's no way she isn't shocked by it, because who in their right mind wouldn't be? But she keeps her face an expressionless mask, because this is Adelaide, and I love her for it. "If not Beck, then who?"

I wince at this. *Who* isn't relevant to the conversation, and I'd rather avoid getting into it. My expression tells her all she needs to know, however.

"Oh," she says. "*Oh*."

I don't like that intonation.

"I suppose it was to be expected," she adds.

"Hardly."

"After all, you *are* married—"

"In name only."

"—and you're living together—"

"Along with five hundred staff!"

"—and he really is a delicious specimen."

"Are you done yet?"

Adelaide attempts to hide her smile, but she doesn't try hard enough. "I'm sorry, poppet. It really is an unfortunate circumstance."

"That's putting it mildly," I mutter.

She gets up to stir the soup. "Why don't you explain the whole thing to me?"

"Do I have to?"

"If I'm to give advice, I need to know the particulars of the situation. Besides, I'm not in the grave yet. Let an old lady live vicariously through your relationships."

"You're not old," I say.

"Of course I'm not." She waves the wooden spoon in the air. "Now out with it."

I give her the CliffsNotes version of my very short-lived, very injudicious fling with Henry.

"He's a scoundrel," she says when I'm done.

"Not exactly breaking news."

"Damn. Why are the good-looking ones always evil bastards?" Grabbing two handmade ceramic bowls from a cupboard, she begins rummaging around for spoons.

"What about Eduardo? You've told me plenty of times how dreamy he was."

Her expression placid, she makes a noise that sounds remarkably like a snort. "He was an evil bastard."

I feel the features on my face extend: my eyes widen, my jaw slackens, my mouth parts. "I thought you loved him madly."

"I did. That doesn't mean he wasn't a horrible husband."

I've always idolized their marriage, although I never had the opportunity to meet Eduardo. He died eight years before Adelaide and I met. Everything I know—or thought I knew—about him comes from Adelaide's stories.

"You lied to me."

"I didn't lie. I strategically withheld information." She nonchalantly ladles soup into the bowls, as if shaking the bedrock of our relationship is something she does every day.

I can't stop gaping at her.

She finally notices when she hands me my steaming bowl. "Close your mouth, poppet. There are worse things than letting you believe I had a fairy-tale marriage."

"But— I—"

She holds up her hand. "I will explain, if you promise to hold your tongue until I'm finished."

I nod and take a mouthful of soup. It's delicious. Maybe the real reason Adelaide doesn't employ a chef is because she can out-cook them all.

"Eduardo and I loved each other. Madly. Passionately. But it wasn't easy. Not by a long shot. They were the best and worst twenty years of my life. I've never loved another person like I loved him." Her eyes take on a far-off glow. "We fought all the time, like cats and dogs. Mostly when I'd find out he was cheating again."

My heart twangs at this information, and I badly want to ask a question. Her sixth sense picks up on this, and she cocks her brow. I obediently take another bite of soup.

"I know you're wondering how I could stay with him. I didn't always. Sometimes I'd leave for a night, a weekend. Once I left for a month. But I always came back." She shrugs her bony shoulders. "He was my best friend. I didn't know how to be without him. I knew I'd never find what we had with anyone else. So we made it work."

What she's describing sounds like the kind of toxic relationship Colleen Hoover would dream up.

"Don't think I was a victim in all of this," Adelaide says, giving me a sharp look. "He had to put up with a lot, too. I wasn't always faithful, either. Sometimes I just wanted something bloody normal. But normal sickened me, and so I always ended up going back. God, the making up afterwards was always worth it. He would—"

"Please stop there." I hold my hand up. "Unlike you, I'm not looking to vicariously live your love life."

She smiles and clasps her hands together on the counter. Her soup sits forgotten in front of her. "Do you hate me now, love?"

"Of course not." I take a minute to untangle my thoughts. They resemble a mess of Christmas lights no one took the time to put away properly. "I'm just confused. What you're describing sounds awful. Don't you think if you had been in a less . . . volatile relationship, you would've been happier?"

"I never told you I was married before Eduardo?"

God, will the surprises ever stop?

"It only lasted three years. He was as calm as a glass of milk. Nothing fazed him. Sometimes I would do things just to see if he'd react, but he'd just look at me like he couldn't understand who I was. There was no fire, no passion. Eventually, we just drifted apart, until divorce felt like the next step. I'm not proud of it, but it did help me to figure out exactly what I wanted from my next relationship."

"At least he wasn't breaking your heart."

"With great love comes great risk. Those we love the most have the most power to hurt us."

"I don't see how they're worth it."

"I have no regrets," Adelaide says. "If I could bring him back, even with all of his flaws, I would."

I consider this. "It just seems unhealthy to love someone that much."

"Henry made you feel more in a month than Beck did in two years."

The truth of that statement strikes home. "And look at me. I'm a mess."

"Would you trade it? Give up every moment to avoid the pain?"

I don't know how to answer that. A lifetime of memories with Henry flit through my mind. Sitting curled together in an armchair, alternately reading pages from *Harry Potter* aloud. Sneaking snacks from the kitchen while the chef pretended not to see us. Building a tiny hut in the forest with scraps we salvaged from the grounds—no proper tools allowed. Tricking Beatrice into using salt rather than sugar in her tea. Kissing him. Falling in love.

"It doesn't matter," I finally say. "He made it clear we can't be together, so I need to find a way to move on."

"In that case, try distraction. Nothing helps you get over a man like getting under a new one."

I close my eyes and take a deep breath. "Thank you for the soup. I should go before you make me regret coming here."

Adelaide guffaws. "You'd die of boredom without me."

As scandalized as I pretended to be by Adelaide's gauche suggestion, it reminds me that I still haven't given Beck an answer. I suppose if I were less practical, I'd be ashamed of having feelings for two men at the same time. But love is complicated, and what I feel for one is so completely different from the other, they can hardly be compared.

And she's right: I need a distraction in the worst way.

Because you can't just approach the king at breakfast and ask for a private word, we do that pretentious thing where my people (Maisie) talk to his people to arrange an official meeting. That's how I find myself in William's office several days later. He's staring at me with the same stoic expression as always, save for a tiny glint of amusement in his eyes, because I've just asked him how one sneaks a lover into the palace.

I almost didn't come. I still can't look at him without remembering what he did to Henry, and right now I'm curling my hands into fists at my sides so I don't do something idiotic like launch myself across his massive wooden desk and rake my nails down that hard face.

As if reading my thoughts, William reaches up and scratches his chin himself, albeit less violently than I would have—there's no blood. "It's not as difficult as you'd think."

For a second I think he's talking about my wanting to attack him, but then I remember my question. "I'd prefer to keep the whole thing . . . discreet," I say.

He grunts and moves some papers around his desk as if he's looking for something. "There are several ways to go about it. He can enter like any other visitor, or an apartment can be arranged."

"An apartment?"

He looks up from the mess of documents his shuffling has only intensified. "There are plenty of empty ones. You can have one commissioned for him."

"And he would just . . . what? Live here?"

"More or less."

I blink. "Like for meals and everything?"

"He'd probably be more comfortable taking those in his rooms."

Nothing can prepare you for a conversation like this with your father-in-law, and if I could transport myself into a room full of fighting cats right now, I'd do it. "Right. Okay. This has all been . . . very informative. Thank you."

A snuffling whine draws my attention to the floor, and for the first time, I realize we're not alone. Argos is curled up on a plush dog bed next to the desk. He fixes me with a mournful gaze but doesn't lift his head.

I kneel down and stroke his chocolate fur. "Hey, boy. How are you?"

"Not great," William says.

"What's wrong with him?"

"Cancer."

"Are there treatments?"

"Not for this."

A different kind of hammer chips away at what remains of my heart. Isn't it enough that humans get cancer? Do animals have to as well?

"You're going to be alright, boy," I lie, and press a kiss between his eyes. He just blinks at me.

I stand and move toward the door, but right before reaching it, I turn back. "Why are you helping me?"

William's attention has already shifted to the thick file he's holding, but he glances up. "Because without you, my son will bodge this whole bloody thing up."

24

"Thinking of You" - Katy Perry

IT'S TIME TO FACE the mess that is my life head-on, like an adult. If I can just pretend it's a haphazardly cluttered filing cabinet, I'll be able to get it sorted in no time.

The first order of business is finally giving Beck an answer. It's been weeks since that day in the park, and I promised him I'd call. I had every intention of doing so, but the coronation is less than two months away, which is code for *I've been so busy I've barely had time to breathe, let alone contemplate my love life—or lack thereof.*

I thought the wedding was bad, but preparing for a coronation makes it seem like a backyard barbecue. Fortunately, my mother has to keep her fingers out of this event. My presence and opinion are required for nearly everything, though, from the crowns to the chairs to the carriages.

I briefly contemplate taking the coward's way out and telling Beck I've been too busy to give his proposition serious thought. But I'm desperate to get out of here and away from the gold filigree on everything in sight. So I ask him to meet me an hour outside the city, in a large forest where, this time, we can be sure no cameras are lurking.

Worthington Park is a small estate belonging to my mother's family, now occupied by her oldest brother. Bea and I spent part of every summer holiday there when we were kids, back when my grandfather was still alive. We stopped going after my father died, and I haven't been back since.

Maisie found me a discreet driver and told him that I need a long, refreshing hike on my own. I text the directions to Beck, hoping my memory serves me well and doesn't get him lost in the woods. He agrees to come. The obstacles have all been slain, except for one.

I don't have a clue what I'm going to tell him.

There is a turnoff before the main drive to the manor house, and my chauffeur drops me off there, the small trail visible through the underbrush. "I don't know about leaving you here on your own, Your Royal Highness," he says. I've assured him I have a ride back to the city.

"I'll be fine. I've hiked this trail so many times I know it like the back of my hand." It's the truth, if you end the sentence at *trail*. I have hiked this trail, yes. Back when I was thirteen.

I fill my lungs with the spirituous scent of damp earth and rotting wood. There is nothing like the forest to remind you there's a world outside your own. I give one last reassuring wave to the driver, who still looks like he's afraid he'll lose his job over this, and set off on the path leading deeper into the wood, my wellies crunching on dead leaves and pine needles.

I walk for a bit before circling back to wait for Beck in the thick covering of the forest. His car pulls into the gravel driveway just a few minutes after my driver has left. I step out to greet him, my heart hammering in my chest.

I offer a tentative smile. "Thank you for coming."

"Did you think I wouldn't?" He pulls me into his warm embrace and presses a kiss to the top of my head. The gesture is so familiar it makes me ache.

I lead the way to the trail and stuff my hands into the pockets of my canvas jacket. The temperature in the woods is at least ten degrees cooler than in the sunshine. The air in my lungs feels strangely void of oxygen, and I'm transported back in time to a similar feeling I had as I sat in his apartment and ripped both of our lives to shreds.

"You never called." His voice sounds loud in the hush of the forest.

"I'm sorry. I've been busy." I seem to have a propensity for half-truths today.

"I meant what I said that day in the park. I want you in my life, Celia, any way I can get you."

I gnaw on my bottom lip, wishing there was a way to make everyone happy. Whenever I turn around, I disappoint people. It's exhausting. Finally, here's a chance to please one person. And so help me god, I'm taking it. "Okay."

"Okay?"

"Okay. Let's do it."

Beck stops walking, and I look over to find him studying me, an expression of mild disbelief on his face. "You're serious? You want to start an affair?"

"Sure, why not?"

His frown deepens. "Okay," he says, stepping closer. He places his hands on my waist and tugs until our bodies are touching. Then he dips his head and kisses me. His mouth is cool and tastes like the cinnamon Altoids he pops every hour. My lips follow his lead, performing a dance they've done many times before. As the seconds tick by, the ache in my heart grows stronger and stronger, until I'm sure it will burst.

He pulls away. The frown is back on his face, and his eyes search mine for an explanation. Words have become foreign to my tongue, and I dream of the ground opening and swallowing me up.

"What's wrong?" There's a plea hidden in his words.

I shake my head. "Nothing. What do you mean?" It's the wrong thing to say. Because I don't want him to explain, to vocalize what we both already know. "Come on," I add before he can answer. "Let's keep going. There's a small waterfall about a mile down the trail."

Beck follows me, but so does the chilly tension between us. The only sound is the crunching of our feet on the path and the forest teeming with life. The waterfall is beautiful, but it does nothing to ease the crackling strain in the air.

I move to continue walking, but Beck pulls me onto a large rock beside him. "Why do I get the feeling you don't actually want to do this?"

I scratch at a speck of mud on my trousers. "I do want to. I'm just afraid of rumors getting out."

"And you're sure that's all that's bothering you?"

"I'm sure. You can't imagine the pressure I've been under."

"It's not too late to walk away," he tells me.

"You know I could never do that."

He doesn't say anything, just looks out at the trees surrounding us. After several minutes, he offers his hand and pulls me to my feet. "And you're not afraid of going to hell for our debauchery?"

If I get sent to hell, it will not be for anything pertaining to Beck. Our love is too sweet, too pure for that. I rise on tiptoes and press my lips against his before any memories can quell the urge. "What debauchery?"

The light has waned, the tree cover bringing evening on much faster. Birds call to their mates to let them know dinner is served. We've been wandering for nearly two hours when Beck glances around and says, "You do know where we are, right?"

"Of course," I reply automatically. The gravel car park should be coming into view any second now, and . . .

I turn around. The trees we just passed look familiar, I think. Didn't we walk this way earlier?

The more I study the forest, the less convinced I become. Everything looks the same, and in the quickly diminishing light, it's becoming harder to discern differences.

I meet Beck's gaze. "I lied. I don't have a clue where we are."

He takes a seat on a fallen log and pulls his phone out of his pocket. After a moment, he says, "There's no service out here. I can't get the GPS to connect."

"Let me try mine." I pull up my map app, but he's right. We are isolated in a forest with no signal. "I am so sorry," I say, and sit down beside him. "I will fix this, don't worry."

I don't have enough service to make a phone call, but maybe I can get a text through. After typing out the gist of our situation, I climb as high as I can on the log and hold my phone up, praying the message will send.

It eventually does, and I rejoin Beck. "I texted Maisie. She'll find someone to get us out of here." Although the more I think about it, the more unsure I am that anyone will be able to find us.

"Do you think we can retrace our steps?" I ask, looking back the way we came.

Beck seems doubtful but agrees to try. I never should have suggested we venture this far. "I'm sorry," I say again.

"For what?"

"For getting us lost. For dragging you out here. For everything."

He helps me across a large mud puddle in the middle of the trail, then takes my face in his hands. Warmth and security pool in my belly. "You don't need to apologize for anything," he tells me, lowering his lips to mine once more.

I despise the numbness that steals over me, and I decide then and there to kiss him with everything I have. I weave my fingers through his silky hair and draw him closer—not an easy feat, since he's a good twelve inches taller than me.

Ever the gentleman, Beck's hands never stray from my face and hips. He kisses me gently, like I'm a delicate china teacup that will break if he does more than brush my skin. Has it always been like this? This June-and-Ward-Cleaver act, with their twin beds and "Hello dear, how was your day?" Is this what I've always wanted? I try encouraging him to ramp up the enthusiasm, but he must misread my signals, because he releases me with a sheepish chuckle.

"We should keep going."

"Or we could spend the night on the forest floor," I say, giving him my best attempt at a flirty look. I *need* this to work. If it unravels, there will be nothing left to hold me together.

He grabs my hand and tugs me along the path. "As tempting as that sounds, I'd better not risk the fallout of keeping the queen-in-waiting out overnight. And in the woods, no less."

We walk for thirty minutes before finally admitting that we're likely no closer to his car than when we started. The forest is inky and mysterious—a completely different creature after sunset. The chill, which felt so good against my skin earlier, has morphed into a cold that has numbed my toes.

Beck suggests trying to find a road instead. "Roads mean people, and people mean phones."

"Yes, but people also mean cameras and bad press," I remind him.

"I'll take a nasty tabloid article over being stuck out here until morning. Come on," he says. "I think I hear traffic."

He leads the way toward the sound, and before long we can see the flash of headlights through a break in the trees. I have to admit, news story or not, I'm elated at the prospect of escaping the forest.

"You stay here," he instructs. "I'll flag down a car. I won't be recognized. They might be willing to drive us, or at the very least tell us where we are." He scrambles through the underbrush and is gone.

I can't see my clothing in the dark, but I'm pretty sure I'm not recognizable in this state either.

Waiting on Beck proves arduous, and I'm just about to walk out myself, bad press be damned, when he reappears in the shadows.

"I thought you said you texted your secretary," he mutters.

"I did."

Without another word of explanation, he helps me shimmy through the scratchy overgrowth. I stumble out onto the grassy strip beside the country road. Our rescuer is still in the car, their headlights blinding me.

It isn't until I'm climbing into the back seat that I realize exactly who has come to our aid.

And with that realization come equal amounts of anger, relief, and an electric buzz that makes me a little nervous to touch metal.

25

"Love the Way You Lie" - Eminem + Rihanna

THE RIDE BACK TO Beck's car is torture. None of us speak as Henry steers down the country roads and in through the gates of Worthington Park. It turns out Beck and I wandered nearly four miles in those woods, and had it not been for his suggestion of heading for the road, we might still be in there.

After Henry parks, Beck and I climb out of the back seat. I wrap my arms around him and whisper "I'm so sorry" into his chest for what feels like the hundredth time.

He presses a kiss to my head, much easier to reach from his height than my lips. "Don't be. I'm not." I look up to find his eyes dancing in the moonlight. "I just got to spend three uninterrupted hours with you. I can think of worse things."

"Say a prayer for me," I say, shooting a sideways glance at Henry's car. "I have to ride with the Grinch."

Beck and I say goodbye, and I climb into Henry's passenger seat. I don't know what I'm expecting on the long drive back with him. I haven't seen him in weeks, not since the night we kissed and he told me he "couldn't" be with me. He might as well have screamed "it's you, not me" from the palace roof.

My body is trembling, both from the cold night air and the buffet of emotions raging inside me. I'm angry, for sure. But I'm also electrified at being next to him. I'm terrified he's going to hurt me again, but I'm also hoping he reaches over, takes my hand, and confesses that he screwed up.

He doesn't do any of that.

We don't say anything for a long time, until finally I can't take it anymore. "I thought you were out of the country."

"I was."

"So why are you here?"

"I'm back."

"I mean, why did you pick us up?"

"You were lost."

"Wow. Thanks, Einstein."

Henry doesn't make a sound.

"Did Maisie send you?" I keep my tone perfectly conversational. I will give up my firstborn child before I allow him to see what he's done to me.

"I offered." His hands are clenched on the steering wheel. If it were someone's throat, they would be on their last gasp of air right now.

"Thank you." I frown at my reflection in the window. "I think."

There's another beat of silence, then he slams his palm against the wheel, startling me so badly I let out a little yip. "No, not thank you. What the *fuck* were you doing, Celia?"

Instantly, my veins are a teakettle, the whistle starting to shriek. "I don't see how that's any of your business." I mourn the loss of my hypothetical firstborn, but there's no way in hell Henry's going to waltz back into my life and pretend he cares.

"You're my *wife!*"

My mouth falls open, and I gape at him, momentarily at a loss for words. However, they don't fail me for long. "Yes, I'm the wife of the guy who said he wants nothing to do with me before his World Tour: Supermodel Edition."

A vein in his neck twitches, and his clenched jaw looks insanely attractive in the shadows of the car. I want to smash it with a baseball bat.

He swerves and brings us to a complete stop beside the road. Before I can ask what he's doing, he climbs out and slams the door.

I wait for him to return. Maybe we hit something, although I didn't feel a bump. Maybe a flat tire? I glance in the side mirror and can just make out Henry's form pacing a little ways down the road. What the hell is he doing?

I get out of the car and prop my elbow on the roof. "Are you almost done ruminating out here? I'm tired and I want to go home."

At the sound of my voice, he swings around and stalks back to me. "You're tired, huh? Maybe because you took a little adventure in the woods without telling anyone where you were, got lost in said woods, and put your life in incredible danger. That does tend to exhaust people." His words are pregnant with anger and laced with sarcasm, but there's something else in them, too.

I open my mouth to respond, but he doesn't let me.

"I'm not done. Do you have any idea what might have happened if I hadn't seen you beside the road? If someone else had come along first? The things people will do for money or fame is insane, Celia. *Insane.* Or let's say you had decided to rough it in the woods overnight. Do you know what the temperatures drop to this time of year? You're not dressed for that kind of weather, and you didn't bring a single blanket with you."

I lift my chin in defiance. "Beck and I would have kept each other warm."

"You're unbelievable."

"I'm unbelievable? No, you're unbelievable." Like a drunkard, I punctuate my words by stabbing my index finger into his chest. "You expect me to stay locked in a tower while you go off and sleep with any woman who will have you. Except for me, of course. *That's* unbelievable."

He scoffs and shakes his head. "One has nothing to do with the other."

"Only because one is you and the other is me!"

"No, because one is a harmless pastime. The other is life and death!" We're screaming now, only inches apart.

"Why do you even care what happens to me? I'm surprised you haven't run me over yourself."

"Trust me, I'm considering it," he growls. "But that wouldn't serve my purposes. I need someone responsible at my side to balance out my image. It's easier to gain the people's trust that way."

I can almost feel the knife. It slips through the soft flesh of my belly and tears through the thick lining of my stomach, leaving a gaping hole, blood gurgling out. It shouldn't hurt—used to it as I am—but it does.

I was wrong. There was no misunderstanding, no hidden explanation. This is who Henry is, who he's always been. "I didn't think it was possible for you to make me hate you any more, but congratulations. You just did."

"I won't ask you to understand."

"What a relief. Because it's beyond understanding." I wheel around and climb back into the car. Let him spend all night out there, for all I care. With any luck, *he'll* be the one to catch hypothermia.

I sink into the rich leather of the seat and adjust the radio until I find a station playing heavy metal—much more fitting for the moment than the jazz Henry had on—and crank the volume so loud that conversation will be impossible.

When he joins me a few minutes later, he immediately lowers it. I wait until he's distracted putting the car into gear before turning it back up. His hand shoots back over, and we keep it up like a pair of middle schoolers. I finally give up after he shuts the power off, not out of defeat but boredom.

His phone is sitting in the cupholder between our seats, and when it vibrates, my eyes automatically flit to it. Before I can look away out of deeply ingrained politeness, Bea's name snags my eye, like a flash of lightning in a black sky.

I grab the device, finishing school be damned. "Why is my sister texting you?"

Henry lets out a resigned sigh but doesn't attempt to retrieve it from me. "I don't know."

"Right. This is just an isolated incident, then?"

"She texts me sometimes, okay? There's nothing going on."

"Do you actually expect me to believe you?"

He looks at me then. "It would be nice for a change."

"Sorry. I'm not feeling generous tonight." I hold the phone out to him. "Prove it. Let me read your messages."

"You have major trust issues," he says, but unlocks the screen and passes it back.

"I wonder why that is."

Henry's phone is a treasure trove, likely the reason it's guarded with three different types of encryption, but I stifle the temptation and only open the message thread from Bea. There have been an astounding number of texts exchanged between them, including pictures my sister has sent, fortunately still wearing clothing. There's nothing overtly suggestive about the messages, but it doesn't stop my rage from bubbling up. I should be angry with her—she assured me she wanted nothing to do with him—but she's not here. He is, and I'm already furious with him, so what's a little more fuel on the bonfire?

"You told me you'd stay away from her. You've been texting her every day!"

"It's not every day, and it's never for long. I feel bad not responding."

"But you don't feel bad about breaking your promise to me?" I toss the phone back into the cupholder and cross my arms.

"How did I break my promise?" His tone has turned incredulous.

"By not staying away from her! You know Bea. She thinks any attention you give her means you feel the same way she does."

"Fine. I'll quit texting her. Happy?"

"Not by a long shot," I snap, and turn toward the window.

Once we're back home, I march up the staircase and down the hallway to my suite, hoping to make it inside before Henry comes up behind me, but he's faster than I am. He grabs my arm before I can open the door.

"Let go of me," I say, trying to pull out of his grasp.

"Not until you assure me you won't do something reckless like that again."

"Like what?" I finally manage to free my arm, rubbing it where his fingers have branded my skin like a red-hot iron.

I see his face in the light for the first time tonight. He looks upset, tired, and stressed—a lethal cocktail. "You know what. Wandering in the forest with him."

"Define *wander*."

"Celia," Henry growls. The power of driving him to the edge is intoxicating.

"Well?" I raise my eyebrows. "I'm just trying to understand what you mean."

"No, you're trying to exasperate me." He moves even closer, so close I get a whiff of that scent I'd sell my soul for. He props his arm against the wall above my head and leans in until I can feel the heat radiating off him. A few more inches and we'll be touching—a thought that is sure to cause respiratory failure if I dwell on it for too long.

"Is it working?" I ask, dropping my voice to a whisper. I swallow hard at the look on his face.

His gaze doesn't leave my eyes, and yet somehow I feel it down to my toes, his eyes orbs of inky darkness. His Adam's apple bobs as he swallows. "You have no idea," he finally says, "how badly I want to—"

"Strangle me? Carve me like a pumpkin? Use me for target practice?"

"God, Celia." Henry closes his eyes briefly. "Do you have to be so morbid?"

I pull myself up to my full height, thinking it will make him take a step back. It doesn't. It only brings our faces closer together. "Why do you care what I do with Beck? You've made it very clear where the two of us stand."

"I don't care. But since we're on the subject, I never thought he was good enough for you."

A loud, mirthless laugh breaks out of my chest. "Not good enough? He's a better person than you by a long shot."

"Probably, but I still think you deserve better."

"I'll be the judge of that, thank you."

Henry rubs a hand over his face, pulling down the skin around his eyes. "We both know your judgment has been a little lacking of late."

"You know," I say, wagging my finger, "I think I'm just a toy to you. You don't want me, but no one else can have me either. That's it, isn't it?"

He pushes off from the wall. "Of course not. I just want you to be happy."

If it wasn't so ridiculous, it might actually be funny. "Happy? Really? That thought didn't seem to cross your mind the night you threw me out of your room."

He runs his fingers through his hair. "Within reason, C." He says it softly, like a caress, the same way he called me "baby" that night. *Baby, are you sure?*

I fight to still my trembling jaw. He will not break me again. "And if I told you Beck makes me happy?"

"Does he?"

"Of course," I say. "I've never been more blissful in my life."
"Then I'm happy for you," Henry says.
Even a child could see we're both lying.

26

"Tailspin" - For You

AFTER THE EMOTIONAL TRAINWRECK of my argument with Henry, I know I need to do something. I won't survive thirty years of this cat-and-mouse game. Hell, I won't survive another thirty *days*.

Leaving Wesbourne isn't an option. I owe it to this country to stay and make a difference. Following Adelaide's advice and distracting myself with Beck provided a temporary reprieve, but his face isn't the one that haunts me at night, no matter how badly I wish it were. I need another way to escape Henry and the strange power he wields over me.

When the answer arrives, it's so simple I'm irritated I haven't thought of it before.

"Wasn't there a collection of old ship logs in the archive room at the Society?" I ask Maisie. We're sitting in my office going over my itinerary for the week.

She looks up from the planner in her lap, realizing I haven't been paying attention to her overview of my upcoming events. My mind is far away. On the shores of Ireland, to be exact.

"They're on the shelf next to the census records. I think. Or they might be filed under Nautical History. Probably that one. Yes, I can almost visualize them in my mind. They're just right there"—her hands jut

221

out in front of her like she's bookending them on the shelf—"between *Wesbourne at Sea—*"

"Maisie. *Maisie.*" I finally get her attention. "That's great. I just need to know they're there."

"In that case, yes, they are there." Her eyes grow quizzical behind her glasses. "What do we need with ship logs?"

"I'm doing some research," I say. "On Queen Helena's mysterious lover."

She rubs her hands together in glee. "I love mysteries. They're my drug of choice."

I cock an eyebrow at this but don't even attempt to hide my smile. I'm in too good of a mood. If my plan works, I might end up being the luckiest girl in the world. "I just need to find a record of him leaving Ireland."

"Why? Oh, are you writing a blog post on the story? I'm sure people would love to hear your side of things! It would—"

"This has nothing to do with my blog."

"What then?"

I wasn't intending to tell her, but I'm so eager to talk about this brilliant plan that the words tumble out before I can stop them. "If I can find evidence that proves Helena had an affair, I can prove my right to the throne."

Maisie begins nodding in comprehension, but then her eyes cloud over. "But you're already being crowned in less than two months. Why do you need to prove anything?"

"Because I'm not being crowned alone. And if I can prove I'm the rightful monarch, I can annul my marriage to Henry and be crowned by myself."

"But . . . why?"

"That part's irrelevant."

"It seems like an awful lot of trouble to go to for something that's irrelevant," she says. "Did you guys have a fight?"

I almost laugh, but catch myself at the last second. "Let's call it irreconcilable differences."

"But you're so good together!"

Now I allow myself a humorless chuckle. "Henry and I are a lot of things. 'Good together' is not one of them. Let's get back to the subject at hand—the logbooks."

Maisie frowns but says, "Do you know his name? Or the name of the ship? What about dates? Any idea when it was?" Her forehead wrinkles as she gets sucked into the project. "Wait. How do you know he came from Ireland, or sailed at all for that matter?"

I give her a condensed review of the letters Henry and I found. "We know she sent him money for the trip. We just need to confirm that he actually left."

"So we'll go to the Society and check all of the logs for a ship leaving Ireland in May of 1837," she says. "It's a brilliant plan."

"Actually, I was planning to go alone."

"Oh, come on! I'm the one who read the diary and told you about it. If it weren't for me, you'd still be sitting at home being nothing but a mere duchess. The least you can let me do is tag along. Besides, you don't even know where the logs are."

I smile. "You just told me. In the nautical history section."

She pulls the worst poker face I've ever seen. "I was wrong. I'm positive that's not where they are after all."

I should bring her along just for entertainment purposes. "Fine. You can come."

Maisie jumps out of her chair and is poised to hug me, but stops when she sees the look on my face. "When do we leave?"

"Tonight. After dark."

She frowns. "Why at night? They'll be closed. Did you forget the hours already?" Her eyes widen as it dawns on her. "Ohhh, you're planning to break in."

"It's not breaking in if you have a key."

A knock sounds at my office door, and Maisie whirls around to answer it. Henry is standing on the other side. My heart sinks, after leaping for the sky.

"I'm sorry," he says, looking at me. "I thought you were alone."

"And I thought you were in Japan." I throw Maisie a withering look. She assured me he was away on business.

"The trip fell through."

"You're just in time," Maisie interrupts, clearly interpreting the tension in the room as something that needs diffusing. "Celia was just telling me everything you discovered about Helena and Philip."

"Was she?" Henry's face is stony.

I try to catch Maisie's eye, but she is focused solely on him.

"And we're breaking into the Historical Society tonight to see if we can find proof of Philip's passage—"

"Maisie," I cut her off. "Aren't we going to be late for something?"

Her poker face has improved in the past few minutes, because she gives me a look of pure innocence. "No, I don't think so."

Henry, meanwhile, has yet to remove his gaze from me. It should be illegal to look at a woman that way, to make her feel so many things with just your eyes and not mean a single one of them. "I'll come back another time," he says.

"No, you have to stay!" Maisie insists. I'm going to strangle her. "Or at the very least come with us tonight. It seems only right."

There is a question in his eyes. He's probably waiting for my approval.

"I'm sure he already has plans." I direct my answer to Maisie, but my focus remains on Henry.

"Actually, now that my plans got canceled, I'm a free man," he says. It's a test to see if I can be in the same room as him and still act like a civilized being.

"Then of course you must join us." My smile feels sweet enough to cause cavities. I do an inner victory dance at the surprise that flashes across his face. Checkmate.

"Great. I'll drive."

I haven't been to the Historical Society since I left my position there and retrieved my things from my office. It looks different at night, foreboding and almost sinister, the bookcases in the archive room casting shadows twice their size and taunting us with the secrets they carry. The familiar scent of dusty manuscripts, ink, aging leather, and Mrs. Grisholm's lemon verbena cleaner ushers in a wave of nostalgia.

"I'll grab the ship logs, and we can go through them at the table," Maisie says, and darts off down one of the aisles.

I pull out a chair, but before I can sit, Henry tugs me in between two bookcases. I spin away from him and hiss, "What do you think you're doing?"

"I wanted to apologize. That's why I came to your office this morning."

"In that case, we'll be here all night." I cross my arms. I'm still irritated that he came along, and as far as I'm concerned, he can participate by being silent and statue-like.

"I'm sorry for the way I ended things that night. And all of the times since then that I've made an asshole of myself and hurt you."

I take great interest in my manicure, ensuring I haven't chipped any polish. If I refuse to meet his eyes, maybe he'll quit talking. The whole thing was weeks ago. I've nearly put it out of my mind.

"I was hoping we could at least be friends," he says. From across the room, Maisie is talking, whether to herself or us, I can't tell. We both ignore her. "Bloody hell, Celia. Can't you at least say something?"

I drop my hand and shoot him a nasty look. "Friends? You want to be friends? You were the one who said our friendship was over."

He sighs and runs his hand through his hair. "That was a long time ago."

"Ten years, to be exact." I resume my nail inspection, although I can't even tell you what color they are. Tears brim right behind my eyelids, but I'll die before I let them fall.

Henry's timing is impeccable. Just when I'm learning how to breathe without him, to be able to go minutes without thinking of him, he rips the scab off and leaves me bleeding all over again.

"I know you have a right to hate me, but it's killing me."

"How do you think *I* feel?"

"C, I'm sorry." His voice is thick with emotion. "Truly."

My monotone belies the thunderstorm raging in my chest. "Don't be. You did me a favor."

I know my words have hit their mark, because a small groaning sigh escapes his lips, the kind of sound you make when disappointment and surprise get together to punch you in the chest. Shoving aside the regret I feel at hurting him, I remind myself that he has hurt me far worse and way more often.

"Sometimes there's more to the story."

"And sometimes the best stories are short and sweet," I retort. "I would love it if, for just once, my life could be uncomplicated. Apparently, that's too much to ask for."

"No, it's not. You deserve that." He sighs again. "But it's not always possible."

Maisie approaches from around the corner, saving me from having to reply. "There you guys are! I've been looking everywhere. I found them!" She holds up a stack of dusty books. "Exactly where I said they'd be," she adds.

We sit at the table and each take one of the ship logs from the stack. "It'll be a lot easier if we check the date first. Philip had to sail in 1837," I say. "If he left Ireland at all."

"So, we're looking for Philip Anderson leaving Ireland in 1837 and sailing to Wesbourne?" Henry has assumed a neutral tone, both of us having silently agreed to put our argument aside for the time being. Forever, if I'm lucky.

I nod and flip open the logbook in front of me. It's dated 1829, so that's an easy discard. The next several are also dated too early to be of any use. Finally, I come across one bearing *1837* on the title page.

"I've got one," I say, looking through it for the passenger manifest.

"Me too," Maisie says.

"And I've got nothing." Henry slides the last logbook onto the dead-end stack. He stands and comes around to peer over my shoulder, barging into my personal bubble. My chair shifts slightly as he braces his hand against the back of it.

For a minute, I forget what I'm doing, and all I can think about is the fact that if I turn my head forty-five degrees, we could be kissing.

But that is the kind of thought that needs murdering.

I clear my throat and those thoughts from my mind and focus on the list of passengers in front of me. The handwritten script of a sea captain isn't the easiest thing to read, but most of the names are semi-discernable.

My finger stops. "Is that *P. Anderson*?"

Henry moves even closer to make out the name for himself. Damn the way he smells. "Sure looks like it." He rises to his full height, and there's a smile in his voice. "Did we just find our proof?"

Without taking my eyes from the book, I move my finger. What I see next makes the blood run cold in my veins.

"How is that possible?" I whisper.

"What?" He leans over me again. I point to the note next to the name, and he freezes. "No. It can't be."

Oblivious to what is happening on the other side of the table, Maisie tosses her log aside. "Well, that was a bust. You guys find anything?" When she sees the looks on our faces, her mouth forms an *O*. "You did, didn't you?"

"Philip Anderson did leave Ireland on a ship named *The Caledonia* in 1837." I slide the book across the table to her. "But according to this, he died at sea and never made it to Wesbourne."

The three of us stare at each other.

Maisie speaks first. "That can't be right. Maybe it meant a different passenger." She studies the manifest even closer, her nose nearly brushing the page.

It's possible. The note simply says *deceased at sea* next to Philip's name. The captain could have written it above or below the line it was meant to be on.

"Let's look through the rest of the book. Surely the captain would have noted something as significant as a death," I say. "*The Caledonia* only had fifty passengers on board."

Maisie passes the log back. "You look. I need caffeine." She leaves for the small kitchen, where she used to be in an intimate relationship with the coffee maker.

Turning the pages as gently as I can, I give each journal entry a quick scan, looking for any mention of death or sickness on board. Henry continues his spine-tingling vigil over my shoulder. Finally, about halfway through, I find the entry for *14 May, 1837*.

6 AM

Light air to gentle breeze from N.N.W. Overcast and pleasant. Average speed of wind per hour 17 miles. Passenger died during the night. Identified as Philip Anderson from the inscribed pocket watch found on the body. Likely cause, dysentery.

"Well, I guess that's it, then." I close the book and lay it aside, and a weight settles in my stomach. "Philip died before he and Helena could be reunited." For some reason, the tragedy of it seems worse than losing the chance to annul my sham of a marriage.

Henry is silent. I glance over as he sits down next to me, looking confused and frustrated. "It just doesn't make any sense. Why would the diary have pointed to Helena having an affair if Philip never made it to Wesbourne?"

I shrug. "Maybe it was someone else?" Even as I say it, I know it's a ridiculous suggestion. No woman as in love as Helena was with Philip would immediately start an affair with another man. It's impossible.

Henry bites his thumbnail and shakes his head. "No. I don't buy that. I don't have an answer yet, but something feels off to me."

"Feelings aren't everything, believe it or not."

"I assume there's some hidden barb in that statement?"

I begin stacking the logbooks that are scattered across the table. "Believe what you want."

"Feelings aside, you'll give up that easily? I thought you'd keep looking."

"Whether I want there to be more to the story or not doesn't mean there is."

"There's always more to the story." His gaze is so intent I have to look away.

"Maybe I'm just tired of searching for it."

Maisie enters the room bearing three very welcome cups of coffee. I accept mine and update her on what we found.

"So it looks like we can lay this whole thing to rest," I conclude.

"Not so fast," Henry says. "There's still the diary."

"Which was probably forged," I say. "Someone found out about Helena's secret and decided to wreak havoc. You said yourself that people will do crazy things for money and fame."

"Or for love," he notes.

"What's your point?"

"I've been thinking about the circumstances of Philip's supposed death."

"*Supposed death*? The logbook says he died. What more proof do you need? The body itself?"

"I told you, I don't buy the story ending with Philip dying on that boat. Helena was too thorough for it to stop there. Look at everything she did to put this whole thing into motion."

He has a point. There was the hidden compartment in the dressing table, her directing letters via her maid. Helena *was* clever.

Henry continues. "I think she was a force to be reckoned with. Think about all of the details she thought of to pull off this affair—arguably the biggest scandal in all of Wesbourne history. These things didn't just happen. My guess is Philip Anderson's death was a decoy."

Maisie jumps up and nearly spills her coffee. "Yes! He was only identified as Philip Anderson because of the pocket watch."

"Seems pretty straightforward to me," I say. The last thing I need is for her to team up with Henry against me.

"Not if you're trying to fake your own death!" She has taken to pacing the room, wringing her hands. "We may never know if they planned it this way or if Philip simply took advantage of the opportunity, but think about it! All he had to do was slip his own watch into the man's pocket. When the name matched one of the names on the manifest, it would have been natural to assume it was the same person."

It's a big assumption, and one I'm not ready to accept. Too much hangs in the balance. "That's assuming no one knew Philip or the man who died. How could Philip possibly have known such a situation would arise? That is, unless you're now implying he killed this person?"

Henry jumps in, almost as animated as Maisie. "There was a small wave of people immigrating to Wesbourne in the early to mid-1800s. Men were coming over because our economy was booming."

"How do you know that?" I ask.

He shrugs. "I read it somewhere."

Unless he's a history buff and has spent hours in the research library—something that is as likely as the king taking up a tutu and ballet—the only place he could have read that is on my blog. I spent an entire month choking on dust to collect the information for that article.

"I don't think it's much of a stretch to assume there were lots of young, single men on board who knew no one else on the ship," he says. "They were going in search of a better life than the one of poverty they'd left behind in Ireland."

He laces his fingers together on the table. I remember with perfect clarity how they felt on my body.

"It's really a brilliant plan, if you ask me," Maisie says. "Philip fakes his own death in order to come ashore under cover. That way, if there was any suspicion about the queen's ex-lover coming to Wesbourne, they would only have had to find the record of his death to put an end to it."

The idea deserves thought. It's far-fetched but not impossible. If Maisie and Henry are right, and Philip did in fact fake his death, chances are good he and Helena would have stopped at nothing to enact their plan to be together.

"Okay. So right now, we have two possible theories. The first, and most likely"—I shoot a look at both of them over the rim of my coffee cup—"is that Philip died on the ship before coming to Wesbourne. Someone found out about Helena's plans to meet her lover and wrote the diary as a way to stir up trouble."

Henry raises his hand. "Objection. I don't think that theory seems *more* likely—"

"Overruled. The second theory is that Philip faked his death, whether it was planned or incidental, and had an affair with Helena, which was presumably the plan all along."

Maisie tucks her hair behind her ears. "I'm with Henry. I think the second theory is more believable."

I purse my lips and exhale through my nose. "It doesn't matter what we want to believe. What *matters* are the facts."

"And really good coffee." Henry winks and holds up his cup in a salute to Maisie, who giggles.

"Don't laugh. It only encourages him." I kick his shin under the table and earn a grunt in response. "We need to be able to prove or disprove one of our theories. Any ideas on how to do that?"

"We could visit Mrs. Schumann," Maisie suggests. At our blank looks, she adds, "The lady who donated the diary to the Society. Well, her grandson found it and brought it in. She might be able to tell us how it came to be in her possession."

"Hasn't she already been interviewed?" I ask.

"They've tried." Maisie takes a big gulp of coffee. "But she adamantly refuses to speak to anyone about it."

I squint at her. "So how is that a viable suggestion?"

"Henry might be able to get her to talk." She smiles at him from under her eyelashes and wraps a piece of hair around her finger. Oh god, is she *flirting* with him now?

"Ah, yes. He is very good at charming innocent and unassuming women. Aren't you, Henry?" I turn my own smile on him, albeit a much icier one than Maisie's.

He looks like he's been backed up against a tree. I couldn't have orchestrated it better myself. "I'm not very good with old people."

"Maybe not, but Maisie's right. You do know women." I pause, choosing my next words carefully. "Unless you think you've lost your touch?"

His eyes narrow ever so slightly. My tactics may not be very subtle, but they are effective. "I guess it can't hurt to try, right?"

27

"Diamond Heart" - Alan Walker + Sophia Somajo

W ITH A BIT OF juggling, Maisie is able to clear our schedule so we can visit Mrs. Schumann in her care home the next afternoon. She sets up the appointment while I pray it will give us some answers.

When I arrive at the entrance to the palace garage, Henry's already waiting, chatting with the security guard stationed there. There's no sign of Maisie. She's likely been tied up by a last-minute phone call.

"Ready?" Henry asks, pushing away from the wall he's leaning against, his hands in the pockets of his dusty blue chinos. He's wearing a white dress shirt, his aviator sunglasses dangling from the unbuttoned neckline. He looks exceptionally good and exceptionally dangerous to a compromised heart.

I glance down the hallway I just walked down. "Have you seen Maisie? She should be here by now."

"She can't make it." He slides on his glasses and holds the door open for me. "Said something came up she has to take care of."

Suspicion floods my veins as I precede him into the garage. "And she told you instead of me? I was just with her fifteen minutes ago."

He shrugs and presses the button on a key fob. The lights of his car flash twice. "Maybe she didn't want to bother you."

I don't believe him for a second, but I'll have to talk to Maisie about it later. There isn't time right now. It will take at least an hour to drive to the village where the care home is located. I slide into Henry's passenger seat without a word and vow to ignore him the entire trip. My arsenal is dwindling, and I need some kind of armor.

The sounds of a dramatic symphony orchestra flow from the speakers as I melt into the buttery-soft leather. Despite his many flaws, no one can fault Henry for his choice in cars or music.

The Wesbourne countryside flies past as we race up and down the rolling green hills dotted with lush forests and ponds. He slows on the cobblestone streets as we drive through several small villages. In one of them, school has just let out for the day. A cluster of children cross the street, all rumpled uniforms and excited chatter, bags swinging from their arms.

Henry munches from the bag of crisps in his lap as we watch them. "You know I've never been asked what I want to be when I grow up?" he says.

I glance at him in surprise. He hasn't attempted to break my silence yet, but there's something about being with him outside the palace walls and the innocence of his comment that makes me give up my cold shoulder, to say nothing about the curiosity tugging at me. "Well, what *do* you want to be when you grow up?"

"A king, of course."

I make the sound of a buzzer. "Wrong answer. Try again."

"If I could do anything? Probably business."

"Business? In what capacity?"

"You know, owning them. Running them. I like the idea of exploring all of the possibilities that make something work."

As a kid, he was always fascinated with taking apart toys, electronics, and anything else he could get his hands on. One summer, when he was fifteen or sixteen, he even dismantled a car and put it back together.

"I'll bet you could do it," I say.

"My father would disagree with you."

"Your father is an atrocious disgrace to humanity. I hope we disagree on everything."

"That's why I stopped trying to please him a long time ago. He'll never be happy with anything I do anyway."

So that's why Henry lives like he does. William is disappointed in him. He destroyed any chance his son ever had at an innocent childhood, and in return, Henry embarrasses him every chance he gets.

It certainly makes more sense than any of the reasons I've come up with to explain Henry's day-to-night change at seventeen. One minute we're best friends, and the next we're living in two separate worlds—he in one filled with women, fast cars, drinking, parties, gambling, and plenty of other things I'd rather not know the details about. Being featured in tabloid after tabloid gave him a worldwide reputation, and he quickly morphed from a sweet and funny boy into a dark and handsome prince.

I, on the other hand, had my debutante season, danced with respectable gentlemen, only kissed three of them, only sipped champagne socially and never more than two glasses, attended art openings and museum exhibitions, completed finishing school, and went on to become the youngest director of the Historical Society at the age of twenty-three.

The fact that I lost my heart to Henry in spite of all of it feels like the plot of some low-budget romcom. He took me apart like some battery-operated toy, found out exactly what makes me tick, then instead of putting me back together, he just left the pieces scattered across the rug.

But he's not the only one who knows how to wield a knife. And if he ever gets within an inch of my heart again, I plan to enact some destruction of my own.

Rousing as the car slows, I sit up straighter and quickly swipe at the corners of my mouth. Fortunately, they're dry. My nap can't have been more than a tiny snooze. Hopefully Henry was too preoccupied to notice.

"You need more sleep," he says. Not preoccupied after all.

"I get plenty, thanks."

He pulls onto a paved driveway, marked by a sign announcing we've arrived at the care home. A three-story brick manor stands on a hill at the top of it, and out front is a car park. Two turrets bookend the house, and various chimney stacks peek out of the roof. Large windows give it a gaping, inquisitive look.

As I move to open my door, Henry puts a hand on my arm. "I'm serious. You'll get sick if you don't get enough sleep."

"I told you, I'm fine." I push the door open and climb into the sunshine.

As we approach the front entrance, I wish for the millionth time that Maisie had come along. I'm uneasy tackling this with just Henry. He's on a streak, breaking my heart. What if he does something that sends me completely over the edge?

Like slipping my hand into his and squeezing. The action sends fingers of sensation through my arm and into my belly. I hate that his touch still has that effect. I'm about to yank my hand away when he drops it on his own.

The foyer of the home is as grand and imposing as the exterior, only it smells of antiseptic and old people. A chill clings to the air like fog, enough to penetrate the blazer I'm wearing. I shiver and glance out the window at a beckoning garden, dazzled in sunlight.

A young receptionist in nurse's scrubs assures us Mrs. Schumann will be right out. She practically trips over her own feet when Henry smiles his thanks. I roll my eyes at her retreating back.

Several minutes later, Mrs. Schumann is escorted into the foyer by a male nurse. We introduce ourselves and each press a kiss to the side of her wrinkled face.

"Oh, I know who you are." Her short, curly white hair bounces as she lets out a chuckle, which morphs into coughing. "I may be in a home, but I still follow the news." She's wearing a bright floral house dress, and someone has applied blush to her papery cheeks, making her look alive and energetic, like an origami crane brought to life.

The nurse motions to a doorway on the left. "Would you like to use our reception room?"

"Actually," Henry says, "I was wondering if Mrs. Schumann might like to take a stroll in the garden." He bestows that heart-stopping grin on our elderly hostess, and she positively blooms under it.

"That sounds lovely," she says, taking the arm he offers and leaving me to follow them outside.

The garden is small but meticulously kept, its wide paths swept free of debris. A gentle breeze wafts a perfectly blended perfume as it rustles through the flowers. The sunlight soaks into my pores, and I silently thank Henry for the suggestion that we leave the cold manor.

Mrs. Schumann's heel catches on an uneven section of the walk, which causes her to stumble, and I step up to assist her on the other side. She doesn't even spare me a glance, still thoroughly enamored by Henry.

"When they told me who was coming to visit, I could hardly believe it. Of course, I know why you're here. Seems the only thing I'm good for these days is giving interviews. The nurses always turn them down for me. I don't want any pesky reporters poking into my business. But with you"—she beams at him—"I'll make an exception."

Never one to resist an adoring female, he returns her ridiculous smile and pats her hand, which is in the crook of his elbow. "I'm flattered you'd make the time for me."

She giggles like a schoolgirl. "Just think what the girls will say when I tell them Prince Henry himself kissed me. They'll be fit to be tied." She chuckles again, leading to another coughing fit.

"Do you want some water, Mrs. Schumann?" I ask, coming to a stop and halting our progress along the path. "I'd be happy to fetch a cup."

"I'm fine. Stay." Her tone holds authority. This woman was obviously a commander of something in her day, even if it was only the local quilting bee.

Henry snorts under his breath, and I glare at him over her head.

"Mrs. Schumann, as you've already guessed, we're here about the diary," I say. There has been enough fawning over Henry to last several lifetimes. "I actually worked at the Historical Society when your grandson donated your items. We would love to know how it came to be in your possession."

A smattering of clouds conspire to cover the sun. Mrs. Schumann's eyes feel like two needles pricking me as she looks me over. There is certainly nothing wrong with her vision, whatever her age might be. I'm currently being turned inside out and thoroughly inspected. I only hope she turns me right side out when she's done.

"It was my grandmother's," she finally says, when she's completed her assessment of me. If her slight lip curl is any indication, I didn't pass the test. She must be Team William, which is ironic, considering she's the reason the diary was discovered in the first place.

"Do you happen to know how she got it?" I add as much sugar to my voice as I can tolerate without gagging.

"She found it."

Pulling my best poker face, I glance at Henry. He meets my gaze, then says in a bored tone, "Mrs. Schumann, tell me more about you. I think under different circumstances you and I would have been great friends."

She positively simpers at him, and her skin becomes translucent in the sunlight. She launches into a narrative of her past, both as a child and an adult. Henry steers us toward a bed overflowing with early summer flowers—delphinium, irises, peonies—while asking questions and chuckling at her answers.

I'm clearly the third wheel, but it's a position I'm willing to overlook, provided Mrs. Schumann tells us something that proves the diary is legitimate.

After the ten or fifteen minutes it takes to wander the entire path of the garden, all filled with anecdotes from her past, Mrs. Schumann slows her pace. "I believe I need to sit down, Your Royal Highness." The clouds are gathering in large quantities now, and the sun has to wrestle them for any small opening through which to shine.

Henry leads us to a small wrought iron bench nestled in the embrace of a giant oak tree. A squirrel scolds our disruption of his sanctuary as we sit down.

"I've certainly enjoyed our chat, sir. But I know you came for more than that, and I'm not going to waste your time. You have a country to run." Mrs. Schumann looks at me before returning her gaze to him. "You want to know how I came to have the diary. Like I said, it was my grandmother's, which is why I was so angry when that nitwit Caleb donated it. He has no respect for history or family. Can't even come visit his own grandmother. Always gallivanting around the globe somewhere." She waves her hand in frustration.

"But I'm getting sidetracked. My grandmother was a housemaid in the palace before she got married. Served under King William II. They had done some remodeling in the servants' quarters, and her room must have been a lady's maid's before, or she'd never have found it."

Henry and I stay silent, hoping she'll continue.

"She said it was wedged in the fireplace, hidden behind a loose brick. She only found it because of a tumble she took one day. Fortunately, it was summertime and no fire was lit. But she tripped and stumbled backwards into the fireplace. When she went to pull herself out, she grabbed onto a brick, but it was loose. That's when she discovered the book.

"Then I found it one day, in the attic of her cottage. I was young, no more than fifteen, enamored by everything about the royal family. I had dreams of working at the palace myself. So when I saw it belonged to the queen's maid, I could hardly contain myself.

"I took it to my grandmother. She was on her deathbed, but her mind was still sharp. She told me the story I just told you, about finding it in the fireplace, and told me to keep the book safe. And I did, until that little twat Caleb got rid of it." Mrs. Schumann scowls at him in belated reproach.

The garden is now bathed in silence but for the gentle breeze in the trees and the twittering of birds. I recognize the trill of a European robin calling its mate. I'm afraid if I speak, the woman will clam up again.

Finally, Henry says, "That's an incredible story, Mrs. Schumann. Did you end up working at the palace?"

He couldn't have pleased her more. "I certainly did. Served your great-grandfather, I did, as housemaid. Not for long, of course, because I fell in love and got married. But those were some of the best years of my life."

"You wouldn't happen to know if there were employment records kept back then, would you?" he asks. "Maybe a book or register of who was hired and their position?"

She waves her hand. "Oh, sure. The butler did all of the hiring in those days. I'm sure it's quite different now. He had a big black book where he kept track of everything. I watched him write my name in it when I joined the staff."

Where is Henry going with these questions? I look at him, but he keeps his eyes on Mrs. Schumann, and a smile tugs at one side of his mouth. "I don't suppose you saw where he put it when he was done, did you?"

She laughs, a shrill cackle that startles the robins. "Of course I did. He had a shelf behind his desk with a whole bunch of books. Don't know what they all were, but I doubt they're still there. Everything's gone to all those computers and whatnot these days."

This seems to satisfy Henry, because he stands and says, "Thank you so much for your time, Mrs. Schumann. It's been the highlight of my week. Now, let's get you back inside."

She titters and blushes at this, something I didn't realize was still possible at her age. We say our goodbyes, and as I walk briskly to the car, I realize that this was my last hope, and now it's gone. I've become society's pariah, Henry's practice target, and a stranger to the people I love.

For better or for worse, I'm stuck in this role I no longer have any desire to play.

28

"Tattoo" - Jordan Sparks

THE AIR HAS COOLED considerably by the time we reach Henry's car. The clouds are churning into a thick gray soup, completely obliterating what might have been a beautiful sunset. A rumble of thunder echoes in the distance.

"She was butter in your hands," I mutter as he opens my door.

"What can I say? I know how to handle women."

"You should hand out complimentary barf bags."

He throws his head back and laughs, and the sound reverberates through the still evening air. After climbing into the driver's seat, he says, "Celia Eleanor, are you jealous of an old woman?"

"Don't flatter yourself. I'm upset she didn't tell us anything useful."

"What do you mean? Of course she did."

"I'm sorry, but were you listening? How is hearing about a baby turtle she once adopted helpful in any way?"

"She told us how the diary was found. Now we know it's legitimate."

I scoff. "Hardly. All we know is that she has a penchant for telling stories."

"You think she made it up?"

"It doesn't matter, because it doesn't prove anything either way."

He looks at me strangely, and I realize that I'm showing my hand with my obsessive need for proof. I can't let him see how badly I need this, or *why* I need it. He would sabotage everything.

"I just like black-and-white answers," I add.

"I know," he muses.

"Why are you helping, anyway?"

He pulls the car back onto the road before speaking. "My father took something valuable from me."

Chills prickle my body. I want to murder King William for what he did.

Henry's knuckles flash white on the steering wheel. "His position as king is the most important thing in the world to him. He's so convinced the diary is rubbish . . ." He shrugs. "I guess it feels like the universe has given me a chance at retribution."

It makes sense, even if it's completely twisted and selfish. I feel a white-hot rage welling up inside me. William stole his son's innocence. You certainly won't catch me telling Henry he shouldn't want vengeance.

Before I'm even aware of what I'm doing, I reach over and cover the hand on his leg with my own. It's warm, and he splays his fingers so mine slip between them, then curls them together. It's such an intimate gesture, my insides clench.

After a few beats, I pull my hand away and tuck it under my leg. The first splatters of rain hit the windshield. "Why were you asking Mrs. Schumann about the employment records?"

"Assuming Philip didn't die on board *The Caledonia*, they were likely going to try getting him a job in the palace, right? To make it possible to be together?"

"You think Helena was going to what—smuggle a gardener into her room?"

"What other choice did she have? He wasn't even gentry."

I should have thought of it myself. I cross my arms over my chest. "He wouldn't have used his real name anyway, so how will the records help us?"

"He could have taken the name of the man who actually died."

"Assuming, of course, Philip himself didn't die."

"Hey," Henry says, "it's a theory we have yet to disprove. I'm sticking with it until we know otherwise."

"So you want to cross-reference the records of the people who were hired after *The Caledonia* landed with the ship's manifest?"

"Can't hurt to try, right?"

No, it can't hurt. But it won't make a difference. Because even if one of the men who was aboard that ship was hired at the palace, there won't be irrefutable evidence that he wasn't exactly who he said he was. Nothing to prove that my lineage is the one that belongs on the throne.

Rattle the shackles around my wrists all you want, but at the end of the day, I'll still be married to the man who is the gasoline on the fire burning me alive.

It's getting difficult to see the road due to the rain coming down harder and a strong wind whipping it nearly horizontal. Even Henry's head-lights make little difference in the blinding wall of precipitation.

"I'm going to pull off," he shouts over the noise.

We're in one of the small villages we passed through earlier. He stops in a car park belonging to a tiny pub. Its lights are only a hazy glow, but nonetheless a beacon of life in the midst of the flood pouring from the sky.

He shuts off the engine. The silence that now fills the vehicle, coupled with the noise of the rain outside, creates the feeling of a warm cocoon. Except that warm cocoon is going to become suffocating very quickly. For some reason, sitting in a car alone with Henry is much worse when said car is not in motion.

"Want to make a run for it?" I ask, with a nod toward the building.

He raises his eyebrows. "We'd get drenched." Glancing into the back seat, he adds, "I have an umbrella, but the way this wind is blowing, it won't do us any good."

I swing my door open, jumping out directly into a giant pool of water. Ignoring my drenched trousers, I dash through the rain toward the entrance of the pub, Henry right on my heels. We burst through it, bringing a spray of water with us.

Inside, dark paneling rises halfway up the walls. Above that, framed oil paintings and black-and-white photographs are scattered in a haphazard pattern. Booths line the small space, their bloodred vinyl upholstery cracked and peeling. An ancient stereo struggles to be heard over the rage of the storm.

When we enter, the handful of patrons sprinkled around the room turn in our direction. All too late, I realize we'll be recognized, even in a small village nearly an hour from the capital. Maybe especially here. I don't know what reaction to expect—do they hate me?—but I desperately want to retreat back the way we came.

But surprisingly, after assessing us, everyone turns back to their meals. I look over at Henry. His normally roguishly styled and tousled hair has lost all of its volume and is matted to his forehead, sending rivulets of water down his face. He actually doesn't look much like himself at all if you aren't used to seeing him up close and in person. The murky interior of the pub helps dilute his features, although the fact that no one seems to have placed that signature jawline is a miracle.

A young woman with an apron, a dark ponytail, and a dozen piercings greets us with a warm, enthusiastic smile. Something like recognition crosses her face, but after a few seconds, she must decide we just bear a strong resemblance to the royal couple. She motions with her hand and leads us to a booth at the back of the room. After sliding onto the sticky vinyl, we take the proffered menus, and she leaves us to study them.

"I am dying for a cup of coffee," I say.

"Warm ale will heat you faster," Henry offers, absorbed in his own menu.

"Do I strike you as an ale drinker?"

"No. That's precisely why I suggested it."

If he thinks I'm about to be coerced into ordering an ale simply because he doesn't think I will, he's wrong. "I'll have a coffee and the chowder," I say when the server reappears.

"It wouldn't hurt you to try something new every once in a while," Henry tells me after placing his own order.

"Actually, it might. But please, swim with as many sharks as you like and eat all the buffet sushi you want."

He just smiles and shakes his head, sending several drops onto the marred wooden tabletop. The server brings our drinks with a smile and assures us our food will be ready shortly.

"I'm so glad we weren't recognized." I warm my frozen fingers on my mug. "I long for the days when no one knew me."

Henry chuckles into his ale. "We were definitely recognized."

I frown and take a sip of my coffee. The heat chugs through my bloodstream. "No, we weren't. They would have said something."

"This will blow your mind, but not everyone voices every thought aloud." He pushes his ale across the table. "Taste it."

I roll my eyes and lift the glass to my lips. The full, malty flavor is intense but not unpleasant. He's right. Instant warmth shoots through my belly, then spreads to my limbs. I set the drink back down and lift a shoulder. "Not bad. I still prefer my coffee, and I still don't believe she knows who we are."

Henry smirks and raises the ale to his own lips, keeping his gaze on me. A familiar tingle rings through me, and I avert my eyes, but it's too late to stop the flush from crawling over my face.

"You forget, I know women," he says.

"If that were true, you'd know her smile meant you're welcome in her bed anytime."

"*Those* smiles I also know quite well. And that one wasn't for me." He takes another swig and licks the foam from his lip. I drag my eyes and thoughts away from them.

In perfect synchronization, the server returns, bearing our plates on her tattooed arms, the food steaming hot and smelling delicious. Henry's stomach growls as she places his fish and chips before him.

"I know this is hugely inappropriate of me," she says, "but tonight is Trivia Night, and I would score so many bragging rights if I brought you." She clasps her hands together in a pleading gesture. "It's so much fun, I promise."

Henry pops a chip into his mouth and looks at me questioningly. The spark in his eyes is unmistakable. "You're the walking encyclopedia. It's your call."

I know he thinks I won't do it, and my first inclination is to decline. But I can't stand his gloating. "Sure, why not," I tell her.

She thrusts a fist into the air. "They're going to freak when I bring Celia Chapman-Payne back. Oh, and I'm Amber, by the way," she says, dropping into one of the most awkward curtsies I've ever seen. "Here, let me grab your plates. We play in the back."

As we follow her out of the dining room, Henry whispers into my ear. "Told you that smile wasn't for me."

I sock him in the stomach with my elbow.

Trivia Night is held in a room that looks much the same as the one we left but is occupied by a louder, more boisterous crowd. They're laughing and tossing back pints of ale. Fried fish, cigarette smoke, and malt all clamor for position as the dominant scent. I feel like a peacock in the desert in my fuchsia blazer.

Amber sets our plates on one of the small round tables dotting the space, which has been divided in half. "You guys take a seat while I get this lot sorted." Her sharp whistle brings the volume in the room down to a hum. "Listen up! It's time to start. Each team will have sixty seconds to come up with their answer. Anyone on the team is eligible to answer, but only the first response will be accepted, so use your bloody noggins and work together. Clive will ask the questions for my team, and I'll ask them for his. Any questions?"

I have roughly twenty, and my hand nearly rises out of habit, but there's no need to attract the attention of the entire crowd. I'll just have to figure it out as we go along.

"What's the theme, Amber?" someone calls from the back.

"Wesbourne history," she replies, throwing a wink at me. At this point, my face is a fire hazard.

I was expecting your run-of-the-mill primary school questions like "Who was the first king of Wesbourne?" and "In what year did Wesbourne gain independence?" But there's nothing ordinary about these ones.

Our team's first question is "How did the crispy come to be Wesbourne's national dish?" I'm positive we won't get it, until a girl with a tangled mass of red hair says a pub owner was closing for the day when a nobleman came in and demanded a meal. Scraping together the only ingredients he had left in the kitchen, he made him a sandwich featuring pan-fried fish, cheese, and jam. The rest is history.

We get the point, and the next five minutes are spent in raucous discussion about the official ingredients for a crispy—red onion slices, shredded lettuce, sliced gherkins, a dash of celery salt, a sweet-spicy sauce, and a brioche bun—until Amber stands to read the question for the other team.

They volley back and forth between the teams, and I can't believe how many nuanced details these people know about our country's history. And not once have they been awkward about having their future king and queen sitting at a greasy pub table with them.

"Drink up," Henry says, pushing his ale toward me. Everyone is facing the center of the room, where Clive and Amber are asking the questions. I'm sitting in front of Henry, ever cognizant of his knees occasionally brushing my back. "It'll help you relax."

He's in his element here: the jostling, the noise, the drinks. I would much prefer to blend into the smudgy background. But I do as he says and take another drink.

Amber appears before me. "Fill in for me? I've gotta make rounds out front." I search for the words to turn her down, but she's already disappeared.

"Come on, C. You got this." Henry squeezes my shoulders.

I walk to the center of the room on what feels like sea legs. I can handle eyes on me, but these ones are different. We come from different planets. I don't make a habit of frequenting pubs, drinking ale, and certainly not participating in trivia nights.

"Give 'em something hard, Your Royal Highness!" someone calls out.

It's the first time anyone has addressed me as such tonight, and the title throws me. It seems as out of place in the room as my blazer. I meet Henry's eyes.

He grins and nods his encouragement. "Don't go easy on them, C!"

Resolve solidifies in my stomach. I walk back to our table and chug the rest of his refilled glass of ale, to much whooping from the crowd. Then I shrug out of my jacket and toss it to Henry. This causes even more cheering. I take my place in the center of the room, wearing only my white tank and blue jeans. I look just like one of them now.

It takes me a few moments to get my bearings, then I address the team across the room. "Where was Queen Helena originally from before she married King William I?"

As they huddle together to discuss their answer, I turn around to see our team's reaction. I'm greeted with grins, thumbs-up signs, and a wink from Henry.

Clive's team guesses France to the amusement of ours. "It's Ireland, you dumbasses!" someone yells. "Don't you read Celia's blog?"

The questions continue, and the more I let myself relax, the more fun I have. By the time Amber comes back, I've been unofficially elected to replace her as team captain. We win and are swiftly accused of cheating by the other side, but they must not be too sore, because Henry and I are bombarded with handshakes and good-natured back slaps by the time it's over.

I was wrong before. Wesbourne is so much more than a country, so much more than the political climate or the brash opinions shared in the news. *This* is the heart of Wesbourne. We're all made of good and bad, the beautiful and the ugly.

"This was the best trivia night we've ever had," Amber says as Henry pulls out his wallet to pay for our meal.

I don't hear the rest of their conversation, because the sight of that palm-sized fold of leather has snatched the breath from my lungs. I can still smell the shop—that earthy, woodsy scent, broken by the occasional whiff of tobacco. The proprietor glaring at me over the rim of his glasses. Pulling out three large, crisp bills to appease him. Watching the engraving machine burn Henry's name into the bottom right corner. The feel of the soft, supple material in my hands. The confidence that he would love it.

It was the last gift I ever bought him.

Fortunately, the rain is nothing more than a slight mist by the time we get outside, but the car seats are cold to the touch.

"You came alive in there," Henry says, cranking up the heat.

"It was just the ale." I try to sweep up the shards of my heart, but they're scattered everywhere, thanks to that stupid bloody wallet.

"You're a natural with people, C. They adore you."

"Not as much as they adore you," I point out.

"Adoration isn't everything."

"Maybe not, but they'd all still pick you over me if they could."

"Then they'd be making the wrong choice. You said yourself I'm not good for much besides parties and women."

Did I say that? "Henry, I—" My own pain is still raw and oozing, but I can't ignore his. "I'm sorry if I made you feel worthless. That was never my intention."

"Don't worry." He sticks a piece of spearmint gum in his mouth. "I have really thick skin."

My lips part, and a sharp, ugly mass rises in my chest. "Please don't say that," I whisper.

"Hey, I didn't mean it." He brushes his fingers against my cheek. His touch tears through my body like a freight train, igniting all of the desires I've been forcing down. "You're the only one who has ever believed in me. That means the bloody world to me."

I don't tell him it's not true, that plenty of people would sacrifice everything for him. Despite my determination to rip him from my heart, I soak up his words like dry ground soaks up rain.

"I've seen the way you are with people, with Mrs. Schumann. There is good inside you, even if you try to hide it," I say.

He turns the key in the ignition. "Sometimes you have to hide who you are to get what you want." Pulling out of the car park, he steers us into the dark night.

"Is that why you made me fall in love with you? So you could throw it in my face?" The words come out wobbly.

When Henry speaks again, his voice is tight. "Is that actually what you think? That I intended for you to fall in love with me?"

My fingers twist and untwist in my lap. I can't bear to look at him. "Why wouldn't I think that, after everything?"

"I would never wish that upon anyone."

Cold air rushes into my open mouth with each breath I take, but I can't make the proper nerves work to shut it. "Do you actually think that little of yourself? Or are you scared of what would happen if you let someone love you?"

"I'm terrified, C. Fucking terrified."

29

"Someone Like You" - Adele

H ENRY'S WORDS HANG SUSPENDED in the silence of the car. *I'm terrified, C.* The only sound is the soft rush of the warm air pumping through the vents.

"Is love really that scary?" I finally say, matching the car's hushed tones.

"You wouldn't understand."

"Oh, because I'm a naive child who doesn't know what it is to love someone?"

"That's not what I meant, and you know it."

"Actually, I have no idea what you mean. You just told me that you hide who you really are to manipulate people."

He reaches for my hand on the console between us. "Celia—"

I pull back. "How am I ever supposed to trust you again?"

"I'm still the same person I was."

"I *loved* you!"

He smacks the steering wheel. "Damn it, C. You think I don't know that?"

"You destroyed me."

Henry slows the car and pulls over to the side of the road. I have no idea what he's planning to do, and my heart mashes the accelerator to the floor of my chest as he turns toward me.

"No, baby, I didn't. You're too strong for that."

His calling me "baby" creates a hiccup in my veins. But it doesn't erase the blinding anger I feel toward him right now. "You have no idea what it did to me. You weren't *there*."

He jabs his fingers into his hair, causing it to stand up at weird angles. "I won't insult you by making excuses."

"How comforting."

"But I *am* sorry."

"Why did you tell them to stop taking care of the Sunken Garden?"

He turns to me with a frown. "How do you know about that?"

"Just answer the question."

It takes him a minute to formulate his response. "That was our spot. And after . . . everything, I couldn't stand the idea of anyone touching it."

It's not what I'm expecting, and I'm not sure what the appropriate reaction is.

"I'm sorry, C. Truly."

I rest my head against the cool windowpane. "Take me home, Henry." Nothing he says can take away the pain. Nothing can erase the past. Nothing can change the future.

We are damaged and broken and beyond redemption. But how do you unspool someone from your heart when they're the very thread holding it together?

I close my eyes, and I'm back there again.

It's one of those glorious days of summer, the kind you only get a handful of a year and that you have to grab with both hands before it's gone. Henry's sprawled in the grass, his feet bare and kicked up behind him, reading aloud from Wuthering Heights, *our latest book. I'm sitting a few feet away, obediently wearing the sunhat my mother insists upon.* The sun is the enemy, Celia. It will not hesitate to ruin your skin.

The Sunken Garden becomes a realm of its own on days like this, everything a little more vibrant, a little more immortal. The whole thing is so sweet it nearly hurts your teeth to think about. The fact that it mirrors the way I feel on the inside is just another coating of bliss on the package.

"Cathy and Heathcliff remind me of us," I say, stripping the rose in my hand of its petals.

"Because I'm a dark-skinned gypsy boy your father brought home?" Henry teases.

"No, stupid." I toss the naked stem at him. "Because they were best friends." I finish the sentence in my head: who fell in love. *We haven't said it to each other yet, but it's there in the way he looks at me, the way I catch him smiling when he thinks I'm not looking.*

"My second guess was going to be because you're an undisciplined hoyden who screams to get her way."

"I hate you."

"You love me."

My entire body freezes. I should do something, say something, but I'm immobile, held in place by invisible chains.

He doesn't even notice, just picks up the book and starts reading again, giving Edgar Linton a nasal voice that would normally have me convulsing in giggles if my stomach wasn't hanging out in my throat right now.

Henry's been inching into my heart more every year, and now he's become my whole world. I have other friends, of course, but it's so much easier with him, the way ordering the same dish at a restaurant is easier than trying something new. I know what to expect with him, and I don't need to fake interest in celebrity gossip or obsess over my latest blowout to feel seen.

Just last week, I gave him a leather wallet for his seventeenth birthday, after months of trying to find the perfect gift. He said it was the best thing he's ever received. I don't even care if it's true or not, because in that moment, it was exactly what I needed to hear.

"You okay?" he asks, looking up from the book. His eyes are pools of melted chocolate in the sunshine, and I could lose myself in them.

"I'm fine," I manage. "Why?"

"You just let me read uninterrupted for five minutes. You're not running a fever, are you?"

I pull the hat from my head and whack him with it. "Why are you so horrible?"

"The question of the year."

We've started calling each other almost nightly. My mum doesn't know, and I intend to keep it that way. She's orchestrated every day I've spent with him, but this feels like it's our own, the only thing we still have control over.

But lately, that control seems to be slipping through my fingers whenever I'm with him. He's been more quiet and withdrawn, and I wonder if it's for the same reason that I've been feeling shy around him, which I never have before.

"Wanna go find something to eat?" he says.

"Do you make all your decisions with your stomach?"

"Duh. It's more fun than making them with your head." He stands and extends his hand.

As I take it and allow him to pull me up, he steps closer. My heart cartwheels around my rib cage as he lifts his fingers to my hair. When did touching him start to feel like touching live wires? He removes his hand and holds up a blade of grass, smiling broadly.

My mouth is full of sand as I look up at him, my heart having given up the gymnastics to go banging around in my chest like it's in a marching band. It's the perfect time to tell him. He doesn't have the courage to go first, so I'll be the brave one this time. I imagine his reaction, the way his face will soften, how he'll take me in his arms and kiss me the way I've been imagining for the past three months. We'll keep our plans secret for a while, away from the prying hands of my mother. But someday . . .

No matter how many versions of the future I spin, there isn't one that doesn't contain him. It will be the best fairy tale.

I take a deep breath, hoping it will steady my nerves. It doesn't. "I—I have something to tell you." My voice sounds small, like a child's. I need it to sound older, more mature.

Henry watches me, his eyes growing darker as a shadow crosses over them.

"I'm in love with you," I blurt out, relieved to have the words off my tongue, where they've been searing the skin right off. The hard part is over.

But he doesn't look happy. In fact, he looks upset. Did he want to say it first after all?

"You can't love me," he says quietly.

My heart skydives from ten thousand feet. "But I do."

"Then find a way to stop."

"What the hell, Henry? You can't just stop loving someone."

"You need to try."

"It doesn't work like that." Hysteria is threading its way through my voice. "It's not something I can just shut off. Besides, I don't want to."

"You're young. You'll get over it."

"Excuse me?" I take a step back as if he's slapped me. I think I might actually prefer it if he had. "Because I'm young, I must not know what love is?"

He looks truly miserable, as if I've just put him into the worse situation imaginable. I had no idea my love could be so off-putting to anyone, especially not to him.

"Celia, you know how it is. We make fun of girls who think they're in love at fifteen."

I shake my head. "It's different for us."

"No, it's not."

"You let me think we had a future together."

"That was your mother, not me."

My mouth falls open. "I don't believe this. You told me I was the only girl for you. You—"

"I meant as a friend."

His voice is an ice pick to my heart, and I fight the confusion swirling through my head. For a second, I think I'm trapped in a nightmare, but the sun on my face is too warm, too real.

"Fine," I tell him. "We'll just stay friends." Even as I say it, I'm battling my inner critic, who says there's no way I can be friends with him after this. But if there's even a chance he'll change his mind, I have to try. I love this boy so much, I would walk across hell if it meant we could be together.

"I don't think that's a possibility either."

For a second, I'm afraid I've said the words out loud, but then I realize what he's referring to.

"You're saying you don't want to be my friend anymore?"

"I'm saying I think we're both too old for this kind of relationship."

He's breaking up with me, and we're not even together.

"Goodbye, Celia."

And just like that, he walks away. Not a backward glance, not a hesitation in his step. Just gone. Out of the garden and out of my life, taking my heart and my dreams and my future with him.

Smashing the fairy tale under his heels as he goes.

I can still remember the bitterness on my tongue as he walked away, that acrid flavor of heartbreak. I found *Wuthering Heights* discarded in the grass where he'd been lying. I picked it up and threw it into the fountain at the center of the garden. The splash it made as it hit the water did nothing to soothe the inferno raging in my chest.

I'm not proud of how I spiraled after that. I would sleep all day to forget, then wrestle with insomnia at night. My appetite fled town, and I dropped five pounds in just over a week. My mother was worried, but it didn't last long, because a bigger issue arose. Two weeks after Henry minced my heart into tiny little pieces, my father was diagnosed with a rapidly growing brain tumor. There was no cure.

Henry was the only person I could imagine talking to about it. He'd ignored all of my texts up to that point, but I thought he would want to know that my dad was dying.

When I rang him, a girl answered. She told me Henry was in the shower, but she'd tell him I called when he got out. I told her not to bother.

Six months later, my father was gone, and Henry had become the world's favorite playboy.

Henry pulls into the palace garage. We didn't speak the rest of the way home, and the silence is tight and thick. Releasing my seat belt, I reach for my purse in the back. He stops me with a hand on my arm, and my breath snags in my throat, clawing but unable to get out.

"C, wait a second." Eros himself couldn't sound more alluring.

Frozen by Henry's intoxicating presence, so close I can nearly inhale him, I can't do anything but breathe and hope he doesn't require me to speak.

"I'm truly sorry for all the times I've hurt you. I know it doesn't excuse anything, but for what it's worth, I regret each and every one," he says, his voice barely above a whisper.

He's right. It doesn't make it better, but a small part of me appreciates the effort anyway.

Lifting my chin with his electrifying fingers, he forces my gaze away from the belt buckle and into his eyes. "Regardless of what I've said or done, you are the best thing that's ever happened to me."

The pull is there. I want to tell him. Tell him that nothing has changed, that I love him more now than I ever did. That a young girl's love is nothing compared to a grown woman's.

But that would only give him the ammo he needs to shatter what's left of my heart. I can't do it. I will never put myself at his mercy again.

So instead I say, "If that's true, you'll let me go."

His eyes grow wounded. "Is that really what you want?"

It's a trap—I know it is—but I falter. For three agonizing seconds, I contemplate what would happen if I told him what I really want. But reality catches up with me, breathless, to remind me that this isn't a fairy tale. There will be no happily ever after in our story.

"Yes. I need you to let go."

"If that's what you want."

"It is," I say, but I don't make a move to get out of the car. Once I leave, it will be over, and I just want to soak up his presence a little longer.

I meet his eyes, as black as the night we just came through, and I feel him rooting around in my soul. "I can't breathe when you look at me like that," I whisper.

"I don't know how else to look at you."

And I don't know how to stop loving you.

30

"The Way I Loved You" - Taylor Swift

I'M IN MY OFFICE finishing up for the day while Maisie updates me on my plans for tomorrow. After Henry and I returned from our trip to see Mrs. Schumann, Maisie confirmed my suspicions that Henry had orchestrated her absence. I didn't mention it to him, because I've discovered it's best for my mental health to avoid him altogether.

Maisie opens the door for a footman, who sets a giant arrangement of white hydrangeas on my desk. It's been a long time since I've seen a bouquet that wasn't a palace-sanctioned decoration. My stomach and heart do this choreographed dance where one sinks while the other skips. I pull the card out with trepidation.

It simply says, *A car will be waiting at 7:00. Wear the long green dress, the one that matches your eyes.*

Apparently, he's back to his cat-and-mouse games.

I toss the note in the trash. "You can have the flowers," I tell Maisie before leaving the office.

Two can play this game, and I've been the mouse for long enough.

I'm reviewing the mission statement of a charity I'm considering patronizing when a text message alert goes off. It takes me a few minutes to locate my phone—still in my purse—and when I do, I'm surprised to see it's from Beck.

> **Beck**: I can't wait to see you tonight. xx

Where am I going to see Beck tonight? I quickly open my calendar app, but the only thing Maisie has scheduled for the rest of the day is dinner in the State Dining Room. I'm about to text back when I remember the flowers. They must have been from Beck, not Henry.

I type out a quick reply.

> **Me**: Me neither! 7:00 right? x

> **Beck**: I'll be there. xx

He must have moved mountains to get a flower delivery into the palace and have a car ordered. If he is willing to go to those kinds of lengths to salvage what remains of our relationship, so am I.

The narrow band of disappointment tightening around my chest can go bugger off.

I ring for Daphne and go to my closet to pull out the dress. I know exactly which one he means, but I'm surprised he remembers it. It's one of my favorites, a draping emerald-green number with thin straps that accent my shoulders and lengthen my neck. Once my hair and makeup are done to perfection, thanks to Daphne's expert hands, I slip into my heels and choose an evening bag.

Tonight is for second chances, and Henry is banned from my thoughts.

I wind my way through the rooms of the palace, lifting the hem of my dress, and realize my heart feels a little lighter. As I walk through the doorway into the Blue Salon, I smack into a hard body coming from the other direction. I cradle my nose as pain shoots through it. I don't even need to look up to know who it is. I'd recognize his scent anywhere.

Henry grabs my arms to stabilize me and pulls back to see my face. "My god, are you okay? I'm so sorry."

I nod, still rubbing my nose. Tears spring to my eyes, the effect of slamming my nose into the brick wall that is Henry's chest. The thrill coursing through my veins, on the other hand, has nothing to do with that and everything to do with seeing him again.

I am a lunatic. A lunatic and an addict.

"You look incredible," he says. "Going somewhere?"

"I have a date with Beck. He's surprising me."

Henry's smile is instantaneous and appears genuine. "Have fun."

"I'm sure we will."

He moves aside so I can pass, but as I do, he stops me with a hand on my bare arm, his touch lighting my skin on fire, the flames running down my entire body. I turn back.

"You look stunning. That dress brings out the color of your eyes."

"Thank you," I say.

"He's a lucky man."

My destination is a private yacht, which is currently docked but will be setting off as soon as I'm on board. As I walk up the pier, I work diligently to keep my jaw from dropping. I'm not entirely successful. How did Beck do all of this?

The upper deck glows with thousands of twinkle lights, dancing like stars against the black night and sea. Bouquets of hydrangeas line the perimeter of the deck, their honey-vanilla scent greeting me like an old friend. Waves lap softly at the side of the boat, and a string quartet performs a sweet Mozart melody on the bow.

I've stepped into another universe, one in which sadness is not possible.

Beck stands waiting for me with that endearing smile I love stretched across his face. He's holding a bouquet of roses. The red of their petals is like blood against the white of the hydrangeas.

"This is absolutely spectacular," I say as he brings me into the security of his arms, warm and safe. It's the polar opposite of Henry's electric touch.

"As spectacular as you are." After a minute, he pulls back. "I'm really sorry for ending things like I did. Truly. I realized the second you left I'd made a mistake, but it was too late."

It wasn't too late, then or now, but I just shush him and rise on tiptoes to kiss his mouth. There are no fireworks, but that isn't an indication of a healthy relationship anyway.

The kiss ends, and Beck smiles. "You look beautiful. Come on, let's sit down."

As we set sail, a server pours us each a glass of champagne and introduces the menu for the evening. No detail has been overlooked. Soft music drifts across the deck, and blankets are ready should the evening grow chilly on the water. There's a different wine accompanying each course, and to end the meal, my favorite dessert, red velvet cake, is served with coffee.

It's perfect in every way.

"Thank you so much for all of this. I still can't believe it." I take one last bite of cake and look around. The lights are reflecting in the water around us, creating an unearthly feeling. It's like we're in our own personal universe out here. "You truly thought of everything."

Beck's smile begins to slip at my words as confusion crosses his face. "What do you mean?"

"This." I motion around us. "The boat, the dinner, the privacy. It's exactly what I needed. You know me well."

His smile disappears completely. "I didn't set this up," he says tightly. "I thought this was your way of saying you forgive me."

"What? No, I didn't do this." I set down my fork and shake my head. "I received flowers and a card telling me a car would pick me up. I didn't even know where I was going."

"I got an email from you telling me to be on board at seven. You're telling me you know nothing about that?"

A searing ache rips from my chest down into my stomach. My first instinct *was* right. There's only one person in the world with the audacity to tell me what to wear on a date he wouldn't even be on himself. Even though he's let me go, I can't escape him.

"No." I swallow. "It wasn't me."

"Then who was it?"

I bite the side of my mouth, considering whether the truth is more dangerous than a lie. "It must have been Henry."

"Why?" Beck spits out the word like it's a bullet.

I shake my head slowly. "I don't know."

"You told me there was nothing going on between you two." His voice has grown as hard and cold as steel.

"There isn't. If there was, he'd be here instead of you."

"Forgive me for not feeling reassured by that explanation."

I stare at the bubbles in my champagne. They're winking at me, daring me to placate him with more excuses and explanations. But I hate lying.

Beck shifts in his chair, growing irritated and impatient. As my eyes slowly rise to meet his, realization steals over me the way the sun breaks the horizon at dawn.

I would rather spend the rest of my life pining for Henry and what we could have had than married to a man I'm constantly comparing to him. I can't imagine anything worse than a life of second-rate happiness and first-rate disappointment.

It will be the second gut-punch I deliver to Beck, but I owe him the truth. "I'm so sorry, Beck, but I can't do this anymore."

The annoyance drops from his face, replaced by pain. "Can't do what?"

I lay my napkin onto the table and walk over to the railing, the words mired in my throat, refusing to come out. The boat sluices through the inky waters, a foaming spray trailing in its wake. The evening is beautiful and perfect in every way but one.

The wrong man is sharing it with me.

I feel rather than hear Beck join me. He pauses a few feet away waiting for me to turn around and give him an answer, to assure him everything is fine between us. How can I do this to him? His only crime is falling in love with someone who doesn't deserve him.

"I love you, but I'm not sure that's enough anymore." I take the coward's way out and keep looking out at the sea. I can't face him, can't see the disappointment and sorrow etched in his eyes.

"Love isn't enough? What else do you want?"

How can I explain to someone else what I don't even understand myself?

"Can you not even look at me anymore?" he says, raw pain sluicing through his voice.

I slowly turn, because the truth is, I do love him. He's exactly the kind of man I envisioned myself marrying: honest, loyal, kind. He doesn't deserve any of this. "I'm so sorry. I never wanted to hurt you."

He laughs without humor and presses his fingers into his eye sockets. "People always say that, don't they? 'I never wanted to hurt you,' as if that somehow makes it okay that they did."

"I don't know what else you want me to say." A strong breeze lifts from the water and blows around us, raising the flesh on my arms. I rub at it with hands that are just as cold.

"How about something along the lines of, 'I love you and want to spend the rest of my life with you'?"

"Even if I can't?"

Beck shoves his hands into the pockets of his trousers. "This isn't the way I saw my life playing out either. Sneaking around, pretending I'm not in love with the woman who's going to be my queen. Always living in the shadows, being second rate, second best. But if it means being with you, in any capacity, I'm willing to do it."

My throat swollen with tears, I say, "You deserve to be with someone who can give you their whole heart."

"You expect me to believe this is all for my benefit? I'm not good at being alone, Celia. I've spent most of my life figuring it out by myself, and I'm ready to do it with someone else. Now you're saying I should be grateful to you for saving me from a life of misery?"

"Of course not. I just meant that you deserve more than I can give you."

He makes a sound of disgust and shakes his head. "It's because of him, isn't it?"

"No," I say automatically, even though we both know it's a lie.

"I'll never be him. I don't *want* to be him, even if it costs me you."

The words sting, although I don't think that was his intention. "I'm not asking you to change. Or to understand."

"You'll regret this someday."

I hope he's wrong. But I'm scared he's right.

The worst part about breaking up on board a yacht is that you have to wait until the boat is docked before you can get off. I spoke to the captain after Beck walked away, and he agreed to turn us around but said it would be an hour before we get back to land.

As I wait, I curl up on one of the sofas arranged on the deck and wrap one of the soft cashmere throws around my bare shoulders. Regret mingles with the salty air, chapping my cheeks and leaving a tang on my lips.

Losing Beck is as different from losing Henry as fire is from water. It is frustration itself, a plan I worked for years to execute falling through at the last minute. Of course I love him, but it's our compatibility, our once-mutual desires and goals, that make it so hard to watch him go. Have I just pushed away the best thing that's ever happened to me?

Losing Henry, on the other hand, was like losing a piece of myself. It doesn't matter that he drives me crazy. I need his humor and that belly-clenching laugh. I need the way he pushes me to my limits, the way he won't put up with my bullshit. I need the way he can take one look at my face and read everything I'm too afraid to say.

It should be easier than this to get over someone who so clearly doesn't want to be with you.

31

"When You're Gone" - Shawn Mendes

A s I'm getting ready for bed after my failed date with Beck, strains of music float from Henry's room. I haven't heard him playing since that horrible night he threw me out.

The sound is mesmerizing, as is the knowledge that he's on the other side of the connecting door, and I walk over and rest my head against it to hear better. I picture him sitting there, completely immersed in the sounds echoing around him, losing himself in the melody. What I wouldn't give to watch him play again.

After a while, the notes die away, and all is quiet again. The only sound is the crazy pounding of my heart, knowing Henry's so close and wanting to see him more than anything. I should at least thank him for setting up such a beautiful evening, right? He doesn't need to know it was the catalyst for the end of Beck's and my already-fragile relationship.

Knowing I'll talk myself out of it if I wait any longer, I knock on the door. What if he doesn't answer? Or worse, what if he tells me to go away? I squeeze my eyes shut. Regret is already creeping in. I should've just gone to bed. What am I doing? The man clearly doesn't want to see me, but like the addict I am, I can't stay away.

I've given up and am heading back to my bedroom when he finally opens the door. Surprised and slightly horrified, I turn around. Cotton pajama pants hang from his hips, and he's tugging a Harvard T-shirt down over his washboard abdomen. "You knocked?"

"I heard you playing," I say as nonchalantly as possible. "It was beautiful."

He crosses his arms and leans against the door jamb. The movement causes the muscles in his shoulders to ripple. I drag my reluctant eyes away.

"I thought you had a date tonight," he says.

"I did. The setup was gorgeous." I take a few steps closer. "Thank you."

His broad forehead crinkles. "For what?"

"For all of it. The red velvet was exceptional."

He studies me for a few moments, then drops his gaze to the floor, rubbing his bare toe back and forth on the carpet. "How'd you know it was me?"

"For starters, Beck greeted me with a dozen roses."

"He doesn't know you hate roses?"

"I've never had the heart to tell him. He loves to give them." I say, shrugging.

"Hydrangeas suit you better."

"The boat was covered in them." I smirk, then whisper, "You may have shown your hand a little." I should be sad, but all I can think is that this must be what it feels like to be on cocaine. Euphoria surges through my blood, all from being this close to him.

Henry shoves his hands into the pockets of his blue pajama pants. "How was I supposed to know he thought you liked roses? Hydrangeas have always been your favorite. I thought this was common knowledge."

"I thought it was you at the beginning, when they brought them to my office with the card. But then he texted me, and I assumed . . ." I bite my lip. "Or maybe I just was hoping."

"I just wanted you to have a good time."

"It was incredible." I should tell him about Beck, but the words lodge in my throat, thick as peanut butter. If I tell him, he might think it had something to do with him, and I can't let him know it did. "I should've known as soon as you made that comment in the hall about my dress."

"You look like a goddess in that dress," he murmurs, his eyes darkening.

His voice, his look, his nearness . . . We're heading into the danger zone.

Henry must sense it too, because he clears his throat and glances away. "You were welcome to one of the state rooms. The boat was yours for the whole night."

I cough in surprise. "I didn't feel like sleeping on the water."

He nods as though it's the most reasonable thing in the world. "Well, I'm glad you were happy. That's all I wanted. It's all I've ever wanted."

I inhale sharply. His eyes are piercing mine again, stealing all coherent thoughts from my mind. How does he do that? I swallow and nod like an idiot.

"Hey, now that you're here, there's something I want to show you." He leaves me at the door and comes back a minute later with a big black book in his hands.

"Is that what I think it is?" I say.

"If you think it's the employment records from 1837, then yes." A starburst of wrinkles spreads from the corners of his eyes as he smiles. Flipping the book open, he moves so I can see over his arm. He points to an entry dated 18 May, 1837.

Mary Hopkins, kitchen maid
Walter McManus, footman
Regina Campbell, housemaid

"What am I looking at?" I ask.

"I took pictures of the logbook back at the Historical Society. Walter McManus was one of the passengers on board *The Caledonia* with Philip Anderson."

"And you think . . . ?"

He closes the book and sets it down on the table nearby. "I think Walter McManus was the man who actually died. Philip saw the opportunity and slipped his own watch into the man's pocket, then came ashore with a new name: Walter McManus, footman at the palace."

"It's still just a theory."

"I know. But a plausible one."

I look past Henry and notice a suitcase open on the sofa in his sitting room. "You're leaving?"

"I have some business in England."

Clearing the emotion from my voice, I say, "When do you go?"

"Tomorrow morning. My plane leaves at nine."

"Have a safe trip."

He opens his mouth as if he's going to say something. Instead, he pulls me into a hug. "Thank you," he says into my hair, his arms wrapped tightly around my back.

I wrap my own around his torso, relishing the feeling of his firm chest under my cheek. The beat of his heart is steady and solid, unwavering. Has he always had the power to shatter me and put me back together more beautiful than he found me?

We stand that way for . . . a minute? Five? I don't know. Time seems to halt. Now that Henry's agreed to let me go, it takes everything in me to let him go.

"Goodbye, C." I miss him as soon as he steps back. Why does it feel like he's saying goodbye forever?

"When will you be back?"

He runs his fingers through his hair. "It depends on how things go. I should know within a few days." His smile causes a muscle near my hip bone to ping. "Don't miss me too much."

If only that were possible. As he closes the door, I get a scary sense of foreboding. He's up to something, and this time I don't think I'm going to like it.

32

"Angels Like You" - Miley Cyrus

THE PALACE IS ABUZZ with that predinner hum I'm slowly growing accustomed to. Staff members halt their various tasks to bow their heads as I pass, something I hardly notice anymore. While I'm certainly more comfortable with the routines of the royal household now and no longer get lost on my way to the dining room, I seriously doubt whether these cold rooms will ever feel like home.

In exchange for becoming a household name and my picture someday being featured on banknotes and stamps, I have given up the chance to ever feel truly at home again.

My heels click a rapid staccato on the tiled floors, occasionally muffled by carpets as I pass through salons and drawing rooms, their drapes now closed against the glow of the setting sun. Dinner will be served in an hour, and Henry will not be present. The reminder stings, sharp and visceral.

I'm walking through the Blue Salon, and distracted as I am by my thoughts, I'm not sure I would have noticed the figures were it not for the whimper. They're huddled together in a corner not yet lit by the lamps.

I stop, the rhythm of my steps coming to an abrupt halt. The king is seated on the floor, a position I've never seen him in, and Argos's chocolate-colored head lies in his lap. William is stroking his velvety ears and murmuring in tones so low I can't make out the words.

If he notices my presence, he doesn't acknowledge it, just keeps speaking in a soothing voice to his dog, who isn't doing well at all. Without a thought to what I'm doing, I move closer. Argos doesn't lift his head, but his eyes flicker toward me. I see pain reflected there. I kneel down and place my hand on his forehead.

"The vet said he won't last through the night," the king mumbles.

"I'm so sorry," I say, settling myself down beside Argos. "Is there anything we can do to make him more comfortable?"

William looks at me, and with a start, I recognize Henry's dark eyes in his. Gone is their usual hard glint; instead, they're overflowing with sorrow. My heart softens ever so slightly.

"Won't be much longer now. A stronger person would've had him put to sleep, but I didn't want him dying on an operating table. This is his home."

I nod. "Do you mind if I stay?"

William's only answer is a grunt, which I take as an invitation. Stroking the soft fur between his eyes, I will Argos to leave this world peacefully and without pain. He just looks at me, his wet eyes luminous and beseeching. Poor baby. I press a kiss to his nose. It's cold.

I study the king covertly, keeping my head down. He's slumped over on the floor, his back to the wall, his legs splayed in both directions. It can't be comfortable, but by all appearances, he's been here for a while. His suit is wrinkled and he's kicked off his shoes, leaving stockinged feet, the sight of which feels strangely intimate.

I want to hate him. I do hate him for what he did to Henry. But at the same time, my heart breaks for him. Right now he isn't a harsh and imposing king or a cold and molesting father. He's a man watching his dog die, and it's killing him.

"I got him when he was a pup," he says.

I feign a stretch to cover my startle reflex at the sound of his voice. "How old is he?"

"Fourteen." William runs a hand over his face in a gesture that reminds me so much of Henry my heart gives a tiny jolt.

I decide to just let him talk. What is there to say, anyway?

"He followed me everywhere I went. Everyone thought I was ridiculous for getting a dog, but I had one when I was young. Best part of my life." He strokes Argos's head, his fingers nearly colliding with mine. I move my hand to the dog's belly. "When I lost that dog, I was a mess. My mother didn't know what to do with me. Offered to get me another one, but I refused. Another dog can't take the place of the one you love, you know?" He looks at me, and I nod, not sure what else there is to do.

"You ever have a dog?" he asks.

"My mum's allergic. I've always wanted one, though."

William grunts—in approval, I guess. It's hard to know.

"They're like people," I say softly. "Once they're in our hearts, it's impossible to root them out."

"They're better than people. Dogs don't hurt you." His words hang in the air, a dark, heavy fog swirling around us.

"Not everyone means to hurt others," I say.

"But some do." The king's jaw clenches tightly. I wonder if he's including himself in that quantification. "My father told me I deserved to watch my dog die if I was going to act like a sissy about it. He'd love seeing me like this." His upper lip pulls into a sneer. "A grown man—the fucking king—crying over a dog," he says, swiping at his nose.

"Sometimes it takes more strength to show emotion than to hide it." I pause to contemplate the words before I ask, "Does Henry know? About Argos?"

William snorts his derision. "He doesn't care about him."

I feel deep trenches forming in my brow as I say, "He loves this dog. He would want to know."

"Nothing he can do about it."

"All the same, I'd like to tell him, if you don't mind."

"Suit yourself."

I pull my phone from my bag to send Henry a text. I'm searching through my contacts before I remember that I deleted his number weeks ago.

I'll message him on Instagram. I open the app, and Bea's story icon winks at me with its colorful ring. I realize I haven't seen her for the past two days. I click on it and immediately regret it.

A photo fills my screen, evidently taken at a club, based on the lights and closely pressed bodies in the background. Henry's and Beatrice's faces beam at me, cheeks pressed together, eyes bright from what was likely an insane number of cocktails. God, they look so good together, with their perfect symmetry and their flawless skin.

I tap to the next photo, taken right after the first. They're in the same position, but this time Bea's planting a saucy kiss on Henry's cheek, her arm wrapped possessively around his shoulders. He's grinning.

I toss the phone back into my bag. Let Henry find out about Argos himself.

No wonder the bastard had to jet off to London. He promised me he'd leave Bea alone, so he couldn't very well mess around with her under my nose here in Wesbourne.

But her betrayal hurts even more. Technically, Henry doesn't owe me anything, but Bea is my *sister*. Blood is supposed to be thicker than water.

If William notices the change in my demeanor, he doesn't mention it. We sit there in silence, stroking Argos, our hearts breaking in tandem. His for the loss of his dog, mine for the loss of everything I hold dear.

33

"Let Her Go" - Passenger

RAIN IS BEATING AGAINST the windows of my suite like a snare drum, sunlight a hazy memory. I stayed with William last night until Argos died, about an hour after I arrived. We were both late to dinner, and neither of us ate much, both of our appetites having fled in the face of heartbreak.

I haven't heard from Bea, even though she can see that I viewed her story. She and Henry will be home soon, and I'll have to face them both, but dwelling on that makes a knot form in my stomach. I'm better off trying to forget about it.

"That'll be all. Thanks, Daphne," I say. She's arranged my hair into a loose chignon for my speech this afternoon at one of the secondary schools in the city. Until then, I have several hours' worth of agendas to review, phone calls to return, and emails to respond to.

I'm slipping my phone into my bag when it rings. It's Maisie.

"Your solicitor just called. He said it's urgent."

"How urgent? Does he want me to call him back?"

"Urgent, as in he's already on his way."

I catch a glimpse of my frown in the mirror. Hearing my mother's voice in my head harping about premature wrinkles, I force my face back into a neutral position. "Okay. I'm headed down now."

I tell my stampeding heart there's nothing to worry about. More than likely, he just has some simple paperwork for me to fill out and this will all be resolved in a few minutes.

Mr. Weston has represented my family since before my birth, having known my father since childhood. I could have used one of the solicitors on staff at the palace, but it seemed the wiser option to use someone from outside.

He's waiting in the antechamber outside my office when I arrive. He greets me with a formal bow at the waist. "Good morning, Your Royal Highness."

"Hello, Mr. Weston. Sorry to keep you waiting." I lead the way inside and set my bag down.

Rather than taking a seat behind my desk, I move to the grouping of armchairs clustered near the fireplace. Mr. Weston places his briefcase beside one of them and waits for me to sit. I try to determine from his face whether I should be concerned, but he gives nothing away. He's one of those men who could be anywhere between sixty and eighty, with a ring of salt-and-pepper fringe surrounding an otherwise bald head.

"How can I help you, Mr. Weston?"

"Actually, ma'am, I'm here to help you."

My eyebrows fly up of their own accord. "I beg your pardon? I was told you needed to see me about something urgent."

He chuckles briefly. "I have good news." Lifting his case onto his lap, he unlocks it and pulls out a file. He also removes a pair of reading glasses and slides them onto his nose. "I was told you've been very anxious to settle this matter."

Is it possible he has me mixed up with another client?

He hands me the file. "It's all in there. Read it over, and then we can move on to the signatures. Your husband has already signed."

As I take the papers from his outstretched hand, trepidation creeps into my chest and lays a ginormous egg there. Mr. Weston's confidence that I'll be eager about this only makes me more nervous to see what's inside.

I flip open the cover. An official document greets me, with the words *In the High Court of Justice, Principal Registry of the Family Division* at the top. The names listed are mine and Henry's, followed by the date of our wedding. An official seal is located in the right corner.

I scan the rest of the pages. This is it, then. The annulment papers I thought were my golden ticket. Henry must have had them drawn up before he left. He's so eager to get rid of me that he couldn't even tell me face-to-face. Not that I was exactly planning to tell him either.

"I don't understand," I say. "The whole purpose of our marriage was so we could jointly ascend the throne."

"Yes, ma'am, that's correct. But I understand Henry found evidence that proves you are the rightful ruler of Wesbourne. You will ascend the throne by yourself in just a few weeks. I'm here to help you arrange everything."

"I'm sorry." I lift a hand to my brow, urging it to soften. "This is all a bit of a shock. What evidence did you say Henry found?"

"Ah, yes. I believe everything you need is in here." Mr. Weston hands me another large envelope, this one less official looking. "He was adamant that you get this."

I slip the flap open and remove the contents. There's a folded piece of linen stationery and a small face-down card inside. On the back, someone has scribbled *My Dearest Philip, 1838.* I turn it over and gasp.

It's a painting of a man in his early twenties with dark eyes and dark hair, a defined jaw, and a strong nose. He's dressed as a member of the working class, which is surprising, as the lower classes often couldn't afford them. Helena must have paid for it herself.

But that isn't the most shocking thing. Most startling of all, startling enough that my blood is thrumming in my ears, is the fact that Henry's face is staring up at me from the picture. There are differences, of course, mostly the result of the passage of time and changes in cultural customs. But there is no mistaking the similarities. Philip is Henry's doppelgänger.

"Have you seen this?" I ask Mr. Weston.

He shakes his head, and I hand him the pocket-size painting. His bushy brows rise to the height of his now-extinct hairline. "Well, there's no disputing that, is there?" He passes it back.

"I don't think so," I say absently, my mind still processing everything. My eyes alight on the piece of paper still in my lap. I can't decide if I'm eager to see what it says or dreading what I'll find. I fiddle with it for a moment, unsure if I should read it now or force myself to fret over it all day.

Mr. Weston rises to his feet. "Why don't I leave you to collect your thoughts for a bit? I have a few calls to make, and if your secretary doesn't mind me sitting on the sofa out there, I'll wait until you're ready to discuss these matters."

I nod my appreciation and return my attention to Henry's letter as Mr. Weston leaves the room. When I can no longer bear the agony of not knowing, I unfold it.

Celia,

If you're reading this, it means your solicitor has given you the annulment papers and the painting I found of Philip. Crazy, huh? It was in the same dresser we found the letters in. It occurred to me a few days ago that, after finding the letters, we never thought about checking the rest of it for anything else. So I went back, and there it was, wedged in so tightly I didn't think I'd be able to get it out at first.

I tried to make it as easy for you as I could. Mr. Weston will handle everything from here. I'm told the annulment will only take a few days to file, and then we're both free to move on with our lives. I'm sure you and Beck are glad of that. I wish you both the best. Despite what I said before, if you are happy with him, that's all that matters.

Please know that hurting you has never been my intention, although it seems like that's all I ever do anymore. Forgive me, C.

I know you're scared to face this new step alone, but I also know you have what it takes. You're the most powerful woman I know, and if anyone can lead Wesbourne to greatness, it's you. I wish I could be there, but my presence would only complicate things. You don't need that, so I'll be watching from afar.

Make her great for both of us.

Henry

P.S. Please don't worry about me. I'm fine, simply keeping my distance so you can do the right thing. I'm letting you go so you can let go.

I read it several times before oxygen returns to my lungs. It's everything I thought I wanted. I should be elated. Instead I feel like I've been kicked in the ribs.

The fairy tales don't warn you about this. They promise a happily ever after and dashing off into the sunset with your hero. They don't mention hearts bleeding on the floor or heroes who hook up with your sister.

They don't prepare you for the dreams that turn into nightmares.

34

"Rolling in the Deep" - Adele

S WEAT BEADS ON THE back of my neck, where the sun pours buckets of heat onto it. I'm dressed in a linen shift dress, but even the loose, light fabric does little to protect against the sun in all of its glory, baking us with these record-breaking temps.

Adelaide squats next to me at the perimeter of the garden bed, similarly dressed and just as drenched in sweat as I am. She digs another hole, about twelve inches deep, with the trowel before tossing it aside and swiping a gloved hand across her brow, leaving a brown smudge in its wake. "Are you sure we're still in Wesbourne? Feels more like the Sahara."

"Go sit in the shade." I motion toward the bench under the oak trees. "I'll finish up here."

She cocks an eyebrow at me. "I told you I'd help, and that's what I'm doing."

In my defense, when I called her to ask her advice on planting hydrangeas, I thought she'd give me a few tips over the phone, and that would be that. Instead, she told me she'd be right over and has adamantly rejected all of my subtle and not-so-subtle hints that she should take a break ever since.

I roll my eyes in amusement and cover the roots of the plant in the hole with loamy black soil. We're planting a new border around the Sunken Garden. I'm determined to bring it back to its former glory. It seemed like a good way to heal a broken heart at 2 a.m. last night, but in this heat, I'm having second thoughts.

Yesterday, after I regained my composure, Mr. Weston and I discussed the evidence that proves my sole right to the throne. He assured me he would see to it that the right steps were taken. Since King William was already planning to hand his crown to Henry and me in a month's time, and Henry already signed away any right to it himself, he doesn't foresee much delay.

The annulment papers remain untouched in their folder on my desk.

"This was a ridiculous idea," I say.

Adelaide gives me a sharp look. "Talk to me, poppet. You are a bundle of nerves."

"I'm fine. Just hot." The thing with Adelaide is, you can never hide anything from her. No matter how hard I try, she always calls—

"Bullshit."

I look at her and blow out a breath, damp tendrils of hair floating away from my face before drifting back to stick to my sweaty temples once again. "You're too canny for your own good."

"Dear, no one says 'canny.' Not even me, and I'm old."

I shake my head and place another bush in the fresh hole she's just dug. "You just want me to tell you you're not old."

She cocks a brow.

"Which you're not," I add.

"Good girl. Now tell me the real reason we're planting hydrangeas in Satan's boiler room."

I sigh and pinch the bridge of my nose. There's no use denying it, not with her. "I've lost everything."

Adelaide clucks her tongue. "I'm going to presume that's a rhetorical statement."

I pull the gardening gloves from my sweaty hands and drop them to the ground, fumbling for my phone and the photo I took of the painting of Philip. Removing her own gloves, she puts on the reading glasses she wears on a chain around her neck. She takes the phone from me, whispering "good god" as she does. Her eyes flash up to meet mine. "Is this . . . ?"

"Queen Helena's lover."

"He's a dead ringer for our darling prince. I'll admit, I wasn't sure where to put my money." She hands the device back and smirks. "Not that I'd ever bet against you, my dear."

I scoff at her obnoxious lie. Adelaide will put her money on whoever she thinks has the greatest chance of success, relationships be damned.

"I pride myself on my incredible intellect, but even I'm failing to see how this means you've lost everything," she says.

I sigh. "I've been trying to prove my sole right to the throne. But now that the proof is here, I feel . . . sad."

"Well, I'm just an old lady, but I'm going to take a guess and say it has nothing to do with finding proof and everything to do with a deliciously attractive man—who I would most certainly fight you for if I were twenty years—."

"Don't say it." I pull my gloves back on and lift another bush from its container. I break up the root ball before placing it in the hole.

"I can say whatever the hell I want, young lady. Now tell me what the problem is."

My shrug dislodges a cascade of sweat down my back. "He filed for divorce. After finding the picture. And then kissed my sister. Oh, and I broke up with Beck. Again."

"Crikey. I'm impressed you're *planting* flowers. I'd be tearing them out right now."

"I tend to avoid destroying things, with the exception of my future."

"Correct me if I'm wrong, which we both know is unlikely," she says, "but weren't you planning to distract yourself with Beck?"

I lob a clod of dirt back and forth between my hands, waiting until Adelaide has another hole ready for planting. She insisted she be the one to do the digging, saying she has the expertise needed for proper hole depth. Apparently, I can't be trusted to estimate twelve inches.

"I tried to make it work with Beck, but Henry brings me to life in a way I didn't even know was possible. When I'm with him, I feel like I'm waking from a hundred-year-old spell."

"He's your great love."

The chasm in my chest shifts, reminding me of its presence, just in case I get too comfortable. "How do I turn it off?"

She cackles. "Turn off love? Oh honey, that would be like turning off the sun. Which I wish was a possibility at the moment," she mutters as she scoots over to start a new hole.

"Okay, then how do I forget about him? For real this time. Not that nonsense about taking a new lover. I feel like I'm drowning on land."

"Why do you need to forget him?" She stares at me with what looks like a quizzical expression on her face. It might just be the sunlight making her squint in spite of the giant straw hat on her head.

"Haven't you been listening to anything I just said? He filed for *divorce*. He doesn't want me. He's currently hooking up with my sister and probably half of London as we speak." I plop the plant down in the empty hole with more force than necessary.

Adelaide grunts as she struggles to pull a large stone from the earth. I'd offer to help her, but I value my own neck too much to imply she needs assistance.

"If you think for a second he filed for divorce because it's what he wants and not what he thinks you want, you're not as bright as I gave you credit for."

I choose not to be offended by that comment. "Let's be honest. Henry isn't the type to settle down and stay married to one woman for the rest of his life. This annulment works as much in his favor as mine."

She tilts her head and looks at me. "No, not just any woman. But I'd bet my villa in the Mediterranean he'd do it for you."

"That's not very reassuring, considering we're currently sweating enough to fill the Mediterranean."

"Do you really think his filing for annulment had absolutely nothing to do with your plans to do the same?"

"He doesn't know anything about that."

"You're positive?"

My shoulders pull downward in tandem with my mouth. "I can't afford to hope for an alternative."

"Celia, I have never known you to give up so easily without a fight," Adelaide says.

"I don't *want* to fight for Henry." I remove another bush from its pot. "It's humiliating."

"Sometimes the greatest battles are won through humility."

I'm not in the mood for thought-provoking quotes or mind-numbing questions. I need a way to move forward. "He's already rejected me twice. I don't have it in me to try a third time." I hold up my hand to stop her next words. "Please, please, don't say the third time's the charm."

A sardonic smile plays at the edges of her mouth. "I was only going to ask if you're afraid of the challenge or the potential outcome."

"What makes you think I'm afraid?"

"Your body language screams it, dear." She waves her trowel at me.

I force my shoulders to relax back into their normal position and soothe the muscles of my face into an expression that hopefully looks less like I want to murder someone. I throw in a smile for good measure.

Adelaide watches this procedure with scrutiny. "Better. But you still didn't answer my question. Are you scared of approaching Henry or of what he'll say if you do?"

"I know what he'll say."

Tossing her trowel to the ground, she turns to face me. "Celia." She would have made a great headmistress. "Think of the most famous love stories of all time. Cleopatra and Mark Antony. Romeo and Juliet. Heathcliff and Catherine. Rhett Butler and Scarlett O'Hara."

"Common denominator?" I grumble. "They all ended in tragedy."

"Wrong." She wipes her brow with the back of her wrist. "Okay, you're right, but the point is, none of them would have been happy with anyone else. Even your own Helena put her life at risk to be with the man she loved because she knew she couldn't be happy any other way. How many people get to experience a great love? You do. And you're throwing it away." She couldn't sound more irritated if I'd told her this heat is staying for the rest of summer.

"It's a little hard to throw away something you never had in the first place."

She presses her lips into a tight line. "Have you actually told him how you feel? Or did you just assume he could read your mind?"

"I'm pretty sure I did."

"Young lady, did you or did you not tell him you love him?"

Okay, I'm pretty sure I didn't say *those* words, at least not this last time, but they were implied by my active participation in . . . whatever was happening that night. "More or less?" I bite my lip, knowing that answer won't be good enough for her.

"Men need things spelled out, poppet. If you want a chance with Henry, a real chance, you need to tell him exactly how you feel. All of it. Then let him do with it what he will." She scoops out another shovelful of dirt. "There's that done. It's all you, love."

I take her place in front of the hole and bury the last of the hydrangeas. Sweat dribbles into my eyes. "I'm not sure I can give him that kind of power again."

"The power to hurt you? But darling, that's what makes love so magical. It's not worth much if you can't trust enough to risk getting hurt."

"What if he sends me away again?"

Adelaide takes a long drink from her water bottle before responding. "Will you be any worse off than you are now?"

"I imagine I'd survive." Although the jury is still out.

"Sometimes the best experiences in life come from the risks we take and our biggest regrets from the ones we don't."

35

"The One That Got Away"
- Katy Perry

L IGHTNING RIPS THE SKY apart, its jagged shards brilliant against the black night. The accompanying thunder booms loud enough to rattle our dinnerware. A few nervous chuckles sound around the room, everyone waiting for reassurance that the storm will blow over soon.

"Dear me," Lady Templeman says from across the table, the emerald at her neck glinting at me. "I do hope it lets up before we leave. Storms are such a nuisance."

King William snorts. "Not likely. They said it's supposed to hail tonight, golf ball size." He pushes a bite of pudding into his mouth, oblivious to the fear on Lady Templeman's face. The grief over losing Argos still lines his own.

"I do hope the gardener remembered to put the hail netting up," she continues. "I just got an order of roses in from Bulgaria, and they are so susceptible to hail damage, you know. I wonder—"

I tune out the rest of her words, my thoughts on the hydrangeas Adelaide and I planted this morning. The hail will demolish them, and

I didn't have the forethought to put up any protection. A damn rookie mistake.

Another roar of thunder shakes the room, and I push my chair back. "Excuse me, please. Sir. Ma'am." I curtsy in turn to both the king and queen before rushing from the room, not caring about the horrified faces watching my escape.

There won't be time to change, so I'll simply have to put the netting up in my evening gown. I kick off my heels beside the door leading into the gardens, then yank it open only to have it wrenched out of my grasp by the wind. Eager to thrust its greedy fingers inside, it slams the door against the wall, and the resounding bang rivals the thunder in volume.

Using both hands, I pull the door shut behind me and stumble to the gardener's shed. I say a quick prayer that it's unlocked and try the knob. It turns under my hand and, now aware of the wind's tricks, I hold on to it tightly as I step inside.

What does hail netting look like? I scan the contents of the musty room, hedge clippers in all manner of sizes taunting me from the wall, a muddy wheelbarrow stubbornly tipped on end as if refusing to be of assistance. Rolls of mesh are leaning against the back wall, and I have to step over more gardening implements than I've ever seen in my life to get to it.

This has to be it. And if not, it will have to work. I just need something to hold it up. I grab a handful of metal stakes and a mallet before ducking my head and marching back into the storm.

It's stupid really, all of this trouble over a bunch of flowers. But I'll be damned before I let all of Adelaide's and my hard work swirl down the drain. I need at least one thing in my life to go according to plan.

The rain has started by the time I get to the Sunken Garden. It soaks me to the bone and makes the moss-covered steps all the more treacherous. Fortunately, the hail is holding off, but who's to know how long that will last. I'll need to work quickly.

Hampered by my sodden dress, I pick up one of the stakes and am just about to pound it into the ground when I hear my name being shouted above the fury of the wind. Who is foolish enough to be out in this weather?

I turn to find Bea stumbling down the steps toward me, as soaked as I am but at least dressed more appropriately in jeans and sneakers. "What are you doing?" I yell as she runs closer.

"I could ask you the same thing," she shouts back.

I motion to the flowers at my feet, a bit bedraggled from the wind but still standing. For now. "I need to protect them from the hail."

Without another word, she grabs the stake from my hand and holds it in place while I wield the mallet. In a few minutes, thanks to the now muddy ground, it's in place. We follow suit with the others, forming a border of sorts around the plants. It resembles a rectangle that's had too much to drink.

"I thought you were in London," I say, picking up the roll of netting, visible only during the flashes of lightning still rending the sky apart. My heart freezes as I wait for her answer, sickeningly eager to see how she'll excuse her betrayal. Bea is the queen of justification, and she hasn't yet been backed into a corner she couldn't talk her way out of.

She helps me unfurl the netting, despite the wind doing its damnedest to tear it from our cold, shaking hands. "I just got back."

"Good time?" I yell as we back away from each other, spreading the netting into a thin sheet.

I can't hear what she says, but she shakes her head. Her blonde hair is somehow still beautiful even as it hangs in wet clumps around her ears. I reach the furthest set of stakes before it dawns on me that I forgot to bring anything to fasten the mesh to the posts.

"Bloody hell!" My momentary loss of concentration gives the wind all the room it needs to slip in, rip the cloth out of my grasp, and send it hurling toward Bea. I chase after it, and between the two of us, we manage to get it pinned to the ground, but not before a wrestling match that leaves us both panting.

I'm exhausted, and my legs are quivering. I slump onto the muddy ground. "What the hell," I mutter. "This dress is ruined anyway."

Bea plops down next to me as the rain's icy fingers trail down my back. I'm shivering uncontrollably, my teeth rattling like marbles in a jar. "Are they worth it?" she asks, pointing to the flowers.

"Probably not." But I've come too far to abandon them now. "You don't have to help."

She looks at me, water running down her face and dripping off her upturned nose, and says, "I think I do." She hangs her head and brushes at the grass between her legs. "I know that you know I was with him."

Here it is—the truth neither of us can hide from anymore. Two sisters in love with the same man. He chose one and rejected the other. I shrug before pushing to my feet. "Is this the part where I offer my congratulations?"

She tugs on my arm to keep me from walking away. "It's not like that. Nothing happened."

"Am I supposed to believe that?"

"Would I lie to you?"

Is she serious? I prop my hands on my hips, and my body temperature rises, despite how cold I am. "As a matter of fact, you would. You *did*. You assured me you'd stay away from Henry. Instead, you flew off to London with him!"

She bites her lip, and to her credit, she actually looks remorseful. "I'm so sorry, Celia. It was an awful thing to do."

"Yeah, you could say that. Now help me get this net up before the hail comes. We'll have to tie the corners to the stakes. I don't have anything else with me."

Working one at a time, we get all four corners attached. When the whole thing is finally up, I stand back and laugh. "We actually did it."

Drenched and shivering hard enough to wake the dead, we stand there grinning at each other like idiots. "What are we doing?" Bea laughs. "Let's get inside!" She grabs my hand, and we run up the garden path as fast as my dress will allow, dodging puddles the whole way.

Our noisy entrance brings a staff member to the door. She retreats to fetch us towels, leaving us in stoic silence, broken only by the sound of my teeth still clacking together and the ping of water hitting the marble floor. Our laughter seems to have been washed away by the rain.

"I really am sorry," Bea says.

I glance at her, and if the rivulets of water running down her face are any indication, she looks genuinely sincere. She did help me in the pouring rain, after all.

"Henry and I didn't go to London together." She toes a puddle on the floor with her sneaker. "I caught him completely unaware. He didn't even know I was in the city. We went our separate ways shortly after that photo, and I haven't seen him since."

Momentarily stunned, I just stare at her. Is this supposed to make me feel better?

"I've always lived in your shadow, and I thought this might help me break out of it once and for all," she says, her voice small.

"What are you talking about?" I squeeze a fistful of my hair and mechanically watch the drops join their siblings on the floor.

"Come on, Celia. You're always the star of the show. Everything I do, you do it better. Everyone adores you. They just think of me as Celia's little sister."

"That's absurd. You've always been the belle of the ball. Half of Wesbourne is in love with you, and the other half just can't say it because they're married."

"Now who's being absurd?"

"Regardless, what does any of that have to do with Henry?"

"Oh, please." Bea rolls her eyes in that annoying way little sisters do. "You two are so close, it's embarrassing to even be in the same room as you."

My snort is loud. "Henry and I are not close. We haven't been for a long time."

"You don't get it, do you? Even through all of your professed hatred of him, when the two of you are together, nobody else matters."

"Bea, that's just not true."

She props her hands on her hips in that saucy way she perfected when she was three. "Really? You're always picking on each other, arguing, fighting. You read each other's thoughts with a single glance. I've fought for his attention long enough to know that as soon as you walk into the room, he's lost to me." Her voice hovers right above a whisper. "I got so wrapped up in trying to be better at something, *anything*, than you, that I thought if I could steal Henry . . ." Her voice drifts off.

I pull her into a hug and wish I could take the pain of the last few months from both our hearts. "You can't steal him, because he's never been mine."

Rubber soles squeak down the corridor and are soon followed by their owners: three maids, each bearing a stack of fluffy white towels. They must think we've brought the entire storm inside.

Once Bea and I are dry enough to traverse the halls of the palace, we head to our third-floor suites. She stops me before we part ways. "He misses you, Celia."

A branding iron shoves its way into my chest. "He actually said that?"

"He didn't have to. The man is clearly miserable."

I shake my head, not wanting to stir up hope I don't deserve. "You can't know that it has anything to do with me."

"I'm not stupid. Henry is crazy about you. He always has been. And if you don't do something about it, you're the stupid one."

36

"When We Were Young" - Adele

I HAVE NO RECOLLECTION of getting to my suite, although I must have, because the next thing I know, I'm curled in one of the armchairs in my sitting room holding a photo album on my lap. My ruined dress is pooled at the bottom of the bathtub.

I flip the pages with no idea what I hope to find there. Proof that I'm not the terrible sister Bea has made me out to be? That I'm not selfish and greedy? That what she said about Henry and me isn't true?

The words he spoke the day he gave me a ride home come back like the ghost of Christmas past. *We're all selfish. We only do something if there's a clear benefit for us.*

Am I deceiving myself thinking I've given up everything for Wesbourne? Maybe that's why Henry's rejection stings so badly. I've been craving admiration ever since the day he stomped on my heart on his way out the door.

I run my thumb over a picture of my dad at the stove cooking breakfast. It was something he did every Sunday morning before church. He'd tell us one thing he loved about us for each blueberry he stuck into the batter of our pancakes.

Your beautiful smile. Your sharp mind. The way you won't let me kill a spider but make me put it outside instead.

That's what I'm looking for. Proof that someone is proud of the person I am.

On the next page, I find a collage of Bea and me in dress-up clothes. We'd dig through the giant trunk our mum kept in the playroom for coordinating outfits, then parade downstairs and beg her to take our picture. Rosalind has more patience than I give her credit for. There are dozens of these photos.

I'm wearing my dad's old uniform in one of them, standing tall and saluting the camera. Something about it looks odd, though, and I study it for a few minutes before I realize what it is. His service ribbons aren't pinned to the jacket, and the more I look at it, the more I'm beginning to think it wasn't his uniform at all. The sleeves hang nearly to my knees, and at eleven, I was getting close to my father's height.

I call my mother. "Do you still have Dad's uniform?"

There's silence on the other end, and I start to wonder if we've been disconnected by the time she finally speaks. "His uniform?"

"Yeah, the one we used to play dress-up with."

"Oh, that. I'm pretty sure I gave it away years ago."

"You gave away Dad's uniform?"

"It wasn't actually—" She stops.

I wait for her to continue, but she doesn't. "It wasn't his actual uniform, was it? Where's the real one?"

Her silence sets me on edge.

"Mum?"

"I think it might be best if we have this conversation in person."

Five minutes, later my mum is at my door, fingers twining together and apprehension bringing out wrinkles on her face that are usually too terrified to show themselves. We sit on the sofa, and I tell myself the worst has already happened: my father is dead, and no news could possibly eclipse that.

She picks up the photo album, and a smile crosses her face. "So many good memories."

"Only half as many as there should be."

She raises her head, and there's pity in her eyes. "I'm grateful we have as many as we do." She turns several more pages in silence, then says, "Your father was a good man."

"I know that, Mum. What does this have to do with the uniform?"

"I just want you to remember your father as you knew him before I tell you what I have to say."

Cold dread grips my spine. "Fine. Just tell me."

"Your father joined the military when he was eighteen. He was so eager to do something courageous, to make a difference for this country. He was young, much younger than a lot of the recruits. He served faithfully for almost ten years, until you were three years old."

And you made him retire.

"He loved it at first. But as time went on"—her voice falters—"it started to take its toll on him. He struggled with depression, even suicidal thoughts. I was worried, but he didn't like to talk about it.

"One day, you and I were in the back garden. Your father was deployed, and I didn't expect him home for another three weeks. I looked up from the flowers you were picking to find him walking across the yard.

"At first I was overjoyed. But as he got closer, I saw the look on his face. He didn't look happy to be home. He looked . . . hollow. He was wearing his civilian clothes, and I just knew. I knew he'd finally done it. It was the least honorable thing he'd ever done, but in that moment, I only felt relief."

There are moments when time seems to hang suspended in the air, everything in slow motion as the pieces fall into place. Like accident scenes in movies, orchestrated to increase their impact.

I reach for the arm of the sofa, afraid it might crumble beneath me if I don't have anything to hold onto. Like everything I thought I knew.

"Dad was a . . . deserter?" I feel like a traitor even putting those words together in the same sentence.

My mother's answer is in her eyes.

"How *could* he?" It's not humanly possible to keep the accusation from my tone.

She places her hand on top of mine. "You have to understand how hard it was for him."

I jerk it back. "I don't understand anything. He deserted his duty, his country, his responsibility. There is no excuse for that."

"He needed help. And he got that after he left."

"Nothing you say can excuse what he did."

She sighs, and I remember the blame I've always placed at her feet for what I thought was my father's forced retirement. "Why didn't you tell me?" I say.

"You worshiped your father. I couldn't take away what little you had left of him."

"So you let me think he was courageous and loyal and *good*?"

Her face is stern. "He was all of those things, Celia, and I won't let you speak about him like that."

"He's the reason I'm in this place! He's the reason we're not at Maison de Lierre right now, the reason I'm married to Henry instead of Beck."

"No, he's not." Mum looks me straight in the eye. "You are."

I flinch, but she's not done.

"*You* are courageous and loyal and good, and that's why you're in this position. A lesser person would have said no. You didn't say yes because you thought your father would have said yes. You said yes because your father raised you to be the kind of person who does what's right."

There are hot balls of tears burning the backs of my eyelids, but I forbid them from coming any further. "It still changes everything."

"If you had known this before, would you have chosen differently?"

I already know the answer, and so does she, but I pretend to give it serious thought. Finally, I whisper, "I don't know."

"Your father lost his courage, yes. But it was that shortcoming that made him determined to raise his daughters to be better, to be stronger than he'd been."

"I'll never see him the same way again," I say.

Mum rubs a perfectly manicured hand over her knee. "Which is exactly why I never intended to tell you."

"But surely people knew? How have I not found this out before now?"

"We paid a lot of money to keep the news from circulating. And to keep your father out of prison."

"The money from the estate."

She nods, and I can see that this secret has aged her. "It was the only thing we could think to do."

It hadn't been enough to stop the rumors. Even I'd heard them. But they never mentioned his name.

"Did he regret joining?"

She starts shaking her head before the words have all left my mouth. "No. He was ashamed of quitting early, but he never regretted the years he spent in service to this country."

It's a small consolation, but it doesn't change what he did.

"How will I ever hold my head up again?" I say.

"You are not your father. You possess a strength and courage he never did. You're going to do incredible things as this country's queen."

"I'm scared." My jaw quivers, and I want my mother to pull me against her chest like she used to when I was little.

She doesn't. Instead she clasps my shoulders and turns me to face her. "Courage is bravery in the face of fear. Your father lacked it, but you don't. Besides, you're not alone in this."

She's referring to Henry, but I don't have the strength to tell her that he's deserted me, too.

Sleep joins the list of deserters in my life. I toss and turn, unable to get the image of my father in his uniform out of my mind. How could he do it? How could he just give up when the going got tough?

I'm secretly glad my mother didn't tell me sooner. I can't imagine living with this knowledge for any longer than I already have. To know that my own father took the coward's way out because he couldn't handle the what-ifs . . .

My conversations with Adelaide and Bea choose that very inconvenient moment to float back through my sleep-adverse mind.

Are you scared of approaching Henry or of what he'll say if you do?

Henry is crazy about you. He always has been.

Bloody hell. They're all conspiring against me.

I mash my pillow into a thicker lump under my head. I close my eyes and count one hundred sheep (the most futile exercise ever created). I climb out of bed and into downward dog position for a few minutes. I sip the lukewarm tea Daphne left on my bedside table. I even try reading a few pages of a novel, but after five minutes, I can't recall a single word.

I unplug my phone from the charger. I tell myself it's just so I can sleep. Desperate times, desperate measures. I send the text to Bea.

Where is he?

37

"Helium" - Sia

MAISIE ARRANGES A PRIVATE flight to England for me the next morning. The royal jet is only available for official Crown business, and unfortunately, chasing my husband across the Atlantic doesn't qualify. She also books the presidential suite at The Lanesborough, Henry's preferred hotel. The royal suite is not available, presumably occupied by Henry himself.

Twelve hours later, I'm crossing the ocean, bound for London. And hopefully some closure. Getting into Henry's suite will be more difficult. I'm nervous he may have given his security team orders to deny me access. When I mention this to Daphne on the plane, she suggests asking Henry's valet for help.

"We are friends, of a sort." A blush stains her cheeks.

"Ah," I say. "Tell him I'm willing to overlook any workplace fraternization if he helps me."

She texts him and, several minutes later, assures me Albright will get me access to Henry's suite.

The hotel is a quick drive from the airport, and I check into my own suite, which is even more opulent than my rooms in the palace. Then I change out of my wrinkled travel outfit and into the emerald-green dress Henry loves. It can't hurt to look good, right?

Standing on shaky legs, I take a deep breath. It's showtime.

I wait in the hotel corridor outside a single door that leads into the valet's set of rooms in the royal suite. Albright steps out, holding it ajar. I whisper my thanks and slip past him into the inner hallway.

I studied the floor plan of the suite on the website, so I know the door on my left opens into a large living and dining room, with a study and the master suite beyond it. I debate knocking, but it's probably better to just enter than to risk meeting one of Henry's PPOs.

I really haven't thought this through.

When I step inside, the state room is empty. I thank the plush carpet for muffling my footsteps. I tiptoe—not easy in heels—past a set of closed double doors leading to the foyer. That must be where the security team is. They aren't going to appreciate my craftiness. I'll have to get Henry's word that no one will lose their job over this.

On the far side of the room, there's another door. It's painted the same color as the walls and decorated with the same intricate gold trim, making it barely noticeable. As I walk closer, the sound of talking becomes distinguishable. Startled, I misstep and nearly twist my ankle. It never occurred to me that Henry might not be alone.

Forcing one foot in front of the other, I approach the door and press my ear against it. I can hear Henry's low voice, and my heart stutters, but I can't make out what he's saying. I wait to hear if the other person is male or female, but there's nothing but silence.

He speaks again, pauses, then says something else. He must be on the phone. I nearly sink to the floor. So far, so good. Now it's just a matter of facing him. The thought leaves me even shakier than I already am.

I opt to forgo knocking and crack the door open. The room is decorated in a cozy matte-red color scheme with lots of wood. The walls are trimmed with gold, the furniture all red upholstery. Henry is standing with his back to me on the other side of the room, facing the window, his phone held to his ear. He's wearing a white shirt tucked into navy trousers. The ambrosial scent of him infuses the room and nearly fells m e.

"What do you mean? Nothing has been done?" he says into the phone.

I close the door softly and lean against it, drinking him in like a lovestruck teenager. It's been five days since I last saw him. Missing him is a physical ache.

He picks up a crystal tumbler from the desk beside him. "That doesn't make any sense. Get me more info." He turns around and lifts the glass to his lips. As he does, his eyes alight on me. The shock registers on his face, and he lowers the tumbler again without taking a drink.

"Keep me informed." He ends the call without taking his gaze off me. "Celia." It floats out on an exhale. Narrowing his eyes, he studies me from head to toe. "I have so many questions, I don't even know where to begin."

"While you're figuring it out, I've got one of my own." I push away from the door and take a few steps into the room. My fingers close around the annulment papers in my bag, and I pull them out. "You filed for divorce without saying a word to me?"

He pitches his phone carelessly onto the nearest armchair. His face is impossible to read. Is he angry? Amused? "Why are you here, C?"

The cotton in my mouth and throat is suffocating. "I need to talk to you," I finally get out.

"Who knows you're here?" He tosses the contents of the tumbler back in one swig.

"Maisie. And I brought my maid. Why?"

"No one else?"

"What does it matter? You still haven't answered my question."

He takes a tentative step in my direction, like I'm a wild animal who might flee if he makes any sudden movements. "I thought I'd save you the trouble of filing for divorce yourself."

"What made you think I would?"

He looks nonplussed. "Give me a little credit."

"Fine. That was my plan, a long time ago. But that was before—"

"Before what?"

Before I realized I can't live without you. "Before I broke it off with Beck."

"So you were going to divorce me, but only as long as you had someone to take my place? I'm flattered."

"That's not what I meant. I broke it off because I realized he wasn't what I wanted. And on some level, he probably is what I need, but . . . I couldn't do it anymore. Not when I feel like this." I clamp my mouth shut before I make the situation worse.

Henry begins pacing, frustration outlining his body.

"Wait, are you mad?" I say.

Stopping in front of the bar cart, he pours another glass of whiskey. He holds the bottle up questioningly, but I shake my head. "I'm not mad," he says, and leans against the desk, ankles crossed. "Just confused."

As he watches me over the rim of the tumbler, I'm unable to look away from his lips on the glass. All I want is to taste them.

"Remember when you said you didn't want me to feel normal?" I say.

He swipes at his mouth, "Not one of my finer moments, I'll admit."

"I don't want to feel normal either."

His eyes flash to mine like lightning streaking across the sky, rending it apart.

"I'm still in love with you." The words linger in the air the way cheap perfume hovers long after its wearer is gone. "But don't worry. I'll find a way to survive if you tell me you don't feel the same way."

He opens his mouth to speak, but I hold up my hand.

"Please let me finish, or I'll lose the courage." I gulp in another lungful of air. "Being with you scares me. Terrifies me, actually. But being without you is one hundred times worse. It's like the life has been sucked from my body and I'm nothing but a shell. I've always said that kind of dependency on another person is crippling and toxic. But that doesn't change the fact that I'm completely and irrevocably in love with you, and it's nearly killing me."

Henry's expression hasn't changed. He's still fixing those fierce eyes on me. The only difference is his hands, now clutching the edge of the desk behind him. His knuckles are white from their tight grip.

"I thought I could make it go away." My voice is growing stronger. "I thought if I stayed away from you long enough, eventually I'd stop caring. But I've never been able to stop loving you, no matter how hard I've tried or how much I've pretended otherwise. You're the color in my black-and-white world, and I'd rather die than live in a world without you."

He pushes off from the desk, and my heart beats a heavy staccato as he closes the distance between us. Pulling the papers from my hand, he sends them scattering across the floor.

"It's okay if you don't feel the same." I'm breathless. "I just needed to—"

My words are cut off by his mouth pressing onto mine, banishing thoughts and words to another planet entirely. Fissures of pleasure rip through my skull as his fingers thread through my hair and hold me in place so his lips can pull at mine, tug, nip, caress.

He tastes of whiskey and spearmint and Henry, a flavor I didn't know was necessary for survival until a few weeks ago. I move my hands up his chest and neck and into those incredibly soft locks I fantasize about. My back arches to meet his body. He groans and pulls me closer. His hands find their way down to my waist.

Will kissing him always be like this, this desperate attempt to get more but never quite being able to satisfy the hunger? His touch is determined and intentional. This is a man who knows exactly what he wants. I pull back just enough to say, "What's happening? I thought—"

He nuzzles a spot beneath my ear that has a direct connection to my groin. "Do you know how bloody hard it was to stand there listening to you when all I wanted to do was this?" He covers my lips with his own again, explores my mouth with his tongue, insistent and possessive and completely intoxicating.

"I thought . . . you didn't . . . want this," I say during tiny snatches of breath.

He draws back and focuses on trailing kisses down my neck. "I said I can't. I never said I didn't want to."

Whatever that means will have to be addressed at a future point. Right now it would take Hercules himself to remove me from Henry's arms.

I tug his mouth back to mine and elicit a moan as I rake my fingers down his jawline. His hands trail along my leg and bunch the silky fabric of my dress. "Every time I see you in this," he murmurs against my lips, "I lose another year of my life."

I wiggle closer in response and feel him tighten. He inhales a gasp, then spins me around. The rustle of the zipper echoes in my belly. It feels like he's unzipping my soul, not just my dress. His fingers feel like flames against my skin. Instead of letting the gown drop to the floor, he carefully turns me around again to face him, holding it in place. His eyes have grown black, and I swallow hard at the intensity in them.

"I'm embarrassed to admit how many times I've visualized this dress pooling at your feet," he says. He slides a finger under each thin shoulder strap, and with a tiny flick, they slide down my arms. He lets out a shaky breath as his eyes traverse my bare body. "God, you are so fucking beautiful."

Then, as if he can't handle another second of not touching my skin, he pulls me against him, dragging his hands over every inch of me until I'm on the verge of crying out in frustration. He slides both hands behind my thighs and lifts me up gently. "Wrap your legs around me, baby."

I do as directed and fold my arms around his neck as he holds me against his chest. He continues his gentle assault of my mouth as he walks us toward the opposite side of the room and opens the door to the master suite.

He carries me to the bed and deposits me on it, then crawls until he's hovering over me. Holding himself up on his hands, he gazes down at me. I spiral and drown in that look.

"Are you sure about this, C? It's not too late to stop." His voice is low and rumbling. It turns my insides to jelly. He's wrong, though. It's much too late to stop.

I reach up and pull his head down, earning a growl of pleasure as he kisses me with the hunger of a starving man.

He directs his attention to my neck and jaw. I squirm and moan under the sweet torture. "That sound is my new drug," he says.

Turning his attention to my feet, he drops my heels onto the floor. The action reverberates through my bones. He grasps my left foot in his hand and presses a soft kiss to the arch, then a grin splits his face. "Remember the night we had drinks in my room? Your modesty was applaudable, but your bare feet were so sexy I had to walk away before I did something stupid."

I gasp as he eases himself on top of me again. His body is a delicious weight. He resumes his exploration, nipping at my skin all the way down to my navel. He leaves a trail of kisses along my waistline. The resulting tremors are an 8.0 on the Richter scale.

When he sits up again, I reach out and fumble with the buttons of his shirt under his steady gaze. I'm a stick of butter. He's the sun. The black ink of his tattoos peeks through as the fabric separates. When I finally finish, he tosses it onto the floor and reclaims my mouth, the separation having been almost too much for either of us to bear.

"Do you know how long I've fantasized about this?" His voice is reminiscent of a pine forest: rough bark, soft needles, enveloping security.

I shake my head, surprised by the admission.

"Too long." He nips at my nose.

I press my palms against his chest. "I want to see your tattoos."

"Right now?"

"Yes. Tell me what they mean. Starting with this one." I trace my fingers over the black arrow symbolically buried in his heart.

"That one has a few interpretations."

"Tell me one."

"A damaged heart can't keep beating." Henry shrugs, and I know that's all I'm going to get.

He leans back as I run my fingers over the ink. His breathing becomes heavier with each touch. I feel myself becoming drunk on the power of it.

"Which one is your favorite?" I ask, after he's told me the meaning behind each one I point to. His answers have gotten shorter as his desperation to get back to the task at hand increases.

"One you haven't found yet," he says. "But that's enough talking for now." He kisses me until the tattoos evaporate from my thoughts.

His warm palm smooths across my stomach before slowly sliding further, his fingers skimming the waistband of my panties. He swallows my involuntary gasp of anticipation.

"I'm going to seduce you, ravish you, and pleasure you," he murmurs against my lips, "and then I'm going to take you."

My heart shudders to a stop before resuming an erratic beat.

"I can't wait to discover exactly what you like." He nuzzles my neck as he says this, and his hand slips lower, until he's cupping me, his warmth seeping through my panties, which are probably soaked by this point.

The pressure of his palm feels too good, and I arch into it. He purrs his approval and slips a finger just inside my waistband, sliding it back and forth along that sensitive line, a promise of what's to come.

His path downward is excruciatingly slow, and I whimper in protest, bliss, agony—I don't even know at this point. He finally reaches his destination after what feels like a lifetime, a journey that has left me breathless and panting for want of him.

Slipping a finger inside me, he shudders out a breath. "Fuck," he moans. "You're going to completely undo me, baby." A second finger joins the first. "How are you so tight? And so wet? God, C." His voice has grown raspy.

I'm unraveling. The way he's moving inside me is unlike anything I've ever experienced, and my climax hits before I can control it. He holds me close while continuing his relentless assault with his hand. When it's over, I whisper, "That ended way too soon."

He grins and takes my nipple in his mouth. I cry out at the biting pleasure. "You're mistaken if you think you're only getting one orgasm," he says after releasing me. "I fully intend to ravish you all night long."

The heat deep inside me grows until I'm consumed with it again. Henry searches my face, and his intensity surprises me. In this moment, I am his sole focus and desire, and the thought makes me melt.

He moves his mouth to my stomach, sucking and licking every inch of my skin. It's impossible to stop the noises that leave my mouth of their own accord. I think this might be heaven.

When he reaches the top of my panties, he stops. "As much as I love these, it's time for them to go." He slips his hands inside and gently pulls them down my legs, the silky fabric no match for his sculpted fingers.

Now that I know what he's capable of, there is no stopping the trembling that has overtaken me. My muscles quiver in trepidation and anticipation. He notices and places his palm flat on my stomach.

"Are you cold?"

I shake my head, because words have failed me at the moment.

"Do you trust me?"

I nod again, surprised to find that it's true. I shouldn't, but I do.

He gazes at me for a few more seconds, then turns his attention back to my body. Dropping a kiss to my navel, he nibbles his way to the source of all of my heat.

He looks up at me from between my legs. "I am dying to taste you," he rasps. I quake, and his fingers gently knead me apart.

I cry out when his tongue touches the most sensitive part of me. It's all the encouragement he needs. He sucks and licks and teases me into oblivion, until the only thing I can think of is the all-consuming fire between my legs. This orgasm hits harder, longer, and more intensely than the first. His tongue doesn't let up its torment until I'm completely spent, a shaking mass on the bed.

He scoops me into his arms like I'm a small child. I feel like bawling. "You are incredible," he whispers into my hair. "A fucking goddess." He bites my earlobe softly and kisses his way down to my collarbone. How I'll possibly survive another five minutes of this is beyond me.

"Henry—" I stammer. "I-I don't think—"

"Shh," he says. "Let me worry about that. Your job is just to feel. And I'm confident you have another orgasm or two still in you."

I've never even experienced multiples before, let alone more than two, and I'm about to inform him of this when he covers my nipple with his mouth and that familiar heat begins to rise again. *How?*

If he was slow and calculating before, now his movements are frenzied, likely spurred on by his own need. He sheds the rest of his clothes, and his naked body is a sight to behold. He catches me staring and grins down at me.

It's hot and slow and seductive, the way he moves over me, building my heat to a raging fire. When I don't think my body can possibly handle any more, he enters me in a single, deep thrust.

It's swift, erasing all thoughts from my mind as we tumble over together. His name rips out of me as he rips into me and the fire rips through me. Somehow, through the blinding bliss, it hits me that this is real. My dream has actually been fulfilled.

We're going to live happily ever after.

It's just like a fairy tale.

38

"Stop Me From Falling" - Kylie Minogue

SUNLIGHT FLIRTS WITH THE drapes, teasing them until they finally relent and allow it to beam in and caress my bare skin. I feel well rested for the first time in an eternity, which is a miracle considering how many times we woke each other during the night. We're like former dieters at a buffet.

Something akin to liquid paradise bubbles in my belly. I realize it's bliss. Complete and utter bliss.

I am sandwiched by warmth: the sun's rays on one side, Henry's deliciously bare chest on the other. The light touch of his fingers drifts up my back. I incline my head and devour the sight of him sleep-tousled and sex-drunk.

Crinkles spread out from his eyes as the side of his mouth tugs upward. "Good morning, beautiful." He buries his nose in my hair and inhales. "God, you smell good."

I prop myself up to drop a kiss on his lips. "You're still here. I didn't think you did the whole morning-after thing."

He grunts and rolls so I'm under him. "I don't." His lips on my throat fly me to another level of heaven. "We happen to be married. Besides, this is my hotel room. You're the one who stayed over."

I pinch the flesh under his arm. He squirms and grabs my wrists. "I can't believe we're here, after all this time," I murmur. My body sighs his name as he consumes me. *Henry.*

"What do you mean?" His mouth travels lower and lower, waking every inch of my skin.

I roll my shoulders back as tingles of pleasure ripple down my spine. "I gave up hope so long ago, and now—" I gasp at a particularly hard nip at my nipple. "It feels like a dream. How did I get so lucky?"

"You are many things. Lucky is not one of them." His voice is low and gravelly from sleep. The sound of it, coupled with the roughness of his stubble against my bare stomach, clenches my insides into a tight ball of pleasure.

"Agree to disagree," I say right before he claims me, and I lose myself in him once again.

When we finally emerge from the bedroom, Henry's designated room butler has set the table for two and kept the food in the warming trays. "Your Royal Highnesses." He pulls out both of our chairs in turn.

Heat climbs my neck, and I wonder how much he heard while setting up. We weren't exactly *quiet*.

Henry smirks at my embarrassment. He leans over to plant what I can only assume was intended to be a chaste kiss on my lips, but which quickly escalates into something much baser. Apparently, his pheromones turn me into an animal.

The aroma of bacon, sausage, and fried eggs must wake his stomach, because it lets out a loud protest. I break off the kiss and grin at him. "Maybe we should focus on assuaging one appetite at a time."

After setting our plates in front of us, the butler gives a stiff bow and excuses himself.

"What kind of business brought you to London anyway?" I cut into my eggs. "Besides escaping me, of course."

Henry narrows his eyes and gives me a sidelong glance. "I wasn't escaping. There's a hotel chain that needs restructuring." He shrugs and spears a piece of sausage. "I'm in the process of buying it."

I lower my fork without taking a bite. I assumed his reasons for being here had to do with Wesbourne and the Crown, not his own personal business. "You're buying it? What are you going to do with it?"

"Hire a competent CEO to run it for me, one who won't run it into the ground like the last one did."

"You're going to keep it?"

He takes a sip of coffee and nods. "Unless it seems more profitable to sell it to the highest bidder. In that case, I'll use the capital from the sale to buy something else." He spreads butter on a piece of toast and pops it into his mouth.

"You sound like you've done this before."

Henry chuckles. "That's because I have."

I set my coffee cup back on the table. "How did I not know this?"

"It's not something I really talk about."

"Why didn't you tell me when we talked about your dreams?"

"You're not an easy person to impress. I wasn't sure what you'd say."

I tilt my head and look at him. "I think it's amazing. Consider me duly impressed."

"It's more of a hobby than anything."

"A lucrative hobby. What do you do with the money?"

He grins and licks the corner of his mouth. "Always so eager for information."

"I want to know everything about you."

He studies me for a few moments, as if trying to make up his mind about how much to tell me, then settles for brushing the crumbs from his fingers. "Why don't we explore the city today?"

Half an hour later, both dressed in jeans and sunglasses, and Henry in a ball cap, we hit the streets of London. He has somehow managed to convince his security team they won't be needed. My heart is thrumming like a bass guitar. I'm finally with the man of my dreams after all these years. Being this happy can't last forever, can it?

"Where are we going?" I ask from the back seat of the taxi.

"Wait and see," Henry says.

"Tell me."

He shakes his head.

"Please?"

"Nope."

"Come on!"

"You need to learn to appreciate surprises."

"I do appreciate them," I say. "I appreciate knowing what they are beforehand."

He laughs and brushes his lips against my temple. "Just trust me."

It reminds me of my conversation with Beck about our honeymoon and how he gave in to me without resistance. Maybe I do need to learn how to wait.

My breath rushes past my lips as the pillars of the British Museum become visible, the Pantheon on steroids. I pull Henry down for a kiss.

He chuckles against my lips. "Told you to trust me."

Between the incredible exhibits, his hand entwined with mine, and the ecstasy that nearly chokes me, I rival a volcano on the brink of eruption. I could stay there all day, but Henry's appetite demands attention.

We grab tacos from a street vendor and eat while walking down an insignificant sidewalk, dribbling hot sauce onto our chins. Plates clatter in a nearby cafe as diners chatter over their fish and chips. Diesel fumes clog the air, cut only by the potent stench of urine and weed. The occasional gust of wind flutters bits of rubbish around our ankles.

It's absolute paradise.

A deflated balloon careens along the sidewalk and punctures my bubble of bliss. Instant revulsion fills my veins. I kick at it violently.

"Easy there. It's just a balloon," Henry says. He grabs it and shoves it into a nearby trash bin.

"I hate them."

"You hate balloons."

I don't answer, just take several deep breaths.

"Because of your dad?"

I look up at him.

He motions toward my bracelet. "You rub it every time you think about him."

"I wasn't there," I say. The nausea roils in my stomach.

"Where?" He brings me to a stop with a hand on my arm.

"At the hospital. When he died." I mumble the words, but the vision comes back anyway.

Henry stays silent, and I venture a peek at his face. It's lined with concern.

"I should've been. But I was angry. Angry at him, like it was somehow his fault he was dying." *Angry at you for leaving me at the lowest point in my life.* "My mum told me to come, but I thought I had plenty of time. I thought—" The words get lost in the sea of emotions in my throat.

Henry pulls me into his chest. "Hey, you couldn't have known." He rubs my back, and the gesture is so sweet, so comforting, I nearly fall apart right there in the middle of the sidewalk.

Instead, I bury my face in his baby-soft T-shirt and remind myself to breathe. "Mum told me afterwards that he was asking for me. He wanted to say goodbye."

Henry's arms tighten around me as the grief tries to pull me under.

"He died while I was on my way to the city."

"Oh, baby."

He folds himself around me, and we stand there on a deserted street in London, oblivious to everything but the bubble that is us.

After a while, he pulls back slightly. "I'm sorry I wasn't there when you needed me most," he says into my hair.

There's no denying the firecracker of pain that whistles through my midsection before exploding with the rest. "You're here now," I tell him.

Our next stop is St. Dunstan-in-the-East, a parish church mostly destroyed in the Blitz during WWII. It's as breathtaking as the museum, in its own way. The steeple soars above the blackened walls in eerie beauty. A curving stone path winds around the park and promises a better view to anyone who will walk its course.

It's a scene directly out of a fairy tale—the harsh Gothic architecture softened by the lush garden surrounding it, horns beeping from the street mingled with birds twittering in the trees, the pungent odor of sewage swallowed by the crisp, clean air of nature. Two worlds combined into one idyllic oasis.

"Let's take some pictures." Henry sits and props a bent leg up in front of one of the immense arched windows. He pats the space between his legs, and I snuggle into the cocoon he's created. The bill of his cap brushes the top of my head, and his arm is snug and possessive around my chest as he snaps selfies of us. We look like sun-kissed, love-drunk teenagers on holiday. I laugh out loud as he kisses that sensitive spot behind my ear, his thumb still tapping the shutter button.

"Mmm, now we'll have something to remember today by," he says into my ear.

I won't need a photo. This day will be seared into my mind as the happiest of my life.

Henry slips the phone back into his pocket and wraps his other arm around to join the first, cradling me against his chest. A hint of black ink on the back of his upper arm peeks out from beneath the sleeve of his T-shirt. I turn it to see better. It's the letter *C* in a calligraphic font, the tiniest hydrangeas twining around it. I trace the smooth skin with my thumb.

"I didn't notice this one last night. What does it stand for?"

A throaty chuckle tickles my ear. "What do you think?"

"I don't—" Realization spreads like a physical sensation through my nerve endings. "Oh. But— How long—" My words are cut off by his lips on my neck.

"A long time," he murmurs against my skin.

The wind picks up and swirls fallen leaves and twigs around the small garden. The sparkly sunlight winks out, and a gray pallor takes its place.

"Come on. We've got one more place to see," he says.

I've heard of backyard cinemas but have never been to one. When Henry ushers me through the first garden tunnel, it's like stepping into another realm, one where everything is possible, even the crazy, explosive love ricocheting in my heart.

Evergreen boughs brush our heads as we walk, the scent of pine so heady it makes me dizzy. Or maybe that's because Henry pulls me into a small alcove and kisses me like the world is ending, his hands cupping my face both gently and firmly.

"No matter what happens, we'll have this day, okay?" he says.

Fear niggles in my chest at his words. "What do you mean? What's going to happen?"

"Nothing." He pulls me to him and cradles the back of my head in his palm. "Let's go watch the show."

Without the protection of our sunglasses, we're much more likely to be recognized here. Fortunately, everyone is too entranced by the magical fairy-tale setting to even consider the possibility of the Crown Prince and Princess of Wesbourne sitting in the back row. Although we don't see much of the movie, ensconced in our comfy bean bag chairs and engrossed in each other as we are.

It seems a waste to be here. I miss having his body pressed against mine.

By the time the show is over, I only want one thing. Henry, on the other hand, has other appetites as well.

"God, I want nothing more than to take you back and devour you," he growls in my ear. "But I will shrivel up before we get there if I don't get something to eat."

"Your perpetual hunger is a real buzzkill," I tease as we leave the cinema to find the nearest restaurant.

He wraps his arm around my shoulders and presses his lips to my hair. "I'll make up for it later, baby, don't worry."

A sharp, sickly sweet spike of pleasure shoots through me. I'm fully aware of how well he can carry out this promise.

The darkened street greets us as we step outside, the sun having gone to bed while we lounged in fairyland. I have the sudden realization that our day is drawing to a close. I can't shake my sense of foreboding, the feeling that this is simply the calm before the storm.

We find seats at a small pub that is buzzing with tipsy patrons, clanking pints, and the live band on the stage. Our booth is in a back corner, partially cloaked in shadows, but we still keep our heads down. We've escaped recognition all day, and being caught now would certainly put a damper on things.

While we wait for our food, Henry clasps my hands across the sticky table. "Did you have fun today?" His thumbs trace rings on the backs of my hands and make concentration difficult.

"London isn't Wesbourne. But it may have been the best day of my life," I say. "Thank you."

"It was amazing, wasn't it?" His grin is contagious.

"Is this how you woo all of your dates?"

"There's only one girl in the world I'd ever do this for." He gazes at me. "She's sitting right in front of me."

That is all it takes. My heart has no choice but to explode into a million tiny pieces. I lean forward and press my lips against his. The amount of PDA I've participated in today is shocking. Even more shocking is my utter lack of remorse. This is what Henry does to me.

It turns out great loves don't always end in tragedy. My own life is now a testament to that fact, and for once I'm more than happy to have been wrong.

There's a sudden commotion beside us, and we both pull back in surprise. Henry comes to his senses faster than I do. He drags me from the table. "Let's go."

The paparazzi follow us out the door, but we lose them when we slide into an empty cab. "Bloody vultures," he says. "Someone must have tipped them off. We should've headed back after the movie." Rage emanates from him and swirls around the back seat of the car.

I struggle to find a reason for his anger. "Are you mad that we didn't get to eat first? We can go somewhere else."

"No, let's just go back to the hotel." He threads his fingers through mine and raises our joined hands to his lips. They curve into a smile that doesn't reach his eyes. Something is wrong, but he isn't going to tell me what it is.

Back in his suite, I kick off my shoes and wiggle my toes against the plush carpet. "Do you want to order room service? The menu's right here." I wave it in the air.

He takes it from my hand and tosses it aside, then slides his fingers around my jaw and through my hair, tugging me closer. "I'm not hungry anymore. At least not for food."

He slowly peels off both of our clothes and leaves them in a heap on the floor. His movements are calculated and slow, a painstaking seduction. I can't read his face. His eyes are dark and shadowed, and his actions the result of deliberate thought.

We are smoke and mirrors, light and dark. Tonight is different from before. Gone is the smiling, playful Henry, and in his place is a man who almost frightens me with his intensity.

Alternating between slow and fast, hard and soft, he brings me to the brink of ecstasy again and again, until I can't take it anymore. We climax together, oblivious to the world outside our own.

"I'm going to brush my teeth," he says when it's over, standing up brusquely and walking to the bathroom.

A chill climbs my spine as I watch him leave. I pull the duvet up to my chin.

For reasons I can't explain, I wait until he returns before brushing my own teeth, and when I get back, I can't tell if he's still awake or not. He has his back turned to me, and the lamp on his side of the bed is already off.

The intense way he made love to me scares me the most. It was like he wanted to savor every moment. Which doesn't make sense, unless . . .

I won't go there.

He won't leave me, not after all of this. He feels the same way I do. He cares too much to lead me on.

I'm being ridiculous.

I crawl into bed and flip off the light and the nagging voice in my head. I curb the desire to touch him and fold my hands under my pillow so they won't get any ideas of their own. It's obvious we won't be snuggling tonight.

We need to have a conversation tomorrow about what's going to happen next. We have a country and responsibilities waiting for us back home. It's time to act like adults.

I sigh and roll over, my back to Henry. It's much easier to sleep on my right side, especially if he isn't even going to look at me. After a few minutes, the bed squeaks as he shifts. Soon, his arms slip around my waist and burrow me into the magical sanctuary of his chest.

"Sweet dreams, baby," he whispers.

It isn't until I'm sinking into sleep that I finally identify the black cloud hanging over our otherwise perfect day. I told Henry exactly how I feel about him, how madly in love with him I am, and how I can't imagine a life without him.

But he has yet to tell me anything.

39

"My Immortal" - Evanescence

Henry is gone when I wake up. I refuse to assume the worst, much to the dismay of the cynical voice in my head, which keeps hammering away at the front of my skull. I sit up in bed and survey the evidence of our late-night activities.

My clothes are crumpled in a pile next to the bed, my shoes discarded near the sofa. Several empty condom wrappers lie on the nightstand, a tingling reminder of Henry's incredible stamina.

Will it ever get old, this feeling of being completely consumed by him? It's like being on drugs, or at least the way I imagine being on drugs feels, except I have the advantage of not coming down from the high.

At least not yet, the nag in my head snarks.

I silence her with a hot shower and the retort that Henry will be back by the time I'm done. When I walk out of the bathroom, he's just coming into the room, carrying a tray of what appears to be breakfast. He's wearing a T-shirt and joggers, a triangle of sweat on his chest. He looks a hundred times better than the food he's holding.

See? I tell my cynical subconscious.

I smile at him. "Hey, I missed you this morning. Good run?"

He nods and hands me the food but doesn't meet my eyes. "I'm going to take a shower." He hesitates for a second, then presses a kiss to my forehead before heading into the bathroom.

Bile surges up my throat. I set the plate on the table with a clatter and take a sip of coffee. I don't know what it is yet, but I can't deny it any longer.

Something is definitely wrong.

A while later, Henry emerges from the bathroom, freshly shaven and smelling like a dream. He grabs a donut from the breakfast tray I don't have the appetite for and demolishes it in three bites.

I cock an eyebrow. "Hungry?"

"Famished," he says, pouring himself a cup of coffee from the carafe. He has yet to so much as glance at me.

"Henry." I wait for him to look up. He doesn't. "We need to talk."

He nods as he polishes off a second donut. "I know." He glances at his watch. "We have about two hours before your plane is scheduled to leave."

My blood runs cold, and my fingers become icicles in my lap. "What are you talking about?"

Instead of answering, he walks into the restroom, and I hear the tap turn on. When he doesn't return, I follow him. He's standing with his hands on the vanity, staring at the marble floor.

I move closer and place my hand on his back. It's warm and strong, and I want nothing more than to wrap my arms around him, but he tenses at my touch and closes his eyes.

"Please talk to me." I drop my hand. "What's going on?"

"I'm sorry." He sighs and finally meets my eyes in the mirror. "For everything."

"You're sorry for everything," I repeat in a monotone. "Even yesterday? Last night?"

"No." Pushing off from the counter, he rubs his eyes. "I don't know."

I make an incredulous sound. "Wow. Okay." I blink rapidly and forbid tears from forming. "How soon are you coming home? Because I can wait. That would give us time to talk about this, and then we can fly home together."

Henry's mouth is a grim, hard line when he turns to face me. "I'm not coming home, C."

Whatever expression I was wearing, I feel it falling as my face melts into a blank stare. "What are you talking about?"

"You heard me. You're going. I'm staying."

"No." I shake my head. "You're not doing this to me again. I'm staying with you."

"You have a country to run."

"Exactly. And I want you at my side."

"That's impossible."

"No," I say, "you're the one who's being impossible. You can't tell me you don't feel anything for me."

"Celia, for the love of god, can you please not make this any harder?" He props his hand against the wall. Frustration radiates off him.

"Tell me it meant nothing, and I'll go." I wait, but he doesn't speak. "You can't, because we both know this is bigger than the two of us. You feel it too. I know you do." I trace his jawline with my finger.

He shudders and pushes past me into the bedroom. I follow on his heels, ready to burst. Grabbing my discarded clothes from the floor, he begins shoving them into my bag on the bed. I yank his arm away from the suitcase, desperate for him to stop and look me in the eye.

He spins around, seizes my wrists, and pushes me up against the wall, his face inches from mine. He's finally meeting my eyes, and I see my own pain reflected in them. We stay like that for what feels like an eternity, and when he finally releases me, I suck in my breath like a drowning person on solid ground again.

Hands on his hips, he stares out the window, his back to me. I ache to slide my hands around him and bury my face in the soft folds on his T-shirt, but I know he'll only push me away.

"Henry. Please." It's a plea, a sob, a prayer.

He slowly turns to face me. He's regained his composure, and his face is now an expressionless mask. "You need to finish packing." His voice is a robot's, cold and impersonal.

I glance at the suitcase, its contents spilling out onto the bed. "Not until you tell me what's going on."

"Nothing is going on, Celia. I don't do relationships. You know this."

I do know this, but like the world's biggest idiot, I thought it was different with me. "You are such an ass!" I scream, pounding his chest with my fists. "Someday you'll meet someone, and you'll give her *everything*. Everything you promised me will be hers."

He removes my hands as if I'm nothing more than a nuisance. "I didn't promise you anything."

A shaky sob spills past my lips. He's right. He didn't. I'm the one who read too much into the actions of a world-renowned playboy. "You knew how I felt. You implied the feeling was mutual."

"I happen to be a really good actor."

"Damn you, Henry!" I grab the universal remote from the nightstand and hurl it at his head.

He ducks it effortlessly, letting it slam into the wall. "Look, if you don't pack, I'll do it for you. It doesn't matter to me. But you will be on that plane."

"Why?" I yell, grabbing his face between my hands. "Tell me why you did it."

He hisses through his teeth like I've burned him and takes a step back. "I thought we'd have a good time, and we did. But this"—he motions between us—"will never happen again."

I didn't think the giant crack in my heart could possibly get any wider, but hearing him confirm my worst fear makes me realize the pain I felt before was just the tip of the iceberg.

I'm spiraling out of control, and there is no stopping it. "You're lying. I know you feel something." I run my hands down his chest. "Kiss me. Prove there's nothing."

He stiffens, then pushes my hands away. "I'm not going to kiss you. And don't touch me again." Turning back to the window, he drags his fingers through his hair.

Had you asked me earlier, I would have said that after the initial pang, each subsequent injury would hurt less. It's the first one that's the hardest. But now I know that isn't true. I know this is it. There is no future for us.

"So you really don't care?" My voice is nothing more than a wobbly whisper.

"I never said that."

"Then why are you throwing me out like some random woman you slept with?"

"Don't ever say that. That is *not* what you are."

I gulp down a shaky sob. "Then why?"

"Because nothing has changed."

"*Everything* has changed. I gave you everything. You made *love* to me."

He hangs his head. "And I've regretted it ever since."

I can't stop the cry that slips out of my mouth. I sink to the floor because my legs refuse to hold me up any longer. The rug beneath me has an intricate design, likely Persian, with splashes of red and blue. I wonder how many hours went into creating its timeless beauty. The fibers look like they would be rough, but they are surprisingly soft beneath my fingertips.

I lay my face down on them and weep.

I don't notice when Henry leaves the room. I eventually open my swollen eyes to see the sun considerably higher in the sky, and abstractly, I wonder if I've missed my plane.

I stand up and study the room. Everything has been tidied, and my bags are packed and set by the door. Henry's wallet lies abandoned on the desk. He couldn't have chosen a clearer way to signal that what we never had is over.

I wander into the bathroom and splash cold water on my face, then turn from my reflection in the mirror. I can't remember ever looking worse.

There's a knock at the bedroom door. I open it, unsure of who I'll find on the other side, but it's only Daphne. The way my heart sinks tells me she isn't who I was hoping for.

Her calm expression never falters, as if finding her employer in this state is something she does every day. "The car is ready to take us to the airport, Your Royal Highness," she says. "I see your bags are packed. Are you all set?"

I want to scream. "Do you know where Henry is?" I ask instead.

"I'm not exactly sure, ma'am, but I don't think . . ."

He's even stolen my maid's allegiance. Will the hits ever stop coming? "Okay," I say. "I'm just going to use the restroom, and then I'll be ready to leave."

I stumble back to the bathroom and hold a cold washcloth to my face. Would that I had a genie in a bottle to magically erase the blotchy stains. I have cried a river of tears over this man. It's time to stem the flood.

Swallowing the giant mass in my throat, I run a brush through my hair. I rub a small amount of moisturizer onto my face and pray the circulation will encourage my skin to return to its normal hue.

While in the car to the airport, I unlock my phone to buy a few minutes of distraction. A smattering of messages clog my inbox, mostly from Maisie and Beatrice, who are concerned by my silence. I don't respond. I'll be home soon enough. Besides, I need every minute I have left before I get there to pick up the pieces and put them back together in a way that somewhat resembles who I used to be.

The latest message from Bea is a link to a London gossip site where the top article features a picture of Henry and me kissing and the headline *Prince and Princess Rendezvous in London*. I click out of it in disgust.

Without even realizing I'm doing it, I catch myself scanning the airstrip for signs of him, but he, of course, is nowhere to be found. So much the better. Seeing him would only threaten the thin veneer I've managed to get into place.

Once we're in the air, I search the oversize tote Daphne packed for something to read. It would take a terrorist attack to keep my mind from agonizing over Henry, but I'll settle for a novel. There is a book at the bottom of the bag. Bless Daphne. I pull it out. *Wuthering Heights*. Damn it. I shove it back inside.

The action dislodges an envelope wedged down the side of the bag. I tug it out, but the familiar handwriting nearly makes me jam it back. Even on a bloody plane I can't escape him. Regardless, I'm like a moth to a flame. I tear it open.

The first thing I pull out is the divorce papers, once again neatly stacked and folded. *Message received, Henry.* The next thing is a letter.

Celia,

I can't think straight when I'm around you. So I'm resorting to a letter once again to tell you what I need to say.

I shouldn't have let you stay in my room. I shouldn't have made love to you. And I sure as hell shouldn't have let you believe we had a future together. Please know how sorry I am for all of it. My only excuse is that seeing you in my suite was my undoing.

I let myself pretend for a minute. I thought maybe there was a chance. And so I made the mistake of allowing you to think something had changed, when I knew all along nothing had. I knew the illusion couldn't go on forever, but I just wanted to live in the bubble a little longer. When we were finally caught on camera, I knew it had to end. We don't belong together.

I wish I had been strong enough to do it right away. I might have saved you some pain. But I wasn't. I wanted to hold you one more night, to make love to you one more time. It was wrong and selfish and, god, I'm so sorry.

It doesn't change anything, but I'll regret it for the rest of my life. It kills me to think of the pain I've caused you. The hardest thing I've ever done was walk away from you lying on the floor of my room, sobbing because of what I did. It took everything in me to not grab you and hold you. But I knew that if I did, I would never let go, and that would be doing you a greater wrong than letting you cry alone.

I know you won't be satisfied with this answer. You never are, my darling girl, but it's going to have to be enough. I can't promise you won't see me again, but I'll do my damnedest to stay out of your life. I know it's the only way you'll be able to move on.

And move on is what you need to do. I've distracted you long enough. Wesbourne needs you, and you're going to go down in history as her greatest queen. Your potential is brimming over. With me out of your life for good, you can finally do everything you were meant to.

Dry your tears, baby, and don't shed any more on my account. In time, you'll find someone who will erase me from your memory. Maybe you and Beck can work things out. Just remember, you deserve the very best, so promise you won't settle. Wait for the one who brings out the best in you. He's out there.

I know you're crying as you read this, and I wish I could kiss the tears from your eyes. Don't cry for me, please. I can't stand to think of you wasting your tears on me.

Be strong. For me.

x Henry

The human heart is a funny thing. It doesn't break the way a dropped water glass does, suddenly and all at once, its pieces scattering across the floor. No, a heart breaks slowly, the fissures only felt at first—sensed—until finally a giant crack opens and pain oozes out. But then it keeps breaking, the chasm opening wider each time and shards breaking off, never to be recovered. Just when you think it's surely over, that the pain can't possibly get any worse, it wrenches yet again and you realize that what you felt before was nothing compared to this latest break, the one that leaves you breathless, aching, panting for relief. The process can last for years, or it can take place in a matter of hours.

Whether I will ever recover is not the point. As the plane flies lower over the country I know and love so well, a bold certainty creeps into my heart. I *have* to recover. And if that proves too difficult, I'll do my best to fake it.

Wesbourne is waiting for me.

40

"Every Day" - Nick Tzios

One Month Later

I'VE NEVER CONSIDERED THE similarities between a wedding and a coronation before, but they are unmistakable. When a person becomes monarch, they marry their country and solemnly swear their allegiance to it until death do them part.

I've had my wedding already—in this exact spot, as a matter of fact. We all know what a disaster that turned out to be. I just hope I will fare better during my days as a queen than those as a wife.

The voices of the choir lift to the rafters as I await my destiny. I don't hear a word they're singing, but I can see their mouths move. The anticipation in the nave is a velvet robe around my shoulders, as heavy as the one I'm actually wearing. From my seat on the throne, I face the Imperial Crown, an extravagant affair featuring gemstones larger than my thumbnail, glimmering and sparking in the light.

This is it. This moment is what I was born for. No longer the Duchess of Whitmere or director of the Wesbourne Historical Society but Her Majesty, *Queen* of Wesbourne. It's staggering. I once thought my small contributions to society were powerful in their own way, but I never dreamed of standing on the brink of this much influence.

I desperately want to shift my shoulders under the cumbersome purple robe and hope my discomfort during this hour-long ceremony isn't noticeable. I can feel my mum's eyes to my left, willing me to remember every lesson in decorum I ever learned. She needn't worry. I'm too terrified to move a muscle.

The archbishop clears his throat, a signal that I'm to fix my attention in his direction. I do so without moving my head. One has to practice for the twenty-two-carat crown to come. He hands me a small book for me to read my oath from.

"Is Your Majesty willing to take the oath?" he says.

"I am willing," I answer. Willing maybe, but am I ready?

"Will you solemnly promise and swear to govern the peoples of the nation of Wesbourne, and of any other territories belonging or pertaining to her, according to their respective laws and customs?"

"I solemnly promise to do so."

"Will you use your power to cause law and justice, in mercy, to be executed in all your judgments?"

"I will."

I think of the changes that have already been enacted during my time as queen-in-waiting. The security at the ports has been increased, and because of that, three drug lords have been apprehended and are now awaiting trial.

At the archbishop's nod, I walk carefully to the altar with my entourage of ladies-in-waiting holding the train of my robe. I kneel on the steps and place my right hand on the large Holy Bible, then recite: "The things which I have here before promised, I will perform and keep. So help me God." I lean forward and press my lips to the book.

I'm once again assisted to the coronation chair with the burden of millions of eyes upon me, both in this room and watching from thousands of screens the world over. They've been following my journey from the beginning, from the shocking news of the diary to my wedding to this—the climax of everything.

The archbishop anoints and blesses me before offering a prayer of consecration. That completed, I receive the orb and scepter, and both are much heavier than I anticipated. The ceremony is almost complete. The only thing left is the crown.

He lifts it from its cushioned resting place. Light dances from every angle. My breath grows thick in my throat as he raises it over my head. For some reason, this feels more momentous than the oath I just took. As I absorb its weight, both physical and symbolic, my heart threatens to burst from my rib cage.

I could never have asked for this, nor dreamed of it. But here it is, handed to me by fate. A far greater destiny than I would ever have chosen for myself. I will do everything in my power for this country I love so fiercely. I will not let her down.

Adelaide was right: few people get the opportunity to experience a great love. I've been lucky enough to have two. Henry crushed my heart, and I'll likely never love another man the way I loved him. But I don't regret a single moment I spent with him, and I'd do it all over again if I could. The time we had outweighs the loss of him.

And then there is Wesbourne. Dear, beautiful Wesbourne. My father gave me an incredible gift when he taught me to love her. She's volatile and she needs direction, but god, is she strong and brave. And she's mine. Mine to care for and cherish, mine to protect and guide. Mine to love until death.

The crowd starts to chant, "God save the queen, God save the queen." Yes, God save me if I let down this country and these people who believe in me.

My mother, now the queen mother, is the first to pay me homage. My eyes burn with unshed tears as she steps forward and bends before me in honor, my position one that would have been hers had my father lived another ten years. She kisses my cheek. "He's so proud of you for being what he couldn't."

Bea approaches next to bow before me. She wears her new title, princess royal, quite beautifully. If she was considered a catch before, her status has risen infinitely more in the past three months, which, as evidenced by the cheeky grin on her face, she doesn't mind one bit. I wink at her, grateful our friendship is back on good ground again.

I clasp the outstretched hand of the archbishop and rise, which brings everyone in attendance to their feet as well. As I begin my recessional down the aisle of the cathedral, heads bow on either side of me. Maisie's blonde head shoots upward for a peek, and I toss her a smile before she lowers it again.

I doubt Beck is in attendance, but I'm sure he's watching somewhere. I wish him well and hope he won't hate me forever. Maybe someday we can be friends again, although we'll never be more than that, regardless of what Henry said. If I ever marry again, it will only be to someone who cares about Wesbourne as much as I do. Maybe I'll even get lucky and find another great love, although I'm not holding my breath.

The former king and queen bow their heads reverently as I pass, something that has to take great strength and humility. They could have chosen not to appear today, but the fact that they did means the world to me, even if I'll never forgive William for what he did. I will be awarding him a dukedom in honor of his service as king for twenty-two years, which means Henry will one day inherit it as well, not that it will make any difference to him.

I haven't seen him since that day in his hotel room, when he left me in tears. Our annulment was finalized the following week. True to his word, he's stayed away from Wesbourne entirely, if the tabloids are to be trusted. I still haven't decided whether I'm grateful or wish he wasn't so good at keeping his promises. Perhaps both.

I've come to realize there's no such thing as letting go. There's only accepting what's already gone.

The cathedral doors are in sight now. On the other side stands a crowd of people—my people—ready to welcome their new queen. Just two months ago, I walked this same path with Henry beside me. This time, I walk alone.

Two footmen stand at the entrance, and security personnel are clustered around in a way I only hope I'll eventually get used to. I take a deep breath.

It's time to face my country.

As the footmen swing the doors open, a flash of movement on my right catches my eye. I turn my head, conscious that the slightest imbalance will cause the crown to topple off. My gaze collides with a face so familiar it hurts. Our eyes lock, and everything I've wanted to say for the past month wells up within me, a tidal wave of emotion.

He came.

A carousel of memories spins through my mind. Henry's in each one, the sun, the breeze, and the storm. He reaches through me with his eyes, down to the basement of my soul, and wakes emotions I've been keeping locked up. A vise squeezes my chest, and I can't breathe.

Finally, he breaks his gaze and bows his head. *My queen*, the motion says. I'm scared my heart will break anew.

I lower my eyes to blink away tears, and when I look back, he's gone.

I step out into the beautiful sunshine, casting beams from the gold orb and scepter I'm still holding, into the crowd, who are cheering my arrival. The clear sky draws my eyes upward. Can he see me from up there? The sun's rays warm my skin like his pride pouring down from heaven. It seems fitting to release the anger and resentment I feel toward him for choosing the coward's way out and instead cling to the good memories I have.

The scores of people facing me are chanting, echoing the one that started inside the church. *God save the queen.* They wave the flag of Wesbourne, its green stripes a vibrant emerald in the sun. Children sit on their father's shoulders, desperate for a glimpse of their new monarch, and swing their chubby fists back and forth in celebration. All around us, phones are snapping pictures.

Do they know everything I've given up for them? Probably not. But that's okay. Great loves are worth sacrificing everything for, even our fairy-tale dreams.

And sometimes the best fairy tales are the ones we write ourselves.

Need more Henry & Celia? Download a bonus chapter for free at https://jessicajude.com/thrones-we-steal-bonus

What's next? Read the second part of Henry & Celia's story in Castles We Save!

Thank you for reading *Thrones We Steal*! If you enjoyed this book, it would mean the world to me if you left a review, even if it's short. Reviews are like tips for authors, and every one helps!

xoxo Jess

P.S. Want to discuss my books, dissect Easter eggs, and spiral with other like-minded readers? Join my exclusive reader groups on Facebook and Discord. We'd love to see you there! You can also join my email list at jessicajude.com/newsletter to receive updates and exclusive bonus content!

Also by Jessica Jude

Thrones We Steal Trilogy
Thrones We Steal
Castles We Storm
Crowns We Save

Hand of Revenge Series
Ace of Betrayal
Queen of Vengeance
King of Obsession
Joker's Endgame

A group of wealthy friends plays poker to determine the victims of their weekly revenge plots. What they don't bargain on? Falling in love with the people who could destroy them.

Embers of Us Series
Flare (coming 9.15.26 – pre-order now!)

About the Author

JESSICA JUDE LOVES NOTHING better than sending her characters on an emotional roller coaster of love, angst, and drama, but in reality her life is very ordinary, drama-free, and probably boring to anyone watching. (Which would be weird. And creepy.)

She married her high school sweetheart at nineteen. Being an author is a dream she's had since she was six years old and wrote her first book, which was ten pages long, about a girl named Mary getting lost in the woods. (It was never published, but good news: Mary was eventually rescued.)

When she's not writing, Jess is reading, reading about writing, or eating ice cream. In another life, she would live in England in a sprawling manor house with hidden passages and secret stairways, but for now, she's content with her old brick farmhouse in the Midwestern United States.

Still a fan? Here are some ways you can ~~stalk~~ stay connected!

https://jessicajude.com/newsletter

Instagram @JessicaJudeBooks

Threads @JessicaJudeBooks

TikTok @JessicaJudeBooks